THE
GLITTERING
WORLD

THE
GLITTERING
WORLD

ROBERT LEVY

G

Gallery Books

New York   London   Toronto   Sydney   New Delhi

A Division of Simon & Schuster, Inc.
1230 Avenue of the Americas
New York, NY 10020

First Gallery Books hardcover edition February 2015

GALLERY BOOKS and colophon are registered trademarks of Simon & Schuster, Inc.

For information about special discounts for bulk purchases, please contact Simon & Schuster Special Sales at 1-866-506-1949 or business@simonandschuster.com.

The Simon & Schuster Speakers Bureau can bring authors to your live event. For more information or to book an event contact the Simon & Schuster Speakers Bureau at 1-866-248-3049 or visit our website at www.simonspeakers.com.

Interior design by Robert E. Ettlin
Jacket design by Laywan Kwan
Jacket photograph © Felicia Simion / Trevillion Images

Manufactured in the United States of America

1 3 5 7 9 10 8 6 4 2

Library of Congress Cataloging-in-Publication Data is on file.

ISBN 978-1-4767-7452-7
ISBN 978-1-4767-7453-4 (ebook)

For Carole and Hugh
and Rachel and Devan
and Dan

CONTENTS

I woke up this morning
and I took a look around
at all that I got
These days I've been
lookin' in the mirror
and wondering if that's me
lookin' back or not

— *Steve Earle, "The Other Kind"*

Part One

BLUE

Chapter One

Blue was restless from the moment they took off. When the plane wasn't bouncing it lurched, a bucking hard-core mosh against the unsteady rumble of the fifty-seater's black fly buzz. Through the worst of it he white-knuckled the armrests. The shape of the plane unnerved him: the vessel tunneled like a mine shaft, like the endless tapering caverns he traveled in his dreams. He ran a pale hand through his tar-black hair and leaned his head against the window, though he'd given up on any chance of sleep, Ambien and a plastic cup of red wine sadly missing from the agenda on the brief morning flight.

All the while Gabe, unfazed, chattered away beside him. Going on about various cloud formations he'd spotted beyond the wing, whether the restaurant would still be standing when they returned to New York, his hope that a nomadic family of Sasquatches might have wandered as far east as Nova Scotia. It was strangely comforting, and Blue nodded when he thought he should. Still, he couldn't help but peer across the aisle toward Elisa, her head buried in her husband Jason's shoulder. Elisa had always hated flying, almost as much as Blue. He wished he were sitting next to her instead, misery and company and all that. Now it was Jason who was at her side, as fate and marital vows would have it.

He figured he'd catch some shut-eye in the rental car, but

once his giddy traveling companions loaded their luggage and piled laughing into their late-model gray Cadillac, Blue knew there would be no sleep until they reached Cape Breton. He shifted in the backseat as the car pulled away from the curb. The glass and steel of the terminal juddered past, and the airport, along with the rest of Halifax, soon receded from sight. The brilliant bold sweep of the swollen Maritimes sky made his vision blur and his legs tremble, as if he had been at sea his whole life and was only now coming ashore.

Elisa settled on her sit bones in the passenger seat. She whipped out her vintage Konica—her constant companion of late—and shot a picture of her husband behind the wheel. Jason bopped his head and tapped his square, well-manicured nails against the steering column, emoting like the heir to Nat King Cole as he sang along to a big band tune on the radio. Gabe's unfamiliarity with the song didn't prevent him from humming his own form of accompaniment. Folded like a crab claw with his spearmint-green Pumas on the back of Elisa's seat, he looked happy just to be along for the ride, busy doodling in his sketch pad with a black Sharpie, his writing hand scarred by a childhood burn. Gabe was a scrubby weed of a kid, not yet old enough to tend bar, someone Elisa and Blue would have gravitated toward back in their nightlife days; indeed, with his sleepy smile and tangled mop of dirty blond hair, Gabe was pretty. But young. In the bright light of day, the twenty-year-old looked strangely even younger than when he'd walked into Blue's restaurant last winter to inquire about the Help Wanted sign in the window.

The four-hour drive stretched well into the afternoon, their destination a vacation house in the vicinity of the defunct Starling Cove Friendship Colony, the former commune where Blue was born. What recollection he had of the artists' community was questionable at best, scratchy images of trees and mountains and possibly the façade of a crumbling brick building, spectral memories that might have been cribbed from photographs. Along the way they stopped at a Tim Hortons for coffee and lunch, then a Needs Convenience for gas and snacks; at a musty used-clothing chain store called Frenchy's they spent nearly an hour. Blue, Elisa, and Gabe darted up and down the aisles to dig through the haphazardly compiled bins, Elisa with the enthusiastic determination of the fashion conscious, Blue and Gabe with the wariness of those who had spent grim youths forced into secondhand clothes. Jason hung back to make small talk with the matronly shopkeeper.

Blue came across a T-shirt of an eagle superimposed over an American flag superimposed over an image of the burning Twin Towers, the words *Never Forget* emblazoned across the front. "Hey, Jason," he called out, and held the shirt up for inspection. "What do you think?"

"It's uncanny." Jason crossed the store and leaned in to scrutinize the garish image. "Seriously, this is exactly what it was like! Except for the giant eagle. Although I was a little distracted that morning." He laughed, snagged the shirt from Blue, and tossed it back into the pile. It was good to hear him joke about it, considering.

"What did I miss?" Elisa emerged from the dressing room wearing nothing but a safari hat and an enormous and ill-fitting hockey jersey that ended halfway down her tanned and olive-skinned thighs, her camera slung from her neck as usual. "Something funny?"

"Extremely," Jason said. "And now you'll never know." He flashed her a smile as he took her hand, and she placed the hat atop his head. Reflexively, Blue leaned past a rack of long coats to check if Gabe was close by; sweet, adoring Gabe, the only one in the world who looked out for him the way Elisa once did, which is to say completely. Why Blue attracted that kind of fervent attention was a different matter entirely.

"Hey, look." Elisa gestured in the direction of the shop clerk. "She has your old 'do." The woman's short and spiky hair had a decidedly blue tinge from a cheapo concealing rinse that bore an uncomfortably close resemblance to Blue's style from his lip-pierce and Manic Panic days. "You've returned to your people," Elisa said, draping an arm over his shoulders. "At last."

Though the name had stuck, Blue hadn't dyed his hair in ages, not since his club kid days ended and he started work in real kitchens. Only photographs remained, and the nickname. "Why don't you go blue again?" Gabe had asked one night in Brooklyn after they'd closed down the restaurant.

"It's not me anymore," he replied, a shoebox of his memorabilia from high school and beyond scattered across the counter. But what he'd meant was, *I'm too old for that.* Thirty years old with hair the color of a circus clown was not only unflattering but desperate. He wasn't the same carefree boy of fifteen or even twenty-five, scraping together money for his daily meal of a single brick-sized burrito and a forty-ounce of St. Ides. "It is a bit childish, don't you think?"

"'When I was a child, I spake as a child,'" Gabe said in his oddly endearing way, and placed an old photo booth strip of Blue and Elisa back into the box. "'But when I became a man . . .'"

And Blue thought he had. But here he found himself, overworked yet near penniless under the weight of crushing debt. He would have readily traded some of his cooking skills for an ounce of business acumen, but, alas, the intricacies of keeping the restaurant solvent had eluded him. Not exactly as planned.

Outside Frenchy's to grab a smoke, his cellphone buzzed. Blocked call, unlisted: his mother. "Hello, my lovely boy," she said, her voice weaker than ever. "How's it going up there?"

"So far so good. How you? How's your new, what do you call it, home health aide?"

"No use complaining." She wheezed, breath heavy against the receiver. "So tell me. Where are you right now?"

"We're still on the road."

"You mean at the airport?"

"No, on our way up to Cape Breton." Silence. "Mom?"

"You . . . You told me you were just going to see the lawyer in Halifax and sign the papers."

"I figured we'd swing by the house first. You know, just to see it."

"No, no, no. Your grandmother . . . No. You barely knew her, Mickey."

"Whose fault is that?" Blue said, and immediately regretted it. *Be nice*, he reminded himself. *You know how sick she is. How much she loves you.* The sense memory of Bengay and Tiger Balm assaulted him.

This whole trip, though, it was colored by his mother and her decision to haul him as a child out of Canada twenty-five years prior. He often felt that she'd robbed him, taken away his claim to his grandmother, the community, and this land as a whole. And now that his grandmother had died, his only connection to her was the house she'd left him in her will, in the hope, perhaps, that he would return to Starling Cove. Little had Grandma Flora known he was so hard up for money that he would have no choice but to sell the house as soon as possible.

He needed the rest of them along to make it feel less mercenary than it really was.

"She's gone," he said softly, and shook away the smell. "Don't worry about me. Besides, it's not like I'm alone, I'm up here with Elisa and Jason." He cast an eye through the store window, though all he could see was his own distorted image reflected back at him from the smudged glass; too difficult to explain Gabe, who the glorified busboy was to Blue, and who he was not. "We'll be fine. I swear."

"Where are you staying?"

"I'm not sure exactly," he lied. "About an hour from Starling Cove, I guess? Elisa has the directions."

"Babe, listen to me for once in your life. Your grandmother, she was a very religious woman." His mother's voice had turned pensive and haunted. "She had a lot of strange beliefs, and some even stranger ones about my friends."

"That you were all a bunch of drug-fiending hippies, right?" He forced himself to squint up into the sun, as if in censure. "That was a joke, by the way."

"Aside from the lawyer, don't tell anyone else what you're doing up there. Trust me on this, please. I know you're curious. But get it done and let that be the end of it."

"Okay, okay." There was no winning on this subject. "Mum's the word. Promise."

"Smart." A long silence, punctuated by the hiss of her bedside oxygen tank. "Just be smart."

Gabe came out of the store. He held the door open for Elisa and Jason, who exited arm in arm, Jason sporting the safari hat and Elisa with two plastic bags stuffed full of clothing.

"Hey, listen," Blue said. "I should go."

"Love you," his mother said, almost as a plea. "Stay safe."

"Love you too. I'll be back in no time, really. The days will fly."

"Who was that?" Elisa said as they got back inside the car.

"My mom. I told her we're heading north."

"Awww, Yvonne. How'd she take it?"

"Not thrilled." Going up to Cape Breton was the latest of many disappointments he'd handed his mother in his quest to individuate himself, a process that began over a decade ago, when he moved out of their cramped Hell's Kitchen apartment after high school. She came down with debilitating osteoporosis soon afterward, the first in a series of infirmities that overtook her in his absence. It seemed as if every time he did leave her side, it triggered some new calamity, a fall in the bathroom or a flare-up of shingles, and these days she was bedridden. Now that he had firmly extricated himself from her, there was an unspoken understanding that it was best he simply kept away.

"I left out the fact that we're staying in Starling Cove proper," Blue said. "She told me not to mention to anyone what we're doing up here, so . . ."

"Well, seeing the house is the right thing to do," Jason said from the driver's seat. "How do you sell a house without taking a look at it?" Jason was ten years older than Blue and Elisa, and thus the reigning voice of reason and maturity; it was reassuring to have his explicit approval.

"It's not about the house." Elisa took a leftover iced coffee from the cup holder and used the straw to fish inside for ice. "Yvonne hated her mother. She doesn't want anything to do with her. Even dead."

"Is that true?" Gabe asked. "What happened?"

"I really don't know," Blue said. "She won't talk about it. Never would, except to say that my grandmother was crazy. My mom and I left for the States when I was five. All I know is we moved so many times that after a while my grandmother couldn't find us anymore. Which I'm pretty sure was the plan all along." Grandma Flora's lawyer had found him, though, hadn't he? Three months since Blue had received word of her death and the house she'd bequeathed him. It had taken some time to pull the trip together.

Blue shrugged and dug inside his bag for his cigarettes. "Anyone mind if I smoke?"

"Actually, yes," Elisa said. "I'm feeling kind of carsick. Sorry."

"That's okay. We'll be there soon enough." He sat back, slid down so his knees were against the back of Jason's seat, and beat a slow tattoo on his jeans. Sure, there was the business with the house, but he chose to focus on the pleasures that awaited them. They were in store for a full week of leisure time he hadn't dreamed of since opening Cyan two years ago: cooking for fun only and board games, whisky and beer, fires to build in the wood-burning stove highlighted in the rental-property listing. It was Elisa who convinced him that he was going to burn out if he didn't take a breather, and Jason who forced his hand by booking the plane tickets. All in all, a welcome reprieve from the oppressive humidity of New York in August. It was the only time of year he'd consider closing down the restaurant.

Across the Canso Causeway and the swing bridge over the canal and they were on the island of Cape Breton. Blue thought about how long it had been since he'd last crossed the bridge, covering the same territory but in reverse, like an unraveled roll of film wound back inside its spool. As highway gave way to green mountain vistas of trees rooted upon jagged rock, a slowly simmering sense of familiarity began to sink in. Not so much as memory, more like he'd carried the landscape inside him, on a cellular level. He started to tingle.

Soon they were deep in the Highlands. Four lanes thinned to two, the road bracketed by balsam firs as well as the occasional hardwood tree, stick straight against the afternoon sky. According to the directions, they needed to circle half of Starling Cove, an inlet of St. Veronica's Bay, before they found an access road that crept up the side of Kelly's Mountain, the quarter-mile-high summit that towered over the cove and the surrounding areas.

The branches parted to make way for an unmarked, leaf-canopied drive, the mountain's peak high above. The Cadillac's square nose pitched up as it left the asphalt, then dropped with a startling thud before the car righted and wound its way around the mountain's base. A hundred yards later, the surrounding trees gradually telescoped until feathery pine bristles began to massage the car's exterior. They rolled into an open field, lush emerald grass bubbled up in mounds. A short side road ambled past overgrown hedges, through which weather-beaten cabins in an assortment of sizes and shapes could be glimpsed; Elisa lowered her window to take a passing shot.

A gaily painted two-story house appeared from the trees, yellow and trimmed with elaborate hatched latticework and wedding-cake eaves, Victorian in inspiration if not origin. Barely visible above the treetops was the slanted roof of another house, a little farther up the hill. This second house had a birch white face, its upper windows a slatted pair of dark and narrowed eyes, watchful. Blue recognized the teeth of its wide summer porch from the rental listing. He sat up and looked out the back window, a cotton padding of fog cast over what he presumed to be the water, the mist draping the bay below with the sun already lowering behind the mountain's distant peak. The overcast sky flared with an abrupt and oppressive bright-ness like light off a mirror, and Blue, blinded, squeezed his eyes shut, shielding them with his hand.

Jason slowed the car and lowered his window as he came to a stop. A woman in her fifties, compact and robust in blue jeans and a purple hempen shirt, emerged from the doorway of a small shack separated from the yellow house by a vegetable garden. She was First Nation by appearances, her face sun-kissed and framed by gray hair tied back in a knot with stray shoots spilling wild behind her ears.

"Welcome to the cove," she said, smiling. "Head on up the hill. I'll meet you in a minute."

By the time they pulled into the small dirt lot behind the white house and hauled their luggage from the trunk, she had made her way up to them.

"Hi there. I'm Maureen." She shook Blue's hand, her face flushed as she greeted them. "Now, which one of you is Mi-chael?"

"That's me. But everyone calls me Blue."

"Oh! Like Blue Edwards?"

"Sure. I guess?"

"Never mind," she said, and waved him off. The others in-troduced themselves and they all followed her up the rear deck and into the house. "This is what is known around here as the MacLeod House. Built and burnt in 1826, built back up in 1852, and restored and burnt and restored again a couple more times, with a full addition in 1973. I redid it as a guest house a few years ago."

The kitchen was pure charm, small but open. The farm-house sink, counters, and refrigerator all glowed a subtle shade of mint, which matched the forested wallpaper, its patterned green boughs an extension of the trees on the far side of the windows. The glass was beveled in a chalet style and skirted with pleated red tartan curtains; the effect bordered on country kitsch, but somehow it all worked.

Maureen showed them the quirks of the various appliances and where the garbage and recycling bins were, how the downstairs shower had to be run for a minute or two before the hot water kicked in. A black wood-burning stove squatted stoically at the edge of the living room, past it a farmhouse table, two couches, and an impressive library surrounded by windows that framed the front porch overlooking Kelly's Mountain and the fog beyond. Up a short flight of solid oak stairs hand painted with fleurs-de-lis were three bedrooms: one bright and pink with a view of the cove, another done up in darker plaid tartans, the third narrow and yellow with a steepled ceiling. The frame of the last room, according to Maureen, was original to the dwelling, and was where they all dropped their bags beside an antique pine crib allegedly crafted by William MacLeod, the man who had built the house. The crib was the only fully intact remnant from the first fire.

"Please, make yourselves at home," she said. "I'm just down the hill if you have any questions. And if you see an older gentleman wandering the lawn with a book and a pair of shears, don't be alarmed—that's my husband, Donald. Wave and he'll wave back, but he'll probably keep minding what he's doing."

Maureen told them about the hiking trails behind the house, the canoes at the dock down the hill, which way to go from the main road to get to the supermarkets, large and small. She was polite and thorough, though she often turned to look down the hill, as if she had somewhere else to be.

"By the way," she added as she opened the front door to leave, "if you all aren't too tired, we're having a little shindig down the hill tonight if you feel like stopping by. Just some food and drink with a few friends, nothing special."

The others got to unpacking, while Blue went out onto the side porch and sat at a picnic table to smoke a cigarette. He listened to the faint sounds of the others inside, the wind soughing through the trees, the chirrup of insects and birds. Along with the cigarette smoke, he breathed in great big lungfuls of air; it was clean and sweetly flavorful, as if it had only just been raining.

∝

Before they started down the hill, it was already clear that their hostess's idea of a little shindig was in fact a full-blown rager, the sound of live music an eerie thrum off the water long past the dusking of foggy Starling Cove. "Holy shit," Elisa said over the skirl of a fiddle as she zagged across the gravel drive, camera in hand and tottering behind the others on stilettos she'd stubbornly insisted on wearing. "They don't mess around here, do they?"

"I could tell Maureen partied," Gabe said. "Something about her screams high spirits."

A dozen revelers had spilled out onto the lawn, where an auxiliary troupe of musicians tuned their instruments as they waited their turn. A few dozen more were packed inside Maureen's crowded living room, along with a band consisting of a fiddler and an accordionist flanked by two guitarists, as well as a drummer rocking out on a djembe. The candlelit room was loud with laughter and drink. Young children ran loose, and as they flitted about in a game of tag, Blue had a ragged flash of memory:

a moonfaced little girl chasing after him as a fiddle played, the celebratory yet somehow menacing stomp of feet and clapping of hands all around . . . He closed his eyes and strained to hold tight to the thread, but the recollection was gone.

Maureen parted the crowd with a drink held high in her hand. "Glad you all could make it! What's your poison?"

"What do you have?" Gabe asked.

"Not a whole lot. Only some beer, and some wine. And some lethal sangria my cousin made. I'd be wary of that. Oh, and some fine old whisky a friend brought. A jug of it. There's some fustier options as well, like schnapps. And possibly sherry somewhere . . ."

Within an hour Blue was merrily drunk, having met what he imagined to be every resident of Starling Cove. Maureen herself was a potter who sold ceramics out of a nearby shop she shared with an abstract sculptor, while her friends included a woodworker specializing in driftwood art that featured in local galleries, as well as a glassblower who lived and peddled his pieces out of a converted century-old barn on the far side of the cove. Starling Cove seemed an ideal spot for artisans to sell their wares, situated as it was on a stray branch of the heavily touristed Cabot Trail. Blue wondered how many of them were castoffs from the former artists' colony, and how many might have known his grandmother, or his mother, or even him. No one mentioned the old commune outright, only that the cove was known for its diversity, a place people gravitated toward from both near and far.

A diminutive and heavily bearded man named Fred Cronin, an ironsmith and publisher of a local newsletter, waited alongside Blue for the bathroom. Though standoffish at first, he soon warmed under the heat lamp of Blue's attention, and spoke of how he had moved to Cape Breton from Detroit as a draft dodger in the early seventies, never to set foot in America again. By all appearances, this self-imposed exile was fine by him.

"This your first ceilidh?" Fred said in a career smoker's rasp, stroking his silver-flecked beard as he leaned against the stone mantelpiece in the living room.

"My first what?" Blue was distracted by the objects scattered across the mantel: a framed watercolor of a white lotus-leafed hexagonal mandala, a pewter tray containing a half-burned bundle of sage, an exquisitely rendered praying mantis crafted from green Bakelite that stared back at him through compound eyes, dark brown bordering on black.

"Ceilidh," Fred repeated. "It's like a Gaelic hootenanny. Could be a barn dance, or even just a house party like this. Basically, a get-together to get drunk and dance around to some old-country-type Scottish music. Lots of old country culture here, even today. They don't call this place Nova Scotia for nothing."

"I was actually born here, so you'd think I'd know that."

"Oh yeah?" The man produced an antique-looking camera from somewhere beneath his beard and took a lightning-fast shot of him, the flash blinding. *This guy should meet Elisa*, Blue thought. "Whereabouts are you from?"

"I'm not sure exactly," Blue hedged, honoring his mother's plea for discretion. "Sydney, I think? Anyway, I've been gone ever since, just about. It's nice to be back."

And it was. Who knew where this would take him? Maybe fortune was intervening, and he was destined to come across some long-lost relative. Hell, maybe this man Fred was actually his father, and Blue had unwittingly stumbled into an unlikely family reunion, right here in the Cape Breton Highlands.

This final thought a bit too close to home, Blue excused himself to refill his sangria, caution to the wind.

On the other side of the room, the informal circle of dancers spun with increasing zeal. Some paired off to execute elaborate steps, while others held hands and simply twirled one another, a few more with their arms linked around the perimeter in a kind of drunken hora. Elisa, her camera and heels long since cast aside, moved effortlessly from group to group. She clapped her hands, swung her hips, partner danced in remarkable approximation, using steps it would have taken anyone else days to learn. Her mimicry appeared effortless, the way someone with absolute pitch could reproduce tone. But Blue knew how hard it had really come, how much dance had consumed her before her body finally said *no more*. Two decades' worth of self-sacrifice and perfectionism, countless failed auditions and the pain of recurring injuries . . . Inside and out, the sheer accumulation of setbacks had taken their toll.

He joined her and led her in a provisional country waltz—not too terribly, though Elisa was intent on correcting his form at every turn. They were a long way from their days as fixtures in the New York club scene. Day shifts working at Pat Field's and Liquid Sky and later in the clubs themselves, nights wrecked as all get-out, dressed like mental patients on the dance floors of USA and Palladium and Tunnel, their MDMA fog not worn off until sometime after their lunch break. A lost decade of tarnished glamour held together with duct tape, spirit gum, and daydreams. It was where he had met Elisa, and what he liked to remember of that most hazy time was pure rapture.

The ceilidh danced on, Blue and Elisa along with it. They tried and failed to coax Gabe out of the kitchen to dance, then Jason, who waved them off and sat on a patchwork leather couch next to a gaunt and elderly man in a burgundy cardigan and black square-framed glasses. Jason was drawn to strangers—in taxis he was fond of the front seat, where he could talk politics with the driver; in diners, the waitress-trafficked counter; he even chatted up token booth clerks. None of them minded either. And he'd successfully pursued Elisa, hadn't he? Picked her up in a bar, no less, no mean feat considering she'd probably been hit on a thousand times in a thousand bars by better-looking men, with better game. None of them had Jason's dogged determination, however, and certainly not his christlike patience. Blue often suspected there was something about him too good to be true.

As for Elisa, if you had told Blue that she would ever get married in the first place . . . And to a man who was stable and secure? A newly minted therapist, well versed in the everyday neuroses of the born-and-bred New Yorker such as herself? Not in the forecast. Yet there Blue found himself not one year ago at the Central Park Boathouse (his date an elfin redhead named Zoë he'd happened to take home the night before), as noted Jewish intellectual and Columbia Law professor Lawrence J. Weintraub walked his daughter down the aisle—handing her over to a man who not only was a gentile but was actually churchgoing! A black (or more specifically, black and Korean) man! Probably not in Professor Weintraub's future projection. But even her father couldn't question Jason's particulars, himself awed in the face of that firm handshake, that quiet confidence, those teeth . . . Jason was everything Blue was not. He was, in a word, husbandly.

"This is Donald," Jason said, already familiar, his arm around the older man's shoulders. "He's Maureen's husband."

"Nice to meet you," Blue said. Donald's handshake was too

hard, Blue's fingers mashed against one another so roughly he flinched, though he tried to mask it. "Thanks for having us."

"It's past my bedtime." Donald turned to stare across the room, head weaving as if searching someone out. "But I haven't gotten permission yet, so . . ." His cadence was melodic, with a storyteller's inflection. Blue looked to Jason, who winked at him.

"I don't think you could fall asleep if you tried," Jason said. "The music's pretty loud."

"I can sleep through anything," Donald said. "During the war they would call me Charlie, because I was the only one who didn't get up for reveille. 'Oh, Charlie, Charlie, get out of bed,'" he sang, straining to be heard above the din. "'Oh! Charlie, Charlie, get out of bed!' At least that's what I'm told."

The glassblower wandered over and launched into an extended monologue about a visit he and his wife had made to Ground Zero. But Donald only stared at Blue, until he leaned over and whispered, "I know you, don't I?" in Blue's ear.

"Oh. Uh, I don't think so. Unless it's from the past few minutes, that is."

"Well, time is a most peculiar mistress," Donald said. His eyes receded behind his thick plastic lenses, until his whole expression was a blur. "Especially amongst the fairies. There's no such thing as time with the Other Kind. Though I suppose you know that already, being fey yourself."

"Excuse me?" Blue let out a startled laugh. *Did this dude just call me gay?*

"Well, you'll be going down, then, won't you?" Donald said, leering and newly agitated. "Down and down and dowwwwwn . . ."

Their small circle fell silent. Jason, placid, patted the man on the knee, though he also tilted his head in a gesture for Blue to take off.

"Better keep an eye on that guy," Jason said to Donald. "He's nothing but trouble."

"Hilarious," Blue said, but he bristled. He gave a little salute, and negotiated his way across the crowded room. Time for some more booze.

After refreshing his drink he headed out onto the side porch to smoke. Maureen soon popped her head out, took a quick look back, then tiptoed conspiratorially to his side. "You have an extra one of those?"

"Of course." Blue handed her a cigarette and lit it for her. "This is quite a ceilidh," he said, faux authoritative.

"That's what we do." She exhaled a sigh of pleasure. "Hey, your friend is some dancer."

"Isn't she? She used to be serious about it, but she kept hurting herself. Recently she's taken up photography. Less chance of injury, I suppose."

"Good for her. You two looked so happy together dancing. You're both glowing."

"We're just friends. Old friends. Elisa and Jason are married."

"Oh, I know. I already cornered your boyfriend and got the lay of the land."

"Boyfriend?" He winced. "I'm not . . . Gabe and me aren't together."

"No? I thought— Well, the way he was looking at you, I just assumed."

"It's okay." Blue snorted, smoke escaping his nostrils. "I'm not offended. Believe me."

Maureen and Donald must have figured they were two couples on holiday. And how far was it from the truth? There had been that one night, after all, a misguided attempt at providing Gabe a modicum of real tenderness. But that kind of justification had gotten Blue in trouble countless times; you'd think he would have learned.

"Gabe's a puppy dog, you know?" he said by way of explanation, not to mention rationalization. "He's had a hard life, not that he talks about it. I'm protective of him. Maybe too much."

"You care about him."

Blue nodded. "So, what did he tell you exactly?"

"He said that you're very kind, and that you like to pretend otherwise. And that you make the best food he's ever tasted."

"That's nice of him to say."

"I believe it. You're different. I can tell. Like I said, you got the glow." She sipped her drink. "Elisa's glowing too, of course. But her glow is common enough. Any idea where yours might come from?"

"Uh, couldn't properly say, really." He blushed and looked away. "Maybe it's the sangria."

She laughed. "You never know."

They smoked in silence. Blue suppressed a yawn, faced the woods, and listened to the sounds of the party blare from the open windows: the creak and slam of the screen door, a cacophony of voices, music, clapping and stomping. He turned to find Maureen gazing intently inside, at Donald, who'd gotten up from the couch and was busy collecting bottles and glasses from the coffee table. "My husband," she said, her tone neutral.

"He's an interesting guy," Blue said. "Very spirited."

"He has Alzheimer's." She stubbed her cigarette out on the inside of a mussel shell set out on the porch railing. "He was diagnosed last year. But I could tell for a while already. I knew."

"Oh, God. I'm sorry."

"Yeah, well, that's one of the perils of marrying someone twenty years older, I guess. Not that I was ever the marrying kind. But after a few decades of take-a-lover, leave-a-lover . . ."

"Is that what you were like?" Blue noticed she didn't wear a wedding ring, nor, he had noted, did Donald.

"That's what a lot of us were like, up here. Our little lost land, back when we still pretended to have ideals."

"There used to be a commune up here, right?"

"Something like that. Where did you hear about that old place?"

"Someone mentioned it before," he said imprecisely. "Were you and Donald living here back then?"

"Sure we were. Donald was actually one of the founders of the Colony. Not that he moved here for that purpose, exactly. He was an entomologist turned rubber-booter, came up from McGill to study ants, of all things."

"Ants? Is there something special about the ants up here?"

"There's something special about *everything* here," she said with a wicked grin. "This has always been a singular place. Not just for the indigenous people, Mi'kmaqs like me, but for everyone who comes through. And that vibe fit the 'live off the land' era just perfect, you know? We had quite the good time. Many years' worth. But if you would've told me then it would come to this . . ." Soundless laughter, a quick jerk of the head. "I've had better years, that's for sure. I just hope they're not all behind me."

He offered her another cigarette, leaned in to light it against the swelling breeze. They separated slightly but stayed close, shoulder to shoulder. "Donald can't read a clock anymore. He knows what the hands are, but not what they mean . . . I have to leave him little notes all around the house. 'This is the oven. It gets hot. Don't use it without Maureen.'" She exhaled through her teeth, smoke scattering in the dim shine from the porch light. "In the spring he found me in my studio and said, 'I have to talk to Maureen about the oven.' I said, 'Okay, what do you need?' and he said, 'No, not you, I have to find Maureen.' I said, 'Darling, I *am* Maureen.' He kind of grumbled and walked back to the house. I figured out what was going on a few days later, when we were going to bed and he said, 'Good night, Barbara.' That's the name of his first wife. She died forty years ago."

"What did you say?"

"'Good night, Donald. Sweet dreams.'" She stubbed out her barely smoked cigarette, then pocketed it. "Thanks for the smokes," she said, and squeezed his arm.

"Anytime. You know where to find me."

She walked back inside, the snap of the screen door absorbed into the wall of noise. He watched her through the window as she gave her husband's arm the very same squeeze, and Donald shuffled off to the kitchen, his hands and the crooks of his arms heavy with beer bottles and stacked glasses. Maureen joined some of her friends in the front room, where they swallowed her into their orbiting circle.

Blue retrieved his drink from the porch railing. The sangria had gone lukewarm; it tasted a bit like blood. He kept at it anyway, the alcohol going to his head, the surface of his skin. He rested his elbows against the railing and listened to the cry of the fiddle. This was followed by applause, then a hush from the house, as if the party was a radio play that had been abruptly muted. The wind whistled through the trees, knotted boughs discernible in the moonlight before a cloud lumbered over the cove. He closed his eyes.

A powerful sense of being watched shocked him to attention. Had he caught a strand of movement in the woods? Probably his imagination, but gooseflesh prickled his arms nevertheless. He kicked back a slug of wine, wiped his mouth, and lit another cigarette.

A light flickered in the trees. A lightning bug? Something alive and in motion, whatever it was, though now it was still, glowing like an ember. Blue stepped off the porch and walked a crooked line to the edge of the lawn a dozen yards from the house, and as he did the light appeared to approach in kind. The densely packed pines rustled, their limbs swaying overhead like water swept by an oar. He squinted into the night, as if he could glean meaning from the forest simply by staring hard enough into its dark and mysterious heart.

The light was gone, but he could hear—no, *feel*—a presence within the woods, accompanied by a wet earthy scent, powerful and fecund. He covered his nose, the cigarette paper a bright stain between his fingers, and the spark of light appeared again like a beacon. The source of the smell was extremely close, within arm's length, perhaps; its proximity left him simultaneously repulsed and intoxicated. He could feel something reaching out to take his hand, stroke it like a lover would. Blue's eyes narrowed, and his trembling fingers spidered forward, as if upon silken strings.

He could see himself. Right there, standing a little way into the woods, the dark surface of the forest freshly and impossibly reflective. There was his own startled face, backlit by the house and the candlelit glow from the windows. The light in the woods, it was the burning tip of the cigarette in his white hand, fingers extended in communion. Was he staring into a mirror?

He stepped forward, and now he could see right through this other self. On the other side of his reflection was the ghost image of a balsam fir, its needled branches held back by a hand. The hand that held back the branches, though, that was not his own—indeed, it was like no hand he had ever seen, the fingers bone-thin, and long, and deathly gray.

In a nauseating flash, it came to him: he wasn't seeing his reflection, nor was it some estranged identical twin. Rather, he was seeing himself *through someone else's eyes*. He was at once inside his body and outside of it, watching from beyond the sheltering trees. He saw himself as he was.

His sight refracted, the branches in his periphery a kaleidoscope of shadow and moonlight. A split-apart image of the forest floor and he listed, then steadied, his vision a mirror fragmented into shards. He pressed his eyes shut but the fractalled images didn't yield, only multiplied into differing angles. He thought of the compound eyes of the praying mantis sculpture he'd glimpsed inside the house as he saw himself from deep in the woods, as well as closer by; a splinter of his chin captured from ground level down the hill; a sliver of the back of his neck viewed from the treetops. He saw himself through a multitude of eyes, all watching from the woods.

His curiosity swelled, then turned to fear, then excitement, rapid pulsations that bled together until one emotion was indistinguishable from the next. His very being cried out in surrender, and he hungered to be disassembled into nothingness, his heart pounding so hard he thought his chest would burst. And all the while the whine and burring of insects, the call of predatory night birds, and the screech of the fiddle in one long and discordant stroke, the final note of a song that refused to end.

A hand grasped his shoulder, and quickly withdrew. "Hey," Gabe said. *How did he get so close?* "Are you okay?"

"What?" He shook his head. "Oh yeah. I was just . . . Nothing." Blue glanced back over his shoulder at the trees. *Nothingness*, he thought. *Surrender. Communion.* "Admiring the scenery."

"Nice." Gabe nodded sagely. "Maureen smoked you up, didn't she?"

"What? No."

"She said she was going to bring by some sticky stuff, so I just figured. Hey, how long have you been out here? We haven't seen you for hours."

"Hours?" Blue looked down. Between his fingers he held a charred cigarette butt, the stub burned down to the filter. He flicked it into the trees, and instantly regretted the trespass. "Has it been that long?"

"It's four in the morning. Elisa's complaining about her feet. She sent me to find you."

"Okay. Let's go." He mussed Gabe's hair somewhere between rough and tender, a bid for normalcy if nothing else, and Gabe ducked away from him. *See? Everything is fine.*

They walked across the lawn. Elisa, heels in hand, put an arm around Blue and the other around Gabe. The three schlemiel-schlimazeled to Jason, who stood with his arms crossed, shaking his head in mock disapproval. Elisa slapped him hard on the ass, and Jason howled as he threw his own arm around Blue. The four returned in a slanting box step to the house on the hill.

Once Jason and Gabe shambled upstairs to bed, Blue and Elisa retreated outside for one last gasp of night air, and for Blue one more glass of wine. "Man, am I beat," he said as they planted themselves on the porch swing. He glanced down the hill, toward the trees at the border of the lawn. "I thought I saw . . . Jesus, I don't know what. It was like I could see outside my body. Like I was watching myself through the woods, but from a hundred different eyes. Something." He rubbed his face and waited, but no response was forthcoming. "Fuck. Maybe I was having a flashback."

He thought he heard her laugh under her breath, but once he leaned in he could make out the sound of anguish as she choked back tears. "Hey," he said. "Hey, are you okay?" She didn't answer, only rested her chin against the heels of her wrists. "What's the matter?"

After a while she said, "Do you ever think you've made the wrong choices in life?"

"All the time. Why?"

"I don't know." Elisa's face was cast in darkness, only a slight suggestion of her features visible in the moonlight. "Never mind. I'm fine, really. Just ignore me, okay?"

"If you say so."

He listened to the wind rustle the leaves, to the solitary warble of an unknown bird darting across the tree canopy. *Awesome Elisa.* More than a decade gone since they met as teenagers in front of the Limelight, where they split a tab of E and danced the night away on a catwalk, looking down at the world below. He saw inside Elisa that night, right to her soul. Not by the yellow glow from the moon but beneath a scorching spotlight, its gels rotating red, green, red. The throb of music from the speakers, clean sweat, the chemical smell of dry ice: he had never wanted that blurry carnival of wasted youth to end. Then he awoke from its poppy-petaled spell, only to find himself cold and alone on the dirty bathroom floor of his midtwenties, wondering how he'd managed to land up there. When he wasn't looking, the lost boys and girls had all grown up.

Beyond the cove, a thin zipper of dawn opened on the horizon over Kelly's Mountain. "Look," he said. "Here comes the sun."

"Please don't sing," she said, and he busted out laughing. Elisa could always do that, penetrate to his core and alleviate the sense of alienation he'd harbored as long as he could remember. What could he say? She still got him. It didn't help that she was as beautiful as ever; that would never change, not to him. He would always love her, if only in regret. Except for that one night in May, right after he'd gotten the call about his grandmother and her house, when he and Elisa found their lips thrust together in need of both consuming and being consumed. Hands fumbling in the dark to remove each other's clothing, the heat of her warm flesh on his, skin on skin. That night regret was a stranger.

Blue slid his hand along the rough wood of the porch swing and interlaced his fingers with hers. Across the cove the distant light strengthened until it sparkled above the water like a disco ball, like glitter thrown from a rafter high above a cavernous and smoke-filled dance floor.

"Glittering," she said softly, as if she'd plucked the word from his mind.

"What's that?" he asked, but she didn't respond, only squeezed his hand before loosening her grip. It was a word he'd long kept close to his heart, one that described a place that didn't exist. A land of belonging he had once searched for across the skin of lovers, at the bottom of liquor bottles, in clouds of pot smoke and granulated powders and pills. His magical home, always just out of reach. She was the only thing left of that world, and already she was fading.

"Elisa," he said, her very name in his voice its own charge of urgency. "If there's something going on, you know you can tell me, right?"

"Sure," she said. "Of course."

"If things with Jason aren't—"

Her breath caught in her throat. "Don't," she said, and moved her hand from his. "I can't. Forget it. I'm sorry."

She stood and went inside the house, Blue left on the jangling porch swing, alone.

Chapter Two

He sees himself again, this time in his dreams. His unconscious, normally a dark pool, is now aglow with moonlight, and the mirror of the night forest appears to him once more. He faces his refractive self-image, and hears his call to himself: a choir of different selves in different voices, but all him. Struck by the same sense of longing he felt outside the ceilidh, he steeps in the fecund scent of his kindred, close by, so close.

They call him Blue, his adopted name; they call him Michael, his given name; and they call him by another, older name, something altogether different, but also familiar. A dream name. Or a christening at last?

His lips move, as if to repeat the word. But only a buzzing sound emerges, a hive of listless bees awakening to life, to be reborn.

∞

Blue opened his eyes to the tartan room's plaid bedding and matching walls. The name was gone. All that remained was a dull thud of sensation: that of being smothered and emerging, an escape from being buried alive, which was how he felt after most of his nightmares. More gloomy thoughts born of Saturn.

He'd neglected to draw the curtains, the square of light from the window next to the bed diffuse but still painfully bright. He slumped back down, a momentary shuddering of trees across his vision before he sat up again, determined to meet the incipient challenges of wakefulness.

Beyond the foot of the brass bed, someone stood in the doorway: Gabe, in a rumpled T-shirt and jeans that hung low over his narrow hips. They both started.

"Oh—sorry," Gabe said. He went to shut the door, appeared to collect himself, and peered back inside. "I was just—sorry. I heard you cry out."

"I was having a nightmare. Don't sweat it. Really." He didn't want any strangeness between them; he had enough to deal with already. "I hurt," Blue said, and rolled over. "What time is it?"

"Noonish. A bit later maybe."

"I feel like I've been hit by a truck."

"I know what you mean." Gabe shut the door and leaned against it. "A little too much schnapps, I guess."

The two had been in a holding pattern for a few weeks, since they'd drunkenly fallen into Blue's bed together, an odd repetition of what transpired with Elisa a couple of months prior. It was the same night he had shown Gabe his old photographs, and nostalgia once again turned into abandon. Blue had done most of the work, Gabe largely passive, almost dutifully so, a ritual display of surrender as Blue hauled him from the bed and into his lap. Blue's hands slid up Gabe's spine, only to rest on a fibrous landscape of raised scar tissue along Gabe's back in beaded threads. Another disturbing indication, along with the mottled scarring on his hand, that Gabe had suffered greatly in his youth.

"What . . ." Blue said that night, but, "Don't," Gabe had replied, and moved Blue's hands down to his waist. Gabe hadn't wanted him to see, and so he wouldn't look. The landscape of

Gabe's back remained fixed in his mind, however, an image of vestigial limbs or perhaps wings, shorn clean from muscle and bone.

After they'd finished, Gabe had put his shirt back on and turned to Blue, traced his finger over the smidge of hair on Blue's chest as if reading something there. Blue drifted off to sleep, and awoke the next morning to find him in the same position, inches away with his ice-blue eyes trained upon him, as if Gabe had remained awake all night doing just that. *Searching*, Blue had thought at the time. But for what, exactly?

"Hey, you know who's great?" Blue said now to break the silence. He had to do right by Gabe, which was why—against better judgment—Blue invited him on the trip in the first place. "Maureen. She's spectacular, isn't she?"

"Absolutely," Gabe replied, eager to agree, as was often the case. "We talked for a while last night. She's kind of like the best mom ever."

"It's true. Though she is a little out there." He took a cautious glance out of the tartan room's bright window, which faced a stand of mighty firs that stretched around the back of the house. "She told me she thought I glowed."

"Well, you sort of do." Gabe hid a sideways smile and stared down at the floor. "She told me something else, though."

"What?"

"That Elisa is knocked up."

Blue's stomach contracted, and he swallowed hard. "That she's *what?*"

"She said Elisa had *the* glow." Gabe laughed. "I don't know what that means about you."

Blue remembered what Maureen had said last night: that they both glowed, but Elisa's was familiar, or common or something . . .

"I wouldn't exactly take her word for it," Gabe said, picking up on Blue's conspicuous unease. "It's probably nothing."

Blue wanted to say he didn't buy it, but the problem was that he instantly and utterly did. This was based on his worldview, having long accepted the truism that if a certain possibility was deeply discomfiting, that meant it was accurate. Not that the kid could be his: despite his inebriated state that night, he had total recall of Elisa reassuring him she was on the pill. But why shouldn't he want Elisa and Jason to be pregnant? It would help cement their relationship, and in doing so abate the shame Blue felt over sleeping with her. He didn't want to be a shitty person. Not to Jason, not to anybody. And he certainly didn't want to fuck up Elisa's life. *She should have the future she wants,* he thought. *And if that involves kids, well, good for her. Maybe I dodged a bullet.*

After Gabe shuffled back to the yellow room, Blue dressed and put the conversation out of his mind; if Elisa was in fact pregnant, she would tell him soon enough.

Downstairs, Elisa was washing last night's dishes, while Jason read in the Adirondack chair out on the porch. And there—past the back of Jason's safari-hatted head, beyond the edge of the porch and down the rolling lawn that humpbacked Maureen and Donald's property—was the shining daylight splendor of Starling Cove. They had arrived under fog, so he wasn't expecting the expansive vista or the magnificence of the open sky, clear and blue, traversed by a lone eagle high over the shimmering water. No wonder so many who wandered up here in decades past had ended up staying. Was this really the place his mother had fled, dragging him along with her?

"So," Blue said. "Are we going to stay here forever or what?"

"You, maybe," Elisa said, drying her hands on a dishrag. "I

wouldn't know what to do with myself. There's only so much ceilidhing a girl can take." She pressed the rag to his chest, casual with the intimacy of the gesture; they were, he supposed, cool again. "And thank God you're awake. I'm starving." She gestured to a pink ceramic mug, no doubt one of Maureen's creations, filled to the brim with coffee. "Light and sweet, just like you. Ha. Jason went to the general store and bought out the place—eggs, bread, cheese. Whatever vegetables they had, which wasn't a lot. Our work here is done. Wow us, please."

"Lower your expectations. I'll see what I can do."

Setting his sights on the pantry, he started by excavating the dusty canned goods and nonperishables left by untold past renters. Gherkins, baby corn, dried beans . . . Pastry flour! Mini-quiches were his first thought, but when he unearthed a package of almond slivers and a jar of cinnamon, he shifted to sweet breakfast buns. Their caramelized, starchy smell soon wafted into the living room, and Elisa begged him to take them out of the oven.

He'd been cooking for more than twenty years, since the days of making hotchpotch casserole dinners for his cuisine-challenged mother, seven-year-old Michael balanced precariously on a stool set against the stove. He loved feeding people, loved the entire process of conception through delivery. Part of his pleasure was the ease with which it came to him. His first béchamel at culinary school (the sauce taught early in the first semester to scare off the dilettantes) had the velvety and complex nature of a master chef's. While the other students scurried back and forth from their notebooks to the stove, he whistled quietly over his saucepan, stirring the bubbling milk around a melting roux. His classmates at the institute initially resented him, then began to scrutinize his work for hints and tips, as in-

structors and visiting chefs gravitated to his cooking station. He
was, in short, a natural.

After graduation, he sous-chefed at a few places before opening Cyan, a storefront dumpling spot in Brooklyn with a couple
of tables that soon fostered a brisk delivery business. There were
write-ups in *New York* magazine and *Time Out*, and a mention
in the Dining Out section of the *Times*. With enough traffic, he
had hoped to move into a larger space, maybe by next year. But
that was before he started borrowing money from men like Vincente Castro, an independent entrepreneur who loaned money
to naive and/or desperate business owners throughout the outer
boroughs. It was only later that Blue came to terms with the
fact that the man's nom de guerre was Vinnie the Shark, and
that Vinnie's friends had witty and hilarious nicknames as well,
names like Jerry Rasputin and Sawed-Off Sal. The only way he
was going to dig himself out now was by signing off on the house
sale.

He found a lacquered wood tray on a high shelf with the
words M. *Benoit* carved into the underside, and used it to bring
the plates, buns, and orange juice to the porch. Gabe propped
open the screen door with a sculpted bear's head mask that
stared up from two blank eyeholes slashed into the dark copper.

"Oh my God." Jason rested his bun on his plate and sat back
in his chair, his eyes squeezed shut as if he were pained. "Oh.
Oh, Jesus, that's good. I want to savor it."

"Amazing," Gabe said, and swatted at a persistent fly drawn
by the buns' honeyed odor. "You should get these on the menu.
I mean, this is just amazing. I don't want to finish."

But they would say that. "You like?" he asked Elisa. She
would tell him.

"It is beyond," she said, and raised a glass of juice in salute.

He tried to glean her physical state, the way Maureen had. Was she chewing too fast? No, slow, deliberate. Mindful. All told, there were no overt signs she was eating for two. And how pregnant could she be anyway? A month? Two? More? Maybe she hadn't told Jason yet, hadn't told anyone. Maybe she didn't know herself. He forced it out of his mind, an itch he refused to scratch, especially the troublesome thought at its center.

It was still only Sunday and he couldn't reach the estate attorney about his grandmother's house, so the day was all theirs. Maureen had told them about the canoes docked at the water, and after clearing the dishes they sauntered down the steep hill, bright sparkles on the stony shore cast by the early-afternoon sun that made the wet rocks appear dusted with glass shards, if not quite diamonds. Jason embarked in one canoe with Elisa at the bow; they cracked jokes and laughed as they coasted out onto the cove, before any of them had fetched paddles. Blue hurried to the dockside shed, which reeked of mildew and animal droppings. The smell reminded him of the earthy stench of the night forest, as well as his dreams. He looked down at the water, his image reflected back from a dozen different vantages.

After cruising the cove for a couple of hours they returned to the house for a late lunch. With a note that read "A few things from my garden," Maureen had dropped off a basket of fresh vegetables, which Blue used to whip up a summer salad that was eagerly devoured. She had also included an envelope of weed and Zig-Zags. "Our very own pot fairy!" as Gabe put it, passing Blue a freshly rolled joint. Elisa and Jason abstained, which wasn't unusual; Jason was pretty straitlaced, and she never did like weed much, probably hadn't smoked since their club days. Still, he tried not to wonder anew about this supposed glow of hers.

They decided to go for a quick hike before it got dark, and took one of the trails behind the house. Tree branches arched overhead like a cathedral ceiling, casting distorted shadows upon the packed ground. Blue had always enjoyed the outdoors, fond memories of idle summers in which he wandered over Oregon railroad tracks or kicked rocks along gravel roads in Iowa, driftwood and shells collected beachside up and down both coasts. Alone, mostly, because he didn't have time to make many friends before his mom would uproot him and hustle him off to the next town or city.

They walked for some time and had fallen silent with the effort, Jason at the lead while the others marched behind at a steady clip. Blue fell back, slowing further to take in a particularly glorious view of a cluster of trees bearing incongruous blood-red leaves amid the lush wall of green. Flycatchers cheeped overhead, darting in and out of the tree canopy. There was a whispering noise from back in the woods, vague susurrations in the vicinity of the red trees. He put an ear to the wind. Someone humming? Or just the dull buzzing of insect life? He started down the path again but the murmuring returned, as abruptly as it had ceased. Words, rushing past . . .

It sounded like a foreign language, every other syllable in a lofty register and accompanied by a throaty animal scratch in an ambiguous, genderless pitch. A single word jumped out at him.

home

He heard it again, twice—*home, home*—and listened for more.

home
home home
come home you are home
you are home

"Listen," Blue whispered, but the others were already out of earshot. He wanted to call out to whomever it was but was afraid of scaring them off. The words beckoned him closer, attempting to draw him into the woods, and though he was frightened he felt nothing so much as seduced.

He tried to step back but his foot refused to rest on its heel so he stepped forward instead, into the woods. The voice magnified and distorted, words layered over one another now so he could no longer glean their meaning. Other voices joined until they formed a jumbled chorus, a static wall of noise. Blue grimaced and closed his eyes, bending to rest his palms on his knees. Right under him was an anthill, its occupants streaming out from the nest in a frenzied torrent, their movements scattered and panicked. Atop the anthill sat a single dewdrop, its domed surface reflecting back a grossly enlarged image of himself. He was all eyes.

"Blue?"

The others had stopped at a fork in the trail about thirty yards ahead. "Are you okay?" Elisa called out, but it was Gabe who dropped his pack and hurried to Blue's side.

"Maybe we should head back," Gabe said, placing a hand on Blue's shoulder.

"I'm fine," Blue said, and righted himself. "Just got a little dizzy." He took a bottle of water from his pack and drank.

"Like last night." Gabe's expression was a riddle. "Last night, when I found you on the lawn, you looked the same. Staring into the trees like you were . . . transfixed."

"I'm fine." He tried to smile, and stepped back onto the trail. "Don't worry about me. Okay?"

Gabe was right, though: the voices carried the very same shock of recognition, along with a powerful feeling of being battered from all sides. He could no longer recall their exact sound; that was lost to him, along with the rapturous sensation that had accompanied them. All that remained was an absence, a void, along with his painfully familiar sense of unbelonging, amplified. He wanted the rapture to return.

Jason approached, followed by Elisa. "Look," she said, and pushed back unruly boughs to reveal a sign, faded green paint flecked inside the grooves of wood. The sign sat atop a tilted iron pole and was crafted in the shape of a lithe Tinker Bell fairy in flight, its folded-back wings and Kewpie-doll face carved in profile. The words *The Starling Cove Friendship Outpost & Artists Colony, Est. 1971* were etched in script along the border. Aside the legend, the fairy's outstretched hand pointed in the direction of the deep woods.

"Catchy name," Elisa said dryly as she took a photograph. "Blue, is this where—"

"Yep. We seem to have found my place of birth." *Home. You are home.*

"Really?" Jason said. "You were actually born here? Out here in the woods?"

"All I know is that I was born in a barn."

"Like Jesus!" Elisa and Gabe both said, then laughed.

"Yeah," Blue said. "But instead of three wise men they probably had a crèche full of chanting doulas. My grandmother must have been horrified."

"So," Jason said. "Want to check it out?"

Following an overgrown path up the hill, they came to a three-story brick building. At over three hundred feet long it was entirely out of scale, the only structure around, yes, but also the largest they'd seen so far in the cove. It looked to be an old mill, its windows devoid of glass. It soon became clear the place was burned out: half a caved-in roof, no intact windows, smoke damage visible around the casings and roofline. The few remaining clay eaves were cracked and charred, creeper vines threaded over cold gray stone and a gaping archway that must have once framed a now-absent set of doors.

Inside, a diorama of vegetation mirrored the surrounding forest, a sea of weeds carpeted by untamed grass. Water damage cratered the ceiling, warped beams yielding glimpses of the upper floors and the late-afternoon sky beyond. Webs of vines grew from the foundation and ran wild along the brick, weighing down rotted tapestries that hung from the waterlogged rafters. Broken bottles and rusty beer cans glimmered beneath the bank of narrow window frames: the ruined structure looked to be a sanctuary of sorts, most likely for bored teens. *I could have been one of those kids*, Blue thought as he eyed the stretch of crude graffiti down the narrow hallway. *There but for the grace of my mother.*

Once they entered the inner chamber, they paused to take in the scene: a series of cracked and peeling but surprisingly intact murals, corner to corner and floor to ceiling along the four walls. Blue crossed the space to the shadowed end of the room, while the others stood in the entryway, painted as the snarling mouth of a coyote. In the dim light he could make out a life-sized illustration of what appeared to be a Russian Blue cat in flight, its wings actual tree branches protruding from its silver-gray fur as it soared majestically toward a sneering yellow-faced sun overhead. He leaned in closer for a better look. The animal wore a tuxedo jacket and ruffled shirt; otherwise it was pantless, with a singed photo of an erect penis decoupaged between its legs, shellacked along with the rest of the mural. The cat thrust forward a rusty corkscrew in its paw; like the tree branch wings, this too was collaged, a real corkscrew affixed to the drawing with its tip protruding from the wall, inches from Blue's eyes.

He snapped his head away and almost knocked into Jason. "Fascinating stuff," Jason said. "Pretty compulsive, wouldn't you say? It looks like, what do you call it, outsider art. Am I right? Hey, wait. Is that a flying cat with a dick?"

"Looks like." Blue put out his arm. "Watch out. You'll stick yourself."

"Yeesh." Jason touched a finger to the side of the corkscrew. "This place isn't exactly childproofed, is it? Was it like this when you were growing up?"

"Honestly, I don't know. I mean, I think I would remember all this." He was beginning to get the feeling that his lack of memory had been necessarily adaptive.

Beneath the cat was a water-damaged illustration of a swirled banner like a map legend, upon which *Fluffy Gray Mirrorcat of the Otherfolk, Fortifier of the Place Below and Protector of Our Queen* was written in delicate cursive. A few feet down the paper's length the cat reappeared; here he bore neither tree branch wings nor human erection but a leash fashioned from a leather shoelace and led by an unseen hand. It was some kind of continuing story, told not only in pictures and words but in associations and archetypes, an ongoing narrative leading from one wall to the next. Alongside the illustrations were passages written in unfamiliar symbols and languages, Gaelic perhaps among them. The images made Blue uncomfortable on a visceral level.

And they were everywhere. His eyes couldn't rest on a single unmarked surface: the walls caked in grime to the dirt floor, the crumbling chimneys all illustrated with honeycombed beehives and diving trout and a tarantula driving what looked to be a police car, frolicking manticores, a nude woman with a red star on her back, the flowering roots of swollen tubers. Though faded by time, the murals were crafted with expertise, broadly characterized but with the precise exactitude of Matisse paper cuts. Images a child might have chosen, but rendered by the assured hand of an adult. All of it was life-sized and perfectly to scale.

Elisa called to them from the stone steps leading upstairs. Blue went to follow, but stopped short of a decrepit kitchen, the relics of an old stove and washbasin blackened with soot. Beyond the kitchen were two battered metal doors. The first was shut tight, but the second was slightly ajar, a dried-out rag hanging from a nail on its back. The dim light from the gaping windows barely penetrated this far inside the building, but through the exposed rafters he caught a faint glinting past the cracked door, a reflective wink in the darkness. With the toe of his boot Blue teased the door open, obscuring what little light he had. He retrieved his plastic lighter from his pocket, its modest flicker illuminating the inside of a closet decorated with the illustrated narrative that had spread throughout the building like mold.

In the center of the left wall was a string of yarn-haired paper dolls, made to resemble children. Hands fused one to the next, their eyes deep pools of charcoal, the children ran from a battalion of what appeared to be fang-toothed fairies, their tissue paper wings afloat like lengths of shed snakeskin over an uneven topography of flaking paint. On the opposite wall was a near mirror image, only here the children appeared gleeful and maniacal, and chased the fairies instead. Their needle-fanged prey, alarmed, fled in the direction of the open door, two of the children shepherded in their midst.

I've seen this before, Blue thought, and stepped inside the closet.

He held the lighter up to the ceiling. A red-skinned angel, expression beneficent with eyes closed in either ecstasy or solemnity, was painted on the scratched boards overhead. Flowing white robes draped the angel's chest like a toga, its red wings aloft in massive crests, cellophane traced through with fine pencil mimicking gold leaf that reminded him of a butterfly's wings. Spiraled in cursive beneath the figure was written *Borealis the Mother was sent up from the Heavens of the Faraway World to bring comfort to the New Children of the Screaming Places* on a curled banner scroll; the words that followed trailed off the ceiling into illegibility.

Above the angel's head, a tiny halo: an actual gold band, like a wedding ring, embedded in the wall. He'd seen this ring before as well. He was sure of it. Could it have belonged to his mother? His grandmother? Or was it always right here, stuck to the closet ceiling?

On the floor was yet another illustration, this one painted across the wooden slats. It was similar in manner to the angel, wings spanning the cramped space from edge to edge. Only this was no angel. Naked skin chalk white, its bright honeycombed eyes stared out from a tapered and sunken face, jagged teeth bared like an insect's mandibles. The wings were leathery like a bat's wings, wide and capped by elongated fingers that ended in serrated claws. Blue squatted and brought the increasingly warm lighter closer to the rendering. The creature's nails and teeth were tiny rusted staples riveted directly into the floorboards, its eyes hollowed-out copper filings hot-glued inside the dark spaces between the slats.

There was a legend beneath this one as well, but it was written on the floor behind him. He stepped out of the closet for a better look when a hand grabbed his arm.

"Do you hear that?" Gabe said, head cocked.

They crept down the hall. Blue thought of the words from the woods, spoken in that unidentifiable yet achingly familiar tongue. The shifting wind through the open windows made any sound difficult to place, and he wasn't sure if his imagination was getting the better of him.

"I think so," Blue said. "Someone whispering?"

"Someone whistling."

Elisa and Jason stole down the stone stairs. They all heard it, a lilting little tune carried on the air, soft and then softer, depending on the direction of the wind. They went out back—not much there but an old covered well, along with some sodden kindling and planks—and stood silent for a few moments, trying to pinpoint the sound. There was a crunch of leaves farther out in the woods, and Jason stepped forward, placing a protective hand in front of Elisa. "Hello?" he called out. "Is someone there?"

The whistling stopped. Another sound now, softer but no longer masked: water, close by and babbling. Jason tiptoed off the path into the trees with Blue behind him, while Gabe and Elisa hung back.

About ten yards into the woods there was a break in the foliage where a small creek wound its way downhill. Beside the water a man in a checked flannel shirt and nylon waders crouched upon a rock; a book was laid open across his lap, but he stared into the distant trees.

"Donald," Jason called out. The older man raised his head and smiled, then returned his attention to the spot where the stream disappeared into the woods. "How are you doing today?"

"Not terribly," Donald said. "Just out here looking. Dry summer . . ."

"Find anything interesting?"

"Not yet."

Elisa and Gabe made their way down the embankment, and Donald tracked them, shielding his eyes from a shaft of sunlight penetrating the leaves. "There's four of you," he concluded. "Bridge numbers." A loud rustling sounded behind him and a large brown dog scampered from the underbrush. "This is Olivier. He was trained as a bird dog, which I grew up calling a pointer. He's a rescue dog. My wife got him for me to 'better my mood.'"

The dog made a beeline straight for Elisa, who tried shooing it away until Jason stepped in and lured it back toward the creek with a branch. "Sorry, doggie," she said by way of apology.

"She's allergic," Jason explained. He tossed the stick a great distance; the dog disappeared back into the brush only to reappear a moment later, branch in mouth and begging for another go. "We once stayed at a bed-and-breakfast in Vermont and she had an attack. After landing up in the emergency room we found out that a dog had been in our room. It was scary. She could barely breathe."

"Actually, it was a cat," Elisa said. "But dogs aren't so great for me either."

"Barbara is just the same," Donald said, and peered at her through his Coke bottle lenses. "She'd never let us have a dog, even though the boys begged for one." His words were punctuated with reverence, as if his former wife and Elisa shared some rare and magical trait. Blue's stomach tightened, and he thought of Maureen.

"Where are you all heading from?" Donald asked, and ran his hands over the dog's hide, dirty fingers dug deep into brown fur.

"We saw the sign," Jason said. "For the . . . community?"

"Ah. Yes. The Colony. May she rest in peace. Folks heard 'artists' colony' and thought they'd find a host of little cottages out here, but we only ever had the one biggie. Used to be an old loggers' quarters, back when you could still do such things in these woods, before all the appalling environmentalists such as myself came along and ruined everything. I still like to come back for a little visit now and again, just to see the old girl. It was a magical place. Fairy-touched, until the end. The wife doesn't like me to go inside in its current state, so . . ." He shook his head. "Coming up from the old logging road, then?"

"Yes," said Jason, who apparently had not only an innate sense of direction but an understanding of local geography as well. "Maureen said that's where all the best trails are."

"Just be careful. It's best to go in a group. Easy to get disoriented. You might not find your way back." Donald shut his book, glanced back up the creek mouth, and stood to face them. "There's all sorts of legends concerning these woods. A fishing captain taught me an old ditty about an Irish moonshiner the mountain was supposedly named after. It goes"—and here he sang—"*Kelly dearly loved the Highlands but he couldn't live alone. For the breezes used to whisper, 'Kelly, boy, you must come home.'*"

The word echoed in Blue's head. *Home, home. Come home, you are home.*

Donald whistled for a moment, tried to find the melody again. "*The breezes kept a-callin'*," he sang, dropping into a near whisper, "*kept a-callin' night and day. Till from the lofty mountain, they lured him far away.*" He looked up at the sky. "So old Kelly went back where he came from. Though I suppose we all must, in due course. Even the queen."

Donald climbed the embankment and stopped to look down

on them, the dog at his heels. The afternoon light dimmed over his shoulder and the treetops above the horizon, his shape a stark and dramatic shadow. "Don't worry," he said, the twin windows of his spectacles frosted white as he looked back at the sun. "You'll find your way eventually. Just remember to take me when you do." With a little wave, he was off.

Gabe turned to Blue as they watched Donald disappear in the direction of the burned-out building. "Didn't Maureen say he had dementia?"

"Alzheimer's, actually."

"So sad. I bet he has a lot of interesting stories left to tell." Gabe let out a sprightly little whistle in poor imitation of Donald as they headed back to the trail.

The temperature began dropping as soon as the sun set. Back at the house, Blue made stew using more salvaged pantry ingredients, served from a green ceramic soup tureen hand painted with bright slices of apple. Once the plates were cleared they collected logs from the rear deck and put a fire on in the living room, which infused the woodstove with a pleasant cedar smell. A halfhearted game of Celebrity followed as they fell one after the next into a collective food coma, lulled to bed by the flicker and heat from the flames. Elisa and Jason dragged themselves off, and Gabe tried to coax Blue along as well, but he would have none of it. "Go ahead," Blue said, "I'll be along soon," and he crashed out on the throw pillows. Gabe placed a quilt over him before he tramped upstairs himself.

❦

Darkness.

Underground. A mineshaft? Hard to tell, but the space is dank and oppressive, the smell of wet earth heavy in the air.

Someone else is there with him, close by, the sensation of hot breath covering him from crown to foot. It's not really breath, though. It's dirt: he is buried alive. Unsure which way is up or out, he knows he should be scared but he isn't. This is what he was made for.

Pushing forward, his fingers knead the earth like dough. His palms flatten, they pull and massage and flatten once more. He extends a finger. Its tip pierces the wall of dirt, forms a small pinprick of light. The finger slims, lengthens, and transmogrifies to fill the breach, a skeleton key of flesh and bone.

He makes a hole big enough to force his head through, slithering forward as if from a primordial pool. The glittering light blinds him. It stings, this shred of dawn's brightness, burns the place where his eyes should be but are not. But still he crawls forth, until his body is birthed from the earth that is his home and shall always be, this land of emerald green and brightest blue.

Even as he lopes through the forest, the insects and birds scattering from his path, he knows that he must change; that is why he has been chosen. He reaches forward with a long and sickly gray finger to pull back the branches of pine, hairs aquiver upon his elongated limbs. He was sent up from the hive to bring new life, his only purpose. Only when he succeeds will he be allowed to return.

A field of grass, speckled with bright pink wildflowers; a distant green clapboard house, tilted upon the hill as if steeling itself against a storm; and the sound of two young children at play, their laughter circling closer and closer to the edge of the woods, where he waits for the others to arrive.

❦

Blue awoke with a start. He thrashed against the quilt, which
had made its way up over his head, and yanked it off, scuttling
crablike from the woodstove. He was soaked with sweat. From
the dying embers, yes, but also from the dream; the two had
become intertwined. He pulled his wet shirt over his head and
threw it before the stove, an offering to the livid god of fire.

One night back in March, Gabe, upon hearing of his recurring nightmares, had posited that Blue had died violently
in a past life; it was as ridiculous a theory as you'd expect from
a young man whose personal belief system was informed by the
Village Voice horoscope column. But there was something about
Blue's dreams that had always held the unshakeable power of
lived experience. His haunting nightmares of an underground
existence had been his lifelong mystery; the woods and the
house and the laughing children, though, those were all new,
and spoke to him of his early years in Starling Cove.

He still held bitter memories of an itinerant youth spent at a
distance from his peers. Most children hadn't liked him. Feared
him, even, though he couldn't understand why. There was a
time he was convinced he gave off some pheromonal signal that
made them walk wide of him, as if he were contagious and to
be avoided at all costs. Adults enjoyed his company, however,
so he would cultivate those relationships, for better or worse.
It was only once he hit adolescence that his classmates began
flocking to him.

At eleven in St. Louis, Marybeth Freemont ran her Blow-
Pop-sticky fingers through his downy black hair during recess
before planting a wet kiss on his lips, the watermelon taste of
her tongue remaining long after she'd hurried away. At thirteen in Atlanta, Ricky Barlow got into bed with him during a
sleepover and sucked him off beneath his blanket before the boy

climbed back to the top bunk, never to speak of the incident again. At fifteen in high school in New York, Melissa Kaufman, a senior girl, asked him to the fall dance; it was during a medley of Beastie Boys songs that she (and this was the only way to put it) deflowered him on the back stairs, where she leaned against the railing, hitched up her crinoline dress, and pulled him out of his pants and into her with a raw hunger that had shocked him.

Apparently he'd begun giving off the right kind of phero-mones. People just seemed drawn to him. His mother took no-tice and, calling him her "good luck charm," dragged him along to job interviews and bingo nights at bars. On a few dates as well, a tactic so disarming that it usually worked in her favor. "I don't know what I'd do without you," she often told him after landing a new secretarial job or getting their latest landlord to forgo a missing rent payment. Eventually Blue left home and she fell sick in his absence, as if he were the root cause of all her fortune, both good and ill.

He stepped onto the porch of the MacLeod House for some fresh air. The cove was tranquil in the muted light from the waning moon, the tower of Kelly's Mountain vigilant in the dis-tance. He hung the quilt over his shoulders and padded barefoot down the lawn, the grass damp between his toes. He stopped at the foot of the trail leading into the trees. The woods where the old Colony building was, where Donald had appeared to be waiting for something, or perhaps summoning it himself.

There was another source of light distinct from the quarter-moon: a sliver of illumination from the little shingled cabin Maureen used as a pottery studio. Blue crept across the drive to the cabin and peered through a slit in the curtains. Mau-reen, her back to him, was at a long, paint-spattered worktable and bent over something ridged and steely gray; he couldn't see more than that. The mono buzz of classic rock on the radio made the entire studio hum, a comforting defiance of the immense and silent blanket of night.

She shuffled to the slop sink on the far side of the cabin, glaze-stained latex gloves raised before her like a surgeon. Blue moved around the back to get another vantage point. By the time he made it to the opposite window, Maureen had unexpectedly turned to face him, her gray eyes bulging with alarm.

He hurried inside. "I am so sorry," he said, mortified. "I couldn't sleep and I just kind of wandered down here . . ." Now that he said it, what was he doing exactly? How bizarre of him to spy on her and scare her like that, dressed in little more than a quilt! Maybe he wasn't fully awake after all, though it sounded like a poor excuse.

"You almost gave me a heart attack." Maureen exhaled, a hand to her chest. "That's not nice to do to an old woman."

"I'm really sorry. I don't know what I was thinking. I wasn't thinking at all." He pulled the quilt tighter around him. "Forgive me, please. And for the record, you don't qualify as an old woman. Not even close."

"Well. Thanks. That does make me feel a little better." She gestured at a stool and Blue sat at the worktable, where an oversized clay mask lay facedown upon stained newsprint. An inverted bowl with twin slits for eyes, the mask was glazed metallic gray, a prism of shadow and color refracted in its bulbous contours.

"Very cool," he said.

"Isn't it? It's going to be a praying mantis. Love those critters. Mantises are the best bug killers around, especially for farms and apple orchards, places like that. I'd tell you it's my spirit animal if I wasn't worried about you looking at me funny." She wiped a hand across her forehead, which left a faint trail of glaze. "Do anything fun today?"

"We smoked and went for a hike in the woods."

"Good stuff, huh?"

"The weed or the woods?" Blue smiled. "They were both nice, actually. Thanks." He picked a stray splinter of firewood from the quilt. "We saw Donald out there. He looked . . ."

"Like he was waiting for someone?"

"Exactly." His heart began to thrum, as if planning an escape. "It was kind of strange, actually, but last night? He said he knew me or something. He seemed pretty sure of himself too."

"That's a new one. I'll have to add it to the list." She opened her mouth and then shut it, and was silent for a few moments before she spoke again. "He's waiting for Barbara, by the way."

"His first wife."

"The very same. She's going to come back any day now. Or someone like her, maybe." She shook her head. "But who knows? A woman who died on the Isle of Skye forty years ago might just stroll on out of there yet. These are some strange woods, after all."

"Donald said as much. Something about a moonshiner, old Kelly, hearing words on the wind?" He paused. "I heard something out there myself. Something in the trees."

"Did you now?" She sat across from him.

"I heard . . . Well, it sounded like words being whispered, but in another language. I could understand it, though . . ." He waved his hand. "Never mind."

"This is sacred ground, you know. From long before moonshining days. My people, the real natives from all over these parts—some of us believe this is the resting place of Kluscap. He was the first man, and also a kind of god. Not much wilder

than any other creation myth, when you think about it. I still
call it Kluscap's Mountain instead of Kelly's, just like the rest of
my family. The story goes that someday Kluscap is going to wake
there from his sleep, and come with the fairies out of the sea
caves under the mountain. The entrance to the caverns is actually called the Fairy Hole." Blue was reminded of the vicious
fairy-looking creatures on the walls of the burned-out Colony.

Maureen reached over and turned off the table lamp. The
only light remaining was from the dull overhead fixture, so that
her face was thrown into shadow. "Of course," she said, "there's
a stranger legend about these parts, one even Mi'kmaqs don't
dare speak of. It's about a dangerous species known to stalk the
land, from early spring through Celtic Colours. Every year, you
can feel them coming as soon as the snow melts, can even set
your watch to it. They might even come to you at night. Watching, waiting on the other side of the window . . ." She leaned
forward, elbows on the table. "They're called the Summer People."

Blue swallowed, hard. "What do they want?"

She burst out laughing, slapping a hand down on the table
like a domino player throwing a bone. "Honey, that's my idea
of a bad joke. The Summer People is what we call the tourists."

"Oh. Sorry." He chuckled uncomfortably. "So basically
you're saying I should have knocked first."

"Next time." She rounded the table and squeezed his shoulders. "Really, though, it's nice to have the company. Like I said,
there's something about you . . . Let's just say you don't seem
like the usual sightseer doing the Cabot Trail for the summer."

He wanted to tell her what they were actually doing in
Starling Cove—that he was born here, and that his friends had
come with him to put to rest a part of his past. But he held his

tongue. All he said was, "I guess I disguise myself better than most," and left it at that.

Maureen finished straightening up and killed the light before they walked out onto the lawn. "Hey," Blue said. "Thanks for letting me hang around."

"Come back another night, a bit earlier, and I'll teach you how to throw clay on the wheel. It's especially fun if you're a bit toasted."

"It's a date. If I can get you back, that is. Maybe I can cook you a meal?"

"Lovely. I heard you have the touch, after all."

"Listen," he said once they neared the drive. "What you said about Elisa, having 'the glow'? Did you mean you thought she was pregnant?"

"Who's been whispering in your ear?" she said, a sly smile creeping across her lips. "Good night, Michael. Sweet dreams."

"Blue," he said. "Blue," but she didn't hear him, only waved good-bye and headed down the narrow dirt path through the vegetable garden until she disappeared around the side of the house. There was a moment of perfect silence before the screen door slammed shut, echoing across the cove like a gunshot.

Chapter Three

Blue waited until Tuesday to call the estate lawyer in Halifax, who gave him the number of the local property agent responsible for the house sale. By the time they finally connected it was already Thursday, leaving him to wonder, with only two days left of the trip, whether it was worth seeing the house at all. What was he going to do, suddenly fall in love with the place? Not going to happen. Every credit card was maxed out, and he was three months behind on rent for Cyan. The problem was that he couldn't keep up with demand, and had no idea how to manage costs or amortize his debts, especially his less savory ones.

Speaking of which, he had received three missed calls on his cellphone in the past few days from Vincente Castro; the fact that the loan shark had ominously failed to leave any messages made Blue's kneecaps itch. Even if he got fifty thousand bucks back for the house after taxes—and that was optimistic—it wasn't much of a leg up. But he had to grab it, and grab it fast. He scheduled a time to view the house the next day and would sign the papers then and there.

Meanwhile, he tried to keep himself occupied. He drove with the others to Baddeck for ice cream and strolled the board-walk along the Bras d'Or Lake, followed by a lunch of lobster rolls and beer at the Water's Edge; dinner at Chanterelle, overlooking St. Ann's Bay; the next day a trip to Joe's Scarecrow Village near Cheticamp and a second pass at the supermarket so they could stock up on provisions for the rest of the week's meals. More nights by the fire, and whisky and wine, though Elisa refrained; he still couldn't bring himself to ask her why. There was more hiking as well, though not for Blue, who refused to brave the woods. His sleep was finally sweet again, free of nightmares for the first time in recent memory.

He arranged to meet the property agent on Friday afternoon while the others were out on a hike. Waiting at the foot of the drive, he halfheartedly smoked a cigarette; in the past couple of days, he'd only had two or three. The taste had become newly awful to him, as if the pack had staled overnight. *Maybe it's time I finally quit,* he thought, and stubbed out the butt beneath the heel of his engineer boot.

A dirty maroon Chevy Suburban pulled over to the side of the road, kicking up a cloud of gravel dust. "You Michael? Stanley Baker," the agent said with a smile. "Ready to go?"

Dressed in a black-and-red-checked shirt, his collar crumpled beneath a frizzy gray ponytail, Stanley bore little resemblance to the pseudoslick salesmen that Blue and his mother had traipsed after into dozens of rat holes over the years. They made small talk on the short drive; it turned out he was also a licensed attorney, so they could take care of the sale as soon as Blue saw the house. "It isn't in great shape," Stanley warned, "but you got a decent price for it. They're foreign buyers, from Belgium. Go figure. There's a lot on the market just sitting, so consider yourself lucky." He went on to offer his condolences, which Blue thanked him for, though he felt a bit of an imposter seeing as how he hadn't seen or spoken to Grandma Flora since he was five.

Near the top of Kelly's Mountain, the elevation caused Blue's ears to pop. They popped again a few minutes later on the other side, where they wound their way down and then up a dirt path, the forest thickening as Portland Road snaked northward. *To grandmother's house we go*, he thought, and grimaced.

Just before the turnoff they passed a ramshackle old church that appeared to have slid into disuse, its birch exterior peeling white with its bell tower half collapsed, the bell itself nowhere to be seen. An enormous anchor rested in the small patch of unruly grass between the church and the road, beside which stood a weathered sign, a stark black-on-white Celtic cross insignia crowning the words *Christ Church 1818 W. Macleod*. The bottom half of the sign was a changeable copy board, a verse of scripture spelled out in a stark red procession of crooked letter tiles.

AND GOD SAID LET THEM HAVE DOMINION
OVER ALL THE EARTH
OVER EVERY CREEPING THING
THAT CREEPETH UPON THE EARTH

Blue felt a tightness in his throat and covered his mouth, turning his head to cough. By the time he looked up again, the church was out of view.

Five more minutes down the road and there, across a vast clearing, was Grandma Flora's house. He'd come to picture it as the dark stage piece behind the Bates Motel, an imposing, widow's-walked home with a shadowy figure visible in the window, if you looked closely enough. But in reality the house turned out to be entirely unthreatening, faded green clapboard with a gabled roof. It was modest in size, akin to a Cape Cod cottage, not sinister as much as sedate. It was the house from his dream: the one past the field dotted by wildflowers, where he had heard the sounds of children at play.

He followed the property agent up the rotted porch steps. As Stanley struggled with the key and pushed against the door with his shoulder, the wood warped in its damaged frame, Blue felt a frisson of apprehension. *Maybe this wasn't such a good idea,* he wanted to say, but instead said nothing at all. The door soon gave, and the agent nudged it the rest of the way open with his foot, yielding a glimpse of the foyer and the staircase just beyond.

"You coming?" Stanley said. He smiled and cocked his head toward the door.

Blue strode past him and inside. The house was musty and dark, with every window shaded, the only light from the open door. The remains of a dozen houseplants lined the hall, where they sagged upon a series of wicker plant stands, littered among an impressive panoply of cracked terra-cotta pots.

"Can we go up first?" Blue asked, placing his unreadiness to explore the downstairs at the feet of a noxious odor emanating from somewhere past the stairs.

Atop the house was an abbreviated atticlike floor, the low-ceilinged space packed with all manner of crap—boxes and busted dressers stuffed with old clothes, hundreds of moldering romance novels piled waist-high, chipped Virgin Mary figurines and other religious bric-a-brac, gold-leaf crosses nailed to the four walls. A futile dam of possessions, assembled to ward off the inevitable.

Downstairs, the makeshift bedroom at the back was dark and smelled like piss and unwashed flesh. "Well . . ." Stanley let the rest of his sentence hang in the stale air, the awkward silence bisected by the ringing of his cellphone. "Got to take this," he said quickly, and backed toward the living room and the porch beyond. Blue covered his nose and ducked inside the room.

Past an unmade hospital bed, two tabletops were nailed across the window frames, the legs sawed off and jammed into the extra spaces above the ledges. The almond wallpaper danced with the thin shapes of sparkle-eyed kiddies busy sledding, or sweeping; they wore wool mittens and little hats and shiny shoes, trailing sacks of twigs for kindling in their wake. In a partially rendered eatery, a cherubic little boy slyly dipped a hand into a cauldron of rich chocolate batter. Some of the children linked arms in jigging circles, while others were alone, curled up in the creases of the walls. Around the windows the wallpaper was peeled away, though thin slivers remained: a bodiless face here, a headless girl there, lending the room a disturbing air of decapitation.

Blue retreated to the living room and its wood-paneled walls, the floor covered in water-stained carpeting. A ratty orange couch sagged behind a scuffed coffee table, its scratched glass surface a murky window over shelves crammed with papers. He sat beside the table and removed a pile, sifted through bills and circulars, tax documents and aged coupon clippings, many older than himself. An entire life, reduced to a pile of papers. What would his own paper trail look like, were his life to end today? The never-ending letters from creditors, faded flyers from his club days, old report cards and loan applications . . . Better to burn it all.

As he returned the papers he noticed a large black binder on the bottom shelf, and dusted off the cracked leather cover. A photo album, filled with pictures of him, younger than he'd ever seen; all his mother's photographs were from their time in America. The first few pages showed him as a chubby-cheeked baby, and later as a boy, sunburnt and giggling at three or four in a field of purple lupines, the colors seventies saturated and over-exposed in brassy photo corners. Occasionally his mother would fall into the frame: half of her alarmingly youthful face, or a drape of her brown and iron-straight hair, a bent arm around him or a knee upon which he rested. But it was clear the subject of the photographer's gaze was the little boy named Michael, who would one day become Blue.

He turned the page. There were leaves of yellowed newspaper taped inside the album, pages of them. He unfolded the first to find the front page of the Friday, October 2, 1981, edition of the *Cape Breton Post*, the headline LOCAL BOY AND GIRL GO MISSING. Below the headline were photographs of two young children, a boy and a girl; his own face was the boy's face, which stared back from beneath a crooked bowl cut, a goofy smile upon his lips.

Blue's eyes narrowed before going wide, then wider, as he read.

Starling Cove—A search was under way Thursday for two five-year-old Starling Cove children, according to police.

The girl, Gavina Beaton, and the boy, Michael Whitley, were last seen at about 10:30 a.m. playing in the yard of the house where Whitley often visits with his grandmother, Starling Cove resident Flora MacKenzie. "We're doing everything we can to locate them," said Staff Sgt. Lewis Connolly of the Cape Breton Regional Police.

Police later confirmed no clues were found, though

the investigation has been hampered by the unseasonable forest fires.

Late Thursday afternoon members of Cape Breton Ground Search and Rescue and regional police's K-9 unit searched the area where Beaton and Whitley were last seen.

The ground search also turned up no clues. A door-to-door canvass is under way.

Michael's heartbroken mother, Yvonne Whitley, along with Gavina's mother, Tessa Beaton, remained at the Portland Road home on Thursday night surrounded by friends and family members and hoping for good news. Both families are residents of the Starling Cove Friendship Outpost and Artists Colony, a communal living collective.

"I'm devastated," Ms. Whitley said. "This is a feeling no one would ever want to have. It's not like these kids to wander off, so we're just really scared for them. We'll keep hoping and praying every minute they're gone."

"You'll know her if you see her," Ms. Beaton said of her sociable daughter, and added that she has a distinctive birthmark on her right shoulder in the shape of a star (see photo at right).

Mrs. MacKenzie was too distraught to comment.

Blue flipped forward and found another headline: ONE WEEK LATER, STILL HOPE FOR MISSING CHILDREN.

The sound of creaking footsteps on the porch shocked him to attention, and he quickly shoved the binder into the crook of his arm. He looked up at the discolored ceiling, the crumbling plaster, anywhere but at the album.

"So, that's about everything," the agent said from the other side of the screen door. "Still want to sell it?"

Blue nodded and stood, not really listening; he was in another place now. The unwanted knowledge seeped into his pores, traveled his veins, coiled around his stomach, where it contracted and clenched like a fist. A flood of awful scenarios washed over him: he and the other child must have been abducted, or otherwise had some sort of ordeal, the slate of his memory erased by whatever horrors he'd endured. He felt a sudden and overwhelming sadness, not for himself exactly but rather for the boy he'd been, the boy who had to forget. Also for the little girl, Gavina; who knew what had become of her? Maybe he would learn from the clippings. And now that he began imagining what might have happened, he could never unconjure the images of violation.

I don't have time for this shit. It was just too much. Not when his business was falling apart, when there was so much else to push through. *Not now. Not now.*

"You want to take a minute?" Stanley said, studying him through the screen door. "I can wait outside if you'd like . . ."

"No. No, that's okay. I'm ready." The agent disappeared down the porch, and Blue went to follow him. But then he stopped, and turned.

Directly facing him was a four-paneled door, paint peeling and padlocked, with three two-by-fours nailed across the frame. *The basement*, he thought, the space a distant half memory. Something inside him—his rib cage? his heart?—reached out for the tarnished brass knob, like metal filings to a magnet.

"Excuse me," Blue said through the porch screen. "Do you happen to have the key to this door?"

It was only after prying the boards off with a crowbar Stanley had fetched from his Suburban that they found the padlock key on the agent's keychain. As soon as the door opened, the smell hit Blue at once: an earthy, fetid stench, mixed with another scent, a heavy musk that was not altogether unpleasant. The pungent blend of rotten vegetation and heady perfume was jarring, and was touched with a tangy iron flavor, like blood. It was oddly familiar. The agent pleaded a bad knee and headed back outside, while Blue lingered at the top of the steps and stared for a long while down the open throat of the stairway.

"Hello?" he called into the dark void, almost expecting a response. His footsteps echoed as he started down the stairs, feeling his way with one hand on the splintered plank railing while the other searched in vain for a light switch, the black album of photos and clippings clasped beneath his elbow. As he descended it struck him that he was in a waking dream, one of his characteristic nightmares but spun in reverse. And then he knew why the peculiar basement smell was so familiar: it was from his dreams as well.

He trusted that he'd reached the last step, and indeed the sole of his boot touched ground on the hard dirt floor of the basement. Just as he knew a sagging series of shelves was lined up against the cracked plaster wall behind him, and that a sump pump was installed in the far corner, opposite the boiler and the water heater. Everything in his mind's eye was oriented from the middle of the room, so that's where he shuffled, a hand held out in front of him. He felt for the pull string of an overhead bulb, but even as he did so he knew there was none to be found. *There never was any light down here*, he thought, and shuddered violently.

After a few steps he put his foot down onto an unstable section of the floor that gave way in a rapid relay, the sound of shifting planks. A *trapdoor*. He jerked back, a large hole exposed in the center of the basement, where the hard dirt floor had only just been. He'd almost stepped right into it. Even in the dark he could somewhat discern the pit—by dawning memory instead of true sight—and got down on his hands and knees to feel his way around its circumference, a good ten feet across, and dug right into the floor. He placed the album beside the hole, dislodged a rock the size of a Ping-Pong ball from its edge, and dropped the rock into the pit. There was a thump of stone on wood and then mud, deep below the house's foundation.

On his stomach now, he leaned over the pit and inhaled. The uncertain smell was stronger here, much stronger. The wet, bountiful aroma entered him, and he pictured himself drawn into the hole; he was surprised to find the thought appealing. At once he hungered for its unknown depths, and knew with complete certainty that he would be welcomed down there.

Home, he thought, *home, you are home*, the words chanted in his head like a mantra. Not in English, but in that atavistic, alien language from the woods. Had he found his home? Not in this land, or this basement or house, but beneath it all, in a place below the world.

He stood too quickly and nearly toppled into the pit, everything a dizzy rush as he tried to right himself, and banged his head *hard* against something suspended from the ceiling—a light fixture? An electrical box? It swung away but arced back, slamming into him again. Blue stumbled forward and inadvertently kicked the photo album into the hole, a thud, then a squelch against the chasm's dirt and rock walls. He put his arms up to protect his face, and managed to catch hold of the hanging thing, much lower and larger than he had imagined. His fingers curved around it, and he held tightly to the cold metal of its vertical rails.

A cage. My *cage*.

And now he is inside of it, looking out at the dank basement through the interstices between the iron bars. His grandmother is at the bottom of the stairs, emaciated and wild-haired, almost feral. She holds a wooden slop bucket in the bent claws of her hands.

"Please!" he cries, but his voice isn't his own, it belongs to a child, a little boy. "Grandma Flora, please!"

"Don't call me that!" the maddened woman shrieks. She hauls the bucket over to the hole and the cage suspended above. "You're no kin of mine."

She lifts the bucket and douses him with water like Dorothy undoing the Wicked Witch, and this water scalds just the same. Boiled, he knows instinctively, on the kitchen stove right over his head. It burns like fire, eats away at his flesh, and he screams.

"Mama!" he gets out through choking sobs, the pain excruciating. His melted skin bubbles and bursts, his tiny hands blistering on the bars of the cage, fingers reduced to angry tissue and bloodied bone. "Mama!" he cries out again, and "She's no kin of yours neither!" his grandmother shouts back.

"You are the other kind. *Fae*," she hisses, the word dragged out like a rusty nail across wood. She drops the bucket and works her hands over the surfaces of the cage, applying a sap-sticky ooze to the iron, the phosphorescent substance reeking of blood and musk. The whole world is burning now, everything raw and blackened in a blinding curtain of agony.

"How are you doing down there?"

A voice, from above. His mother? No, a man's voice. *What is it saying?* "Hello? Mr. Whitley? Everything okay?"

I'm okay, Blue thought, and, "I'm okay," he called out, his hands fixed to the cage bars. Not from the inside, he was surprised to see, but from without. "Everything's fine!" he shouted, more to himself than to the man upstairs, whose voice he now recognized as belonging to the property agent.

When he tried to remove his hands from the bars, however, he found that he could not, his skin fastened to the iron like a mouse stuck to a glue trap.

leave this place

A voice in the unknown tongue, the alien language, spoken in the otherwords. His words.

go now

go

He focused on his hands. His attention telescoped, and he ignored the mounting dread that accompanied the enervating force from the iron. It was like being incrementally murdered, how a lobster must feel in a gradually boiling pot. He concentrated his strength, suppressed a scream of pain and terror, and pulled away.

With a wet squelch he lifted his hands, the skin of his fingers and palms sloughed from muscle and tendon like braised meat. Stuck to the bars were the outer layers of his hands and forearms, left behind like a discarded pair of ladies' evening gloves. All this he could see, in this black hell; he could see everything down in the dark. And still the alien voice rang in his head, his own secret voice. And it said

go

leave now

go

go

Blue staggered to the stairs, his hands and arms a mess of

bloody cartilage and pulp. As he climbed the steps, though, his fingers twitched, and they glimmered as if threaded with gold filament. He watched in shock as his hands began to change, skin muting from angry red to rose to pink. One last glance at the cage and it really was there, suspended like a noose over the pit in the middle of the room, the flayed skins of his arms draped there as well, as if hung out to dry. Those too began to shimmer, and they faded into the darkness.

By the time he threw himself through the basement door, his hands were as he knew them. His familiar alabaster pallor restored, neither bloodied nor scarred: he was whole again. He wanted to lay his hands on the property agent to see if they'd leave marks on his shirt, but instead Blue barreled past him, nearly falling through the screen door as he tried to get it open.

"You all set, then?" Stanley said, looking at him askance. Blue could barely meet his eyes, afraid that the man would see the panic there, which would make the fear all the more real.

"Sure. Let's go." *Go. Leave. Now. Go. Go.*

"Why don't I run down and get the paperwork?"

"That's okay," Blue said. "I can sign everything in the car."

A painful minute later, the other man climbed into the driver's seat, Blue already inside. "Sorry," Blue said, "I just remembered I'm late for something. Really late." Stanley put the key into the ignition, turned it once, twice, a third time. *Please go,* Blue prayed, sweaty palms gripped onto his knees in the crash position. *Please. Please. Please.*

The engine caught. Blue closed his eyes and drove his palms into his eye sockets, where a jagged electrical storm flared at the corners of his vision. Finally, the Suburban lurched and began to roll forward, downhill toward the main road.

The drive was interminable. After a few brief and fumbling

attempts at small talk the agent stopped trying, and they rode the rest of the way in silence.

At the bottom of Maureen and Donald's hill, Blue signed the authorization papers for the sale in a daze. He didn't feign reading them, only scrawled his messy signature on dozens of dotted lines throughout the thick stack of legal documents.

"Congratulations," Stanley said. "You just sold a house." He handed Blue his copy of the contracts, as well as a large packet from the estate lawyer. "And last but not least," he added, producing a separate envelope, "the cashier's check. Keep an eye on that, it's like cash."

Blue, without thought, slid the envelope into his breast pocket and opened the passenger door. He tentatively touched the toe of his boot to the road, afraid that something might reach up and grab him, pull him down into the earth like Amy Irving at the end of *Carrie*. His mind stuttered: at once he thirsted for the truth behind the newspaper clippings, and the memories that had surfaced in the basement. But a moment later he wished it would all just go away. *I should have listened to my mother*, he thought, and the words hummed in his head as he headed up to the house. *I should have listened*. The knowing and the not-knowing was splitting him in two.

He made his way toward the MacLeod House, Gabe's halo of blond curls visible over the porch railing. Halfway up the hill, Blue whipped out his cellphone and dialed his mother's number in New York. It took three tries for the call to finally connect.

"It's me," he said. His voice was flat, that of a stranger. "It's Michael."

"Mickey? What is it, baby?" his mother croaked; she sounded sicker than ever. "What's wrong?"

"What happened to me, Mama?" How long it had been

since he called her that, since he cried out for her the way he had in that basement, so many years ago. "When I was little? When I was taken? What happened to me? Who took me? Do you know?"

"Where are you?"

"The cove. I'm here, in Starling Cove."

"Oh. Oh, my baby boy. Why did you go back there?" She stifled a cough, blew her nose, and wept. He buried his face in his free hand, the paperwork from the sale pinched beneath his elbow, as the photo album had been not one hour earlier. "It's not what you think," she said meekly. "You came back to me. To the world."

"Did I?" He was crying now himself. "Are you sure?"

"She lured you, Mickey. I told you! She lured you back, just like I knew she would. Even dead she won't leave it alone. Even dead . . ."

"Mama, what am I?" he said. "Tell me what I am."

"An angel, baby. You're my little angel. Always have been, always will be."

we

are not

of the fallen

A voice in his head, spoken in the otherwords.

though

we

have been called

many things

"Mickey?" his mother said. "Are you there?"

"I'm here," he said, numb. "I'm here."

we

have always been

here

The voice was no longer solitary but part of a chorus of voices, a multilayered incantation. Blue's vision began to refract, and he squeezed his eyes shut.

here
before the first traveler
here
with only
the sound
of rushing wind
and buzzing bees
and insects that
burrow and bite
and so
we
shall always be

It was the greatest truth Blue had ever known.

"Fly back," his mother was saying, but it was hard to hear her, interference jamming the line. Or was that the sound of the voices in his head? "Hurry back to . . . and we can be . . . again." She coughed and inhaled. "You were never supposed . . . I knew it would hurt, when you finally . . . I just didn't know how much."

"Hello? Mom? Can you hear me?"

She said something else but it was garbled, an onslaught of digital scratches and pings.

"Listen, I'm losing you," he said. "If you can still hear me, I'll call you from the landline."

Blue wiped his face, filled his lungs with great big gasps of air, and let his breath erode the thoughts racing through his mind. A histrionic jolt of opera music thundered from one of the small cabins beside the trail, and he reflexively looked heavenward. Clear skies. He took another minute to collect himself before continuing up the hill.

"So, how did it go?" asked Gabe, rocking on the porch swing with his feet upon the railing. "What was the house like?"

"Nothing special." Blue was shivering; unable to look Gabe in the eye, he stared out at the cove instead. "It was a dump. You didn't miss anything."

"Was it two stories? Did you walk around the property? Is it really on ten acres? I want details."

"Yes, no, yes. Nondescript, really. Kind of depressing. I signed the papers, so it doesn't much matter anymore. Happy?" That Gabe tried and failed so miserably to hide his injured pride melted right through Blue's hastily erected armor. "Sorry. I just . . . I guess I'm weirded out by being up here."

Don't tell, he heard; was this his mother's voice, now? *Don't even tell yourself.*

"Going into my dead grandmother's house," Blue hedged, "when I never got around to seeing her alive? It's a shitty feeling."

"I wish you had let us go with you," Gabe said. "Just to, you know, support you."

"That would have been smarter. Thanks." Blue moved next to the swing but couldn't bring himself to sit, so he dropped the contracts from the sale down in his stead. "I don't belong here," he said, and it was as if someone else had spoken through him, made him say the words. "I have to go."

"So we'll go," Gabe said, his blue eyes brilliant with empathy. "We're out of here. Tomorrow."

But that wasn't what Blue meant. He didn't belong in New York, either. And he didn't know where in the world to go next.

"It's beautiful here," he managed to say. "Almost painfully so, you know? But I'm ready to get the hell gone." *And never look back.*

A loud crash echoed down the hill. Gabe jumped up, and Blue looked to the road to see if there'd been a smashup. There was another crash, and then another, a clatter like glass breaking, only duller and coming from Maureen's studio. A figure emerged: Donald, arms flailing and disoriented, the glint of the setting sun caught in the squares of his eyeglasses before he disappeared back inside. Another racket ensued, the sound of more pottery being shattered, until Donald reappeared and staggered down the path into one of the small cabins on the far side of the drive.

"What is he doing?" Gabe said. "Should we do something?"

The screen door of the MacLeod House flew open. Jason rushed down the porch stairs in a half stride, half jog, face grim with his eyes fixed on the cabin down the hill. Elisa, barefooted, followed soon after, Gabe and Blue along with her. The three struggled to keep up, as if they were merely bouncing along yet another hiking trail with Jason as their intrepid guide.

"Donald?" Jason called out as he entered the cabin. "Donald, are you all right?"

Blue and the others stood in the doorway, the subdued light at dusk doing little to illuminate the forlorn space. Donald sat in an office chair, hunched between a framed poster from a production of Gilbert and Sullivan's *Iolanthe* and an open rolltop desk, which held what looked like a ham radio. He combed the fingers of one hand through his thinning gray hair, while the other clutched a book, the words *Entomologia Generalis, Vol. II* printed in gold on its cracked purple cover. His bird dog, Olivier, ran against Donald's trouser legs, first one side, then the other, a figure eight of brown fur. Jason placed a gentle hand upon the older man's shoulder and crouched to whisper in his ear.

"I hear you," Donald replied. "But there's only so much time I have left." He removed his glasses, resting them upon the book. His voice was weak and feverish; he appeared newly ancient. "I can't find the hive without my memories. My . . . maps? Is that what they're called? They were penciled inside one of my books. But this is the wrong volume. And it's all going now . . ." He pressed his eyes closed and shook his head. "They're only going to grab what they want and be gone, so how can I ever find my way back now? There's smoke on the air already . . ."

Donald looked up at them. He squinted into the light before his eyes went wide and his jaw slackened. Returning his glasses to his face, he stood and covered his mouth. He was staring directly at Elisa, framed in the light of the doorway. "Barbara?" he said, his voice aquiver.

He reached out to her, hand trembling. The dog barked and darted across the floorboards, unsettling a frayed throw rug. "You're back," Donald said. "They sent you back for me . . ."

"Oh. No. I'm—" Elisa tried to back away, but was trapped against Blue and Gabe on either side of her.

Donald's shoulders heaved, and he withdrew his hand as if he'd touched it to a hot stove. "Don't!" he shouted, and let out an anguished moan as he lurched toward her. "Don't leave me here!"

Elisa swallowed hard, then went to him, taking Donald in her arms. He fell against her, and the two of them slid to the ground. He sobbed as she rubbed his back. She shushed him, rocked him like a child with night terrors. Blue thought of the word *sundowning.*

"It's okay," Elisa said. "I'm not going anywhere. I'm here. I'm here."

The dog, hungry for inclusion in their circle of two, nuzzled against Elisa, and settled its snout on her calves. They remained in place until Maureen, frantic and soaking wet in a towel, came hurtling across the lawn. "Where is he?" she cried. "Did you see him?" She crossed the threshold and froze at the sight of Elisa and Donald in their tender pietà.

After an uncomfortable silence, she stepped inside and helped Donald up and out of Elisa's arms. "Darling, we're going to take a bath now," she said firmly. "Come with me to the house." Donald nodded, a reluctant acceptance.

As she walked him out with her arm around his bony frame, she peered at Elisa over her shoulder. "Thank you," she whispered.

Blue and the others left the cabin in a ghostly silence. The sun had fully set and it was immeasurably darker, as if a curtain had been drawn across the sky. Halfway up the hill Elisa sneezed, then lagged behind; closer to the house she wavered and pressed a closed fist to her chest.

"Shit," she said. "The dog . . ."

Blue moved toward her, as did Jason, who knocked into Blue in his haste. "Are you all right?" Jason asked her.

"I'm fine." But then Elisa sneezed again, so hard that she began to cough.

Jason placed a hand on her back. "Why don't you just take a minute to catch your breath."

"Because I don't want to get eaten alive by mosquitoes?" she snapped, and shrugged him off. "I said I'm fine. Let's just go inside."

But she wasn't fine. It was clear an hour later that close proximity to Donald's dog had cost her. Elisa curled up with a week-old gossip magazine, prone beneath a quilt on the couch. Blue put a pot on the stove and assembled the makings of a broth, something he could brew with garlic and herbs as a restorative, Elisa's wheezing audible from the kitchen.

It helped to keep busy: as long as he was at the stove, Blue needn't think about anything else, and could at least feign a sense of calm. Jason, on the other hand, was visibly restive and at a total loss for what to do, having already foisted tea and Benadryl upon Elisa; it was as if Donald's manic agitation had gone airborne. Elisa, for her part, seemed to refuse Jason's care with an almost perverse sense of withholding, until his level veneer began to blister and crack.

"You *swore* to me you were going to get an EpiPen." It occurred to Blue that he'd never heard Jason raise his voice in anger before, and certainly not toward Elisa. "If it's not too late, maybe I can find you one in—"

"I don't need you to find me one!" she shouted between long wheezes; the sickly sound of her voice reminded Blue of his mother and their thwarted conversation. "Stop infantilizing me," Elisa rasped. "I can take care of myself."

"But you can't!" And there Jason was, authentically shouting, his soothing therapeutic disposition evaporated. *Welcome to the other side*, Blue thought, but quickly admonished himself. Gabe emptied the dishwasher, gathered wood for a fire, borrowed Blue's lighter to hide out on the porch so he could smoke the end of a joint, all to avoid the mounting tension. Blue wanted desperately to join him, but was too wary of risking the crossfire in the living room.

"I wish you could take care of yourself," Jason muttered.

"Leave me alone already." She waved him away. With a

groan and an exasperated thrash of his arms, Jason stormed up-stairs, his indecipherable grumblings scarcely audible before he slammed a door somewhere overhead.

After another minute of wheeze-tinged silence, Elisa sat up. "Too mean?"

"What?" Blue said. "You? Never." She smiled and winced, slid her small frame down the couch. "How are you feeling?"

"Honestly? Pretty lousy. Consumptive, even." She took a sip of tea and used the mug to warm her hands. "Goddamn aller-gies. Can't take me anywhere."

"It was for a good cause, though. You were really sweet with Donald."

"Maybe that's why I'm acting like such a bitch. I must have used up what little charm I had left."

"You want some more tea?"

"No, thanks. But you can run me a hot bath. A good soak might do the trick."

"Sure." A saucepan on the stove began to bubble angrily, and he turned down the flame. "You mind if I ask Jason? He's begging to be of use."

"Knock yourself out."

After Jason ran the tub, he escorted Elisa to the bathroom and hurried back down to the kitchen. "Blue, listen. I phoned the pharmacy in Baddeck. They have EpiPens there, and we don't need a prescription. Normally I wouldn't feel the need to manage her, but she's just being so stubborn." Blue looked up at the ceiling, unsure of where this was going. "I'm just going to make a fast run into town and pick it up. That way, if she's not feeling better in an hour or so . . . Well, we can cross that bridge when we come to it."

"No worries. I'll hold down the fort."

"Thanks, man."

Shortly after Jason headed out to the car, Gabe popped in from the porch and placed Blue's paperwork from the house sale down on the dining room table. "Hey, I'm going to ride into town with him. Is that okay? He looks like he could use the company."

"Of course." Blue was consumed with peeling, chopping, paring; as long as he was at work, nothing could be wrong. Not when he had the cashier's check in his pocket and could leave this place behind. *Tomorrow*, he thought. *Just hang on until tomorrow.* "We'll be fine. I'll have dinner ready and waiting."

Once Gabe and Jason left, the house fell coolly silent. Donald's tantrum and Elisa's subsequent allergy attack had been enough to temporarily forestall the inescapable, but the nauseated feeling that had surfaced in his grandmother's basement came roaring back. Worst of all, it made some sort of sick sense: Blue remembered so little of his life before leaving Cape Breton that he must have wiped his memory clean, his nightmares the only trace he had failed to extinguish.

Not even cooking could distract him. He was suddenly alone, and afraid, and above all cold. Gooseflesh raised along his arms, and a chill settled in from an unearthed slab of ice deep inside his chest. He struck a kitchen match and set fire to the pile Gabe had prepped in the woodstove, newspaper and kindling aflame as the bittersweet scent of cedar smoke permeated the room. He thought about calling his mother back, but the prospect seemed too daunting. She would simply lie to him, the way she always had. Anything to keep him tied to her. She had said it best, after all: he was her little angel, and always would be.

After a few busy minutes of chopping tomatoes and mincing

garlic for the sauce, he could no longer take the solitude and headed upstairs to check on Elisa. "Knock knock," he said, a drumbeat knuckled against the bathroom door. "How are we in there?"

"Come on in," she called, faux seductive. "The water's fine."

Suspended in bubbles up to her neck, she appeared dismantled, her hair a fan of eels in the cast-iron claw-foot bathtub, face adrift on a sea of pinkish foam. *The head of Orpheus*, Blue thought, recalling a painting he'd once seen. He flashed back to his grandmother and the disembodied, Hummel-esque children on her wallpaper, her gnarled fingers on the handle of the slop bucket. And her voice, her baleful, murderous voice . . .

"Feeling better?" He moved a towel from the chair beside the tub so he could sit.

"Better, yes. A little regretful is all." Elisa blew a spray of bubbles from the back of her hand. "*Non, rien de rien*," she sang to the heavens, her voice old-vinyl scratchy. "*Non, je ne regrette rien . . .*" She coughed and stared at the ceiling. "Would you do me a favor?"

"What's that?"

"Could you grab my camera? It's on the bed."

He brought her the old Konica. She dried her hands and began to take pictures from the bathtub of the room's corners, its slanted ceiling, the patchy topography of the worn terry-cloth bath mat, and the chipped toilet seat; she tried to shoot Blue as well but he pulled the towel over his face.

"Show yourself," she implored, and he did, mugging gamely for her as she snapped away. "You have such a pretty face. Don't hide it."

"You're the one hiding."

Elisa peered at him over the top of the camera, and he slowly reached out and took it. She disappeared below the water, only a dark corona of hair visible before she surfaced, the bridge of her nose snaked with foam. Through the camera's viewfinder, her face looked bisected and veiled, half masked. He shot her face, her breasts, her hand on the lip of the tub. A parting of the bathwater revealed the dark thatch of her pubic hair, and, barely, the small mound of her belly.

"You're lingering," she said.

"Sorry." He tried to chuckle. "It's been a long day."

A popping noise downstairs: the crackle of the fire, or the sauce as it ran over the side of the pan. Could he trust her with his secrets, after all this time?

"Listen," he said. "We're still best friends, right?"

"Sure." She waited, then said, "Of course we are. Why? Is there something going on?"

"I don't even know where to start." He hung the camera off the back of the chair by its strap. "I've been feeling strange, ever since we got here. Like I'm being watched. Or more like I'm being . . . manipulated." He was holding back from her, something once upon a time they'd both sworn they would never do. "I've been getting a feeling like vertigo, or at least what I imagine vertigo must feel like. Except it's mixed with déjà vu. You know?"

"Not really." She eyed him doubtfully, and all of a sudden he was unsure any of it had truly happened. "Are you okay?"

"I have those nightmares, right? The ones where I'm buried alive? I think they might actually be memories. Maybe I— Maybe I was underground, you know? Or trapped somewhere, or something. But I don't just feel it when I'm sleeping. Not up here. I mean . . ." He decided to start over. "That day we were in the woods and ran into Donald? I had this feeling. That first night too, at the ceilidh—I was outside and I kind of spaced out, but there was this sense that . . ."

She scrunched her face; he wasn't getting through to her. "I found some newspaper clippings at my grandmother's house," he said. "They said I disappeared as a child."

"*What?*" Her mouth hung open, and for a flickering moment it became a gaping hole, ridged with crooked stalagmite needles. "You're kidding me."

"'Boy Goes Missing.' Actually, boy and girl; it happened to someone else too. 'Frantic Search Under Way.' That sort of thing. Pages and pages of this stuff."

"What happened to you?"

"I don't know. I mean, obviously I was found. But the strangest part is that even though I seem to have gone missing for days, I don't have any memory of it. Forget the fact that I'm thirty years old and my mom has never seen fit to mention it to me. She must've taken me to the States soon after it happened."

"Who could blame her? So, where are the clippings?"

"I . . . left them there." An image of the cage swinging above him, followed by the sound of him kicking the photo album into the hole, the hollow echo as it plummeted into the carved-out depths beneath the house. Elisa couldn't know about all that, not yet. "Maybe I'll go back for them. Tomorrow, before we leave."

"Well, maybe you should ask your mother what happened. She's the one who seems to be keeping things from you, no?"

"Believe me, I tried. She wasn't very forthcoming." He rested his head in his hands. "I feel pretty dead. I can't really think about it right now."

His thoughts traveled down a dusky path. A stranger—his father, perhaps—at the foot of Grandma Flora's drive, beckoning Blue and the little girl Gavina down to his car. A cabin in the woods, a mattress on the floor. The man's hairy white hand on Blue's cheek, and then on his inner thigh . . .

But that didn't happen. Not at all. And if he could imagine such a scenario so vividly, who was to say what was the truth? Even his authentic memories had been distorted to the point of invalidity, like some kind of grotesque funhouse mirror; he might never know what had taken place, not really. Maybe that was for the best.

They both sat in silence, still but close, no sound but the leaky tap as it dripped out water one drab at a time.

"I'm pregnant," Elisa said. She stared straight ahead at her clear polished toenails, feet crossed on the far edge of the tub.

"Wow." So there it was. "Is it . . . Jason's?"

"Of course," she said, stung; he wished he hadn't asked. "Why would you bring that up? I told you—"

"Sorry! I'm sorry. That was wrong of me. Really wrong."

"Forget that," she said. "Forget it." She drew her legs up and used her knees to shield herself from him. "I'm six weeks along, as far as I can tell. So relax."

It had taken him this long to figure out he was secretly holding out hope they were pregnant together. The realization hit him like a body blow. What had he been thinking? That the two of them would run off together? The idea was laughable. Wasn't it?

"I'm sorry," she said, her face concealed. "I didn't mean to interrupt what you were saying before. It just seemed like we were sharing, and . . . I needed to tell someone. Someone besides Gabe, that is."

"You told Gabe?"

She nodded. "The other night. He came right out and asked

me, said the two of you had been speculating." She lowered her knees, her eyes trained on him. "Quite frankly, I'm surprised you didn't ask me yourself."

"I just—I guess I thought if you wanted me to know that you'd tell me."

"Which must be why you don't exactly look surprised."

"Well, I'm not. I mean, yes, I thought you might be. You have been acting a little strange lately. No offense." She was staring at the ceiling again. "So," he said, "I guess the word I'm looking for is congratulations."

"I suppose."

"You don't sound thrilled."

"Let's just say it wasn't planned. I mean, so much for getting back into dancing, right?"

"Not necessarily. You could start up again, if you really wanted. You could do anything."

"Sure," she said, absent of any conviction whatsoever. "Sure I can."

"What does Jason think?"

"I haven't told him yet."

"Elisa . . ."

"I know. But can you imagine what he'd be like if he knew I was pregnant? He'd have me on bed rest by now."

"He did just sneak into town for an EpiPen."

She rolled her eyes.

"Okay," Blue said. "Let me get this straight: You've stopped drinking and smoking, which leads me to believe you're keeping it. But you're not telling your husband, who, yes, would be irritating and yet obviously supportive and a complete prince. So instead you're being freaky and passive-aggressively angry at him, even though he's really done nothing wrong."

"That pretty much covers it."

"And you wonder why I won't settle down."

"If you had settled down with me, things would be different. For both of us." She reached out her hand. He took it, traced her palm with his thumb, her heart line, the life line, fate. "We used to have a great time together, didn't we?"

"We still do," he replied. "Always."

"Maybe you're right," she said, and withdrew her hand, let it fall beneath the surface of the water with a splash. "What you said that first morning? Maybe we should live here forever. Just stay. And leave everything behind."

"We could do that." He pulled the cashier's check from his pocket. "We could go anywhere."

"What's that?"

"The proceeds from the house sale. It's about enough to cover my debts, but fuck it, maybe we should skip town and never look back. Head off to Newfoundland. Or Greenland."

"Or outer space." She laughed. "What? It's just as likely."

Something rattled and clanged downstairs: the saucepan lid as it slipped off and clattered to the floor. "I shall return," Blue said, and tucked the check back into his pocket as he leaned down to kiss the crown of her head.

There was a dryness in the air, a barometric shift as he exited the room that made his brain ache for hydration, if not a stiff drink. A tightness pulled at the corners of his cracked lips. Elisa was right, of course. They could never be together, not now, not without the both of them feeling as if they were usurping what was not theirs to take, or give. It would remain a fantasy.

Blue skipped down the stairs to the kitchen and turned the heat off the range, retrieved the fallen lid from the floor where it sat in a ruddy pool of boiled-over tomato sauce. He put the lid down on the counter, turned on the cold water valve, and bowed to drink straight from the faucet, his thirst boundless. *Just drink*, he thought. *Drink and eat and most of all sleep. And when you wake up, everything will be normal again. No worries, no pain. Tomorrow, you're out of here.*

He turned off the tap, went to put the lid back on the pan, and froze. The sight of the sauce, bubbling gory red and pulped, brought him back to the basement and the boiling water that had burned him, the bloodied gristle mess of his small hands as they clung to the bars of the cage.

He placed the lid on the counter and, without another thought, plunged his hand into the scorching sauce.

He saw white with pain and shut his eyes, nearly blacking out. But only for a moment: just as quickly as it hit him, the pain began to recede. A tiny dark spot formed in his mind's eye, and he focused upon it; the spot began to grow, until what was once the size of a pencil point became the black mouth of a tunnel through which his consciousness climbed, the hurt already memory. He lifted an eyelid to find his hand still pressed inside the pan, the sauce a stormy red sea around his wrist. There was no pain, not anymore; it had been an illusion.

He stood there for some time before he yanked his hand free, and in doing so toppled an open bag of flour from the counter. The powder rushed down his legs like an avalanche, hit the floor, and rose up again in a mushroom cloud of white fallout. The smell of seared flesh threaded the air, a taste in his mouth both earthen and sanguinary, as if he'd bitten his tongue. But all he could do was stare at his hand, at the burned, mutilated marrow and the shocking raw pink of his fingers as the skin there stirred, and swelled, and changed.

A few moments later, his hand returned to its familiar state.

No blood, no scarring, no sign of being burned at all. Just the persistent smell of cooked meat, and above it that of the tomato sauce, still simmering in the pan. He'd cut and burned himself in the kitchen a thousand times over—as recently as last week—but it only now occurred to him that he bore no scars whatsoever.

He wasn't who he thought he was, not even close; he'd been wrong the entire time.

He turned to the small window over the farm sink, his reflection transposed over the branches of the pines swaying past the property. *Who are you?* He gave himself a cold, clinical look, a scientist observing a specimen in a petri dish. *Who are you really, underneath it all?*

He put a hand to his face. He moved it along his cheek, slowly, in a caress, his fingers touching upon the crooked swell of his nose. It had been broken ten years ago, when he was walking Elisa to a cab and was jumped by some dudes early one morning outside the Roxy. Most of the time, though, his nose didn't appear broken at all.

He let his hand come to rest below his right eye socket, where he hooked his fingernails into the tender area below. He grasped a fold of skin and pulled downward, tearing into himself, a narrow runnel dug along his flesh. There was no pain this time, not as he stripped away a flap of skin from his cheekbone, the tissue below exposed to light and air. He'd been wearing this camouflage for so long he must have forgotten it was a disguise in the first place.

This isn't me.

A brackish liquid that stank of seawater squirted from the wound and left a spray of pinkish fluid across the window and the clay sink. He listed at the smell, not because it was repellant but because it was intoxicating, exhilarating. He steadied himself, a pulsing light flashing beneath his skin, his skull surrounded by an undulating membrane of foliage, the leafy tissue interlaced in a tangled briar the color of lichen.

He continued peeling at his face. It was like deboning a fish, or prepping a chicken, something he'd done in the kitchen on countless occasions. The surrendered parts of his disguise lay strewn all about: thick hanks of black hair stuck to the sink, mealy strips of skin run down his pant legs and along the floor in wet slug paths. But as he contemplated these castoffs, the ragged bits shimmered and began to melt, thinning to dewdrop-sized particles before vanishing from sight altogether. Where he had expected carnage, he found beauty; he was beautiful, underneath it all.

I'm not human at all.

All that was left of his old face were two unchanged eyes, two white and green-lensed orbs that stared back at him from the window like a pair of hard-boiled eggs. They were what remained of the masquerade, relics of this too-bright world. And past the twin white orbs, beyond the muscle and protein and all the rest of this pretend human squander, there was his secret self, his real self. Arms sickled like the forelegs of a mantis, his fingers birch-gray branches of transmuted flesh and bone, he tensed and released as his uncovered form rippled like a wave upon the shore. He was made of this place, of the night sky and grass and the woods on the far side of the glass. He was made of this land. And he would never forget that again.

He plucked his eyes from their sockets, and everything changed.

The air went out of the room, as if the entire world had become a vacuum. His mouth fell open and a wall went up. He was a creature caught in a net of feeling beyond feelings, all pervasive and alive, a thousand pricking needles in search of a vein. Chest pulsating with ecstatic sound and energy, he was made of lightness, and light.

The kaleidoscopic visions, refracted images of himself and the woods and the landscape that he'd glimpsed since his first night here: he was seeing out of the eyes of the others that were like him, of him, the many eyes of his kin. Others just as he was, a tribe of himself.

In a multilayered image he saw the outside of the house, through their eyes. They waited beyond the trees, as they'd waited for years, ever since he first left them and emerged from the forest disguised as a little boy. They were the ones from the woods, from the place below the world. His people.

And how glad he was. How thankful that they'd waited with such patience, and his heart, near bursting, swelled with joy. There were no doubts, not anymore. He no longer belonged to this wasted aboveground landscape of iron and greed. His people, they would teach him how to shed the remains of his disguise once and for all, to let go of who he had once believed himself to be, Michael and Blue both. They would show him how to return to all he had forgotten: his real family. And now he would go to them.

Out and down the porch steps, a cold wind whistled over his newly exposed face. The crisp evening air was tinged with the smell of smoke, the acrid odor an affront to his new consciousness that reached him through someplace other than the blunt, barklike coating where his nostrils used to be, but no longer were. And with the recognition of the smoky scent came low whisperings, accompanied by a new spectrum of light visible in the darkness, past blue to bruised purple and darker. He pored through every color now, all the way down beyond black. He saw, really saw, for the first time since he'd left their side.

One was there, by the edge of the property. Its branchlike arms were extended, prehensile bristles tugging back snarled leaves to peer over a hedge. And there was another, high up in the tree canopy, its hind legs curled like snakes around the slender bole of a pine. One more flat to the ground by the peony bushes, with two more beside it, erect and slimmed to the narrowest of widths. They watched him watch them watch him, all with the same honeycomb eyes.

They greeted him in his language, and he in theirs; they shared the same tongue. They shared the same mind as well: a hive mind, alive with unified intelligence. *Here with only the sound of rushing wind and buzzing bees, and insects that burrow and bite.* He was of another kind, like his not-grandmother had said. This was who he was, finally and at last. They called to him by his secret name. And so he went.

He crept toward the woods, then stopped.

The mind of the tribe drew his attention back toward the house and the whining electric glow from the bathroom window upstairs, its artificial light a glaring impurity against the moonless nighttime sky.

There was another. Like him, or rather soon to be. He wasn't the only one they had come for.

Part Two

———

JASON

Chapter Four

Jason, hunched over the farm sink, scrubbed at an egregiously burned frying pan with a shred of steel wool. He'd tried making scrambled eggs, but the result was a brown-and-yellow hash that tasted like a salt lick, its remnants unyielding in their death grip upon the skillet. He was afraid of scratching the bottom— couldn't damaging the coating cause minute fragments of metal to leach into the food the next time the pan was used? Better to tread lightly, delicately, make smooth, circular gestures and coax the pan clean. Maybe he'd go down the hill and use Maureen's internet connection to find out the proper way to clean vintage cookware. Vinegar? Baking soda? Or a simple soap-and-water solution?

Jason's hands started to shake. He placed the pan down carefully in the sink, a tinny reverberation of iron against clay. Ten days gone since they were supposed to be back in New York. But that was another lifetime ago.

Car wheels on gravel and Jason tried to keep his breath steady as he strode to the door; he refused to allow himself to imagine who might be coming up the drive. "Come on, come on," he said, and stopped, startled to hear the words spoken aloud.

A Cape Breton Regional Police patrol car crept toward the house, and his heart drummed inside his chest. It was Detective

Jessed, one of two first responders that night. This time he was unaccompanied and in uniform, a shallow smile and a raised hand behind the windshield.

Only a smile and a wave. Jason's stomach churned, then settled, a dog jerked on its chain. *That means they haven't found them.*

"Good morning," the officer said, mounting the porch steps. The air was thick with smoke from the forest fires, still visibly raging along a crooked ridge high on Kelly's Mountain. "Do you have a few minutes?"

Jason invited him inside and offered Jessed a seat at the table while he fetched them both coffee. He wanted to give the detective a minute to survey the room—he'd straightened it up late last night—to show that he had nothing to hide. Of course he would be open, and amenable. He would be beyond reproach.

"Here we are," Jason said, and set down two mugs, along with a small ceramic pitcher of cream and a matching bowl of sugar cubes. "I take it nothing's turned up?"

"Unfortunately, no." The officer removed his black leather gloves and blew across the surface of his coffee, a little whistle of air before he sipped at it, catlike, with a slight dart of the tongue. "Obviously we haven't had the resources to recanvass on foot, but we are still searching by air."

"So I've heard." Every day the cove was buzzed by a low-flying prop plane of the *North by Northwest* variety. It wasn't solely for their benefit, however: the authorities were also searching for a missing group of hikers and on high alert due to the fires still blazing up on the mountain. "I appreciate that."

"Anything we can do." Jessed uncrossed and recrossed his legs, ankle over knee. Upon his last drive-by, he had implied that Blue and Elisa would owe the department one hell of an explanation if this turned out to be a misunderstanding. Search and Rescue was having enough trouble with the forest fires as it was.

The detective produced one of the flyers Jason and Gabe had been distributing, the word *Missing* in red boldface above enlargements of Blue's and Elisa's passport photos. "I see you've been conducting your own canvass."

"Yes, well, we thought it might be useful."

"You should coordinate with our office. More efficient that way." Jessed placed the flyer facedown on the table without taking his black eyes off Jason. Though he probably had a couple of years on the detective, Jason couldn't help but feel patronized. "I'd like to ask you again about what happened that night when you got back from the pharmacy," Jessed said, "if that's okay by you. Standard procedure and all that."

"Please." Jason smiled and considered opening his palms but decided the pose was too pious. "I completely understand."

"Now, you said the downstairs lights were on when you pulled up. Did you see any other lights anywhere?"

Jason thought about the moment he'd cut the ignition and opened the driver's side door, the sound of Gabe crunching gravel beneath his sneakers, the paper drugstore bag as it crinkled in the boy's hand. They went up the porch and it was dark, but not terribly so; he pictured smoke wisping beneath the light. But that was an inserted memory: he hadn't seen or smelled the not-so-distant forest fires until much later that night, closer to dawn.

"Just the porch light," Jason said, though he wondered as to its importance.

"Okay. Now, you came up the front, is that right? Not

through the side and the door there, where your car's parked now. Why is that?"

"I parked near the front of the house that night. Normally I would've pulled the car around, but because my wife wasn't well I felt more of a sense of urgency."

"But Mr. Peck had the bag with the EpiPen in it. Not you."

"That's right." The pharmacist had handed over a clipboard with a signature sheet that Gabe scooped up and signed before taking the bag, which sat on the dash during the drive. *That goddamned EpiPen.* She hadn't even wanted it.

"And you came right home, without stopping. Is that right?"

"Yes. We were worried."

"Both of you."

"Well, no," he said, thinking back. "Actually, Gabe was fairly blasé. Though that might have been because he was trying not to alarm me. You'd have to ask him."

"And Mr. Peck is . . ." Jessed leaned over in his chair to take in the staircase.

"Still in bed." Jason shifted in his seat. "This hasn't been very easy for him. For either of us."

"Understandably." Jessed nodded slowly, his gaze penetrating. Jason understood that he was—at least in part—being interrogated. Although who could blame them? Jason had seen countless television shows, police procedurals and docudramas, all of which played the same refrain: when an adult woman goes missing, look to her personal life, especially her significant other. And here they were, hundreds of miles from home . . . What other explanation was there? But there was one, and it had to be found.

"So tell me," the detective said. "What happened next?"

Jason told him once more how they'd come through the

door, and the first thing he'd felt was an immeasurable vacuum of stillness and silence. It was as if the entire house had become a hermetically sealed vault, with the flat, long-buried smell of a subterranean tomb. He told Jessed about the cinders flaring in the woodstove, and the pan overheating on the range beneath a swelling crest of bubbling red foam, the evaporating remains of tomato sauce. The unmanned rudder of a wooden spoon had fallen over the burner, dangerously close to the flame.

In front of the oven, a toppled bag of flour was spilled across the terra-cotta tiles, a topography of whitecaps upon a shellacked orange sea. Through the spray of powder, a set of shoeprints shuffled toward the sink and continued in the direction of the door. Blue's boot prints, obviously. Whose else's would they be?

At the time, Jason hadn't allowed himself to believe anything could be very much wrong. Not even the most likely scenario: that Elisa's condition had worsened, and that Blue—lacking the rental car Jason and Gabe had taken to Baddeck—had called an ambulance, or maybe commandeered Maureen's Toyota. Jason's only thought was that Blue must be tending to Elisa upstairs. The two of them laughing about God knows what, most likely yet another inscrutable tale of wild clubland nights that made his own youthful follies seem banal by comparison.

It was then that he had felt Gabe bristle behind him, frozen by the front door as if sensing some unspeakable presence. Jason avoided turning to him. There had to be some kind of mistake. There couldn't be anything wrong with Elisa, not *really*. He denied the very possibility.

Upstairs, the bathroom door was closed. He knocked, said her name, called it louder. He knocked harder, until the door relented and the latch sprung open. One last look at the bot tom of the stairs, at Gabe and his saucer-wide eyes, before Jason pushed open the door.

The sweet smell of bath products filled his nostrils. That and also something heavier, a damp earthy scent. The lights were on, everything still save a film of soap bubbles floating on the surface of the bathwater like the boiled-over pan on the range downstairs. Beside the tub was Elisa's camera, hung by its strap from the post of a ladder-back chair, a dry towel across the seat.

He ducked into their bedroom, then Blue's, and finally Gabe's, the yellow and slant-roofed one with the twin beds and pine crib. He turned on every light, threw open one door after the next, searched the cellar by flashlight: the house was barren of life. The certainty of her absence was immediate and profound, white space heavy around her missing form, like the perforated border of a paper doll cutout. She was gone. And so was Blue.

"Tell me what happened next," the officer said, his voice low and patient. And what was a detective but its own kind of therapist, with a more pointed version of the talking cure? Jessed didn't seem to care that he'd heard it all before.

"By then, I knew something was really wrong," Jason said. "I just knew. I ran down the hill to find out if they'd been there. I thought maybe Elisa had decided to go to the hospital. But they were nowhere to be found. Maureen had put Donald to bed and was straightening up in the kitchen. She could tell how panicked I was."

"And then she decided to put the call in."

"That's right. You were here, I don't know, maybe three hours later?" He tried to say it without bitterness, but of course he'd spent that time cursing the police, screaming Elisa's and Blue's names into the woods until his throat was ragged, pacing up and down the hill in case the police had gotten the address wrong and driven past. He'd called the police himself a half hour later. The dispatcher politely but firmly stated that according to Jason, his wife and friend had only "just gone out" not two hours earlier, and no one could officially be reported missing for twenty-four hours. But still he knew. He knew. And he'd been right.

"You called very quickly after coming home."

"That's right." *How long should I have waited?*

"And you didn't think that they might have gone off on a little adventure?" Jessed said, not for the first time. "Just on impulse, on a whim."

"She wasn't feeling well. And as you know, their money and credit cards were left behind. It doesn't seem like they were going very far to me."

"The cashier's check from the house sale, though, they took that with them. And Mr. Whitley's credit cards were maxed out as it was. Were you aware of the fact that he was heavily in debt?"

"That was the point of selling the house. So he could keep his restaurant afloat." Jason left out the fact that it was his own idea that Blue drive up to Cape Breton and actually view the property before authorizing the sale. Now look where that had gotten them.

"Mr. Peck reported that the restaurant was recently cleaned out."

"It was robbed, yes." Gabe had placed a call to another restaurant around the corner from Cyan, only to learn that the storefront had been broken into and ransacked. The burners, the cash register, the dishware and silverware, the tables and chairs, all of it taken in the night. No one claimed to have seen anything. "Blue owed some not-so-nice people a not-so-small sum of money."

"So it seems. If that does prove to be the case, it's certainly a possibility that he 'took the money and ran,' you might say."

"What about my wife, then?"

"They liked having a good time, am I right? Out partying all night . . ."

Jason tried not to grimace. "They're not those people anymore."

"But based on the history of their relationship."

"I don't understand."

"That they're very . . . close." The officer let the last word hang in the air so heavily it could have brought down a clothesline.

"I don't know whether you're inferring anything—"

"Not at all."

"—but Blue and Elisa were friends. They only have history as friends. Close friends, yes, but nothing more." Where had he gotten the impression otherwise?

Jessed slid a manila folder across the table. Inside were a series of Elisa's photographs from the vacation; the police had come back for her camera and undeveloped rolls of film a few days after she and Blue went missing. Jason flipped through the stack: shots of the trail behind the house, the cove at night, a close-up of a bee alighting on a pink peony with a blurry Donald in the background as he tended garden down the hill. Why she refused to so much as try the digital camera he had bought her last year, Jason still couldn't fathom.

The next few pictures were of the upstairs bathroom, all taken from what looked like the vantage point of the bathtub, the tub's heavy lip visible in some of the shots. Then, a photograph of a man's face, obscured. Jason's heart skipped, and he quickly turned to the next photo. It was only Blue, a towel wrapped around his head like a turban, his lips pulled back in a leering parody of a smile. He could immediately tell Elisa had taken the picture; no one but her could make him smile like that. It was an effect Jason knew all too well.

A few more shots of Blue—the stack was thicker than he'd figured, exactly how many were there?—and suddenly there she was. His wife. His girl, which is what he called her though she was most certainly a woman. Her angular, exquisite face smeared in bath bubbles, slender neck jutting from the foamy water. Her breasts. Her stomach. Jesus Christ, her pelvis, her fingers, her wrists . . . Every part of her was achingly familiar and yet, viewed separately, rendered alien and obscene.

A seizure of memory: the sound of water running, back in their New York apartment. Elisa in the shower, the early-morning light of late June filtering through the rectangular bank of bedroom windows. Her flip phone jangles on the nightstand, and Jason rolls over to see who's calling at this hour, but when he opens the phone to check, the call is put through. It's her OB/GYN's office, confirming her appointment for the next day.

"Will you be coming too?" the cheery receptionist asks.

"No. Why, should I?"

Silence. "Just make sure Mrs. Howard gets back to us."

"Uh . . . Okay." After he hangs up he tries to put the call out of his mind. He couldn't have possibly heard properly. Hadn't woken up really, still susceptible to all manner of misunderstanding. The receptionist probably misspoke. Surely she wasn't implying Elisa is pregnant. That isn't possible, after all.

Is it?

He never mentioned the call to Elisa. Now, many weeks

later, the shadow fell across his mind again, the one that reminded him that he and Elisa hadn't slept together in months. Not since his birthday in January, when she deigned to let him do more than kiss her. She claimed it was her antidepressants, that they were screwing with her libido, but really he knew it must be him. The only answer was that he repulsed her.

Blue, he thought. *Fucking Blue.*

Before he could stop himself, he exhaled loudly, his even-keeled composure cracked like an eggshell. *Well played, Detective.* Because of course he'd harbored suspicions about them. How could he not, when Elisa was on the phone with Blue until all hours, when they'd had a whole life together before Jason had stepped on the scene? And then that phone call from her doctor's office, the one he tried to blot out of his memory, but which still haunted the dark corners of his consciousness.

But what could he have done, confront her? Divorce her without any substantiation? He couldn't have prevented what had happened, if she was in fact pregnant with Blue's child. The unspoken deal between Jason and Elisa was that Blue was part of the package: Jason had to take Blue, or leave her. So he went along with it, told himself all the while that Blue was a certified mess, a closet case, no real threat to their relationship. He told himself such things with greater frequency after they married and Elisa became depressed, when she and Jason stopped having sex and she turned to the aid of an uptown psychopharmacologist, referred by Jason himself. It was too easy for him to see all of this as his own fault.

"Mr. Howard, forgive us," Jessed said. "We need to explore every avenue."

"I understand." Jason smiled tightly, returning the pictures to the folder. "But these don't mean anything. I mean, look at them. They're joking around here. Hey, you don't know them, they're a funny pair. When they get together, they're like a couple of kids. There's nothing more to it than that." He said the words, but he didn't feel them, his mouth cotton dry; he was helping to prove Jessed's theory. Jason had always known that Blue held an unshakeable power over his wife, that they shared a connection that could never be undone; it was only a matter of time before it bit him in the ass.

After the interview was over and he walked Jessed to the door, Jason inquired if the police might be returning Elisa's camera anytime soon. "When we spoke with Ms. Weintraub's mother, she told us to keep it as long as we needed," the detective said, using Elisa's maiden name. "It shouldn't be much longer."

"You mean when she came up last week?" They hadn't even asked for the camera until after Elisa's mother had departed.

"She came by the station yesterday."

"In North Sydney?" He knew Diane was planning on returning to Cape Breton, but to do so without telling him? That wasn't like her. "Is she still in town?"

"It was only a day trip. We had a few more questions. Administrative issues, mostly." Jessed paused. "She did mention that her daughter was on antidepressants. Is that right?"

"Zoloft. Yes. Half of New York is."

"And you would say your marriage is a happy one."

"I would. Absolutely."

"I have to ask." Jessed smiled weakly. "Thank you, Mr. Howard. We'll be in touch."

Jason stayed on the porch to watch the cruiser disappear down the hill. Had Elisa's mother said something to the police about the state of their marriage? It was bad enough when

Diane had showed up last week, lost and frazzled and as understandably bereft as any mother whose daughter had gone missing. Jason had driven her from the airport to the police station
himself. Upon leaving her interview with the police, however,
she was distant and distracted, the change borne out during subsequent conversations in which she seemed unwilling to discuss
Elisa or her whereabouts. They must have told her something,
information they were withholding from him that had reassured
her of her daughter's well-being. Either that or they'd instructed
her not to speak to Jason.

It was the only answer he could come up with. Diane hadn't
returned his calls the past few days; he'd managed to catch her
on her cellphone only the day before, a blip of a conversation
that ended abruptly when she pleaded a migraine and begged
off the line. Had she in fact been mere miles away when he'd
reached her? And why did Jessed so purposefully fail to conceal
this from him? It was hard not to feel suspicious, though he
tried with all his might, certain as ever that paranoia would be
his eventual undoing. Which was, as it had always been, completely unacceptable.

The early-morning mist was already burning off the cove.
If Jason stared at the landscape long enough, the idyllic scenery turned menacing, swirling waters and murky shadows surfacing like dark creatures risen from the deep. He looked for
Maureen and Donald puttering outside their house, but then
remembered that they'd headed down to their flat in Halifax
for a series of Donald-related appointments. Maureen had implored Jason to call her if he needed anything, as if she didn't
already have enough to manage. "You can stay on as long as you
want," she'd said the day before as she rubbed his shoulders on

the porch swing, a gesture so warm and unexpected he found it uncomfortably sexual. "Until they come back. Until you find them."

He went back inside the house, through the kitchen to the stairs. And there was Gabe, seated in shadow on the top step; he was draped in a light cotton patchwork quilt, a little boy who'd snuck out of his room to eavesdrop on his parents downstairs. The effect was aided by his too-large T-shirt and sweatpants, the cuffs of which were rolled into thick rings below his knees: he'd taken to wearing Blue's clothes, culled from the closet in the tartan room.

"Are they gone?" Gabe said.

"It was Jessed, by himself this time. He left a few minutes ago."

"I take it he's not exactly pursuing all leads?"

"Taken correctly." Jason cleared the dining room table and set out paper and pens, while Gabe shuffled over inside his papoose of a quilt. "Well, then. Want to get started on today's business?"

They gathered the castoff materials that had accumulated over the past week—color-coded aerial photos, topographic maps, land surveys—and arranged them in order of proximity to the house. The rest of the morning was spent as usual: writing up detailed notes on the previous day's canvass. They'd started their own search four days prior, when it became clear the authorities' attention had drifted toward the missing hikers. The police had covered the neighboring woods and fields, as well as the mountain base and the marsh shallows of the bay. But there were many more doors to knock on, a seemingly infinite amount of ground to cover, and Jason came to accept that a proper search would fall to them. Realistically, this could only succeed if one of the locals had seen something, anything that might give them a starting point.

Their route was plotted using the aerial maps, spiraling out from the MacLeod House and the Cabot Trail in a carefully orchestrated canvass covering as wide an area as possible. Jason drove them in the rental car along the winding main road, where they would stop to introduce themselves at each house along the cove. Rarely was such an introduction necessary. It seemed as if most everyone in the community knew who they were by now, a subject of local gossip and a steadily shrinking item in the *Cape Breton Post*. The brushfires and missing hikers were still front-page news, whereas Elisa and Blue, even at the start, hadn't warranted an article in the paper higher than page five. It was as if only one group of people could legitimately go missing at a time, and the hikers had beaten them to it.

Jason placed a follow-up call to Stanley Baker, the property agent who had showed Blue his grandmother's house the day he disappeared. When they'd first spoken, Baker had told Jason that if he wanted access to the house he would have to go through the police and a justice of the peace with the authority to issue a search warrant. Either that or the new owners, who were abroad for the remainder of the summer. Though Jason and Gabe had snooped around, the house was locked and they'd failed to find anything of note on Flora MacKenzie's property. It had officially been sold.

Jason asked the agent once again if he could remember anything at all about Blue's disposition that afternoon, and this time Baker described him as "acting jumpy."

"Jumpy? Really?"

"Truth be told," the agent said, "by the time I left him I thought he might be on something. Came flying out of the basement like a bat out of hell. Real edgy. Maybe that's a New York thing, though. I don't know. There was even this smell about him, on his hands maybe . . . It was like I got a contact high."

"And you just remembered this."

"Look, I already told the police everything. Hey, if it makes you feel any better, the detective sounded pretty sure they just took off." After hanging up the phone Jason kept his hand on the receiver, as if holding on to it could help him better absorb this new information. He'd been in touch with a private investigator in New York whom he'd met during his stockbroker days, and made a mental note to call him later in the day.

In the dining area, Gabe sat drawing in his sketch pad with his leg bouncing madly beneath the table. "The real estate agent," Jason said. "He mentioned Blue seemed jumpy that afternoon. Does that sound right to you?"

"Jumpy? I don't remember that. Kind of the opposite, actually. He looked really drained."

"Did he say anything when he came back from the house? Anything at all you can think of?"

"He did say he felt strange being here. Coming home, I guess. He didn't want to talk about it. Like I said, he pretty much just wanted to get the hell out of Dodge."

"And you told the police that?"

"Sure. But I didn't get the feeling they were interested." Gabe shrugged. "Maybe because I didn't push it. It didn't sound so great that one of the last things Blue said to me was that he wanted to take off."

"You don't believe they left on their own, though."

"Nope. And neither do you."

Gabe popped a sugar cube into his mouth, his restless leg still jittering under the table. This livewire energy wasn't Gabe's natural state, as far as Jason could glean; the boy had changed in Blue's absence. A distinct possibility, Gabe being a prime example of someone who had lost himself inside of Blue. Just like Elisa once had.

Jason thought some more about what the property agent had said. This was the first time since the disappearance they'd heard anything significant regarding Blue's behavior. Donald's freakout and Elisa's allergy attack aside, Jason hadn't noticed anything atypical that day, certainly not in relation to Blue. But so what? Blue's appearance and affect often altered from moment to moment. He was a kind of human Rorschach blot who could make one person conspicuously uncomfortable, while others might dive right into his orbiting sphere of influence, only to give themselves over completely. Jason himself had felt strangely unnerved upon first meeting Blue, not terribly long after Jason and Elisa had started dating. *Typical pretty boy*, he'd thought at the time. But really he'd been put off by Blue's mercurial beauty, as well as his hold on Elisa, not to mention what Jason cynically presumed to be Blue's unearned (and downright freakish) mastery of cooking. Jason had been, quite frankly, jealous of him.

There were times when, at Elisa's invitation, Blue would join them at an upscale restaurant or bar and arrive oily-haired and reeking of cigarette smoke, unshowered in leather pants and a moth-eaten sweater; Jason would want to crawl under the table. But right as Jason finally worked up the courage to say something, Blue would run a hand through his matted black hair and everything would fall into place. At once he would emerge artfully arranged, the change so swift it was disturbing. As was so often the case with Blue, Jason would be left to wonder if he had somehow misinterpreted.

And as for what the property agent had said, even Blue's smell was weirdly mutable. His pungent musk of nicotine and kitchen grease could perfume in a single moment to a light sandalwood, the scent of a holy censer about him, of sacred space. It was this same distinctive smell that haunted Jason these past few days upon waking, his head heavy with dark dreams. Nightmares of someone at his bedside in the pink room, a long-limbed figure with a face cast in shadow. Pale and reedy fingers pressing upon him, forcing him down until he could not scream, could not breathe.

They were dreams of being swallowed alive, of death. In his heart, he knew they were dreams of Blue.

It wasn't the first time Jason had endured recurring night-mares. There'd been worse ones, but then he had Elisa to help him through. That was soon after they first met, back when Jason was a trader and he and his fellow stockbroker buds had stumbled drunk into the Slipper Room, their fifth stop on a late-summer pub crawl through the Lower East Side. There was some kind of burlesque show going on, an open-mic night for "performance artists" and "gender illusionists," basically a motley crew of exhibitionists with props. The mustachioed drag king MC, her three-piece suit accentuating her Weeble-like shape, was in the middle of doing a bit on the difference between male and female genitalia when Steve Berry from M&A set down a drained tumbler of Jameson and stage-whispered, "Is every bitch in here a dyke or what?" a little too loudly.

As if summoned by mystical means, a breathtaking young woman in a strapless black-and-white Marimekko-print dress appeared beside their booth, sparkling dark eyes set like precious stones against kohl-smeared olive skin. Berry smiled up at her, mesmerized. She smiled back before she reached over, grabbed Berry by his necktie, and dragged him from his seat to applause from the surrounding tables. Near the entrance he pushed her off. She pushed back. Jason got between them and ushered Berry in the general direction of the door.

"Your friend is an asshole," she said to Jason, more than ready to tussle, despite her significant height and weight disad‑ vantage.

"I know," he replied. "Sorry about that."

"Why are you even here, anyway? For God's sake, go to a strip club where you belong."

She headed to the bar, but he intercepted her before she could get the bartender's attention. "Let me make it up to you," he said. "Please. Can I buy you a drink?"

He smiled, showing off his new teeth; once a crooked, orthodontia-neglected mess, they'd recently been capped. She eyed him with no small amount of skepticism. "Well. Okay. But only because I don't have any cash on me."

She said her name was Prudence. They spent the next cou‑ ple of hours in a booth in the corner, talking, then necking, the rest of Jason's colleagues long since vanished. At two in the morning she asked if he wanted to go home with her.

"Most definitely," he said. "But let's wait. Will you have din‑ ner with me this week?"

He'd always been good at reading people, and, as much as it would have thrilled him to bed her that night, he knew that if they slept together he would never hear from her again. He would become "that black broker guy I fucked," a funny story for her friends, instead of a man who might mean something to her. He could already tell that she meant a great deal to him.

Indeed, his reticence had intrigued her. They went on a few more dates, one in which she told him her name was in fact Elisa, and another over a mind-blowing home-cooked meal at her place in Alphabet City that consisted of two varieties of paella and an amaretto flan for dessert; only much later did she reveal that Blue had prepared everything for her in advance. The next night, their obvious and electric sexual connection was consummated. Following dinner and a movie, they'd gone back to Jason's apartment in Brooklyn Heights and spent hours in bed—kissing, fucking, spooning, everything hot and tender and beautiful, just right. He couldn't remember the last time he'd felt so blissed out, so centered and sane. He was in heaven.

In the morning he left her in his bed. He quietly showered, shaved, and dressed, kissing her on the forehead before he slipped out the door. Because of a call from his sister's hospital he was late getting on the train at High Street, and stepped out of the World Trade Center station to a commotion at the mouth of the subway entrance. People pointed up at the Twin Towers, smoke and flames spewing from the higher floors of the North Tower, where Jason's office was. He used his briefcase to shield his eyes from the morning sun and watched as pieces of things fell, debris. No. No, bodies. Jumpers. One, then a few moments later another: a woman whose skirt had blown off, two others holding hands, a fourth, a fifth, a sixth. Each eternal descent was followed by a rat-a-tat crash, the sound of matter meeting the earth, followed by screams at street level, then stifled sobs.

A man hanging from one of the building's girders was waving something in his hand, a desperate semaphore in the direction of those staring up from the ground, the object a black square of darkness against the piercing blue sky. An unknown force made Jason shove his briefcase under his arm and sprint toward the tower, dodging gawkers and cars alike: something about the sight of the man, a thousand feet overhead, had compelled him. And then the man let go, his limbs pinwheeling in the wind, and it was like watching someone trying to swim against a deadly current. There was no more noise, everything silent, the man flung around the side of the building as the object flew from his hand at the last second.

Jason was less than fifty yards from the base of the tower when he recognized the thing the man had refused to relinquish in his final moments, the holy object he must have held so dear. It was a simple black briefcase. Jason stared down at his own black attaché, identical in every respect, and looked on from outside his body as the briefcase slid from his grasp and hit the pavement soundlessly. He backed away from it, slowly, then turned and ran.

By the time he finally made it over the Brooklyn Bridge and reached home, Elisa was waiting by the door in one of his dress shirts. The cordless phone was dead in her hand, the TV blatting prophecies of doom from the other side of the apartment. They embraced, and Jason couldn't stop shaking his head, kept saying, "Oh, Jesus, oh God," over and over. Elisa shushed him, kissed him, said, "I'm here, I'm here." She held him tighter, ran her hands up into his closely cropped hair, across his neck, down the back of his sweat-soaked shirt. "I'm here. I'm here."

And she was. When he woke up from nightmares of falling, the earth spinning out from beneath him; when he called his firm a few weeks later to say he wouldn't be returning to work at their new location; when he sought a therapist specializing in PTSD. He'd known so many of the dead. Thirty-seven personally, including Steve Berry from M&A, who, in his own drunken and heedless way, had introduced Jason to his future wife.

With Elisa's encouragement, he researched accelerated programs in psychology, a new calling. Because of his insane family he'd always had a vague appreciation for mental health professionals, but now Jason understood the vital need for their services firsthand. He wanted to help others the way he had been helped, back to life, and to love.

Elisa, flaky and obstinate as she could be, was a godsend. Once he started grad school, she made sure he ate properly and exercised, never complaining about the long nights he spent at the library on his thesis or interning at the Brooklyn House of Detention. She kept him sane, and, best of all, laughing, attending his graduation at NYU in a cap and gown, robe shredded and refashioned as an avant-garde wrap dress with the mortarboard hung jauntily from the side of a fresh asymmetrical shag cut. Elisa allowed him to throw himself into his work, innately grasping his need to problem solve, to puzzle out other people. In doing so she avoided—to both her credit and her advantage—becoming the problem or puzzle herself.

Still, it wasn't enough. He had to analyze everyone, not only his clients but his friends, his family, and of course Elisa. He needed to dissect everything around him in order to avoid taking a scalpel to himself. Was that what her disappearance was, a final, vituperative rejection of his overbearing nature? Or was that thinking too much of himself? Yes, he had provided her with stability and kindness—indeed, with love—but he'd let the passion slip away; it was no great wonder she began to drift.

But now the time had come to pack down the guilt and focus his energy on bringing her back. Let that be his redemption.

In the days following Detective Jessed's follow-up interview at the house, Jason and Gabe continued to canvass the cove with even greater urgency. They spoke with an elderly couple of third-generation Cape Bretoners, both of whom had a lovely Gaelic brogue; a flophouse of teenage meth addicts, where Gabe did most of the talking; a cabbage farmer who asked Jason if he happened to be the son of a football player who played for the Patriots back in the seventies. There were so many others, a blur of compassionate faces. And while each resident was largely polite almost to a person, not a one had much to share, other than their sympathies. *At least they aren't treating me as if I were some kind of murderer*, Jason thought. *Just a run-of-the-mill cuckold, like any other.* He wasn't sure if this was a relief, exactly.

On a bright Tuesday afternoon—the thirteenth day after the disappearance—their canvass brought them to the far side of the cove. They pulled past a mailbox plastered in bright stickers of plump cherubs and up a dirt drive to a prefab minihome, a beat-up yellow Volkswagen Beetle on the lawn with a faded 9/11 decal in the back window that depicted an exhausted firefighter slumped on a street curb and flanked by a pair of translucent, consoling angels.

Jason killed the ignition. "Who have we got?"

"Tanya Darrow," Gabe said, reading from the clipboard in his lap. "Thirty-something single mother, according to Maureen, although she wasn't completely sure about her age. Her husband died in a car crash and she mostly keeps to herself."

Bare platform steps led up to the entrance. Twin wind chimes in the shape of seraphs swayed like hanged men on either side of the stairs, an Annunciation scene crocheted on the seat cushion of a wicker chair beside the door. Jason knocked and stepped back, while Gabe loitered a few feet away on the lawn. A harried-looking woman came to the door. She was lanky with crimped red hair, dark bags under clearwater eyes that squinted fearfully into the midday light. A moment later three young children appeared, circling her as if she were a covered wagon under siege.

"Hello, Ms. Darrow? My name is—"

"Oh, I know who you are," she said. "You're the one whose wife . . ." She wasn't going to finish.

"Yes. Jason Howard. And this is Gabriel Peck," he added, poking a thumb in Gabe's direction. "Do you have a minute?"

She shooed the kids inside and shut the door behind them. "Sorry to bother you," Gabe said from the lawn. He held his scar-blemished hand behind his back, as he often did. "We're going door to door, to see if anyone might have heard something about our friends."

"I was wondering whether you were going to come this far around the bend."

Jason smiled. "News travels fast."

"Fast as an echo. But sorry, I really don't think I know anything useful. It's just the strangest thing that happened, isn't it? How awful. It's like the earth opened up and swallowed them."

Swallowed them, Jason thought. *That's exactly what it feels like.*

"Of course," she went on, "I hope there's been some kind of mistake. I wish you all the luck in the world."

They'd had the same conversation with seventeen other Starling Cove residents that very afternoon, and Jason had long tired of the ongoing lack of substantive information. There had to be someone who knew something, anything. It was time for him to step up his game.

"It's been so hard for us," Jason said, affecting a more somber tone as he forced tears at the corners of his eyes. Was he really going to do this? *Forgive me,* he pleaded to the dead, if not to God himself. "Not knowing where they are. We've already been through so much, coming from New York and all. So many lost. Almost five years past now, but for us it still seems like yesterday."

"I'm so sorry." She put a hand to her breast. "You weren't there when it happened, were you? On 9/11?"

"I was. Right there. Under the towers." He proceeded to tell her the entirety of his experience that day with every possible dramatic flourish, including his tearful reunion with Elisa back at his apartment, which had the woman welling up herself. By the end of his story, she had taken his hands and was lost in his eyes, her breath erratic as she choked back tears. He was disgusted with himself.

"Sometimes I think—" Jason stared up at the late-afternoon sky before he continued. "Sometimes I think they've become angels. All of them who died that day? Maybe they're floating through the firmament right now! Tucked inside the Lord's heavenly embrace, for all eternity. And they watch over us, even though we can no longer see them . . . I know that they're here just the same. Our guardian angels."

"They *are* angels now!" the woman said. "You poor thing. You poor thing . . ." She squeezed his hand. "You'll be in my prayers. And so will your wife."

Back in the car, he could barely make eye contact with Gabe. "Wow," Gabe said from the passenger seat. "That was . . . something." Jason couldn't tell if the boy's tone expressed revulsion or admiration, though most likely it was a combination of the two. "Did you make all that up on the spot?"

"Not as much as I would have liked. For what it's worth." He was surprised Blue never told Gabe, but in a way he was touched; it was Jason's story to tell, after all, and he respected Blue for recognizing that.

Jason started the engine and was already pulling out of the drive when the woman appeared beside the car and gestured for him to lower his window. "Just one thing," she said, panting. "Did you speak to Fred Cronin yet?"

Jason looked to Gabe, who shook his head.

"Ask him." She looked back at the house for a moment before lowering her voice. "Ask him about the Other Kind."

Chapter Five

"Darkening my door, I see." Fred Cronin spoke with a weariness that suggested Jason and Gabe were not only expected but were in fact late. Were they supposed to know him? They had met so many locals lately. He did look somewhat familiar, what little Jason could see of him through the cracked door, a squat troll of a man with cavernous ruts in his face and an unkempt beard, a swollen nose, and bulging hazel eyes. Though Jason vaguely recognized him, he had the thought that it might be from a television show or movie, rather than from real life.

"How nice of Tanya to invite you over," Cronin said. "That girl, that girl . . . Jesus holy hell. Well. What are you going to do. Anyhow."

He disappeared from view, the door left an ambiguous foot ajar; it took Jason a few moments before he summoned the nerve to step inside. Gabe followed, daylight vanquished when he shut the door behind them. The outside of the single-story cottage may have been weather-beaten white, but aside from a stark bulb overhead the interior was dark as midnight, ancient roller shades drawn over the windows. Every surface was obscured, buried beneath books and documents and newspapers, stacked in some places to the rafters. A *hoarder?* Jason wondered, not sure where to rest his eyes. He tried to avoid Gabe's nervous and sidelong glance.

"I run my own printing press out of the cellar," Cronin said, and swept his arm in the direction of a perilous heap of papers on top of the woodstove. "Back issues of my journal. And I'm the only one who doesn't charge storage." He pulled two pamphlet-thin newspapers off the top of a nearby stack and handed one to each of them. "So, let's get this over with, shall we?"

Below the ludicrously ornate nameplate of *The Starling Cove Believer* was the bold headline SEARCH FOR WHITLEY AND FRIEND CONTINUES, the subheading "Still Missing after a Week." And there, reproduced in faulty black and white, was printed a recent photograph of Blue and Elisa. They were dancing, her arms around his neck with her back arched in a spasm of unmitigated bliss. It was like looking at Detective Jessed's pictures all over again, the ones from Elisa's camera. It was like seeing a pair of ghosts.

Now Jason remembered where he knew the man from: Fred Cronin was an artisan friend of Maureen and Donald's he'd met at the ceilidh. An ironsmith, if memory served. He must have taken the photo that night.

"Beautiful girl," Cronin said, and he cocked his head, his grizzled beard sweeping the front of his stained waffle shirt; Jason failed to detect any hint of lasciviousness in his voice. "That might be why they wanted her."

"Why they . . . ?" Jason wasn't sure he'd heard properly.

"You might as well stay awhile." Their host moved a massive cairn of spiral-bound newspapers from a black velvet-upholstered couch so they could sit. For himself he produced a warped plastic chair from beneath a sagging card table covered in emptied beer bottles. "Tell me," he said, pausing to light a cigarette. "How much do you two know about these parts?"

"You mean Cape Breton?" Jason said.

"I mean the cove." The man couldn't have been much past his midfifties, but he looked positively decrepit. "Have you noticed how different this place feels?" he said, hissing smoke through his teeth. "How the air smells, the unusual sound the wind makes as it whispers through the trees? The way the water tastes, even?"

"Yes," Gabe said at once, much to Jason's surprise. "It's like everything is more . . . alive here. More energized."

"So you do feel it," Cronin said. "Not everybody does. Only the sensitive," and he cast a baleful look at Jason. "When I first moved up here I figured the cove was hyperoxygenated. The way places like Big Sur are, with all the runoff into the lakes and waterways, you know? Locations like that, they tend to attract specific kinds of people, since back in the day. Seekers and such, the occasional religious freak. And Starling Cove is no different. Take the water, for example. That's why we've always had the best screech."

"Screech?" Gabe said.

"Shine. Moonshine. You could make a decent living bootlegging in these parts, right through the eighties. Lots of the houses around here, they still have the old gin stills in the basement, or rum-running tunnels that lead down to the water. And believe you me, the Colony made the best screech of all."

"The commune," Jason said. "Were you a part of that place?"

"Not as such."

"But they made moonshine there? At the Colony?"

"Most everyone did around here. None better than those folks. Donald's secret recipe."

"Donald was part of the Colony? Maureen's husband?"

"Part of it? Hell, he founded the damned place."

"He did?" Gabe said. "But he seems so . . . professorial."

"That was the type back then. Like Leary and Ginsburg and Castaneda, middle-aged guys with that father figure thing working for them. And Donald with his pipe and elbow patches . . . Worked like catnip, especially when it came to the ladies. Take a look at Maureen! She was a local girl, native Mi'kmaq even, only stopped in to the Colony for a visit one day and never left. Not until the fire, that is." He watched the smoke from his cigarette curl around the plastic light fixture and its single dim bulb. "What did your missing friend tell you about life in the cove? About growing up here?"

"Not much," Jason said. "He hardly remembered a thing about it."

"And you believed him."

"Why wouldn't we? He was only a boy."

"That's what his mama kept saying." He chuckled. "Should've known who he was when I laid eyes on him. Sensed he was one of them. But I was thrown by the name. Not to mention the fact that our workaday world seems to have rubbed off on him. Poor little Hansel . . ."

"Hansel?"

"Sorry. Michael. Or *Blue*," Cronin said, in a theatrical tenor redolent with sarcasm. "I mean, what was he going to tell you about his people, if he even could? The real question is why he came back after all this time. Why now?"

"He came back to sell his grandmother's house." Jason tried to settle on the couch.

"Yeah, well, how'd that work out for him?" He lit another cigarette off the first and stubbed the spent butt into the side of an overflowing crenellated ashtray, browned filters bent into the shapes of scoliotic spines. "He's probably still alive, if it's any comfort. Flora was a crafty one, but the Other Kind are craftier."

"The Other Kind." Jason looked to Gabe. "Tanya Darrow said something about that."

"They're the ones that live here. Under the ground."

"Under the ground?" Gabe sat up in his seat.

"Underground, under the bay, wherever they are. It's hard to say exactly. They're tough to put a finger on, since the land around these parts has a funny way of adapting whenever it suits the Kind. They live somewhere in the earth, but you'll never find them down there unless you raze the mountain. Not without one of them to take you. And not a one ever will. Anyway, most everyone knows they're here. Either of you gents want a beer? No?"

As if he'd said nothing unusual whatsoever, the odd little man got up and wandered off to his kitchen. He spent such an interminably long while retrieving a cold one from the fridge that it was hard not to feel he was toying with them.

"So you were telling us about the Other Kind," Jason said once Cronin finally returned to his chair, beer and bottle opener in hand. "About the . . . I'm sorry, the ones underground?"

"Right."

"Right what?"

"Are you messing with me, son?"

"Not at all." *What is up with this guy?* "Please, go on."

"As I was saying, nearly everyone around these parts has heard of them. Old country folks call them the Fae, but really they're talking about the Other Kind."

Fae. Jason recalled Donald using that word, at the ceilidh. "So, they're out there somewhere," he said. "Under the bay, maybe. But what are they?"

"Do you mean they're like nature spirits?" Gabe asked.

"Hard to say for certain, since they're not meant to be

known. But they're here all right, as sure as the seasons change. They just don't like to be seen. That's why if they come, they come at night. They like to take things. Laundry off the line, bottles from the recycling, a hood ornament now and again . . ." He leaned back in his chair. "No one knows what they are exactly, but everyone's got a theory. At least I do."

"Tell us. Please." Gabe was breathless, and Jason recalled the *Weird Creatures of Atlantic Canada* paperback the boy had picked up at the airport newsstand in Halifax. "What do you think they are?"

"See, that's the funny thing." Cronin ran a fingertip along his chair arm, a landing strip cleared across a thick pad of dust. "Because what I think they are is the same thing everyone else does. But most people don't know that. They haven't thought it through. Take the old-timers, like Donald. They tend to be the more open-minded types, the ones willing to admit that there's a presence here. They mostly think the woods are harboring fairies."

"Fairies." Jason said it with a straight face, but his inner clinician triggered the diagnostic process. Delusional disorder, for starters; possibly a more severe paranoiac element to boot, with a potential for schizophrenic tendencies. And a chronic alcohol abuser to be sure, a constellation of red capillaries broken across the man's bulbous nose. "You think fairies took my wife."

"Let me finish," Cronin said, his annoyance undisguised. "That's just how some people identify them. It's *cultural*. In the old country, that's what the common people called those they couldn't begin to fathom. The Fae. The Good Neighbors. The Silent People. In Ireland, they're the Aos Si, the people of the mounds. Lots of names for the things that live among us, but aren't *of* us. Some of the Mi'kmaqs around these parts, they call them the stone dwarves."

"But those are superstitions," Jason said. "Folklore, basically."

"Some of it, sure. But not all. Sometimes, late at night, we'll get *dreags* over the water. You know, like corpse candles?"

"Will-o'-the-wisps," Gabe chimed in. "Ghost lights, or something. They're like little UFOs, right?"

Cronin nodded. "But I for one would hardly think aliens would come down from the celestial heavens to buzz a foggy little cove in Cape Breton, do you?"

"I suppose not," Jason said. It was actually fascinating to have a conversation with someone of such heightened pathology outside of a clinical setting.

"Isn't it funny," Cronin said, "that the elders see fairies? Folks today, though, we talk about the whole alien abduction thing. Or maybe by now it's all about mass hallucinations, or government experiments, whatever the flavor of the day may be. Whereas I personally prefer the term *ultraterrestrials*. Do you see where I'm going with this?"

"I think so," Gabe said. "They're all just different ways of explaining similar phenomenon."

"Exactly. Because here's the thing: they're all the same, man. Grays, little green men, the Fae, whatever? Hell, maybe even the goddamn angels and demons! They're different names for the same thing."

Jason crossed his legs, which their host seemed to take as some kind of covert sign of disrespect. "Look," Cronin said, "I'm not some backwoods yokel. I'm from Detroit. All these terms, they're names for whatever it is that walks these woods. Real beings, no matter where they came from. And they're near impossible to describe."

"And you know this how exactly?" Jason said.

"I've seen 'em." He lit another cigarette and let the smoke drift from his nostrils. "Only once up close. I was driving over Kelly's Mountain late one night, twenty-five years ago now. I rounded a corner near the peak, and at first all I saw out of the corner of my eye was a pinprick of light, like a lightning bug but greenish. Only as I kept driving, the light stayed there, hovering past the driver's side window. Hanging over the side of the mountain too; it couldn't be a light from a house or anything, and what's more, it wasn't going anywhere, even as the car kept moving. Impossible to tell just how close it was. It was like the light was following me, like the moon. Tracking me."

A *light*, Jason thought. *Detective Jessed asked if I'd seen any lights the night they went missing.*

"I was so rattled I nearly drove off the road," Cronin continued. "I pulled onto what little shoulder there was, and there it came again, this strange green light. It stopped just like I'd stopped, but it was still floating. It felt so close I could reach out and touch it. I rolled the window down a crack and suddenly I heard this giant burst of sound, like dialing through the world's biggest radio, searching for a clear signal. I went to roll the window back up but it stuck, so I covered my ears, hoping my eardrums wouldn't bust."

He coughed violently, then collected himself. "After a while—a few seconds maybe, but it felt like whole minutes—the light started getting brighter. And then I heard voices. Whispering voices, coming out of the wall of noise. I could hear them talking. Laughing and moaning too, like maybe they had started screwing or something . . . It made me feel sick and horny all at once. It was like I was on fire, and it felt so fucking good."

Jason bristled, but held his tongue.

"Well, the light got even brighter, so bright I thought I was going to be burned by it. It was like a monster green sun, burning itself into my corneas, even with my eyes shut. And then I saw what looked like people, standing in the middle of the light. Still with my eyes closed! They were climbing on the side of the mountain, kind of hanging there at a twisted angle, almost like trees growing right out of the earth. All different shapes—some long, some squat, but it was hard to tell because they would look puffed up one second, then deflated the next. Their shapes shifted along with the light, but also with the sound. Rising and falling, like a beating heart. There were two of them, though, both about three feet high, the size of children. They were in the middle, like they were important. Like they were being protected by the others."

"Had you been drinking?" Jason tried not to use his therapist voice. "Or dropping acid, maybe?"

"Probably both," Cronin replied with a chuckle, his lower register an emphysemic rasp. "But believe me when I tell you it happened. I saw what I saw. They're something you can't perceive exactly, like they weren't made to be seen with human eyes. I could only catch parts of them—*glimpses* of them—the parts they allowed me to access."

"And you thought they were aliens?"

"At the time, yeah. Like I said, this was coming off the seventies. Alien culture was all over the place back then. *Close Encounters*, the Mothman, all that jazz. But eventually I realized I was wrong."

"You realized they're actually ultraterrestrials."

Jason maintained a neutral tone, but Cronin's lip curled anyway. "All I'm saying is that they're not from some other planet, or from heaven or hell or any of that bullshit. They're from right here, and they've been here all along. A lot longer than us, I'm guessing. They own the place. Not us. Them."

"Why do you think they would want my wife? And her—our friend?"

He shrugged. "Not my place to conjecture."

That's all you seem to be doing. Jason couldn't stop himself from grinning, and Gabe shot him a glance. *You've told us fuck all, except that one long-ago night you got wasted and nearly ran off the road. Thanks a lot for nothing.*

"Please," Gabe said. "We're listening."

"Well," Cronin said, "from everything I've learned, it doesn't seem like the Other Kind are capable of reproducing on their own. They need to crossbreed to survive. So I figure that because they took them both, it's most likely because they want to breed them."

"Okay, then." Jason stood. "I'm sorry, but we have a lot of ground to cover. And since it's getting late . . ."

He turned toward the door but Gabe shot up from the couch. "Wait," the boy said, and grabbed Jason's arm. "Please."

Jason stared at Gabe's hand for a moment before he shook it off. "Let's go."

"Jason!" Gabe lunged to take hold of his arm again. "Please. Sit down."

"Others have been taken," Cronin said, standing himself now. "The cops won't admit it but it's documented. Your friend—you might not know who he really is, but I do. He's one of them. The night I saw the lights—"

"I've heard enough." Jason stepped to Cronin so fast that without so much as laying a hand on him, the man fell back into his seat. "We can't start chasing phantoms right now. I need some concrete answers. Something real, you know?"

"Suit yourself." Cronin shrugged and stared at his scarred knuckles, his cigarette burned down to the filter. "If you're not ready, you're not ready." He looked at Gabe. "But when you are, we can discuss it further."

"Thank you for your time," Gabe said. He shook the man's hand and waited for Jason to follow suit, which he did, finally and reluctantly.

On their way out the door, Cronin handed Gabe a stack of yellowed papers that reminded Jason of the mimeographed worksheets from his elementary school days. "A little bedtime reading," Cronin said. "For those with an open mind."

Jason could feel the man's eyes burning a hole in the back of his head as he and Gabe walked to the car, the sensation lingering long after they pulled out of the driveway and onto the main road.

As the car ascended Kelly's Mountain, the sky blue but for a thread of gray clouds over the horizon, Jason thought about Cronin navigating the very same route that long-ago night. As delusional as the man was, he was no liar; he really did believe he'd seen the mysterious beings he had tried to describe. But if magical alien fairies really did take Elisa and Blue—to *breed* them, Jason thought, and laughed out loud, howling up through the Caddy's open sunroof—then there wasn't a goddamned thing anyone could do about it.

An image shuddered inside his head, one of Blue and Elisa. Their hands upon one another, hungry and desirous like rutting animals, all flesh and savage sex . . . It was an imagined home movie that Jason had rewound and replayed many times over many months, never more so than the past few days.

Jason pushed the thought away. "Ultraterrestrials," he said. "Can you believe that guy?"

Gabe let out a quiet titter from the passenger seat, imitative of a laugh. Other than that, he was silent, absorbed in Fred Cronin's decomposing papers.

"Wait." Gabe clenched the pages in his hands. "Wait a second. Stop the car."

"What? What is it?"

"Pull the car over. Now. You have to see these."

∝

Jason's first thought was that the newsletters were a hoax. Fred Cronin could have come up with the story only yesterday, spun it whole cloth after Blue and Elisa's disappearance. But no. The crumbling circulars emblazoned with the *Starling Cove Believer* nameplate were authentic, dashed off years ago on a dinosaur of a printing press. Twenty-five years come and gone since a boy named Michael Whitley vanished, in this very stretch of woods. The first time.

They pored over the documents, pages and pages of reflections on various supernatural occurrences in and around the cove, including the disappearance of "The Starling Cove Hansel and Gretel," as Cronin had dubbed them. In October 1981, two young children, Blue and a girl named Gavina Beaton, went missing one afternoon without a trace. Cronin included references, quotes, and reproductions of articles from legitimate press like the *Cape Breton Post*. Though there was a local panic involving vague accounts of a drifter seen camping in the vicinity, the authorities seemed to have had few leads. Eerily, the search was hampered by forest fires, then as now.

Two weeks after the disappearance, Blue and the Beaton girl wandered out of the woods. They behaved as if nothing had happened; both claimed to have no recollection of their time away, in the woods or otherwise. According to Cronin's account, however, there was far more to the story than the police, the media, or the children's families would let on. His papers didn't claim to have any firm answers, though they contained a great deal of loony speculation about who might have wanted the children and why.

The newsletters were peppered with references to local media coverage, ink-smudged phrases with erratic capitalization: "WHAT The CAPE Breton POSt does NOT want you to KNOW is that tho there was no SIGN of abuse the children were found NAKED. This indicates a possible GENETIC and/OR personality RECONFIGURATION such as is found consistently in abduction LITERATURE across the GLOBE." As the story developed, Cronin's dispatches became increasingly bizarre, insisting that despite all appearances, the children who returned from the woods were not the same as the ones who had gone missing. "THEYre rePLACEments. THEYre reCONSTRUCTEd BEings, disGUISEd and possibly malEVOLent. Why do THEY NEED us?!"

"Sure, he's a bit of an oddball," Detective Jessed said over the phone as nightfall settled across the cove. "But Fred's harmless. Trust me on that."

"I wasn't saying he might be involved," Jason said, though his implication in calling the police had been exactly that. "I just thought it was interesting that he was the only one who put together the fact that as of thirteen days ago, Michael Whitley has gone missing in these parts not once but twice now. Don't you find that unusual?"

The detective breathed into the receiver; it might have been a sigh of exasperation. "We're aware of Mr. Whitley's history in our community."

"*What?* Since when?"

"It's nothing to be concerned with at this time. We've asked the press not to report on certain details of the case—extraneous or otherwise—that might jeopardize the investigation. Of course, that never stopped Fred much. Excuse me one second." Jessed sounded as if he was thumbing through papers. "In any case, you should rest assured that the department has been exploring every angle. We want you to know that we won't stop until we've found the both of them. But as you know, we have our hands full with the fires on the mountain."

"The fires. Right. Tell me, how often do these forest fires happen?"

A long silence. "I understand why you would want us to pursue this angle, Mr. Howard. But let's focus on facts, and not go chasing after the Devil."

"All I want—" Jason's voice caught. "All I want is for you to find them."

"Of course. Of course. And we will make every effort."

After he hung up the phone, Jason brooded over their past conversations, searching for a clue as to what the police believed had actually happened. Did they really think that Elisa and Blue had skipped town? He suspected from the start of the whole ordeal that they would be stonewalled, seen as outsiders by the authorities. But now that he grew to understand the cove and the dynamics of its population—mystics and philosophers and draft dodgers, sweat lodgers and marijuana growers and meth cookers—the entire community's reticence made more sense. How do you go missing from a place people go specifically to get lost?

"That didn't sound good." Gabe fed the woodstove before returning to the cracked leather club chair in front of the fire.

In his lap were the faded copies of *The Starling Cove Believer*, which he read and reread with the focus of a code breaker attempting to crack an encrypted cable.

"They already knew about Blue disappearing as a child," Jason said. "Makes you wonder what else they're keeping from us."

Or who else. It was bad enough trying to get in touch with Elisa's mother, but he had even less success reaching Blue's. The woman didn't pick up her phone. The only time Jason had managed to speak with her was the day after the disappearance. Jason was well aware of her deteriorated physical state and tried his best not to alarm her, but she despaired at the news nevertheless, and in spectacular fashion. "I told him!" she cried in a mournful wail that fast dissolved into a tubercular cough. "I told him. I told him . . ."

"I wouldn't worry just yet," Jason had said by way of reassurance. "I only thought you might have some idea where they might have headed. They probably, you know, went on an adventure," he added, parroting the line the police had used on him.

"Not the first time," she muttered, and not much else.

Not the first time. Now Jason knew what she had meant.

He picked up the phone again and called the *Cape Breton Post* reporter who had interviewed him in the days following the disappearance. The woman essentially confirmed Detective Jessed's account, saying she had been asked not to report on the prior vanishing. When Jason asked her what she thought might have happened, the reporter pleaded ignorance and suggested he take it up with the police. This fresh angle, like all the others, was going nowhere.

He tried to clear his mind by returning calls to his clients, the ones he hadn't already referred to a colleague with whom he shared offices. *At this rate*, he thought, *I might not have a practice to go back to.* "We can pick up right where we left off," he promised Walt Kerner, a sixty-something phobic with a debilitating case of OCD who refused to be treated by anyone else; it was enough work getting him to his scheduled appointments. "One more week and I'll be back."

Jason cursed himself for lying. How could he ever go back to New York, when Elisa was still out there somewhere? But he felt a queasy thrill at the thought that he could hit the road and put the Cape Breton Highlands in the rearview, disappear himself and let someone else clean up the mess for once. Gabe, for example, who would probably stay forever, in his own rudderless way. How terribly unexpected it would be for Jason to up and leave! How very out of character!

Which was why he knew he could never do it. Jason was far too adept at his role, the One Who Makes Everything Better. Even if that phone call from the doctor's office had meant what he feared (and he was intermittently able to convince himself that in fact it did not), he could never leave. Not unless he was forced.

It was well past dark when Jason finally ended his last phone session. Gabe sat before the woodstove, scribbling furiously as usual in his sketch pad amid an increasing array of reference materials: Fred Cronin's newsletters, maps and local histories, apocryphal lore culled from the local library and the shelves of the MacLeod House, a growing collection of scrawled-upon pages scattered all around. Jason studied him. They'd gotten along quite well these past few days, the shared activity of the canvass having brought them closer. Though the twenty-year-old was technically a man, Jason couldn't help but see Gabe as a child, one mixed up in something he had neither the depth for, nor the constitution. Jason had lost his wife, but at times it was Gabe who was distraught to the point of seeming widowed, when he had only lost, what, his boss? A friend? Or more?

In truth, Jason actually didn't know Gabe terribly well; the boy seemed to have no friends or family to speak of, as if he'd sprung fully formed out of the ether, having just kind of shown up in their lives one day. The day, Jason supposed, that Blue had decided he needed someone else besides Elisa.

It was a subject of gossip—unclear, even to Elisa—if the connection between Blue and Gabe was romantic or not. Blue had drawn more than his fair share of admirers, but their relationship appeared rooted in something greater than base attraction, at least on Gabe's end. It was obvious the kid adored him, the same way Elisa had. Now here Jason was, stuck in this deceptively bucolic purgatory with no one to lean on but a virtual—and exceedingly young—stranger.

"What?" Gabe caught him staring, and snapped his sketch pad shut. *Is he drawing me?* Jason wondered. "What is it?"

"Just thinking." Jason shook his head. "You hungry?"

"Nope." Gabe raised his beer bottle. "Thanks, though."

Jason reheated some grilled chicken from the previous evening, food he had set aside for Gabe. Gabe, who never so much as considered eating it, who didn't seem to eat much of anything anymore, save a handful of sugar cubes or a candy bar here and there. Jason microwaved the plastic-wrapped plate and sat down to eat at the dining room table, mere feet from Gabe and the woodstove. He took his time tasting each bite, allowing the food and a freshly opened bottle of Pinot Noir to rouse him from thoughts of bad endings.

People, after all, had a tendency to vanish on him. His fa-

ther had cut out on his mom soon after she'd given birth to
Jason, having simultaneously knocked up another woman. Even
years later, Jason's mother would drive up to Harlem to deposit
him and his older sister, Deirdre, on the doorstep of their father's apartment as a kind of passive-aggressive reminder of his
former family. One night, their mother brought a rusty-handled
revolver as well, and blasted a hole in the door, nearly killing
their father in the process. Seven-year-old Jason could hear the
neighbors laughing at his mother—"Check out this crazy little
Oriental bitch!"—as his father's second wife cursed them down
the hall and into the elevator.

They returned the very next day. Their mother waited for
a neighbor to exit the building before she slipped inside and
marched them upstairs to their father's hastily repaired door.
She stood them behind her and banged on the dinted metal
until her knuckles welted red. "What in goddamn hell do you
want from me?" their father shouted, yanking the door open.
His expression shifted from anger to fear when she pulled the
revolver from her handbag, then shifted again to shock as she
raised the gun and put the barrel to her temple. "I told you!" she
shouted. "You did this! You did this!"

Jason went for the gun, but it was too late. In an explosion
of sound and dust, his mother's brains were spattered across the
sickly green walls, along his outstretched arm, his face, bits of
meat in his sister's hair and against the wall, everywhere. Their
father dropped to his knees over her body, pant legs soaking up
the blood that pooled on the dirty-white linoleum. Though it
was their mother who had died, they never saw or spoke to their
father again.

They moved in with their mother's mother in Bay Ridge,
where they lived with her for the next fifteen years. It wasn't

long after their grandmother passed away that Jason's sister—never the most reality-based soul—finally lost it altogether. Deirdre was diagnosed with paranoid schizophrenia and admitted to Clearside Hospital in Queens, less than six miles from their mother's gravesite in Flushing Cemetery. Jason had faithfully made his weekly pilgrimage to his sister's ward for two decades now, another responsibility he'd shirked in the past three weeks. Did Deirdre, in her Trifluoperazine-induced haze, even grasp that he had failed to show, had in fact failed *her*, as he was now failing to find his wife?

The closest he ever came to seeing their father one last time was in high school, when he was on the Brooklyn Tech track team and had a meet with Thurgood Marshall High in Harlem. "Hey, Howard," his teammate Brian had said while scanning the draw on the coach's clipboard, "I think you're supposed to race yourself." At first he thought the duplicate name was an error, but sure enough, there was a boy on the Thurgood Marshall team named Jason Howard.

He scoped out the competition, and there was no mistaking him; it was like looking into some kind of distorted mirror. The moment he laid eyes on the sixteen-year-old—his same height and build with his father's same eyes, an all-black version of himself, as if the Korean half had been bled out of him—he knew what had happened, and who the kid was. His father's other son, the very same age and also named Jason, after his father's father.

Jason had begun to shake. He eavesdropped on the boy and his teammates, on this other imposter Jason who could talk cool; not like Jason, who prided himself on his locution. It was easy for him to brush off the ribbing he got from some of his reverse 'round-the-way friends for sounding white, since he knew he was going places, but seeing this other Jason rattled him to the core, made him feel he was lesser, half a man. This other Jason, he was what their father had always wanted; he was the son good enough to keep. And then the thought hit him like a punch to the stomach: *What if my dad is actually here?*

His heart racing, Jason turned toward the stands. He scanned the half dozen rows of bleachers, his watering eyes straining as he searched for angry or bewildered stares, the only expressions he could remember ever seeing on his father's face. But everyone looked so pleased. A wall of beaming parents, cheering students, younger siblings jockeying for a better view of the field. All so happy and proud.

And then he found him. Second row from the top and grinning like a big old fool in a Thurgood Marshall baseball cap: *Dad!* Jason was about to call out when he saw the man seated beside his father had the exact same features: the square jaw, the pronounced, leonine cheekbones, his big brown eyes. Not only him, but the woman right below them, and also the toddler she had balanced on her knee. They were all him now, every single person in the stands was him, each wearing the same shit-eating grin. *Dad and Dad and Dad and Dad.* A sea of his father's faces, and now they were all laughing as well. And just like that, the bright sky above went midnight dark and Jason swooned, taking a knee as he dry heaved beside the dusty green track.

"Howard?" Brian appeared beside him and placed a hand on Jason's back. "You okay?"

"I'm fine," he said, and shrugged him off. But as he tried to get up he listed, then keeled over and passed out. When he awoke he was being loaded into an ambulance behind the sports facility, an EMT adjusting an oxygen mask upon his face and exhorting him to breathe, just breathe.

Even then Jason craned his neck out the back of the ambulance, a vain attempt to try to catch a glimpse of his father, who probably wasn't there in the first place.

He never ran track again.

"Jason?"

He looked up from the table to find Gabe watching him. "You okay?"

"What's that?"

"You're trembling."

Jason raised his hand. Sure enough, his fingers were shaking, a hummingbird blur of motion.

"Are you cold?" Gabe asked. "Do you want to sit by the fire?" He started to get up, but Jason gestured for him to sit.

"I'm fine," Jason said, and clamped his hand to his knee. "I feel hot, actually." He wiped a glaze of sweat from his brow. "Wow. This is . . . unexpected."

"You want to get some fresh air?"

Jason lowered himself onto the porch swing. Gabe was in silhouette against the railing, the nearly full moon bright in a cloudless sky. They sat in silence, listened to the sounds of birds and insects flitting about the cove, the low breeze in the grass, the trees. The wine warmed Jason's skin, and he settled a bit; he'd had a few panic attacks before, and knew the symptoms both personally and professionally. *That's what you get for dwelling on the past.* No wonder he preferred peering inside other people's heads instead.

Gabe stared off into the woods beyond the house, and soon Jason found himself following suit, accompanied by a nagging sensation that something was staring back. This place was getting to him.

"Feeling any better?" Gabe said after a while.

"Yes, actually. Thank you. I'm just tense."

"I know what you mean." Gabe sipped from his beer, then spat over the railing. "Ever since Blue—ever since they both went missing—I've felt . . . different. Emptier. Like a part of me is missing too."

Jason tried not to look at the trees.

"So what next?" Gabe said. "More canvassing?"

"Couldn't hurt. I also want to find out more about Blue's grandmother, and what happened when he went missing. The first time."

"Shouldn't we ask Maureen and Donald about it?"

"Absolutely. It would be nice to have some light shed on all this. We should also track down the one who went missing along with Blue, the little girl."

"That's going to be tough, unless you've got a Ouija board. According to the newsletters, she drowned a few months after they walked out of the woods."

"Jesus. Her poor family . . . Can you imagine, after going through all that? Well, maybe her folks are still around. I'll ask Maureen when they come back from Halifax."

"What about Fred Cronin?" Gabe said. "I'm sure he has plenty left to tell us."

"No doubt. But that's not the kind of path I want to travel down."

"Why not? I know he sounds kind of crazy, but still. If we want the police to pursue all leads, shouldn't we be doing the same?"

"That guy is clearly delusional. Not to mention a serious alcoholic, from the looks of it. And on top of that, he's probably messed up from drugs as well. For all we know, he's another one of those crankheads."

"That doesn't mean he's wrong."

Jason couldn't keep from raising an eyebrow. All this nonsense reminded him of what it was like trying to reason with his sister, in the months leading up to her institutionalization.

"I'm just saying," Gabe went on undaunted, "Fred's the only one who seems to have some idea—any idea—of what might have really happened. So I wouldn't, you know, discount everything he says just because it doesn't fit into your worldview or whatever."

"I'm sorry, but it's not in my job description to indulge people's fantasies. Quite the opposite, in fact. Especially when said fantasies involve my missing wife and, *you know*, mythological creatures."

"Well, maybe there's something to it. Have you heard of the Green Children of Woolpit? A boy and girl in England—no one knew them—they just walked right out of the woods. A total mystery. That was a thousand years ago, but it's the same kind of Hansel and Gretel story, only in reverse. Apparently they were both green-skinned and spoke in their own weird language. The boy died, but the girl integrated into society."

"So were they aliens, or fairies, or what?"

"Exactly," Gabe said and nodded, in a strange little imitation of Fred Cronin. "I've been reading up on different kinds of unexplainable disappearances, centuries' worth. It seems the two most common types of abductees are young children and pregnant women."

"Well, nothing to worry about there," Jason said, a little too quickly.

Gabe lowered his eyes, then raised them to the woods. He opened his mouth but failed to speak.

"What?" A shuddery image of Blue and Elisa flared behind Jason's eyes before fading. He blinked, hard.

"Nothing," Gabe said, and shook his head. Jason just stared at him. "It's just—I don't think we should be so dismissive of Fred's theories."

"You know what? It's getting late." Jason stretched his hands over his head. "I should catch some sleep. See you in the morning?"

"Sure." But Gabe didn't look at him. He only stared off the porch at the trees, until Jason eventually stood and went back inside the house.

❧

Darkness.

On the lawn in front of the MacLeod House, a spiteful wind blows across the moonlit cove. Jason feels eyes upon him: there's something out there, watching from the woods. A magnetic pull draws him closer to the trees, his feet on the tips of their toes and stuttering forward against his volition. The pines sway, dull gray bristles swept beneath the starry cupola of nighttime sky, the stench of smoke heavy in the air. How could this be a dream, when he can smell the forest fires from the mountain, when his senses are so alive and everything is so very real?

The curtain of branches draws back, and Blue steps naked from the woods. Body youthfully slim and taut, cock flaccid yet impressively sized, his musculature accentuated by an irradiated cobalt glow. He is lit from within.

"You're letting yourself go," Blue says. His mournful gaze travels Jason's body, and now Jason sees that he is naked himself, suddenly so cold in the crisp Maritimes night. He looks upon his own sagging and distended skin through the younger man's eyes and is ashamed. "You've stopped walking the old paths," Blue says, "stopped searching the hidden places. You've given up . . ."

"No," Jason says, the frigid air burning his lungs. "Not at all. We've been pursuing every avenue. But all we've found are fairy tales."

"Some fairy tales are true." Blue circles him in a close ring. "Doesn't seem quite right, how we disappeared, does it? Sorry for cutting out on you like that." His voice drops to a halting whisper. "But once I opened our eyes and saw, really saw . . ."

"Where are you? Where's Elisa?"

Blue stops in front of him. "We're fine. For now. As long as we can hold back the flames. Harder this time, since they made it all the way down to the locus of the hive. As above, so below. And so it goes."

"I didn't ask how you are, I asked *where* you are."

"That's really the same thing, though, isn't it." A halfhearted smile, and Blue commences his circling.

"Don't get philosophical," Jason says. "I asked you a simple question."

"A simple question," Blue echoes, his voice so doleful and tremulous that it causes Jason to quiver. "We're in Tír na nÓg. In Elphame. Beneath the Great Mound, under the roots of the ocean. But we are not of the Mound. We are of the Hive Queen. And we are birthing anew. Does that sound simple to you?"

Jason tries to laugh but his chest is too heavy, too packed with ice. "So you're in Fairyland, huh? How do we get there? Second star to the right and straight on till morning? No, wait, of course . . . I'll never be invited because I don't believe."

"That's sarcasm."

"Yes. That's sarcasm."

"I remember what that is." Blue grins. "Wouldn't you say it's something of a defense mechanism?"

"That should be my line."

"You can let down your guard with me. We're safe here. For now." Blue cuts the air with his finger, makes a sound or maybe it's a word, an utterance in a guttural, incomprehensible language before he speaks again. "You should be honest. Tell me that you only want Elisa back, that you want me to stay gone. Go on. It won't hurt my feelings."

"That's not true." The air grows colder still, and Jason holds himself, assurance of his essential corporeality. "I would kill to get you back. Both of you. Even after what you did." *Why am I trying to reason with him?* Jason thinks. *It doesn't matter what he says, what I say. This is just a dream.*

"There's no such thing as *just* a dream," Blue says. "Only nothingness. And surrender. And communion." He stops once more. "And reproduction."

The sound of water running. Elisa's cellphone ringing. The receptionist's voice. *Will you be coming too? Just make sure Mrs. Howard gets back to us.*

Jason winces. "You ruined my life," he says, and how good it feels to finally say it out loud. "Do you know that? She's *my* wife, you little shit. And you fucked her. You, what, impregnated her? And then you took her away from me. Why?"

"I couldn't help it." Blue lowers his head. "It's what I was made for."

"To breed," Jason says, using Fred Cronin's word.

"Yes. To breed."

Elisa and Blue, running off to have a baby together; it's as close to his worst nightmare as Jason is willing to go. That vivid imagined film flares before his eyes, the scratchy conjured images of the two of them in bed, limbs tangled in a mad dance of lust. Between them a spark of life begins to pulsate, a light so small, but one that nevertheless manages to brighten like a steadily fanned flame . . . All because Jason wasn't man enough to keep her.

"It's not your fault," Blue says, each word an aching thrust. "She was compelled."

"I didn't say it was my fault." But of course he'd thought it, hadn't he?

Blue steps closer, inches away. "It didn't happen the way you think it did, for what it's worth. But now that I've returned to the hive, there's no going back."

Roaches check in, but they don't check out, Jason thinks, and this makes Blue laugh. Jason tries to laugh too, to ignore the creeping tendrils of dread and frost that make his teeth chatter, even as his lips stick together.

"It's okay to hate me," Blue says, inside Jason's head now, his icy blue lips no longer bothering to move. "For my betrayal. But don't hate Elisa. It's not her fault, any of this. She's going to need time to adjust. You too. Everything's different now. So be kind to yourself. For once in your life."

How does he know me? My hidden self? Jason curses his unconscious. The dream is deteriorating into the worst therapy session of all time.

"I don't think you should still be here," Blue says then, shaking his head. "Maybe it's for the best that you move on, get gone. Move on," and the words echo in Jason's head. *Move on, move on, move on.*

"Please," Jason says. "Please get out of my head."

"But that's the hive mind. We're all inside of one another, and we dig deep. Besides, that's what you're good at, aren't you?

Getting inside people's heads. So go on, then. Dig deep, get inside a few heads. If you're ready to hear the truth, that is." He places a blue palm on his flat blue stomach and grins. "I have to say, there are things you don't seem ready to hear."

"I asked you a question before," Jason says. "There are things you don't seem ready to answer."

"Okay, then. You want to know where we are?" He shrugs, sadness in eyes. "That's easy. We're under the ground."

"Under the ground?"

Jason pictures a grave. His mother's body in the earth of Flushing Cemetery in Queens, her bleach-white skull and bones inside her pine coffin. "My mother. She's dead," Jason says dully, and shivers. Ghostly vapor issues from his lips, as if he's releasing his own spirit into the air.

"If she was really dead to you," Blue says, "you wouldn't still be searching for answers. But I can tell you what you want to know. I can do that for you now. Get you inside her head."

Blue's glowing expression is drowned in grief as he moves his hand from his stomach to the side of his face. Jason knows what he's about to do, but he can't manage to look away. Not even as Blue digs a long and sharpened finger against his very own head and burrows a bullet-sized hole inside his skull, a round and winking and bloodless tunnel to an unknown world.

"She's sorry for leaving you and your sister," Blue says. "She doesn't want you to worry, not anymore. She's in a far different place now. Can you see that, the way we can see?"

"Where is Elisa?" He grabs Blue's arm and yanks it out of his head; it's like plunging his hand into ice water, impossibly cold. Jason's teeth crack, he shakes. "Where is my wife?"

"I told you. She's down in the ground." Blue smiles, his

toothless mouth its own gaping rift, though his eyes remain
haunted and fearful. "Just like the rest of us."

∞

Jason stirred, his sleep disturbed by a great clatter downstairs.
The sound of the refrigerator door slamming and empty bottles rattling atop it, followed by the tinny buzz of music from
the kitchen radio. Dream residue floated inside his head, and
he tried to dislodge it, all that his self-sabotaging mind had
conjured. He rolled over and folded the pillow in a crescent to
cover his ears, but he was already wide awake.

He shoved the dream back down as best he could. Forgetting
was an act of divine mercy. Sometimes it felt like all he had left.

He pulled on a sweatshirt and pajama bottoms and went
to the top of the steps. An old country song was playing on
the radio downstairs, a woman singing something about hurtin'
words, and above it he could hear the faint susurrus of whispers.
He peered over the railing. Gabe was stretched out on the floor
in front of the fire in the woodstove, a beer beside him and the
cordless telephone cradled on his shoulder. As usual, the boy
was drawing in his sketch pad as he quietly spoke.

"It's getting cooler, though," Gabe said, oblivious to Jason
crouching on the stairs. "It's almost September." A tapering spiral was forming beneath the tip of Gabe's pen, the page darkened by a churning storm of feverish scrawling, a swirling black
hole of images and words. Jason thought of Dream Blue, how
the naked man had encircled him like a tightening rope or a
coiling snake, and the passageway carved inside his skull.

"I've seen a few signs, yeah," Gabe said into the phone.
"Well, more than a few. No. Not during the day. At night, when

I'm alone. Traces. Tracks, maybe. Out in the woods." He took a swig of his beer. "I feel them out there, you know? It's so strong here. It really is." A long silence. "Right. Right. Well, yeah, I tried talking to him about it, but he wouldn't listen. Right. I will. I'll be there. Please, just wait for me, okay?"

Jason crept from the stairs and back across the landing to the front bedroom, where the other landline sat on the windowsill. He brought the receiver to his ear and waited for Gabe to continue his conversation. Instead, he heard the screen door slam downstairs, followed by the sound of footsteps across the porch and down into the dark pool of night.

"Hello?" Jason whispered into the receiver. "Is anyone there?"

For a moment he thought he could make out the sound of someone breathing. After a long minute in which he heard nothing else, however—only a hollow vacuum of noise, devoid of texture and tone—he decided the line was dead.

Chapter Six

When Gabe finally awoke the next day and came downstairs around noon, Jason asked when he'd be ready to leave for their daily canvass. Gabe begged off, saying he was going to hang around the house, as he wasn't feeling very well: something he'd eaten the previous night that hadn't sat right with him.

"I can handle it," Jason said. "Rest up, okay? We need you at full strength." He said good-bye, headed out to the car, and started down the drive. Maureen's red Toyota was parked across the lawn in front of her studio; she and Donald must have returned from Halifax sometime in the night.

When Jason reached the bottom of the hill, instead of pulling onto the main artery he took the small dirt road that led into the woods. He parked a hundred yards in—past a meandering bend that rendered the car undetectable from the property—and walked back on foot, sticking to the trees so he couldn't be seen from the house.

He waited. Gabe appeared twenty minutes later via the rear deck, a six-pack of beer cradled like a baby in his arms. The boy walked toward the rear of the MacLeod House and through the tall grass, where he disappeared into the stand of firs skirting the lawn. Jason let another minute pass before following, and trailed after Gabe through the brush.

After some time Jason heard the sound of voices and slowed,

crouching to peer through the foliage. He spotted Gabe sitting cross-legged on a patch of packed grass beside the creek; it was where they had come across Donald their second day in the cove, directly behind the burned-out remains of the Colony. This time instead of Donald it was Fred Cronin in his place, the little man perched upon a rock with a walking stick thrust into the ground beside him like the stylus of a sundial.

Through the tangled briar, Jason made out a small arrangement in the center of a circle of stones: an apple, a loaf of barmbrack, a black-and-white bandanna tied in a knot, as well as a plate of half-devoured meat, bones jutting from decomposing flesh. It had the appearance of an abandoned picnic, or some kind of offering. A lure, perhaps, for an animal. The circle was laid out close to where the pair sat, though its placement gave the distinct impression of separation. Jason couldn't hear what they were saying, only an occasional word as it floated on the wind like a dandelion seed. *Daylight. Indigenous. Essence.*

As he leaned in for a closer listen, a dog began barking from the opposite bank of the creek. Jason stumbled back, broke into a trot as he moved quickly through the bracken, and kept running after he hit the path. He jogged for a mile or more, brooding over Fred Cronin and Gabe's secretive meeting. It had probably been Cronin on the phone last night with Gabe, filling the boy's head with more talk of the Other Kind. Grimm tales of swapped children and glowing lights, all the legends that only a fellow local could either corroborate or contradict.

Jason emerged from the woods between Maureen's house and her studio. And there she was, hanging laundry on the clothesline, linen tablecloths and wrinkled old napkins trembling on the line like stripped bark. He thought of the desiccated meat inside the circle of stones.

"Out for a run?" Maureen said as he approached.

"Yes. Well, an impromptu one." He gestured to his khakis, sweated through at the knees. "I didn't think to pack workout clothes."

"I'm sure we can manage to rustle up whatever you need. Free of charge."

"Thanks. Hey, I didn't know you were back from Halifax."

"We're only here for a brief stay, unfortunately. I would have come found you but things have been so hectic. Donald hasn't been doing so well lately. He hasn't been the same since—well, since that night."

"I'm sorry to hear that." Jason had figured as much, what with all the appointments. "Is there anything I can do?"

"I think I should be asking you that instead, no?"

"We'll call it a draw." He looked over his shoulder and back at the trees, and felt that familiar and uneasy sensation of being watched from the woods. The sound of skittering through dry leaves, of pencil on paper.

Maureen placed down the plastic laundry basket and wiped her forehead. "Tell me, how is your canvass going? Find out anything?"

"Heard a few things. Some of them pretty strange, actually. As in, Body Snatchers strange."

"You didn't happen to speak to Fred Cronin, did you?"

"Indeed. He told us something about people living under the ground. Ultraterrestrials?"

She laughed. "Is that what he's calling them this week?"

"What's his story, anyway?"

"Oh, Fred's always been something of a character. Even as a young man, he had that lone gunman bit down to an art form. But he really does believe in all that stuff."

"I can tell."

"It's of a certain time, I suppose. He's full of it, like a lot of the folks that have moved here over the years. Free thinkers that sometimes think *too* freely. It's all devils and fairies to that lot."

"Fairies . . . I've been hearing that word a lot lately."

"There's a ton of fairy talk around here. Done in private, mostly. Honestly, I never would've thought in a million years Donald would be a believer, but even he is. Surprising, for a scientist. But it was passed down to him in early childhood."

"So he's basically in Fred's camp, then."

"Well, funnily enough, Donald first came up here to debunk some of the more bizarre theories about the cove. That it held special power, contained a vortex of spiritual energy, like Stonehenge or down in Sedona, ley lines or what have you. We do have a great vibe going, I can tell you that—this is the only place I truly feel creative, for one thing. Is Starling Cove a magical place? I suppose. But who can say for certain?"

"So you don't think there are otherworldly creatures inhabiting these woods."

"If I did, I wouldn't go around talking about it. That's how you land up in the funny farm. Others, of course, have no such concerns." Her face was still, tightening for a moment before her expression slackened and she smiled. "Start asking enough people in these parts what they really think and you'll be waist-deep in baloney by dinnertime. There are some folks in the Highlands who think the CIA has a secret underground station out here. No kidding. They would blame a seasonal flu on the U.S. government if they could get away with it. This lady who sells native jewelry, down at the docks in Ingonish? She goes around telling anyone that'll listen that the mussel factory in

St. Ann's Harbour is a front for a military experiment in psycho-tropics. She's not alone in that one either."

Jason had forgotten how reassuring it was speaking with someone who shared his skepticism. "I try to be a patient lis-tener," he said. "It is my profession, after all. But sometimes it does become difficult."

"I hear you. Donald's always liked to talk nonsense about the cove. Mostly that's how he passes the day, though not so much as of late. He may not be from these parts, but he once knew as much about the Highlands as any local historian. There was a time when the mere mention of the name William MacLeod was enough for him to chew your ear off."

"William MacLeod? You mean the man who built the house we're staying in?"

She nodded. "Donald used to collect all these wonderful old MacLeod artifacts. Maps, legends, you name it. I cleared out the attic last year and donated it all to the Gaelic College. Tech-nically the MacLeod House is our guest house, but it's far older than ours, at least the back half. The night MacLeod finished building it for his daughter and her family, or so the story goes, he banged his last nail into the wall, put his hammer down, and set fire to the place. Then he walked out into the woods, never to be seen again."

"That seems to happen quite a lot around here."

"Don't people ever go missing in New York?" She sounded perplexed, and maybe a little offended. "Anyway, that was al-most two hundred years ago. It's a legend, which is pretty much code for claptrap. But hey, who knows? Maybe it is true." Mau-reen stared across the lawn at the trees. "Like I told you a couple of weeks ago, these are some strange woods."

"Did you?" Jason thought for a moment, listening to the

wind in the leaves, the snap of a pair of faded brown corduroys on the clothesline.

She looked down at the ground, the laundry basket. "Oh. No. I suppose not. I mean, I did say that, only not to you. I must have said that to someone else. Some time before . . ." She shook her head. "Anyway, I would hardly think to mention it. Not to put too fine a point on it, but what do you think people do up here all winter? They drink, my dear. Been doing it since the Scottish landed, and long before that, I'd wager. And what most of them do in the winter, half do in the summertime as well. So if what they say about MacLeod going off into the woods is true, believe me, he had a bottle in his hand as he went."

She stared past him, over his shoulder; it was a gesture of pure obfuscation. *Dig deep, get inside a few heads*, he heard Dream Blue say. *If you're ready to hear the truth.*

"Blue was born here," he said. "Did you know that?"

"He was?" She said it somewhere between a question and statement, and began fussing with the laundry basket, her fingernails, anything to avoid Jason's eyes.

"Yes. His real name is Michael. Michael Whitley."

"I—I knew that . . . He booked the house under that name. It's been in the papers as well."

"But that's not the only reason you know it."

She froze. Jason put a gentle hand on her arm; outside the confines of his practice, he was free to make physical contact to facilitate intimacy. There were no firm rules of ethics here, professional or otherwise.

"Maureen," he said, and all of a sudden he understood. "You knew, didn't you? You knew he was one of the children who'd gone missing in the cove."

"Yes." Her head wobbled, and steadily gyroscoped into a sort of nod. "Oh yes."

"Why didn't you tell us that? Why didn't you tell me?"

"I suppose I didn't want it to actually *be* him, back after all that time. I thought he'd gotten away."

"Away from what?"

She allowed herself a faint smile. "Come inside the house. I'll make us some coffee. Or something stronger if you're interested."

They went in through the back. Halfway down the hall abutting the living room, she stopped to peer inside an open bedroom door. Donald was seated on the edge of the bed in only a pair of white briefs, his aged skin spotted and wrinkled; he was hunched over a book, its purple cover cracked along the spine.

"The first volume, gone," Donald muttered into the pages. "It's gone."

"We'll find it, darling," Maureen said wearily, pulling the door halfway closed.

Jason averted his eyes and followed her into the kitchen. They sat at a small table, its surface bare but for a green ceramic napkin holder and matching salt and pepper shakers, the table's yellow leaves folded down like a wilted tulip. She poured them two mugs of coffee, and spiked hers with whisky; she tilted the bottle in his direction but he declined.

"I should have said something," Maureen said after a while. She scrutinized the inside of her mug, a tea leaf reader searching for a sign. "To Michael, most of all. But I couldn't. I just couldn't. I could tell he didn't know anything about what had happened to him, and the thought that he was going to start digging around and unearth what's best left buried . . . I couldn't stand it. Especially since I was close with his mother, back in the day."

"Yvonne," he said.

"Yes. How is she holding up?"

"Not well."

"I'd imagine not." A bird cawed stridently from behind the house; the cry of a hawk, maybe, as it circumnavigated the cove. Maureen sipped from her mug, and it was a long time before she spoke again. Which was fine; Jason knew well the distilling power of silence. If need be, he could wait all day.

"So, yes," she eventually said, as if she'd caught her breath, though her voice had a fresh undercurrent of defensiveness. "I pretended that he was just another tourist on a summer get-away. He didn't exactly volunteer what you all were doing up here, that he'd come to sell his grandma's house. But I knew. I figured the second I got the inquiry about the rental that he must be coming to settle some business of Flora's. So I didn't say anything."

"You didn't want to stir up what had happened to him as a boy in the woods."

She looked at him funny. "The woods?"

"What happened when he went missing."

"Well, sure. But really because of what happened after that."

Jason shifted in his chair, puzzled. Maureen sighed and rested her hands on the scratched wood of the tabletop. "I wanted to protect him from Flora."

"From his grandmother? But why?"

"She was a troubled woman. Very troubled. Even before the kids went missing. She could never get a handle on her daughter, who was truly wild before she had Michael, just wild. Yvonne and Flora weren't on speaking terms, what with Flora being very old-time religious and Yvonne being your average hippie girl. But then she got knocked up, and they softened to each other. When Yvonne would go on one of her magic mush-room trips—quite frequently, I might add—she made sure to drop the baby off with Flora for the night. Sometimes for up to a week, or more. I'd say Michael lived at Flora's place as much as at the Colony."

"So you *knew* Blue, before. Back when he was Michael."

"He was a lovely little boy," she said quietly. "We were crushed when he went missing. It was like someone had cut a knife right through the heart of the cove. It was probably the first and last time the Colony felt any kind of real love from the surrounding community. But then the kids came back, thank God. To be honest, most people didn't look too closely at what had happened, me included. We were just happy they were safe and sound."

The enduring trauma was plain in Maureen's expression, her gray eyes so clouded that Jason reflexively glanced out the window at the fog milking over the cove. "Did the children say what had happened, where they'd been?" He asked the question in a near whisper, and she leaned in closer to hear.

"All they said was that they got lost. Didn't say if anyone took them, or what they'd been eating for two weeks, nothing."

"Was it true they came back naked?"

"There were rumors. No one really knew for sure, except Flora."

"Why her?"

"She was the one who found them. Flora was baby-sitting for Michael and the girl, Gavina, who was the daughter of another Colony girl. The kids disappeared off Flora's property, and came back to the exact same spot where she last saw them, like hom-ing pigeons. Or so she said."

"You didn't believe her."

"I did at the time. But then she and Yvonne started fighting over Michael. One time not too long after the kids came back, Flora had him over at her place for a visit but wouldn't let Yvonne back inside to get him. His mama had a couple of the Colony boys kick Flora's door in. When they broke into her basement, they found him locked inside a cage hanging from the ceiling."

"Jesus." Had Blue's visit to the house that day set him off? So much so that he hit the road to parts unknown? And he convinced Elisa to go along for the ride . . . It did fit the police's scenario, as well as the property agent's account. "And that's when Yvonne took off with Blue?"

"No. That's when the custody battle started. On one side was Flora MacKenzie, an upstanding member of the community, and on the other her drugged-out, good-for-nothing daughter. That was the narrative, at least. Who would entertain the thought that this woman kept her grandson locked in a cage? It sounded preposterous! So at this point, the legal fight between Flora and Yvonne became a battle between the community and the Colony. In-fighting started dividing us. And then in the middle of all that tension, the Colony went up in smoke. Literally."

"Sounds like it might have been arson."

She peered in the direction of the darkened hallway. "No one knows exactly what went down. Lord knows there was enough conjecture. What else is new, right? The fact is it happened in the middle of the night, and no one saw anything. Fortunately we all got out, but with not much more than the shirts on our backs. We camped for a while, but as it got colder people started looking for real shelter, and real work. So began the Colony's diaspora days. Eventually we got absorbed into the greater population. We're all really lost souls at heart, and a lot of us just kind of stuck around, trying to feel the old magic again. Since the fire, none of us have really been connected in the same way."

Maureen waved her hand as if shooing an invisible fly. "But that's all ancient history. Look at me, chewing your ear off! I must sound like my husband." She dropped the last word to a whisper.

"I love listening to you talk," Jason said. It came out sounding more flirtatious than he intended. "Like I said, this is what I do for a living."

Her loneliness was written across her face. "What was I . . ."

"You were telling me about the Colony. We were up there our first week, actually. We ran into Donald out back."

"He spends a lot of time there." She spiked her coffee once more and took a quick slug. "Lots of memories. Some good, others . . . not so much."

"That place is something. The murals of the animals, and angels and demons . . ."

"That was all Gavina Beaton's stuff. She was the most precocious artist I've ever seen. She did all that work before she turned six."

"You're kidding me."

"That's when we really started getting worried about what had happened in the woods. Before they went missing, Gavina used to be Miss Congeniality. Always doing a little dance, putting on a performance. Girlie little showoff. But after, she was changed. She wouldn't talk to anyone, wouldn't look you in the eye, wouldn't so much as go out on the porch unless Michael was by her side. It was like she'd become a deaf-mute, though I guess now you'd say autistic? That was when she started the paintings. She would sit inside all day and cover one wall after the next. All those crazy scenes, violent and sexual. It was like she'd suddenly aged a thousand years."

"And what about Blue?"

"He had always been shy. The timid type. In his case it was much harder to tell how he'd been affected. Flora, though, she was sure he was different when he came back. *Real* different. She had her old-world beliefs about good and evil, the kind that are near impossible to rid yourself of, once they're entrenched. She convinced herself that her grandson was an imposter. That he was evil."

"Did she think that he was—was what, possessed by the Devil?"

"Nothing that Catholic, no." She took a long sip from her mug and stared out the window. "She thought he was a changeling."

"Like a fairy in disguise?" He vaguely remembered the term from Fred Cronin's newsletters.

"Fairies are said to swap out human children for their own kind, yeah? So changelings were an old-country way to explain problem children. Deformed ones, the mentally handicapped, crib deaths, even. People can reason anything away, can't they?"

"It's certainly easier than facing the truth."

Blue and Elisa in bed together, sweat and semen and saliva.

The shrill cry of Elisa's cellphone on her nightstand, the chipper voice of the doctor's receptionist.

Just make sure Mrs. Howard gets back to us.

Jason winced. "It's no wonder the boy seemed different," he said. "He'd been lost in the woods for two weeks and was traumatized by the ordeal. Why would his grandmother feel the need to create an entire fantasy around it?"

"Can't say. But if you knew Flora, you'd know she wouldn't let it be."

"I don't understand. If she thought her grandson had been replaced by an imposter, why in the world was she trying to get custody?"

Maureen leaned in, close enough to kiss. "She felt she had need of him. Flora was first generation, her folks over from Scotland. Fairy wisdom was ingrained in her belief system. According to legend, the only way to get back a child stolen by fairies is to trade back the changeling for the real child. Some lore says even worse than that. That you have to kill the imposter in order to make it right."

She sat back in her chair. "Faith and family, they both make you do crazy things. Combine the two, and you're in some really twisted territory. Yvonne was worried. Really worried. And then Gavina died. So she ran."

"What happened to Gavina?"

"She drowned. Not too long after the fire at the Colony. At that point she was living with her family in a trailer parked at the beach, just down the road. Her poor mother only ran up the hill to use the telephone, left the girl by the water with her big brother. But he wandered off. I think that's why Daniel eventually went into law enforcement. It was his way of dealing with the guilt over his sister. He had a hard life before he found the Mounties, got into a lot of scrapes. Became something of a vandal as a teenager, if I recall. I suppose that's often the case, though. Cops and robbers, flip sides of the same coin." She drained her coffee and set down the mug.

"I'm sorry," Jason said. "Who are you talking about?"

"Daniel Jessed. He was one of the police officers who came

by the night Blue and Elisa went missing. He introduced himself, didn't he?"

∝

According to Maureen, Detective Jessed's mother had taken off after Gavina died, leaving the boy on the doorstep of a convicted felon in North Sydney presumed to be his father. After the man was later arrested for drug trafficking, eleven-year-old Daniel was taken in by a local family, the Jesseds, whose name he eventually adopted. As a teenager, he ran into all kinds of trouble—underage drinking, disorderly conduct, breaking and entering—before he straightened himself out and joined the police academy.

Maureen wasn't clear on the details, only that Gavina had been left in her brother's care and had drowned. But what was Jason supposed to do about it? If there was anything he knew from being raised a black kid in New York, it was that messing with the police was never a winning proposition. The mere possibility of a connection between Jessed and his sister's death—between the officer and Blue and Elisa's disappearance—was enough to set him on edge.

Later that afternoon, he got tired of being alone in the house and sped off to the Gaelic College. Inside the main building and past an archway strung with a banner that read *Ceud Mìle Fàilte*—"A Hundred Thousand Welcomes" in Scottish Gaelic— he found the Great Hall of the Clans and its exhibits of Scottish clan history, as well as the stories of the first families that settled in the region. It wasn't long before he found William MacLeod's name on a set of artifacts, including the pastor's yellowed and well-thumbed Bible. According to the display copy, MacLeod founded the once-powerful Christ Church and was a fanatical religious leader who ruled over the community with unyielding tyranny, as teacher, preacher, and judge. There was no mention of his supposed disappearance into the woods, only that he was believed to have set sail for Australia with his infant grandson in 1826 after his daughter and her husband died in a fire. Nothing in the exhibits about superstition or changelings or missing children; this was the official record, after all.

The farther Jason walked inside the Great Hall, the closer the events recounted in the exhibits approached present day. Following the immigration of Highland Scots on the heels of the English came an influx of other settlers, including many Irish immigrants seeking better fortunes than their homeland could provide. It wasn't until Jason reached one of the final exhibits, however, that he was brought to a halt. *The 1960s–1970s,* the accompanying placard read, *Back to the Earth.* Among the photographs reproduced behind the glass display was one of a gathering in front of a large brick building. The colors were so bold and deeply saturated that the print resembled an inked animation cel or a pop art canvas, and for a moment he wasn't sure he was looking at a photograph in the first place, let alone one of the Colony.

But there it was. The Starling Cove Friendship Outpost and Artists Colony in the days before it was rendered uninhabitable by fire, its exterior brightly painted and bursting with Day-Glo color. Its front steps were still intact, wide pine planks leading to a carved archway. A pair of broad doors were decorated with an enormous image of a praying mantis, the tibiae of the insect's forelegs curving around the iron door handles. Spread out along the steps in an insouciant sprawl were the commune's two dozen or so denizens, most of them in their twenties with a smattering of babies and toddlers, Blue perhaps among them. Maybe the black-haired one racing across the lawn at the bottom of the frame, rendered as a blur of motion. In the center of the small crowd and planted between two comely young women was a proudly smiling Donald, a good three decades younger but wearing the same familiar style of square-framed glasses, a book resting upon his knees.

It took Jason far longer to place Maureen. She stood in a second-floor window, her youthful face pressed to the pane so that her features were distorted, cheek mashed against the glass like an overripe tomato. It was her, wasn't it? It had to be. Her eyes had that same hooded shape, her nose the same gentle curve, narrow and regal. He brought his face close to the display. The glare from the overhead track bulbs spotted the print through the glass so that it appeared as if stars were shining among the trees behind the brick building. Pinpricks of light dappled the leaves and branches, the photograph shimmering like one of those 3-D winking Jesus pictures that shifted depending on your perspective. He began to dizzy and had to turn away.

The Great Hall fell silent. Jason withdrew to find a bench on which to rest, the enormity of the room lending the impression of being inside the hull of a ship, accompanied by a resultant seasick sensation. He dropped his head into his hands and drew slow and deep breaths, performing the practice he had clients execute if they found themselves overcome by anxiety.

The whole intrepid sleuthing bit—canvassing the cove, hunting down Fred Cronin, questioning Maureen, even—it all seemed more futile than ever. None of these people wanted to help him, not really; possibly because they had something to hide. Certainly Daniel Jessed did. Learning of the detective's personal connection to the case had triggered Jason's paranoia, already uncomfortably heightened since Elisa and Blue first went missing. Obsession and distrust were exactly the kind of red flags Jason had tried to ignore in his sister, Deirdre, before she was first institutionalized, almost twenty years ago. That he might share her same demons, and after all this time, was simply not allowable. Which was why he had rarely discussed his sister with Elisa, nor the circumstances behind his mother's death. It was too much for him to share. He, whose entire profession was built on sharing, on excavating the events of his patients' pasts in order to manage the present.

He placed his palms on the hard wood of the bench and willed his breath to slow. *I am not my patients*, he told himself, as he often did at his lowest moments. And he had never been lower. *I am not myself sick, in the head or otherwise. I am my own person, free from irrationality and fear. I am not my patients, not my sister, not my parents. I stand free of them. I stand alone.*

So move on, he thought, the secret words a force command inside his head. *Move on, move on, move on.*

Jason stood, ignoring his queasiness as he strode toward the exit. He wanted to make it back before nightfall.

❧

Never much of a drinker, Jason had already put away an entire six-pack of beer and was well into a fifth of scotch by midnight. The side of his face itched from no-see-um bites he'd suffered in the woods that morning, one irritated patch in particular that he scratched at until the skin broke. A filament of blood blossomed beneath the tip of his fingernail, and he stared at its shocking bright color in amazement.

With Gabe nowhere to be found, Jason had the house to himself, alone in night's silent embrace. All alone, except that intolerable feeling of being watched from the woods. Alone, but never alone, haunted by all-too-familiar ghosts. He stood and stared out the windows, into the blackened pitch; all he could see was the dim outline of pine trees, casting shadows upon the moonlit lawn. He'd had enough of waiting.

Flashlight in hand, he slipped out and down the porch steps and rounded the side of the house to the hiking trail. Though it was a temperate night, there was also a steady breeze, which kept the insects off him as he made his way into the woods. After a spell of wandering he left the path, and not long after heard the familiar sound of water rushing through the trees. He realized with a start that he was nearing the creek where he'd found Gabe and Fred Cronin earlier in the day, where they had spotted Donald weeks earlier. He was back behind the burned-out brick walls of the old Colony building.

He approached the circle of stones where he'd seen the pile of effects in proximity to Cronin and Gabe: an apple, a plate of meat, the knotted-up bandanna, and more. The flashlight's beam crossed the ground. The circle was empty now, the collection of offerings gone, nothing there but dirt and a spray of pine needles. "Where are you?" he whispered. He stepped inside the circle of stones, cut the flashlight, and listened.

"*Where are you?*" Jason screamed it now, the flashlight cast aside. He took hold of one of the circle stones and flung it in the direction of the creek, the sound of rock on dull wood. A moment later he picked up another stone and threw that one as well, then another, and another, pelting the black corners of night. Rock hitting water, trees, brush, a shower of baseball-sized meteorites crashing to earth.

"Where!" he howled, throat raw and voice hoarse. "Show yourselves! Show me where you are! Show me!"

He cried out, over and over, until he could scream no longer, out of breath as the mosquitoes found him and began their inevitable working over. He dropped to his knees, brought his hands together, and began to pray. He prayed for Elisa, and for Blue, for his sister and his mother as well. For all of them to find their way, to let in the light of the Lord, on Earth as in Heaven. But not for himself. Never that. *If you pray for yourself,* he thought, *then God will never listen.* It was something his mother had once said, the only thing he remembered her teaching him. It was a lesson he dared not forget.

"It really is okay to pray for yourself, you know."

Blue's voice, measured and present. Jason turned, and even in the dark he could tell there was no one there. Were the words inside his head?

"Don't be afraid," Blue said, and now it sounded like many voices, many Blues. *A hundred thousand welcomes.* "We're trying to tell you our journey has been set in motion, so you can take leave before what is to come. Because soon, you'll have to face us. And that would make us real. Which would make you unwell, wouldn't it? By your very own criteria, that is. Delusional. Paranoid. Schizophrenic. Are you prepared for that awareness? Better to take your own journey home first, no?" The disembodied chorus of words threaded through the air, weighty inside the broken stone circle.

"I have nothing to say to you." Jason was most assuredly awake, and knowing that made it far worse. "You're not real. And I'm not crazy. So fuck off."

"Keep on cursing the dark, then." Blue's voice alone, closer now; Jason could feel breath upon his cheek. "Better to switch on a flashlight, though, isn't it? Better to see our true face. If not, maybe it's time for you to move on."

The last two words echoed loud enough to rattle Jason's

teeth, and he flinched. *It's not him*, he thought wildly, *it's the woods. Whatever it is that lives out here, it's trying to make me leave*. But the thought was fleeting, dissipated by the sense that he really was losing his mind. *It's time*, he thought. *It's finally time*.

Footfall sounded in the underbrush nearby and Jason fumbled with the flashlight. He turned it back on just in time to catch a figure emerging from the woods, on the opposite side of the shallow skip of water.

"Gabe?" Jason said as the boy crunched through the leaves, jacketless and pale with his own flashlight in hand, though his was switched off. "What are you doing out here?"

"I followed you. What goes around comes around, I guess." He squinted and shielded his eyes from the beam, until Jason lowered his flashlight. "You okay? I heard you . . ." He didn't finish his sentence.

"I'm fine." Jason got to his feet. "Just needed to get something out of my system." He brushed himself off, the knees of his khakis wet with mud. "So." The darkness around them was too heavy for silence; it demanded to be broached. Still, it took him some time to ask what he really wanted to know. "Care to tell me what you've been up to out here with Fred Cronin?"

Gabe exhaled. "I don't expect you to understand."

"Try me."

He shook his head. "I don't think I can."

"This is about the Other Kind, isn't it? Fairies, or ultraterrestrials, or whatever. Cronin's been putting ideas in your head."

"There's a lot you don't know about what went on up here. With the Colony, the missing kids, even before all of that. This place is special."

"So I've heard." Jason laughed, the bitter and hollow sound reverberating through the trees. "I was talking to Maureen earlier. She told me some interesting things. Like how Gavina Beaton was Detective Jessed's sister. Maybe you heard that one already?"

"I was going to tell you," Gabe said quietly. He flicked his flashlight on, then off, and on.

"When? What the hell were you waiting for?"

"I should've said something, I know. But there's all sorts of things you don't know about. Starting with Elisa."

"What's that supposed to mean?"

Gabe looked down at the flickering glow of his light. "There are things you don't seem ready to hear."

It was exactly what Dream Blue had said. "Gabe." He blunted his worn voice. "Come on. It's me."

Gabe lifted his eyes. "Elisa is pregnant."

Jason opened his mouth but nothing came out, not for a while. "How do you know?" he managed to say.

"She told me, a few days after we got here. She made me swear not to tell anyone. Not even you."

"She's pregnant." So it was true. He knew that already, knew it in his heart, though he'd tried so hard not to believe. But there was no more running from it. "I just . . . She told you that? Why?"

He shrugged. "I asked her."

"Did she—did she say how far along she was?"

"A couple of months, maybe. I am so, so sorry."

"No, it's okay. It's okay."

But it wasn't okay. The baby, it wasn't his. It couldn't be. And Gabe probably had no clue. To Jason, it was like hearing he didn't matter, or even exist.

They stood unspeaking for a long while, their flashlights' circles upon the earth the only evidence of human presence in the dark until Gabe broke the silence. "'The night is far spent, the day is at hand: let us therefore cast off the works of darkness, and let us put on the armor of light.'" After his recitation Gabe smiled kindly, his flashlight now winking on and off of its own accord. "We should head back. We don't want to get stuck out here."

"Sure," Jason said, "sure," though the word sounded as if it had been spoken by someone else, from the other end of a tunnel. "Let's go home."

They circled back to the house in silence. But there were voices in Jason's head as they went. Words from the trees, the wind, the ground beneath their feet, a chorus of voices struggling to be heard.

Go home, he heard Blue say, the way a neighbor might speak to an errant youth caught playing in the streets after dark. *We're a part of something greater now. We've created life from nothingness, and now we can never be undone.*

Fly home, his patient Walt Kerner said. *I'm worried I'm going to do something bad.*

Come back, his sister, Deirdre, said, her affect flattened from years of psychopharmaceuticals. *You need to make sure I'm being taken care of.*

Move on, they all said, separately and together. *Move on, move on, move on.*

∽

Jason poured himself another tumbler of scotch, turned off the porch light, and took the drink upstairs to his bedroom. Everywhere he looked were remnants of Elisa, her possessions rendered artifactual: a hairbrush on the dresser, thick with dark brown strands; four pairs of shoes lined up between the twin windows, their toes pressed neatly to the baseboard; two plastic bags, still stuffed with used clothing from Frenchy's; a pair of jeans tossed thoughtlessly on the bedpost, atop the safari hat she'd bequeathed him. She wasn't coming back, was she? Not after this long. How could she? No matter what had happened, he didn't see a way.

He pulled their suitcase out from under the bed, began to gather his clothes from the closet and dresser drawers, checked under the bed to make sure nothing had been neglected there. He took a slug from his drink, wiped a stray trickle of whisky from his chin, and tried not to grieve for all that he had lost. His father to another family, his mother to suicide, his sister to insanity, colleagues to a cataclysm of smoke and twisted metal. And now Elisa. When would it all finally end? *When you're dead*, he thought. *Not until you're dead. Maybe Mom had the right idea after all.*

Go on, then. His own voice, plain as day. *Wouldn't be such a great loss. Who would even miss you once you were gone?*

He didn't know. He actually didn't know.

Then do it. You know you've been wanting to all this time. It's time for you to move on.

Maybe it would be easier that way. If he drove up Kelly's Mountain and peeled off into the guardrail, the rental car flying free from the road in one brief and final moment of beauty and weightlessness. Then he would be free, at last.

He began to cry. Silently at first, but then in a low sorrowful wail, the dim lamplight of the pink room gone jagged and crystalline. He knocked back the rest of his drink and tossed the glass aside. The tumbler bounced on the crumpled bedspread, rolled off the side of the bed and across the floor, too heavy to break.

Jason wiped his eyes and staggered into the hallway to stand at the entrance to the tartan room, the room Blue had once slept in but Gabe had since adopted. He leaned against the closed door and pressed himself to the splintered grain, the surface rough beneath his large hands.

"Gabe," he whispered into the wood. His voice had cracked, he'd said it too quietly.

But "Yes?" a voice whispered back, from the other side.

"If I—if I were to go . . ."

He couldn't finish; there were no more words. A few moments later the door slowly opened. Gabe stood there in an oversized T-shirt, baggy soccer shorts, and a pair of too-big Vans, all of which made him appear slighter than he already was. He was dressed head to toe in Blue's clothing.

"Don't," Gabe said. It was all Jason needed to hear.

Gabe sat him down on the bed and rubbed Jason's back, his shoulders, his neck, how a parent would soothe a young child. And Jason couldn't help but wonder whether he would ever have a child of his own to comfort, to care for the way his father had failed to care for him. Now that Elisa was gone, now that he'd been left so alone in the world, he had lost the foundation of this hope. He would have to try to rebuild it in another place, at another, unknown time. And so the world had to move on as well.

He was shivering now. Gabe made him lie down and pulled the blankets up and over Jason's shoulders, fetched an extra down comforter from the top of the closet to cover him. "Get some rest," Gabe said. "Just rest." The boy perched himself on the foot of the bed, where he remained, motionless, until Jason began to calm.

After a few more minutes Gabe rose and turned off the

lamp, the only light from the full moon beyond the curtained windows.

"Wait," Jason said, fear edging his voice. "Don't go."

"It's okay. I'm here." Gabe stretched out on the bed beside him, against him, and Jason could smell the woods on his skin, a damp and earthy musk. And also another scent: that of Blue, his bittersweet sandalwood fragrance rolling off the boy in irradiated waves.

"I'm here," Gabe repeated as Jason drifted off to sleep, the boy's breath brushing the back of his head, the words a soothing lullaby. "I'm not going anywhere. I'm here."

∝

A weight presses down on him in the dark. He cannot open his eyes, cannot even breathe. He can only listen as Blue's multilayered voice, soft yet insistent, whispers its way through his ears and inside his skull.

We tried to explain it to you, and then we tried to warn you away. But you don't seem to want to listen.

A creeping dread crawls up Jason's legs, along his chest and arms. The sensation is relentless, as if he is being overtaken by an army of ants.

We were here before the first traveler, here with only the sound of rushing wind and buzzing bees, and insects that burrow and bite. Do you know what we are? We are inevitable.

Pressure upon his face and cheeks, and Jason squirms as his eyelids are lifted against his will. He catches a glimmer of fractalling light, a passing shadow between himself and the night sky, the moon full to bursting overhead.

You still don't see.

Blue is close enough to touch, the words everywhere at once.

You can't see us with these eyes.

At once, a stinging sensation eclipses him; he tries to wriggle free but cannot move, his body cocooned in a web of total paralysis.

We can help you with that . . .

Unseen tendrils dig into Jason's eye sockets, slender and probing fingers taking hold of the fragile eggs that are his eyes. He tries to scream, tries to wake, anything but this. Anything at all.

His eyes are plucked from him with a rending of tissue and skin, the slippery wet worms of his optic nerves snapped back inside his skull. He cries out but all is silence, and he falls farther into the nightmare, further inside himself. *Move on*, he mouths, *move on*, and finally he hears, the words a steady drumming of horse hooves through his otherwise disintegrating unconscious.

~

Jason awoke in the tartan room. Judging by the muted light outside, it appeared to be dawn. Gabe was asleep on the bed beside him. He got up carefully so as not to wake the boy, and eased the door shut behind him. Once downstairs, he made a quick beeline for the bathroom and the shower. It ran cold as usual but he turned the tap colder: he needed the water to rouse him, to help reassure him of his fundamental wakefulness. He had to keep himself together if he was going to leave without causing a scene.

His mind began to race with the logistics of how he was going to extricate himself—from the investigation, from Gabe, from this entire country. The fragile membrane that had kept at bay the voices and dreams of madness—the inheritable condition that was his family legacy—it had nearly been permeated.

He had to go, and do it fast, before this place finally rose up to consume him entirely. The land was the one that held the power here, and always had; the only difference now was that Jason was finally ready to admit it.

He went upstairs and dressed, filled the outside pocket of his suitcase with the remainder of his dirty clothes. There would be phone calls to clients regarding rescheduled sessions, and to Elisa's parents and the police as well, who would surely want to know he would be leaving for the States. He told himself he was going to speak to the authorities in New York, formally hire on that private investigator, contact his congresswoman and other representatives to get them involved. He could always come back, but for now he was moving on. He couldn't stare into this heartless forest forever.

Jason carried the suitcase into the hallway and stopped outside the tartan room door, a hand pressed to the rough-hewn pine. He would leave Gabe a note explaining his need to leave, for the sake of his clients' well-being. He would take the rental car to the airport and book his ticket there—Gabe wasn't insured to drive the car anyway, let alone the fact that the boy had no license to begin with. Gabe could hold on to Elisa's things, reliquary them the way he had everything Blue had left behind. It made sense to leave—completely logical, unremarkable sense. That was the only thing he could tell himself.

He took the suitcase downstairs, retrieved a pad and a red felt-tip pen from beside the telephone, and began to write. *Gabe,* the note began, but he stopped there. Jason stared at the four letters and their succeeding comma, which stared back at him, the venous ink severe and accusing. A dull pain flared behind his eyes and he pressed them shut; this was followed by another, sharper pain, as well as a ringing sound in his ears, as if the air pressure in the room had precipitously dropped. He faced the front door and the adjacent windows, the morning sun's radiance abruptly swelling to pierce the fog over the cove.

But there was something else. Another sensation, a wholly foreign one. It was like seeing a new color or tasting a new flavor, but it was also entirely placeless, unattached to any specific sense. Jason left his suitcase and stepped onto the porch to scan the sky, the water, the rolling lawn down to Maureen and Donald's house. A placid breeze rustled the tree canopy and the grass, rocked the power lines above the road; the stuttering cry of a kingfisher sounded from far off in the woods. He waited. And then, he saw.

A hundred yards down the hill a shape emerged from the trees. It stepped tentatively onto the dewy grass before it continued, its gait awkward and unsteady. For a moment it looked like an animal, stooped and feral, but once Jason squinted he could see that the figure was upright. It wasn't an animal; rather, it appeared human in design. A tremor of fear seized him, eyes watering as he crouched behind the porch railing. It must be what Fred Cronin was talking about, an alien life form or maybe one of Donald's fairies, whatever it was that haunted these godforsaken woods. *We should never have come here*, he thought. *I should have listened*. His instincts commanded him to take flight, but to where? *I never should have come*.

The thing stopped, a brown stain against the lush greenery as its neck craned to face the mist-padded cove. A living shadow, it had a thick, ropy mane that disappeared into jutting shoulder blades. Its back arched down to a rounded posterior, where Jason expected to see a tail, though there was none. Was it covered in scale or bark or flesh, reptilian skin or the matted fur of a mammal? The creature faced him, and cocked its head;

it appeared to detect his presence, smell him, perhaps, rather than sense him by sight.

It began a staggered procession up the hill, arms limp at its sides as though it had no real use for them, its limbs rendered vestigial. Jason wanted to scream for his life but was struck silent. Instead he stood frozen, digging his fingernails into the porch railing until they scarred the wood. The thing gained in human likeness the closer it came; he could see the whites of its eyes, though they gleamed blood red. The way it moved was both terrifying and fascinating in equal measure, patches of putty-colored stains visible upon its dark and meaty surfaces. His stomach dropped out. He could no longer remember how to breathe.

The creature was passing Donald's cabin when Jason's world went negative. It wasn't a creature at all.

"Elisa?" he whispered. Air returned to his lungs with the single uttered word.

He rushed forward and fell from the porch stairs. Now he was the wild animal, loping down the hill fast, faster. The branches sang as the wind whistled through the trees, his feet an erratic gallop-stamp on the uneven grass. "*Oh God, Elisa?*" he screamed, mere yards from her. Her eyes were closed beneath a mask of dirt, hair knotted around her shoulders. But for the mud caking her skin, she was naked.

"Oh, Jesus." Jason grabbed her, held her, gently lowered them both down to the grass. She was cold, so cold, and as he kissed her forehead and her neck he breathed hot air upon her face, willing her back to him. "You're okay," he said, "you're okay. It's going to be okay." He aimed for a tone of reassurance, but it wasn't convincing; he sounded panicked and frightened, a little boy lost in the dark.

Her head lolled back as he stroked her, brushing dirt from her eyelids with the tip of his thumb. "Are you with me?" he said. "Are you here?" There was no response.

"Help me!" he screamed, giving in to the fear, his neck craning wildly as he shouted in the direction of the MacLeod House, then toward Donald and Maureen's, up the hill and down, at the trees and the road and the sky. He didn't want to move her or leave her for a single moment, not yet, not after she'd been gone for so long. "Someone help me, please!"

She cracked open her eyes, and gazed so fixedly over his shoulder he couldn't help but turn.

On the porch of the MacLeod House, in the same spot at the top of the stairs where Jason had just been, stood Gabe. He was wearing Jason's NYU sweatshirt, one Jason was sure he had packed away in his suitcase, along with the rest of his belongings. The boy had the sleeves rolled up, the hood pulled over his head; the sweatshirt was so large on him that it hung halfway down his thighs.

For a solitary moment from this distance downhill, and despite all their many differences, Jason had the unnerving sensation of mistaking Gabe for himself.

Part Three

ELISA

Chapter Seven

———

"Open your mouth, please."

She did as she was told. The stainless steel scraper rooted past her lips and slid between her teeth. Though the tool was unblemished, she nevertheless tasted rust against her tongue.

"Just take a deep breath, and hold it," the doctor said.

She winced. His voice was pitched to salve but his dark eyes were eerily void, like polished stones. The whole of her had become specimen.

"There we go." He slipped the instrument from her mouth, the sample collected. The doctor made a show of wiping the scraper's tip with a square of cotton mesh and tossed the square with a flourish into the metal waste bin, the lid clattering shut when he released the foot pedal. "All done now. In another few minutes, you should be good to go."

The doctor smiled and vanished from the sterile and windowless examination room. Jason, the man she called her husband, took her hand and stroked her fingers atop the hard table and its roll of disposable sanitary paper. The touch of his flesh, of metal, of paper: it was all unfamiliar, every point of contact a fresh pinprick. It was as though she had been lifted from suspended animation, ripped from a place where nothing could touch her at all. Everything would have to be relearned.

Jason massaged her palm, her wrist, her forearm. She shud-

dered and tucked her hands beneath her elbows, where her jagged nails caught on the starchy fabric of her hospital gown. How
many had worn this very same gown before her? How many of
them now dead? *You're lucky to be alive,* they kept saying. But
she wondered.

"Sorry," he said. "I didn't mean to . . ."

"It's nothing." She shrugged, her voice unfamiliar, hoarse
from either misuse or neglect, she wasn't sure which. "I'm just
cold."

They sat in silence. She reminded herself that she knew
Jason, and knew him well. And to a lesser extent Gabe, the
young man in the waiting area down the hall, his baby face gone
chapped and bearded blond in the two weeks since she'd been
gone. She watched Jason watching her. His mind was somewhere else, though, hands held fast to the arms of his chair,
fingers tensed as if eager to be put to use.

He thinks he wants to take care of me, she thought, *but really
he's the one who craves comfort.*

Not a recollection exactly, more like a truth she'd learned
over many lifetimes, from a hundred different angles. He smiled
at her, and she smiled back, reflexively, for the first time since
she had come out of her daze two nights prior.

Earlier, the attending physician had told them there were no
signs of sexual abuse, nor had the preliminary blood work indi-
cated sexually transmitted disease or pregnancy; there was no
indication she'd ever been pregnant at all. "Thank you," Jason
had said with relief, as though it were the doctor's doing. He
turned then to look at her plaintively, and she saw in his expression that he knew what had happened between her and Blue.
The hurt in his eyes was unambiguous, along with a secondary
flare of fire, of pride, perhaps. Or maybe it was affirmation, that

what had happened was a terrible mistake the universe had seen fit to undo, having blighted her with some kind of karmic miscarriage. And that was that. She couldn't argue with a blood test, could she? So she grimaced and turned away, curled into a ball, and held herself with her knees tucked under her chin, in—fittingly—the fetal position.

There had been a flush of embarrassment, followed by a more acute feeling of unmitigated shame. She yearned then for the comforting touch of Jason's firm hands upon her shoulders, the soft cadence of his voice, the consolation one might provide a child. But his touch didn't come until later, and he left her in that moment the way she had left him: alone. And maybe she deserved no better.

All this in front of a police detective named Jessed, whose presence made Jason noticeably anxious. When the doctor added that she showed no particularly troubling symptoms of dehydration or malnourishment, the detective lit up, as if this helped prove some hypothesis she wasn't yet privy to.

"Is there anything you can remember?" Detective Jessed had asked, yet again, for what seemed like the dozenth time.

"No," she answered. "Nothing. I think I fell asleep in the bath . . ."

In truth, she actually remembered quite a bit, if only in flashes. Just not in the way they meant, not in a way she could properly communicate. It was as if that which she did recall needed translation—not so much from another language, but through a second set of senses, resembling the usual ones yet altogether different. A dark light washing over her that tasted like tangerine; the smell of fire as it bled bitter in her swollen eardrums; the touch of frenzy and morning and moon. And a shadow that resembled a face in the dark, one so blinding and bright it was impossible to truly see, yet so beautiful she couldn't dream of ever looking away.

For two days she'd been forced to listen to specialists (Jason included) volley theories back and forth across her bed like some kind of diagnostic Ping-Pong match: dissociative fugue, amnesia, depersonalization, PTSD . . . The word *alienism* came to mind.

How could she tell them that none of their assumptions applied to her? Her experience was not of the real; it was of the otherreal.

She no longer belonged to their world of words. Now she belonged to the ones below the land.

The doctor popped back inside the examination room to tell them she was free to go. "Back to her room?" Jason asked.

"Back to her life," the doctor said. "We're discharging her."

She allowed Jason to help her from the examination table, his hand beneath her elbow as he walked her across the hall to the bathroom. She locked the door behind her, stood in front of the mirror, and stuck out her tongue, which was caked in a layer of lichen-colored film. Her olive complexion was starkly pale under the fluorescents, hair scrubbed clean but lifeless, a dull brown frame for her round face. She brushed a stray lock behind her ear and the light caught the metallic clasp on her hospital bracelet, her name typed in the space between her date of birth and a scannable bar code.

Howard, Elisa. Her last name first, by all rights that of her husband, followed by the name her parents had given her (the parents she made Jason convince not to rush to her side, that she would fly home right after she was discharged). Her date of birth, her sex, the date she was admitted to the hospital, the name of the medical center: all the essential data, printed beneath the clear plastic band. All of it equally meaningless.

She met her own gaze in the mirror. Her eyes were lighter than she remembered; weren't they darker, once? Now, instead of deep pools of brown, the irises were flecked with sparks of green, similar to the oxidized color of the scum coating her tongue. The pregnancy had changed her body in ways large and small, but of course that wasn't the entire story; she'd been changed in other ways as well. She looked away, down at her torn fingernails and the chipped lip of the sink, everything the same unhealthy shade of green.

She washed and dried her hands, and paused for a deep breath before opening the door. Jason was waiting on the other side.

"Everything okay?" He put his hands upon her waist, and she tried not to flinch.

"Sure." *Now smile.* She smiled. "Let's get going."

Jason, never more than an arm's length away, followed her down the hall and into the waiting room. Gabe spotted them and stood. He appeared disoriented, as if roused from a vivid dream. "How are you feeling?" he asked, and wiped at his bleary eyes with the backs of his hands, which clutched his spiral sketch pad and a pen that dangled a ball-bearing chain.

"Better," she said. "Better." She embraced him—unexpected, at least to her—and she did so tightly, too tightly. As she held him she realized that he smelled of Blue. Of his funk and stale cigarette smoke, sesame oil and cilantro and kitchen grease. She drew in the scent as if drowning and starved of air; it was impossible to let him go.

"We're going to find him," she whispered into the curved shell of Gabe's ear. She said the words, heard them from her lips and spoken in her own voice. She didn't know why she had said it, only that it was true.

She pulled back at last. Gabe was startled—unsure, it
seemed, of whether he'd understood her. Before he could respond, however, Jason placed a hand on her elbow and led her
toward a back room to change.

∞

As soon as she walked through the front door of the MacLeod
House her skin began to itch, the nicks and scrapes across her
thighs and shoulders all humming with unease. She turned back
toward the windows and looked out at the familiar vista, the
cove wet with mist and the dusky remnants of a late-afternoon
rainstorm. She had to remember to breathe.

"Want some tea?" Jason rattled the black porcelain kettle
over the range.

"Sure," she said, though she did not. *This place*, she thought,
it feels like a trap. "Thanks."

She forced herself to call her parents. Her mother pleaded
with her yet again to return to New York, her father shouting,
"Make her!" in the background. But she couldn't. She couldn't
see them. Or rather, she couldn't see them seeing her, tracking
her movements as though she were a wild animal that might
bolt at any moment. "I'll be back soon," she said. "I just need to
get my legs under me."

"Knowing you, that might not ever happen!" Her mother's
words daggers; they always were. "Who knows what happened
to you? If you do, you sure haven't told us."

She groaned into the receiver, a teenager again. "I can't
leave yet, all right?"

"But you're fine abandoning us?" Fear in her mother's voice,
and choked-back tears, those of a frightened child.

"I haven't abandoned you," she said. "And I won't."

"But you did. You have. Why can't we see you? Why? That's it. I've had enough. I'm flying back up there."

"Mom, don't. Please. I'll be back just as soon as I can."

She wondered which was worse: believing that her parents were strangers now, or being wrong about that fact and feeling it regardless. Because to look upon them would be to know that she was no longer their daughter, and from that admission there was no turning back.

There was a heavy sigh on the other end of the line. "Just tell me you're safe now. Please. I need to know that. At least give me that, Elisa."

Elisa. Hearing her mother say the name was like being spoon-fed dirt. *You chose wrong,* she wanted to say. *You gave me the wrong name.*

"I'm safe," she said instead. She looked out the window and caught a starburst of late-afternoon light at the foot of the drive, glinted off the windshield of a patrol car as it slowed and passed. "They're watching out for me. The police, the doctors, Jason . . . I'm fine. I need some time, okay?" *Time.* She didn't know what that meant anymore.

"We miss you," her mother said. "Julie misses you. She says you haven't even seen the kids since Mandy's birthday. Long before all this."

All this. She wanted to scoff, but the guilt-tipped arrow found its mark. It was true, she hadn't seen her sister or nieces in months, though back home they were only a short subway ride away. They only wanted to see her face. *Selfish Elisa,* she thought. *Selfish little bitch.* She felt awful. Maybe she was still human after all.

"I'm sorry," she said. "Tell Julie I'll visit them as soon as I'm back."

Elisa got off the phone and sat on the couch, unmoving and unmoved, as her mug of chamomile tea steadily cooled. She pretended to read a decrepit Italian fashion magazine she'd unearthed from the bottom of the log trunk, and tried very hard not to watch the windows and the trees beyond, the impenetrable woods that had rebirthed her into this discordant and too-bright world.

Every once in a while she caught Gabe, pen in hand, eyeing her from his perch in front of the woodstove, the glow of flames on his lean face as twilight sputtered out over the mountains. He would look away, into the fire or down at the yellow-paged volume in his lap, the words *Entomologia Generalis Vol. I* embossed on its battered purple cover. Jason made no bones about his own surveilling, however; his hard eyes stayed upon her, to the point where she ceased to provide him the satisfaction of noticing. And suddenly it seemed like a familiar game: the granting of attentions, followed by their withholding, a cross between a tango and a tug-of-war. Apparently not much had changed between them.

"I'm wiped out," she said at last, and let out a convincing yawn. "I'm going to take a bath and get some sleep." Jason began to rise but she stared him back down. "It's okay." She tried to smile. "I'll be fine, really. It's not like I'm going to get sucked down the drain. You know. Again."

She crept upstairs, filled the cast-iron tub, and eased herself into the steaming water, first with a moan of pain, then relief. She tried to recall what she'd been thinking when she was last here: in this bathtub, this room, this house. The more she tried to remember, however, the more her memories of that night seemed to dissipate. She was worrying rifts in her mind, fingering greater holes in an already moth-eaten sweater.

In the bath, talking to Blue. Talking and laughing and taking pictures: her of him, him of her, of the walls, the floor, the toilet. Talking about, what? His return to the cove, and disappearing as a child. And then, the pregnancy. Which she told Blue was only six weeks along. Which was a lie.

The child, as hard as it was for her to believe even now, would have been his. Theirs. The embodiment of a connection greater than friendship, or sex, or indeed love. Their union, Elisa had long known, had echoes of the divine. The night in May they got wasted and he told her about his grandmother's death, how sad he felt that he would never get a chance to see her again, not to mention how conflicted he was that she'd left him her house. Would he be going back to Cape Breton, after all these many years? The possibility seemed to release a powerful grief in him, and from Elisa a resultant wave of compassion, an effect that bordered on the chemical; that night she was doubly intoxicated. She had hitched up her skirt, and Blue gave her a nervous smile that said, *Are you for real?* and she stared boldly back as if to say, *Yeah, let's do this already.* She stood there waiting, as if in surrender. And all of a sudden they hit the bed and they began to fuck, wildly. Blue tried to slow things down but she told him everything was fine, that she was on the pill.

Which was another lie. She'd gone off it a few months earlier for no real reason; she just finished her supply one day and never refilled her prescription. She didn't understand—then as now—what exactly had made her deceive Blue. All she knew was that she had felt compelled.

Since then she'd been unable to be intimate with Jason (although they had already been sliding down that chilly slope as it was). The growing lump of cells inside of her had weighed heavily on her conscience, its presence seemingly felt before sperm had so much as punctured egg. The baby had later taken on an air of predestination, something to ruminate over while Jason retreated into his work, or into himself. Everyone, it seemed, had their own secret place to go.

But now the source of her daydreams was gone, Blue along with it. Just gone. It was hard for her to digest that she had lost the baby, but what kind of mother was she ready to be anyway? *Maybe it's for the best.* At least that's what she told herself. The alternative was too distressing.

She closed her eyes and let her head slip beneath the surface of the water. Its warmth lulled her, and the pressure mounted as she held her breath, the water hardening around her like a mold; she imagined it shaping her into an elongated, reedier form. A birch tree, perhaps. One tree among many, gray bark peeled back from her eyes and mouth to reveal a dark and flinty substance beneath: mossy black marble, or maybe blood-speckled stone.

She opened her eyes. Hovering above the water's surface was a dark figure, its skull crowned with a nest of sharp nettles like barbed wire, vast and green-tinged eyes cast upon her like twin mirrors reflecting an unseen light. *Blue.* His face obscured, the way it was that night, but still. It was Blue. She would know him anywhere.

Behind him were the others, only hazy shadows but *I remember them*, she thought. They had touched her, caressed her face with needle-fingered yet surprisingly supple hands. They spoke with no sound, but still they spoke. *Home*, they had said, *you are home.* But not to her.

Elisa shot upward in a spray of water, her hands fumbling for the lip of the tub. Her chest was tight, lungs heaving and ravenous as her eyes darted about the empty bathroom.

Once Jason settled into sleep, Elisa slipped from the bed and out of the pink room, easing the door shut behind her. She retrieved her vintage slip dress, beige and embroidered, from a hook in the bathroom, pulled it over her head, and tiptoed down the stairs to the kitchen, her red ballet flats waiting on the braided rag rug beside the back door. Off the rear deck and down past the woodpile, she stopped short in the drive to take in the cove, glowing bright beneath the waning zinc moon. There had been total darkness the night she was taken, half a lunar cycle lost and gone forever. Tonight, everything was painfully clear, including how alone she was.

Blue. She missed him. Deeply, terribly missed him. She missed his cooking! Lord, how she missed that. How he seemed to put a little bit of himself into every one of his meals, the taste of each dish unlike any other. It made so much sense now. Of course his food was extraordinary; it was because *he* was extraordinary. She felt his absence, conversely, as a weight in her stomach, a tumorous growth gone metastatic, the compression constant beneath her skin. Blue had vanished, yes, but he also remained. The way he had remained for more than a decade, twelve years gone since that ravishing boy appeared to her from behind the Limelight's tattered velvet rope like some kind of saintly apparition (outside a nightclub that had once been a consecrated church, no less). His hair black-edged and knotted, a cerulean halo above a pale gamin face, one of his two front teeth skewed but perfectly misaligned, as if by godly design. And when he had smiled at her, her heart snagged. She had been safe, as long as he was near.

She closed her eyes as if blinded, and opened them anew to the cove and the shocked round mouth of the moon. A warmer light caught her attention down the hill, from the narrow cabin on the south side of the drive. She skulked over and peered through one of the windows: Donald, hunched over a scratched-up desk beneath a tarnished metal lamp, his brown dog curled at his side. He sat in front of what appeared to be a ham radio, one hand upon a dial with the other cupped to the padded earpiece of an enormous set of aviator-style headphones.

As if sensing her presence, he turned to face her. Startled, she backed into the dark pool of night, but he strode to the cabin door and threw it open. "Who's there?" he called out as she darted for the trees, her feet crunching over a carpet of pine needles on the edge of the lawn. He remained in place, peering out into the gloom, and she felt foolish hiding from a man who probably only wanted company, or perhaps consolation. *I can do that for him.* She remembered how she had cradled him on the floor of his cabin as he wept. *I brought him comfort once before.*

The dog bounded after her, but stopped halfway across the lawn and cocked its head. She made her way back toward the cabin. As she neared she caught sight of Donald's expression, his eyes unfocused, jaw held crookedly as if pained; there was confusion upon his face. That, and fear.

"My memories," he said, his voice hesitant, tremulous. "Are you the one who stole them?"

"Donald," she said, "it's only me. Elisa." But as she mounted the steps he staggered back inside, fumbling for the door. He slammed it in her face, the dog shut out alongside her, followed by the sound of the lock being engaged, of a chair dragged across the cabin floor and jammed against the door handle. *I'm dangerous,* she thought, and had to resist rattling the knob. *I'm not to be let in.*

She placed her ear against the wood and listened. There was muttering on the other side, but she was unable to make out the words; all it sounded like was "Fae." *Fae. Fae. Fae.* The same word, repeated at varying distances. She pictured him pacing the room like a caged beast.

Elisa lowered herself to the steps and sat. The dog nestled its head against her, and she stroked its fur. She knew she shouldn't because of her allergies, but couldn't stop herself; it felt too good, and right now she needed something she could love without thinking about it. She scratched beneath the dog's snout and let its warmth wake her memory.

I'm in the bathtub. An ecstatic poison seeps through her veins, a netting of liquid light enveloping her in a tightening web of paralysis so she can't scream, can't breathe. She finds herself without need of air, as if she is already one of them herself. She floats from the tub, cradled in their elongated, branch-like fingers. *Light as a feather, stiff as a board*, just like the slumber party game. They rush her downstairs and out the back door, the world a black void streaked with starlight through the trees as they navigate the path to their hiding hole. An endless, rushing night.

But when they near their burrow, the sickening smell of burned earth forces them back. There are fires above, as well as below, heat emanating in thick waves from the flames. There are other ways into their warrens, however, other points of access, and so they backtrack and circle toward the cliffs overlooking the bay. Their ecstatic energy continues to course over her, through her, like nothing she's ever felt. Everything is light. Unable to move of her own accord, she knows she should be afraid, but instead she only feels alive.

They scale the mountain toward its summit, another entryway that might yet be accessible. Near her—right beside her—is Blue. Only she is still frozen as if in amber, so she cannot turn to look upon his face. His true face, she knows now, after all this time. She can't see him for what he really is.

A melody played in her head, erratic yet also indelible. It took a few moments for her to determine it was Donald, singing close by, on the other side of the door.

> *Will-o'-wisp before them went,*
> *Sent forth a twinkling light,*
> *And soon she saw the fairy bands*
> *All riding in her sight.*
> *She was as me touched by the Fae,*
> *Not one of them by sight,*
> *For what remains of time below*
> *Is laughter and the light.*

The lamp went out inside the cabin. She lay down in the grass and stared up at the stars, listened to the breeze whisper through the rustling leaves and her untamed hair. And all the while, the steady thrum of the dog's heartbeat thumped against her like an external organ, its paws kneading her side as if trying to extract milk. She was enthralled.

Unseen insects and their droning stridulations, murmurs of waves lapping upon the shore down the hill, the swift rotation of the planet on its axis: she sensed all of it in a new way, and for the very first time. The whole of creation one vast organism, flushed with blood. She never knew how really to feel, until now.

∽

In the morning, her head swimming with chiaroscuro dreams of shadows and light, she awoke in the pink room of the MacLeod House. Jason was already dressed, and stared at her from the foot of the bed.

"Where were you last night?" he asked stiffly.

Elisa opened her mouth, only to find she had no ready answer. *I'm running through the woods.* Images of tree branches vibrated in her head, calcified and gnarled boughs that reached out with whetted tips as if to take hold of her. *But I am fast, too fast, I will never be touched again.*

"I woke up and you were gone," he persisted, the injury in his tone poorly disguised as concern.

"Oh." She rubbed at her eyes; the trees, they were only a dream, a remnant of a sliver of a memory. She must have fallen asleep outside Donald's cabin alongside his dog, her return up the hill forgotten. Was that what had happened?

She sat up and stared at her hands: they appeared the same, but they should have looked different this morning. Her fingers, they should be stiffer, her palms wider, their surfaces thicker and more coarse; her skin should be rough, and it should itch. Her throat should be constricted as well. *Because you were with the dog,* she remembered. *Shouldn't you be having trouble breathing, like last time?* Her mind was playing tricks. She lowered her hands, tried to sneeze but it failed to materialize.

"I just wanted some fresh air," she said, and adjusted one of the pink peonies in the copper-glazed ceramic vase beside her bed. "Cooped up in that hospital room . . ."

"Sure," he said. "I get it."

He stood and went to the door, and by the time he got there his face appeared untouched by distress, smooth and unlined, synthetic. *How quickly he changes.*

"Are you hungry?" he said. "I can bring you something up here if you'd like . . ."

"That's sweet." *Now smile.* She smiled. "I am hungry. But you know what? I'd really love some diner food. The greasier the better."

They snuck down the stairs and out to the car. Jason eased the Caddy downhill, but slowed to a stop when they spotted Maureen emerging from her studio. She had showed up at the hospital the previous morning with the vase bursting with peonies; the smell had been so ambrosial that Elisa had brought them back with her, returned to the very garden that had birthed them.

"Well, hello there!" Maureen wiped her hands on her work apron as she rounded the car to the passenger side. "I heard they let you out for good behavior. How are you doing, honey?"

"Great." *Smile.* "Really great. Thanks."

"I'm so glad. I know you're still recovering. Still . . . figuring it all out."

"I was down in the ground," Elisa blurted out. She had to stop herself from covering her mouth.

Maureen jolted. "You were down in the . . . ?" She looked to Jason, who clenched the steering wheel and stared straight ahead, toward the road and the dark sky beyond. "The whole time?"

"I think so. Maybe?" She laughed then, apropos of nothing. A former therapist of hers had pointed out that she often laughed when discussing difficult emotions, an unconscious derision of her pain . . . or was that something Jason had once said?

"I really don't know," Elisa went on. "I don't know why I said that. I suppose it must be true, though. Where else could I have been?" *Don't tell them anything more. Otherwise they'll try to follow you, when it's time to go back.*

Maureen nodded as if she understood on some deeper level. Because of Donald, perhaps. Elisa thought of last night again, the elderly man on the far side of the cabin door and the lilting ballad he had sung to her, its galloping melody. And the memories she allowed herself of being spirited through the woods. How frightening it had felt, and how right.

"Donald," Elisa said. "How is he?"

"Not so hot." Maureen whipped her head to the side as if struck. "He hasn't been talking to me lately. Although who knows? Maybe he doesn't have much to say."

Why would he speak, Elisa thought, *when he can sing?* The simple song about time spent below, the laughter and the light . . . Donald thought he knew what she was, what she had become. He thought she was one of them.

"We're off to grab a bite," Jason said. "If Gabe ever wakes up, tell him we'll be back soon."

"Oh, he's gone out already," Maureen said.

"Already?" Jason sounded perturbed. "Where to?"

"He came down the hill earlier to say hello. Turns out Donald didn't bring Olivier back last night, so Gabe was kind enough to search for him out on the trail."

The dog. *A flash of fur, sticky slick with sweat and oil and blood. Fevered rabid, and chasing. They scamper in a matched stride and she keeps speed, howls with laughter and communion. They are each other's familiars, nursed from the same mother . . .*

"I hope that damn dog comes back," Maureen was saying. "I would hate to have to bring Donald any bad news. I'm not sure he could take it."

"It's interesting," Jason said as they continued down the drive, his eyes on Maureen as she headed back to her studio. "Gabe, that is. I felt like I was really starting to get that kid. But now?" He grimaced. "Not to mention the company he's been keeping. Very sketchy if you ask me. He's changed a lot since you . . . disappeared."

"How so?" Though of course they had all changed, hadn't they?

"The way he talks about Blue being gone, for one. Like he's lost a limb. And since you came back alone it's been pure despair. It strikes me as being out of scale." He reached for her hand and held it before returning his attention to the road. "I shouldn't judge. I'm sure he just hasn't been himself."

"Well, how do you know?" The cove unfurled before them in an aquatic panorama of shaded blues and greens, the surface of the water incandescent beneath the morning sun. "How well did we really know him before?"

"True." Jason thought for a moment. "And obviously he and Blue must have had something going on."

"Blue and Gabe are *friends*," Elisa said, the word entirely banal; she could as easily have substituted her name for Gabe's. "Maybe a bit more than that, sure." She didn't know what else to say.

They pulled into the Lobster Landing, a roadside spot near the Gaelic College. The restaurant was busy for this early in the day, and they slid into the only empty booth, by the window. Elisa and Jason made small talk. About the ominous clouds in the sky, the likelihood that New York had turned beautiful in September, the steady stream of cars on the Trans-Canada Highway and how much of the traffic was still from tourists. Eventually a fiftyish bottle-blond waitress with a name tag that read *Patricia, Here to Serve You* appeared with two glasses of water. "Busy today," she said, and stole a momentary glance at Elisa before she flicked Jason a pair of menus and hurried back behind the counter.

"Friendly," Elisa said.

"We've made ourselves something of an attraction to the locals." He handed her a menu. "It seems not all of them are admirers. To be honest, I think we were more sympathetic when you were missing. There's been some speculation that we might have been the ones who started the fires in the woods."

The forest floor blackened, tree bark coiled in strips and bruised purple, like parchment held over a candle. Paper birch, gray birch, yellow birch, all of it tinder. Nothing safe aboveground, nowhere to go but to stay down, stay down, down.

But it's worse down here. Thick plumes of smoke, heady and overpowering. A tidal crest of choking clouds billowing through the warrens, unyielding in its rush toward the throne room . . .

She squeezed her eyes shut. When she opened them, she found Jason looking at her askance. "Sorry," she said. "Just thinking."

She focused on the specials insert clipped inside the menu and tried to make herself hungry, but nothing looked very appetizing. In fact, the entire enterprise of eating was so daunting it verged on the insurmountable. "So, you were saying. About all the attention . . ."

"That we've become local celebrities, yes. Or really more objects of curiosity. There's this free press, called *The Starling Cove Believer*? It's birdcage liner. Bat Boy sightings and alien abduction testimonials. Weirdo gossip and rumors."

"'Missing Woman Returns, Hungry for Lobster Roll.'"

"Something like that." Jason grinned.

So happy, she thought, *so relieved*. He made it all look so easy.

"So," he said, "is that what you're in the mood for?"

"Actually," she replied, plunking down the menu, "I think I'll be fine with just water."

"I thought you were hungry."

"I thought so too. Maybe I only wanted to get out. Be around people."

But that wasn't right. After a cool appraisal of the room, she decided the crowd had about as much appeal as the menu. Lots of dusty plaid shirts, prairie skirts, overalls, and dull work boots . . . Nothing shined here. Least of all her.

Come back to us.

She looked to the window. Trees waved at her from the other side of the road, pine branches rippled like water as if combed by an unseen hand. She had to dig her nails into the corked underside of the tabletop to keep herself from rising.

"You sure you don't want anything?" Jason asked.

"I'll pick off your plate," she said, and forced herself to smile, yet again. *False*, she thought. *False false false.* "Get whatever you want."

He ordered a cheeseburger and fries, and waited for the waitress to disappear again before leaning forward. "I talked to your mother this morning."

"She called?"

"Actually, I called her. She wants me to check in, keep her posted on how you're doing."

"What did you tell her?"

"I said you were well. That you still couldn't remember where Blue took you, or . . . You know. Whatever may have happened."

"Where he *took* me?" She made a sour face. "What is that supposed to mean?"

"Nothing." Jason paused. "Look, I really don't know. I just thought that . . . Well, really, it was the police that thought— they thought that maybe you two had . . ." He feigned a laugh. "They suggested that you two may have run off together."

"Did they."

He waved his hand dismissively. "Your parents, though. They really want to hear from you, Elisa."

"You seem to have taken care of that already. *Jason*."

"I only spoke to your mom. You haven't actually reached out to your father, not once. He's still really shaken up. He wants to hear from you."

"I didn't realize you were acting as their go-between."

"They're worried about you!" He pushed against the table, but since it was bolted against the wall, it only caused his side of the booth to rock back. An older man behind him let out a startled yelp. "Sorry," Jason said, and raised a conciliatory hand. All eyes were on their table, until a moment later the scrutiny of the patrons scattered, as quickly as it had amassed.

"Stop berating me," Elisa said. "I'm not a child."

"I'm trying to understand." Jason lowered his voice as he leaned in once more. "Really I am. But you owe it to them to stay in touch. Every day. Every hour, if that's what they want. Stay connected, for your own well-being."

"Is that your professional opinion?"

He crossed his arms and turned toward the window. They sat in silence until the waitress brought his order, and Jason grabbed the burger before the plate hit the table.

The food smelled like death. Cow's blood bubbled at the corner of his mouth, and he gnawed away at the meat like a

combine harvester, consuming everything in its path. Four minutes later the food was assimilated. Soon it would be metabo-
lized, shit out as waste, and forgotten. It was disgusting.

"And for the record, I'm not berating you," Jason said after a
while, as if he had continued the conversation inside his head.
He spun a french fry in a puddle of bloodied ketchup. "I can't
begin to imagine what you've gone through."

"Yeah," she said. "Me neither."

"The important thing is that you have people who care
about you, really care, no matter what." He swallowed, palms on
the table. "I don't . . ." He took a deep breath and stared down
at his plate. Was he going to cry? "I don't have that."

"But you do." She took up his hands so quickly she almost
knocked over her water glass. "You do. I care about you."

"Do you?"

"Of course," she said without thinking. His hands were so
much warmer than hers; it was like cupping two beating hearts
in her palms.

Jason looked up at her and his face brightened, the sadness
in his eyes softening back to affection. "Let's get out of here," he
said. "Let's go home."

"Okay." She cast a cursory glance inside her handbag, to
make sure she wasn't leaving anything behind. "We'll light a
fire, see if Gabe can give us some privacy. Maybe we can draw
a bath . . ."

He seemed irked. "I don't mean back to the house. I mean
home. Our home. New York."

It was only an act; this was all a trap. And she'd almost fallen
into it.

"Let's go home," he said again. "It's time. For both of us."

"I told you already, I'm not going to do that." Elisa shook her head; she could just as readily return to New York as she could travel back in time. "You know I can't."

"Why not?"

"Because of . . . Blue."

"Blue." Now Jason was the one shaking his head. She thought she could see him repeating Blue's name on his lips, below his breath. "Of course."

"I can't leave him out there. Don't you get that?"

"Actually, I don't." He hid his hands beneath the table. "What do you think you can do for him by staying? Gabe can stay. Maureen said she'll put him up as long as he wants. He can move into their spare bedroom, help out with Donald. And then she can rent out the MacLeod House again. She has bills to pay, believe it or not. I know nobody is talking about that, but it's true. Speaking of which, our rental car? We might as well have bought one for all the time we've been stuck here."

"Cars," she said. "You're talking about rental cars." She couldn't help but laugh. *Rental cars.* He wasn't talking about anything real. But then again, how could he? So she went ahead and laughed. In disbelief at his nerviness, yes, but largely at the absurdity of his suggestion. She could never leave, not if Blue wasn't found; the possibility was unthinkable.

And it wasn't only Blue. There was something else she had left out there, something indefinable, another part of herself that remained beneath the land. There would be no leaving, no.

And then she laughed louder. The other patrons didn't turn to stare this time, not even as her laughter raised to a crescendo, a wicked bellow, a witch's cackle. The old man behind Jason laughed himself then, a little titter at first that blossomed into a string of violent staccato huffs. The gentleman across from him laughed as well, loud and louder still. The woman beside him picked it up, followed by the diners at the counter, the whole restaurant alight in a chain reaction of manic, animalistic hysteria. *Like swarming insects*, Elisa thought, *signaled by collective command*. The chorus of laughter soon drowned out her own.

Their waitress stepped through the kitchen saloon doors. A pot of coffee slid from her grasp and shattered across the tiles. She clutched the doorjamb with one hand, the other at her stomach as she squealed and fell into a squat. It looked like she was peeing, a steaming puddle of coffee rolling out in a black tide. Shattered glass coruscated around her, a glittering spiral that refracted the electric white from the overheads. Elisa remained fixed to the sticky cracked vinyl of her seat until a firm grip on her arm lifted her from the booth.

"I think it's time to go," Jason said. Only he wasn't laughing. Not at all. He reached into his back pocket for his wallet, pulled out a Canadian ten-dollar bill, and tossed it onto the table. Stone-faced, he hustled her to the entrance, one hand on the small of her back while the other held her bag.

"Did you see that . . . ?" Elisa said. But Jason didn't answer, or didn't hear; he simply walked out the door ahead of her.

She trailed after him but froze at the entrance of the restaurant. On the far side of the open door, the overcast sky was an oppressive wall of gray that made her throw an arm across her eyes, her only protection against the diffuse and menacing light. For a flickering moment she lost her equilibrium, unsure of whether she was looking up at the bulging cloud cover or down into a vast and churning sea, or if there was even a difference between the two.

Elisa lowered her head and hurried across the blacktop in the direction of the car, just as it started to rain.

Chapter Eight

She is underwater. The current presses her down, then to the side, shakes her like a child with a doll it cannot unhand. Cobalt waves lap above, visible in a gleaming thread of sunshine; all else is darkness. A wild jerking and she rises, thrust up toward the sky. Upon breaking the surface she finds herself surrounded not by an ocean of water but rather by a tarry black sea, far darker than the depths below. What she had thought was water only a moment before is in fact much thicker, the viscous substance coagulating around her shoulders and neck, sticky clumps in her hair that carry with them the carrion stench of rotting meat. She scrambles for a rock, for driftwood, anything that will keep her from sinking below the surface once more. She is cold, and alone.

Bobbing, she thrashes and the gelatinous bile fills her mouth, her nostrils, ears; it coats her eyes as well, the putrid film rapidly hardening into a mask. Finally, contact—a length of what might be a tree limb, bristling with a coarse fiber like pine needles. She tries to climb the limb but it lifts her from the mire instead, a gnarled arm bending to bring her against its rigid form, cradling her like a newborn. *You are safe in our arms,* a temperate voice says in its secret language, and she is surprised that she understands. *You are safe so long as we are here.*

Her rescuer begins to clean her. Starting with her mouth,

bristles scour her, hard and fast, brushing away the sludge. Wetness upon her face as a slithery tongue licks at her lips, takes up fluid as a hummingbird takes up nectar. Her nose and cheeks are scraped clean; her ears swabbed, and now she can hear a click-clacking of something at work, the sound of shell on hollow bone. *Click-clack*. The filth from her fingertips is scrubbed away, as it is from her breasts and belly, her body damp but drying in the hot air. She feels exposed, oxygenated. *Click-clack*. At last, the black mucus is licked from her eye sockets, and she lifts her heavy lids. Blinded by the light of a dozen distant suns high above, she tries to focus on the face of her savior, her redeemer.

Its eyes are onyx domes, black as the surrounding sludge. For a moment she swims in them, lost in their polyhedral depths, each facet of which appears to hold many more eyes. Each unblinking eye examines her within and without, the spindling branches of her redeemer's fingers lingering upon her dimpled navel. Now she can see more of it towering above her, the rest of its red and ridged crest of a skull, twin horns quivering upon its crown like fat grubs wriggling in a mound of sodden dirt. Aspects of it seem impossibly large—two pairs of great sheltering wings, aglow with bioluminescent scarlet chitin, its trijointed limbs alive with twisting hairs, jagged jack-o'-lantern jaws moving sideways like a pair of garden shears—though its exoskeleton is slender, a narrow cage of interlocking muscle and bone.

The Queen, the Queen. She trembles in her presence. *She has birthed me anew.*

Her reverie is broken, but still she cannot scream. She can't scream. She can't wake up. She can't wake or scream or cry, so she twists from it, its gangly limbs loosening their grip. She falls away, back toward the dark pool of life, the cavern lit by engorged tubers that sway from tangled roots draped in diaphanous webs. She spins downward, and right before she hits the liquid surface she spies her reflection in the black water, her mouth a crooked slash warped with shock.

She is a gnarled but graceful tree. A tall gray birch, pale skin peeled from her flesh in strips to expose her lichen-flecked bones.

∞

Elisa jackknifed awake. Her fists released damp clumps of bed-sheets and moved to the stem of her throat, where she ran her fingers along its length, felt for the familiar contours of bone and cartilage. She was herself again. But she no longer knew who that was exactly, and was unwilling to hazard a guess; she'd been wrong too many times before.

She rose from her nap. It had been raining for days, and the sameness of the weather only exacerbated the disconcerting sensation of endlessness she'd felt since her return. Time worked differently now, every hour accordioning down into interminability. Still no sign of Blue. She vaguely recalled telling Jason he could go ahead and book their tickets back to New York, just to get him off her back. But were they scheduled to return tomorrow, or the next day, or was it in fact next week? She couldn't remember. Not that it mattered to her, since she had no intention of leaving. But the indistinct date grew ever closer, and soon she would be forced to tell Jason that should he leave, he'd be going home alone.

She dressed in a red tank top and chocolate brown balloon shorts and went to the dresser to retrieve her camera, the one Detective Jessed had delivered to her hospital room with a pointed knowingness she couldn't place. When she drew back the curtains of the pink room, she was surprised to see the clouds had evaporated, the cove bright with sunlight; the rains had ended at last. A moth was pressed to the outside of the window, where it slowly beat its wings against the screen like a black and dying heart. Elisa flicked at it with her finger until it took to begrudging flight.

She spooled a fresh roll of film into the old Konica and headed downstairs. Jason was on the phone with a patient, one of the dozen or more strangers who depended on him. Elisa drank a cup of coffee and eavesdropped on the session, and was struck by Jason's deliberate and measured tone, the one that said everything was going to be okay. Which of course Jason relished. His clients' desperate clambering for his reassurances was his own source of relief; he needed to be needed. Which must be why she found herself pathologically denying him of it, especially when she needed him most.

She absently brought a hand to her flat belly, then forced herself to return it to her side. Soon, she would bleed. And then she would bleed again.

Elisa went out to the porch, the door swinging shut behind her. *Click-clack.* She stopped short on the far side of the threshold. *You are safe*, she thought, *so long as we are here*.

Gabe was on the porch swing, hunched over a library book and drinking a beer, his golden hair a corona of bright curls in the late-morning sun. The cover of his book depicted a stone carving of a pagan nature spirit, the primitive sculpture's chipped and leering face distorted by protective cellophane.

"Hey." Gabe pointed his chin in her direction. "How are you doing? You need anything?"

"I'm all good, thanks." She looked out at the cove and its emerald sweep of trees, the sunlight glinting off the misted gray water. The pristine beauty of this place was intoxicating; it was easy to see why people were drawn here, and why they ended up staying. She remembered then how Blue, as a joke, had asked her their first morning whether they were going to stay in the cove forever. How dismissive she'd been, how afraid to so much as imagine such a thing, lest her carefully constructed world come tumbling down. Which of course it did anyway.

Gabe eyed her camera. "Going to take some pictures?"

"Thinking about it."

"I was just going to take a stroll by the water. Give me a minute to grab my shoes and I'll go with you."

She motioned to Jason that they were headed to the beach, and he gave her a little wave before going back to his call. Elisa turned back toward the vista and started to shift into a little pirouette as she did so, but she stopped herself.

You don't do that. You don't dance.

But why not?

Because you don't. Not anymore.

But oh, how she loved to dance; she would never stop, not ever. How could she? Just because she no longer pursued it professionally, that didn't mean she wasn't still a dancer at heart. A lifetime spent spinning in studios and on dance floors, in performance spaces and theaters and bars; she would dance in meadows and down country paths, in another place and time. Anything to feel her electrified muscles surging with the life-giving energy that movement provided her. It didn't matter if no one was paying, or even watching. *Only when I'm dancing can I feel this free.*

She had thought she was the girl in "The Red Shoes," that she would dance and dance, maybe even after she died. But then her nemesis, that reliable fiend plantar fasciitis, crept in like Rumpelstiltskin to snatch the temporary gift she'd foolishly considered hers to keep. She should have taken better care of herself, but as was the case with so much in her life, she'd pre-tended instead that everything was just dandy, that there was no reason she couldn't keep on dancing forever, without any true cost. Hubris had gotten her in the end. It was a slow enough process, however, that she saw that ending's arrival long before it came. She'd grown tired of living in an illegal sublet with four other roommates, of the demoralizing and endless audition process, all for projects that only paid half the time, if she was lucky. She began to feel old, and tired, and poor. And suddenly, there was Jason, and she'd, what, chosen him? Or chosen to give something else away?

Gabe returned after a few minutes and they walked down the drive, gravel dust clouding the tips of her ballet flats; Gabe's sneakers, once vivid green, were now a dullish brown, caked in mud and dirt. "I've been spending a lot of time in the woods," he said, noticing her attention. "There are all sorts of interesting things out there. If you know where to look."

She pointed the camera at his feet and released the shutter. *Click-clack.*

As they passed Donald's cabin, she could hear the subdued sound of a barking dog over the blare of opera music. "Donald's dog," she said. "Where was he?"

"I found him two days ago, digging a hole out by the Colony. Going at it like his life depended on it. Took me a half hour just to coax him onto the trail. The poor thing was soaking wet. He was frantic."

"Maybe he was burying something." Gabe didn't reply, only grinned, without showing his teeth.

They walked toward the main road and the rocky beach be-yond. She paused at irregular intervals to shoot pictures: two sandpipers on an electrical wire, the sunlit fringe of leaves atop the tree canopy, Maureen and Donald's place up the hill with the MacLeod house in the background, now some distance away. "I'm glad you found the dog," Elisa said after a while. "Maureen was worried that something might have happened to him."

"I was worried too." Gabe gave her a strange look. "I saw you that night, you know. Last week? Outside Donald's cabin."

"Saw me . . . ?"

"With Olivier." She walked ahead of him without answering. "You were allergic to him," he went on, unimpeded. "Before."

"I must have forgotten," she said; she had no real explanation. She returned the viewfinder to her eye, obscuring her face. "Say cheese." *Click-clack.*

They headed down to the dock. Elisa left her shoes on top of one of the wood pilings and lowered herself onto the thin stretch of beach, while Gabe dropped right into the shallows, sneakers and all. "Let's go this way," he suggested, and pointed up the shoreline, away from town. "There's a sandbar about a half mile from here. You can walk on it and see trout and stuff, just hanging out."

They continued for some time without speaking. She was forced to acknowledge that all they had left to talk about—the only thing they really *should* be talking about—was Blue. "It's okay, you know," she said, breaking the silence. "We can talk about him. If you want."

"Who?" But Gabe couldn't sell it, and stared out at the bay. He pulled a candy bar from his pocket and gnawed on it, while she stuck to the shore and her camera. The water was menacing in its placidity, a hostile sheen with murky shadows moving restlessly beneath.

"I'm so alone," Gabe said then, quite matter-of-factly. He

looked at her, his light blue eyes honing in and penetrating, almost fearsome. "Without him, I mean. You know?"

"Yes." She lowered her camera and shot him from below, allowing him to see her face. "I know exactly what you mean."

"He was special, wasn't he? How he made me feel. Made *us* feel," Gabe qualified, though still in the past tense. "From the second I met him, I felt caught up in something larger than myself, larger than anything I'd ever known." Blue had the same effect on her. He had been her grounding wire ever since their clubland days, her port in those hedonistic rough waters. And she needed him still.

"You love him," Elisa said, and shivered in recognition. She stopped in her tracks, the wet sand cold beneath her bare feet, and took another shot of Gabe's face.

"Come on," he mumbled, and turned away. "The sandbar is right around this bend."

He convinced her to wade beyond the nettle of creeping brambles that clung to the shoreline, the frigid water to her waist as they made their way forward. The sandbar came into view: a five-hundred-foot shoal of pebble and silt jutting out into the bay, its sloping mass disappearing into the water like the neck of a diving loon. There was a near vacuum of noise as they approached: no gulls overhead, no rumble of the occasional flatbed truck from the main road. The shoal was isolated from the rest of the cove, the only way back the same way they had come.

"Peaceful," she said, but didn't mean it. The stillness and seclusion set her on edge.

They went out on the sandbar, the small rocks pinpricks on the soles of her feet. Ignoring the sting, she photographed the path ahead and the intricate pattern made by mussels alongside

the wet polished stone, rendered visible by the receding tide. Gabe kept his attention on the water, his eyes darting back and forth as if in REM sleep, searching something out. There was the faraway sound of a motor as a fishing boat rounded a bend in the cove, its needle-nosed prow a bright lance in the sunlight.

"I like you," Gabe said, eyes fixed on the boat. He scratched at his arm and a bleeding sore there; bug bites stippled his arms, raised red tracks up the twin burrows of his T-shirt sleeves, along his scar-mottled hand. Now he was the one who seemed nervous.

"Thanks." She shielded her eyes; the boat was approaching, headed in the direction of the shoal. "I like you too."

"You said . . ." He coughed and cleared his throat. "You said we were going to find him."

"I said . . ." The boat continued to race toward them. She looked through her camera's viewfinder and zoomed the lens; there were two stooped figures onboard, a small bearded man in a fisherman's cap and someone else. A woman, maybe. "What are they doing?" she whispered.

"At the hospital," Gabe said, ignoring her. "You said that we were going to find Blue."

Was that what she had promised? How could she have said that? She couldn't remember why she'd done such a thing, what had moved her to such certainty. Such a grand declaration, when she no longer felt certain of anything at all.

She lowered the camera and started to back down the sandbar, only to come within inches of colliding with Gabe, who made no attempt to move out of her way. Sweating profusely now, he had a queer expression on his face, obstinate and not a little crazed. "Of course we will," she said, trying to remain calm. "We'll find him. We will."

"I'm really sorry, Elisa." It was hard to hear him over the mosquito whine of the boat's engine. "But don't worry, okay? Nothing bad's going to happen to you. They promised me."

"What are you . . ." The boat was less than twenty yards away before it slowed and turned, a wave kicked up by the wake crashing hard against the shoal. It had come for them. For Elisa. She tried once again to get past Gabe but he blocked her; there was no choice but to stand her ground. Either that or run the other way down the sandbar, the boat coming to a stop beside them. Where else could she go? Right into the bay, the water bracing even in September? Like a butterfly beneath a descending net, she could only watch as it fell.

"Get her up here." The bearded and haggard little man at the wheel reached around the windshield and motioned to Gabe. Closer to the stern was a middle-aged woman, her head obscured by the hood of a yellow rain slicker. She stretched her hand toward Elisa over the side of the boat.

"What the hell is this?" Elisa yelled above the engine. She held herself, the camera strap wound around her arms like tefillin bands. It was an ambush of some kind, though she wasn't scared so much as astonished.

"She doesn't know anything," Gabe said to them. "She doesn't know what she is."

"Get in, sweetheart," the woman said, and this time she thrust her hand out with an unmistakable air of impatience. Now Elisa recognized her: it was their waitress from the other morning at the Lobster Landing, the rude one. She tried to remember the name on her plastic name tag.

"No way." Elisa shook her head as if attempting to loose it from her neck. "I'm not going anywhere with you."

"We can help each other," the bearded man said, his eyes

steely and unreadable. "We can help you figure out where you've been. You'll be safe with us."

She turned to Gabe, and he gave her an imploring look. They wanted the same thing. If this could help find him, how could she refuse?

"You don't have to," Gabe said meekly. "It's your choice."

"Some choice." Elisa unraveled her camera strap, slung it around her neck, and reached for the woman's hand.

∞

The boat's guttural engine drowned out any attempt Elisa made to question her unlikely captors. She settled onto a hard bench at the stern and looked out at the water, tried to get her bearings in case she needed to find her way back. No words were exchanged, not until well after the boat was docked on the opposite side of the cove. They walked a single-file line along a thin wooded trail—the bearded man in front, Gabe and the waitress bringing up the rear—to a ramshackle cottage set amid a copse of diseased-looking birch trees.

The little man introduced himself as Fred Cronin, and the cottage as his house. A local ironsmith and newsletter publisher, he was a friend of Maureen and Donald's; Elisa remembered him now from the ceilidh, and how he'd taken pictures all night, his vintage Leica almost an extension of his long beard. She stroked the lens of her own camera and thought to do the same.

Inside the cottage, the smell of stale cigarette smoke hung like cobwebs from the rafters. The clutter was staggering—newspapers stacked to the ceiling, sagging shelves of books and nautical maps and heavy chunks of crystalline granite, complicated steel contraptions of unknown provenance shoved into every corner. By the door, a half dozen identical hiking packs rested against the wall, each one crowned by a mining helmet and a lengthy coil of what looked to be rope for rock climbing or spelunking.

A jittery woman, bright red hair and about Elisa's age, jumped up from the floor at the sight of her. "You're beautiful," the woman exclaimed, then covered her mouth with one hand, the other fingering a golden angel pendant on a chain around her neck. A skinny teenager with a constellation of acne at the corner of his mouth paced before the shade-drawn windows in a narrow lane cleared of debris. He reminded Elisa of her first boyfriend, but when she gave him a little nod his gaze moved from her face. Beneath one of the windows was a wrynecked boy of five or six, his eyes lost beneath a shaggy tangle of brown bangs. He took no notice of her whatsoever.

Fred directed Elisa to a dilapidated black couch. The pimply young man and the waitress sat on either side of her, Fred in an adjacent plastic chair; Gabe remained standing, while the red-head returned to her spot on the floor. Their host poured what smelled like whisky-spiked tea into a thermos lid and placed it before Elisa. "We were waiting for you to get out of the hospital. But then the rains came," Fred said in a raw voice, and sipped straight from the thermos, sunken eyes trained upon her. He lit a cigarette with quivering hands, waved out the match and tossed it onto the coffee table's scratched glass surface, missing an overflowing ashtray. "We have a pretty simple request. We want you to take us to the place where you and your friend were hiding out all this time."

"I don't remember where I was," Elisa said. "But even if I did, I doubt I would tell you. I don't even know who you people are."

Fred laughed weakly. "Fair enough. But just so you know, we come in peace. Give us a chance to put your mind at ease."

He introduced the redhead as Tanya; the Lobster Landing waitress as Patricia; and the young man as Patricia's son Colin, and now Elisa could see they shared the same equine features. Patricia said the boy by the window was hers as well; he was occupying himself with a set of rusty-bladed safety scissors and a magazine, its pages freshly serrated and foxed with mold. Other than the little boy, they were all staring at her, rapt.

Fred dragged off his cigarette, the smoke corkscrewing heavenward from the ember's tip. "At the end of the day," he said, "we're people of like mind and common purpose. I guess you could say that we're a group of believers."

"Believers in what?" Elisa said.

"Well, one thing we all believe in is you."

"What's to believe in?"

"That remains to be seen." Fred bent over the side of his seat and rummaged along a low makeshift bookcase of bricks and boards, as Gabe looked on with unease. Eventually he surfaced with a stack of decomposing newspapers, sorted a few from the pile, and handed them to her. "Take a look at these," he said. "I'm not sure how much you know."

Beneath the *Cape Breton Post* nameplate and the edition date of Saturday, October 2, 1981, was the headline LOCAL BOY AND GIRL GO MISSING. Elisa scanned through the papers, then went back to the first article and the photograph of the boy. It was Blue's five-year-old face beneath a mop of black hair, so young but still utterly, painfully unmistakable. She glanced up at the little boy at the window before she touched her fingers to the faded newsprint and the photo of Blue, his picture printed beside that of a moonfaced girl named Gavina, as well as a detail of the star-shaped birthmark on her shoulder.

"Blue didn't know any of this," Elisa said, and shook her

head. "He only found out when he was going through his grandmother's things. That very day, before we were taken."

"Taken." Fred smiled, his teeth brown and decayed; one
tooth flashed silver, while a few more were missing altogether.
"So you do remember something." He lit another cigarette from
the end of the last. "Tell me," he said, and leaned across the
coffee table, close enough that she caught a whiff of his sour
breath. "What do you remember about being taken?"

*A rolling shadow across the bathroom ceiling, and she gasps. Ev-
erything slowing to near stillness as the bathwater rapidly solidifies,
trapping her like a fly in amber.* "I hardly remember anything,"
she said.

"Tell us what you do remember." Fred coughed and cleared
his throat, expectorating into a black-and-white bandanna he
discreetly produced from the breast pocket of his discolored
shirt.

"Please, Elisa," Gabe said. "We need to make sure you're . . .
okay."

She looked away, avoiding their pleading eyes. The cork-
board beside the mantel teemed with alarming images: thumb-
tacked sketches of insect parts that were almost perversely
magnified; a photograph of the dark mouth of a cave flooded
with water; what appeared to be a desiccated old fruit label,
adorned with an illustration of a Cottingley-style fairy seated
upon a rock. She shuddered and turned from the wall, and the
sight of Gabe's expectant face hollowed out a new groove in her
chest.

Elisa didn't trust any of them as far as she could spit, not
even Gabe. But she needed them, for their knowledge if nothing else. She closed her eyes.

"I was in the bathtub. I remember . . . a face. Someone leaning over me." *Not someone,* she thought, and pressed the heels of her wrists into her eye sockets.

A wide face with saucer eyes made up of smaller aspects, the compound eyes of an unclassifiable insect. A face she knows well, though stripped of its mask of muscle and pale skin.

And as she breaks the water's surface—just before its sinewy fingers lengthen to cup the back of her skull—she sees inside it. Right through its patchwork casing, the tarnished grim birdcage of its chest where no heart beats but instead rests a heart-shaped stone, ripped from a hole in the earth. She sees right into it.

"Blue," she whispered. Her hands moved from her eyes to her mouth, short and brittle nails tugging at her lower lip. "The thing that took me . . . It was Blue. There were others too, others like him. But they weren't . . . He's not . . ."

"Human," Fred said, and nodded. "He isn't human."

"Yes." She swallowed hard, took a cigarette from Fred's pack on the coffee table and stuck it into her mouth; it took him a few moments to realize she was waiting for him to light it. It tasted awful, poisonous, but she smoked it anyway. "So what is he, then?" she asked.

"He's Other Kind. Old-timers here, they call them the Fae. We believe your friend was a replacement. That he was swapped out for Michael Whitley, when the boy and Gavina Beaton went missing."

"That's crazy," Elisa said. But her words had no conviction. Memories flooded her mind, of Blue as she once knew him. Of his fingers around her waist as she pushed him onto his unmade bed, her own hands gripping the hard muscle of his sweat-slicked arms as he bucked beneath her. She couldn't wrap her mind around it. It did make some kind of bizarre sense, though, as if Blue were too radiant a thing to be born of man. Yet they had always been a pair, an undifferentiated dyad. Shouldn't that mean she was radiant as well?

Elisa looked up at the expectant faces of the believers. "He didn't know what he was," she said. "He thought he was like the rest of us."

"Sound familiar?" Patricia said under her breath.

"Excuse me?" Elisa said.

"Put a lid on it, Patty," Fred snapped. "You know how this is going down."

"Don't you talk to her that way," Colin said.

Elisa glanced around then: at Fred, the mousy and wild-eyed Tanya clutching her angel pendant, the sardonic waitress, Patricia, and her gangly, surly son. They were all buzzing with nervous energy, their skulls in frantic motion; they resembled a band of bobblehead dolls. Gabe vibrated as well. Only the little boy was relatively still, busy mutilating his magazine by the window. The sound of his clacking scissors was hypnotic, and she tried not to close her eyes, not to let the darkness pull her back to the place below the world and its spiraling catacombs.

"The thing is," Fred said, "we need you to take us to them. This is a real big opportunity for us. Some of us have been waiting a long time for a proper guide, and a lot more have gone before us and never returned. So basically, you're our best chance. And we don't have a lot of time."

"They're dying," Gabe said. Patricia shot him a look. "Fred and Colin both."

Elisa stared at Fred in disbelief. The man turned toward Colin, whose eyes were fixed upon the floor. Fred reached out and clapped his hand to the teenager's shoulder in an affectionate gesture, a surprise considering they were just at each other's throats. "We've got cancer," Fred said. "I got it in both lungs. Final stage. Colin has lymphoma."

"They've given me two months." Colin shrugged the shrug of any teenager. He was hard to look at in that moment, his vibrant glow so deceptive that Elisa wanted to cry.

"There's always been talk about the Other Kind," Patricia said, her voice tender for the first time. "Them and their healing properties." She swallowed, hard. "They can change a person. Make a new version of them, a better version, body and soul. No more disease, no more pain, no nothing." Patricia peered at her son with adoration. "We thought that maybe, since you were . . . *with* them, then . . ." She let her thought hover in the air.

"Then what?" Elisa said.

"Then maybe we could be with them too. Then Colin and Fred, they could be changed. We could all be changed, if we wanted."

"Changed?"

"Yes. Like you were."

"What are you talking about?"

"Come on, girl," Patricia said, her harsh tone returned. "No need to pretend, not with us. We've seen your kind before. All the signs are there."

"You're different now," Gabe said. "Admit it. You're obviously different now."

"If not actually one of them," Colin added.

"I'm not *one* of anybody," Elisa said. "I'm only of me." *Go*, a voice inside her said. *Just go. Make a run for it. And never look back.*

"That's what Blue thought, though," Gabe said. "Wasn't it?"

Fred coughed, sudden and violent, then gathered himself.

"Is there anything else you remember, about how you left? When you went, was it down inside the Fairy Hole beneath the mountain? Or through the old rum-running tunnels, maybe?"

"It's hard to say." She shook her head. "They took me through the woods, I don't remember where. But when we got there I could smell smoke. Something was burning . . ."

"Goddamned Christ Church strikes again," Patricia muttered. "Still trying to burn them out. Every time the Kind show their faces, some Christer reaches for his torch. When are they gonna learn?"

"When we get them all off the force, that's when," Fred said. He returned his attention to Elisa. "Go on, then. Tell us what else you remember."

She stared at him. Past him, through the walls of the battened-down house and all the way into the woods, the swaying trees a gate through which she could pass at any time. She forced herself to focus and looked down at the floor, her bare feet, took a final and deep drag off the cigarette, which made her light-headed. The last remaining dirt cleared from the coffin of her memory, and Elisa prized open the lid.

"There . . . There was something I left there," she said quietly.

Beneath the ground, in the place below the world. Down here the earth is cool, the dirt moist from their excretions, like wet dough between her fingers. The sound of heavy dripping, of movement nearby. She tries to lift her head but it's fixed to the vertical bed of shale beneath her, a striated shelf adorned with petrified boughs of knotted birch and carved with arcane sigils.

The ones that brought her gather around, elongated faces rendered as dark shadows along the cavern walls and lit by their own bioluminescence. Their hands upon her, feeling her. And where she suffers their touch she is anesthetized, numbed by a thousand injections of paralyzing venom.

Branchlike fingers upon her belly, her thighs, creeping tendrils moving up inside of her . . .

"Oh, Jesus." Elisa doubled over and retched. She tried to expel the feeling—the appalling sensation of invasiveness beneath her skin—but all that came up was a bilious strand of saliva and mucus that stank of seawater.

"They took it," she said, her mind racing. Her unborn child, it was still alive. There was no question in her mind. "They took it out of me . . ."

"What is she saying?" Colin said. "What does she mean?"

"A baby," Patricia said. "She's talking about a baby."

"I told you," Gabe snapped. "I told all of you. She really was pregnant."

"Doesn't matter," Fred said. "If there was a baby, it was never really hers."

"What are you talking about?" Elisa rose to her full height and stared them down, bored holes inside each and every one of them, Gabe included. "Whose was it, if not mine?"

"The girl you replaced," Fred said. "Elisa Howard. Not you."

"I am her!" she shouted, more afraid than anything that she wanted them to be right. *No. They're wrong, they must be. They're all insane.* "I am Elisa," she pleaded, if only to herself. "Have you lost your minds?"

"They probably have her right now," Fred said. "Sent you out into the world as her double. Just like they did with the kids." He spoke with tenderness, real sorrow in his eyes. "You need to get back there, though, don't you? Find your friend. And this baby."

"They took it out of me," Elisa whispered; it was all she could think of to say. She was sure of it, defiance solidifying her judgment, fueling her sense of violation as well. She was sick at the thought, all else rendered insignificant by comparison. How could Blue have helped them do that, no matter what he had become?

The matters of these supposed believers no longer held meaning. She needn't prove herself to them, didn't need them for anything whatsoever. *Fuck Blue. Fuck them all.* Below the earth, in the place below the world, was something that had belonged to her, and had been stolen. A child. Her child.

But there was something else she'd lost beyond the child, beyond Blue even. The inability to give voice to it made her increasingly despairing, and furious.

"Show us, then." Fred's face flushed red, and he brought it close to her own. "Go on. You can do it. Take us under the mountain."

"Just do what he says, sweetheart," Patricia said, agitated to the point of twitching. "This doesn't have to be difficult. Just do what he says."

"She will." Fred seized Elisa by the arm. "Even if it takes a little convincing."

He hauled her toward the door, and Patricia and Colin jumped out of their seats. They were all standing, all of them yelling. Neither Fred nor Elisa paid attention to the others. Fred focused only on her, while Elisa went inside herself, to that faraway place beneath the land and waves.

"You're going to take us there," Fred said, and threw open the front door with his free hand. "And you're going to do it now. Colin, get the gear."

"Get off me." Elisa yanked her arm loose, her hands bending into claws. "You touch me again and I'll kill you. I will fucking end you."

"Leave her alone," Gabe said. He made a move toward Fred, but Colin pushed him toward the middle of the room. Gabe stumbled and fell in a dust cloud of newspapers before he sprung up, a feral glint in his eyes. Patricia leapt in front of her son to protect him, but Tanya yelled, "Stop it, just stop it!" and jerked Patricia sideways by the hood of her slicker. The waitress snagged Tanya by her hair and pulled her yowling back down to the threadbare rug.

Is it me? Elisa took in the chaos unfolding around her. *Am I the root of all this?* She felt her emotions radiating out from her in viral pulsations, her wrath and righteousness a boiling wave of anger burning whomever it touched; her fury had spread to the others. It was what had happened at the Lobster Landing, only this time instead of a frenzied delirium she was channeling a white-hot rage, powerful enough to scald. All she could see was flames.

Fire. Choking smoke. Scorched catacomb walls and the throne room aflame as the warning blares through the hive and the warrens. Protect the Queen, protect the Queen . . .

Elisa trembled and covered her face with her hands. Another crashing wave, another transmitted message, a signal sent by collective command. *Go. Just go. Run.*

"Are you okay?" Gabe, at her side.

"I think . . . I think I have to go." She moved so quickly she fell against the screen door as she bolted onto the porch.

"Not so fast," Fred said, already upon her. He grabbed her by the wrist and twisted, and she dropped to her knees, her camera slung over one arm so the strap dug into her bare shoulder and tangled in Fred's iron grip. The world listed around her, the cracked eaves and crumpled rain gutter and the darkening sky beyond, her stomach churning like a storm-tossed ship. She shielded her face with her free arm, and something moved in the corner of her vision. She turned in its direction, the scattered motion coalescing into the shape of her husband as he ascended the porch steps.

Fred, exposed in the doorway, released her as Jason reached forward with both hands. He took hold of Fred by his stained plaid shirt, and in one graceful, balletic motion, swung the little man over the porch railing. Fred crashed through the overgrown hedges with a cry of pain laced with shock. Elisa crab-crawled back and flattened against the cottage's vinyl siding, a queasy thrill of delight roiling her.

A flash of light beamed over them: the red and blue spray of a police siren from a CBRP vehicle parked in the drive. Jason, his eyes narrowed with determination, marched down the porch stairs. Another man was waiting there, a uniformed police officer. It was Detective Jessed, the one who had interviewed Elisa at the hospital; he and Jason must have arrived together in the patrol car. Jessed dragged Fred up from his knees, only to drive him back down with a blow to the side of the head. He followed with a second punch, and a third, Fred trying to push away, to protect his face. The entire scene felt unnervingly removed. It was as if she were watching a nature documentary, one about predatory birds, perhaps, bright flashes of plumage masking talons and beaks. Gabe and Patricia and the others spilled onto the porch and froze, all of them silenced by the sight of Detective Jessed whaling on Fred, until Gabe screamed, "Stop it! He's going to die!"

Jason, startled to attention, looked at Gabe in bewilderment, then to Colin's little brother in the doorway of the cottage. The boy just stood there watching, the shredded remains of his magazine clutched in his hand. Jessed relented and let up on Fred, only to push Jason back toward the porch, as though he were the one doing the beating.

Gabe knelt at Elisa's side. "I am so sorry," he said. "Please, are you okay? Elisa?" But he didn't seem sure of what to call her.

Fred spat a mouthful of blood onto the wet grass, as well as what looked to be a blackened tooth. "You attacked me," Fred gargled through swollen lips, and glared in Jessed's direction. "Right here, in front of everyone. They all saw it."

"Save it, Cronin." Jessed thrust forward an admonitory finger, his hand sheathed in a menacing leather glove that matched his shark-black eyes. "Not another word out of you. Not one." He cast a sideways glance at Jason, daring him to speak.

"We know you're special, no matter what you are." Tanya, no longer able to contain herself, threw herself before Elisa, a supplicant kneeling at an altar. "We need you," she said, and began to weep. "We meant no harm. None at all. Don't judge us too harshly. Please." Tanya choked back sobs, closed her eyes, and pressed her hands together. "We look upon the people of the mounds and see only God's face in their design. We see only his merciful angels . . ."

"Jesus and Mary," Patricia said, rolling her eyes. "Here she goes again."

Jason stepped back onto the porch. "Did they do anything to you?" he asked Elisa. "Did they hurt you?"

She shook her head fiercely; not in answer, but because his words no longer had meaning. All their words were meaningless, as was the sentiment behind them. Who were these people, coming to blows over her as if she were chattel, a prize offered up in a contest? She belonged to none of them, to no one in this world. She only belonged to herself.

"Please," Jason said, "Elisa," and he reached for her, his fingers inches from her face. *A trap*. All of it just another trap to keep her tied to this wearisome place, where she could only be wife, or daughter, or mother. Who knew how long ago it had been set?

She rose and backed down the porch steps. One step, then another, and a third, bare feet on wood, then gravel, then grass. And then she turned and ran, the camera strap flung over her shoulder, the Konica case thumping against her with every stride. Jessed called out for her to stop. She heard footfalls behind her but she kept running, straight for the trees at the back of the house.

Elisa crashed through the bracken and into the woods, and instead of resisting her the branches parted, limbs clasping shut in her wake as if to protect her. The sound of those giving chase echoed through the brush. Despite the rains, she could still smell the burned musk of the forest fires smoldering in the distance, and the bitter scent enlivened her, awakening her senses. She felt free, for the first time since she'd returned.

These woods, they could be her home now, and perhaps they had always been, only waiting for her to accept their verdant embrace. She knew how well the dark forest would hide her, if she asked in its own language. If only she asked, she would never be found again.

Chapter Nine

She awoke in the woods before dawn, the cloud cover bruised violet with diffuse moonlight. Back arched like a cat, she stretched on all fours and ran her hands along the forest floor, across pine needles and beetle shells and acorns, rocks and wet leaves and muddy clumps of dirt, as well as the hard cracked leather of her camera case. She curled into a ball and pushed herself into child's pose, the earth beating beneath her in a slow and steady pulse that echoed across the tree canopy.

There was something else, though. A stubborn barb that tugged at her subconscious, extracting a terrible sensation of loss. She had been down there, in the place below the world, and they had not kept her. Blue hadn't kept her. The rejection was coupled with a whisper in her own voice—incanted from the trees, on the wind, within the flutelike cries of thrushes—all of it saying, *You are still Elisa.* She didn't know who that meant anymore, only that the thought had wriggled into her mind and embedded itself there. In place of her unborn child, perhaps, the one extracted like a splinter from beneath her skin. How much of her had they kept?

As the sun rose and the low mist began to burn off, she continued through the woods, a powerful, lodestone draw pulling her forward on bare and battered feet. By midday the peak of Kelly's Mountain was visible through the trees, the sheltering branches throwing shadows across the forest floor. When was the last time she had eaten? She couldn't say, only that she felt hunger as a dull void, close to her without quite being imperative. Her thirst, though, that was ever-present, and she followed the sound of rushing water to a snaking creek, where she left her camera atop a large rock at the crest of the bank. She scooped her hands into the shallow stream and brought the salve to her parched lips, as well as to her muddied face and neck, its revitalizing coolness a gift from higher ground. She washed her feet, her thighs beneath her shorts, her arms, skin glistening as she padded back up the mossy bank.

She froze. Unquestionably, she knew that she was not alone. She took cover in the undergrowth and grabbed her camera from the rock, crouching to hug her arms around her dirty red shirt for fear it would give her away. Whether she was more afraid of the supposed believers or the so-called Other Kind was uncertain. *Keep me from what I am not*, she thought, and she grinned, though her flesh was pebbled with fear.

Above the call of birds and the whirring of insects there was a rustling sound in the brush, accompanied by a stench of decay, like rotted vegetables. She covered her nose and peered through the thicket.

An ashen, wraithlike shape lumbered through the grove. Though its pace was middling at best, Elisa struggled to track it behind the dense shrubbery. It ambled into a sunlit clearing not fifty yards away, and rested against a tree trunk, pressing itself to the bark as if to slink its way inside.

It was a woman. She was tall and thin and nude, her skin pale white where it wasn't caked in grime, hippie-long hair matted down in a snakelike plait against the side of her face. Elisa stepped from behind the bushes; her first instinct was to see if the woman was hurt. Once she showed herself, however, the stranger's head snapped to the side. Elisa recoiled: the left side of the woman's face, the one previously obscured, bore the brutal scarring of fourth-degree burns. Most of her hair was singed free from her ruined scalp, the flesh there bubbled like melted candle wax. She looked as if she might have stumbled from the scene of an accident, though there was a disturbing and unmistakable sneer upon her lips.

She's a slave, Elisa thought, a flare of recognition ignited inside of her. *A human worker for the hive. I've seen her kind before.* She didn't know how she knew this to be true, she just knew that it was. In the same way she was sure there was an explanation she hadn't been rendered a slave herself. Elisa had come back for a reason.

The woman approached from across the clearing, skin blotchy and red. By the time they were a few yards from each other, Elisa could see her milky left eye, a dribble of yellow pus down her cheek. The fluid collected in a raised ditch of soft tissue above her exposed clavicle, bones dirty-gray against raw and bloodied meat. The burned woman shuffled toward her, but when they were about to collide she shunted past, attention drawn farther into the woods. As she wandered from her, Elisa caught sight of the woman's exposed back: there on her shoulder was an angry red birthmark, the scarlet blemish shaped like a five-pointed star.

"Gavina?" Elisa recognized the distinguishing mark from the newspaper clippings, though it hardly seemed possible, she had drowned twenty-five years ago.

But no, Elisa thought, *that had been a replacement.* The one that had died, that was something else in disguise, like Blue. This was the real Gavina Beaton, the original one, the human girl who had wandered into the woods with Michael Whitley. Still alive, albeit injured in the recent fires, and all grown up.

Goddamned Christ Church strikes again, one of the believers had said. *Still trying to burn them out.*

The woman stopped. She slowly torqued her body with another unnerving snap of the neck that made Elisa grit her teeth.

"Can you speak?" Elisa asked softly. "Can you?"

She groaned in response, a wretched squall of mourning that echoed like thunder through the trees. She was weeping now as well, watery runnels carving channels down her dirty cheeks, the pain of hard labor written across her face. It was Gavina, Elisa was sure of it, the woman's eyes wet and glazed. Stupefied in her servitude to the Other Kind, she saw things that weren't really there. One eye was cataract pale, while the other contained a pupil that was barely discernible, almost lensless, like a pinhole camera.

My camera. Elisa had forgotten she had it, its stiff leather strap weighing down her neck. She flicked off the lens cap and shot from her chest. Gavina flinched, and rotated her head back toward the close-set trees, followed by the rest of her blistered body.

Through a daunting obstacle course of clustered foliage Gavina shuffled forward, Elisa on her trail and continuing to snap pictures. Gavina gained in speed, first a trot and then, despite her obvious injuries, accelerating into a full-blown gallop. Elisa struggled to keep up, the camera dropping to her chest as she raised her hands to shield her face from the trees' lashing boughs. Faster and faster they careered into the heart of the forest, weaving their way between crowding firs, Gavina moving with the inborn grace of an animal negotiating its native environment.

Soon, the vegetation began to lighten. The now-cloudless sky widened in broad blue patches above the thinning treetops, the ground roughening beneath Elisa's bare feet. A whistle of wind, the smell of the sea and the smoldering forest fires, and Gavina hurtled through the tangled briar and disappeared into thin air.

Elisa barely had time to stop. She scrambled for leverage with the help of a weathered root and managed to halt her momentum. It was only once her eyes focused in the bright and unshielded light that she saw she was perched atop a craggy precipice overlooking the bay. Far below, Gavina was in free fall above the waves. Forty feet, fifty and more, her previously unwieldy form arrowing at the last moment into the clean line of an expert cliff diver. The woman vanished into the water, the aggressive red burst of her star-shaped birthmark the last thing visible, barely a ripple left in her wake.

Elisa stared down at the waves. Their silvery caps glittered in the wide-open light, the sun bright above the peak of Kelly's Mountain. The mountain was suddenly so close, oppressively so, hovering over the water like a massive, glutted seabird. *Down there is refuge and communion*, she thought, *below the mountain and sea*. Gavina seemed to believe that as well, and a stab of envy pierced Elisa's chest.

She scaled up a tangled mass of foliage, edged herself toward the lip of the cliff, and dangled her foot out over the crashing waves. Her soles bloodied and bruised, as her feet so often were, back when she was still a working dancer. More than two months since she'd last gotten a pedicure, when she stopped into a nail salon down on Hester Street back in New York, her clear polish grown out quite a bit in the weeks since to reveal the unvarnished white crescent slivers of the lunulae beneath.

A *pedicure*. A stupid eighteen-dollar pedicure. Elisa clung to the memory of it: the ladies gossiping in Chinese, the acrid smell from the dryer, the rattle and buzz of the air conditioner over the door. And that transparent nail polish, still on her feet . . . Could they—the ones that had birthed Blue, in whatever way he had been made—could they have been so subtle, so precise as to replicate a grown-out pedicure? Could they have recreated something so cosmetic, so artificial and mundane?

She felt real all of a sudden. A real woman, with real memories, and all-too-human feelings. The same woman who had gotten that pedicure downtown, who had a best friend named Blue and a husband named Jason and a whole life ahead of her, with or without them. Children or no, career or no, yes or no or no. She was who she was, for better or worse; she was who she had always been. The believers had been wrong.

Let divers dive, she thought, and stepped away from the edge. *I'm not one of them, whoever they are.* She knew this now.

Elisa sat at the cliff side. She would never be one of the Other Kind, not really; she would never be made of this land. But still she wondered if she could live without what was stolen from her body, as well as the ecstatic reverie the Other Kind provided in unending supply, down in the place below the world.

Could she live without Blue, and the state of amazement he himself had given her? So much wonder, and light.

Years and years ago the two of them, high on ketamine, had stumbled early one morning out of the Roxy and onto the hot summer pavement. As they tried to hail a cab, a group of soused frat boys stumbled past and one of them reached over and pinched her hard on the ass. She yelped, and Blue, barely able to stand, spun around to confront them. "What the fuck?" he'd said, staggering forward. "You got a problem?"

"Yeah, you, faggot," a second one said and sucker-punched him in the face. Down he went, and before the bouncers could intervene they had piled on and gotten a few kicks in him as well, though Elisa had tried her best to beat them back. Blue was badly shaken, and as they sat on the curb to collect themselves she watched his nose begin to swell.

"You okay?" she asked, and rubbed slow circles upon his back.

"Sure," he said, "sure I am." But when he brought a hand to his nose it came back red. Blue stared down at the blood and his eyes went wide: the wet stain on his fingers was interlaced with a thread of prismatic material. The shining fluid was denser than the blood surrounding it, and seemed to move of its own volition, the iridescent strand writhing eel-like inside a dark scarlet pool. Elisa's throat caught. Her heart heaved, along with a lust so powerful the whole of her body shook. She opened her mouth, but couldn't speak.

A moment later, the luminous substance shimmered and melted into the red smear upon his fingers, disappearing from sight. They stared at his blood-slicked hand in silence.

"Did you see that?" he eventually said. She was about to nod, but when she met Blue's gaze she was shocked to find his nose had contracted to its regular size. But then it swelled again, and just as quickly shrunk once more, as if deciding whether or not to appear broken. It was the drugs, it had to be. What else?

"See what?" Elisa said, the coward's route. But it couldn't be unseen.

They sat on the curb until Blue's fear receded, and she had tamed her own panting breath. And then a rat scurried past them, and she screamed, and he cackled hysterically as he got down in the gutter on all fours. "Go get those fuckers, Ratsy!"

Blue shouted, and suddenly she was laughing so hard she couldn't breathe.

Could she live without Blue? *Look what happened to his mother*, Elisa thought, and shook her head. The moment he'd left her home, the poor woman began wasting away. Was that Elisa's fate as well, to die alone and apart from both Blue and her own not-yet-a-child, the one they had made together? And if she were to return to the Other Kind, what would that make her? A mother to her child, or a slave, like Gavina? She had no way of knowing.

She turned back toward the woods, and the air before her rippled, like heat off a tar road. The trees lurched, fearfully, though all else was still; even the ocean fell quiet. The hair on her arms stood at attention, as if she'd crossed into a field of static electricity. The silence was pierced by a rumbling cacophony, a ferocious braying fused with a rapturous buzzing that lashed the branches and sent a startled squirrel scrambling from its burrow. Everywhere at once there was a charge of movement, as the forest widened its mouth and screamed.

An onslaught of assorted figures crashed through the verdant foliage. Partially nude men, their clothes tattered and burned, one with his foot clomping inside a laceless hiking boot; soot-stained dogs, their hides singed by fire; a scatter of red foxes, a small black bear, a pair of hawks, a large gray cat; and more. They were running from the fires, or perhaps from something else. Slave workers all, a wild hunt of living creatures that had fallen under the Other Kind's spell. They came in such a rush that Elisa barely had time to drop to her knees and cover her head with her arms. In and among them was a swarm of green lights, a rush of blinding incandescent forms flittering about as the stampede of life surged past her, over her, a dazzling migration tumbling over the cliffs in a wave. *Will-o'-wisp before them went, sent forth a twinkling light* . . . Donald's lovely melody battered her as she was nearly swept off the precipice herself, the sound of whistling wind and bodies pelting the water below.

The land fell silent once more. She dared to lean over the edge, the rippling water illuminated by fading contrails of brilliant green. *And soon she saw the fairy bands all riding in her sight.* Her heart raced, it sung; she was terrified, but also strangely, powerfully high. She stood to watch the fading web of radiance dissolve beneath the waves, like a school of diving jellyfish.

Elisa waited for some time before she turned with reluctance from the cliff. But still she wasn't alone. A figure formed in her path, a sparkling beam of light birthed out of nothingness, from an incision slashed through the air. Something had stayed behind.

It was difficult to see in its entirety—indeed, it was impossible. Relatively human in shape, it was a shadow that lacked concrete form, one that used the surrounding landscape to delineate itself. About half a foot taller than her, slit-thin while still manifestly solid, it was a murky, reedy creature that stank of semen and saltwater, of mulch and rancidity and putrefaction. Its lean appendages hung like felled branches at its narrow sides, like Gavina's lank and ravaged arm.

This is no dream, Elisa thought, and wiped both sweat and tears from her cheeks. *This is a thing of terrible beauty.*

She shuddered, and the being stirred as if in response, raising its left arm in a stilted gesture. She mirrored it, raised her right one in imitation. Its spindly arm tapered and concaved into a rough sickle shape; this she mirrored as well. It slunk forward and conversely became harder to discern, but for the pronged shapes its feet left on the damp moss. She glided in its direction, an arm cupped before her as if preparing for an embrace.

It's just like dancing. Like Madame Farber's ballet class in fourth grade, when she first learned how to move with a partner. As the creature shifted closer, its swampy reek sweetened, citrus tanging the air. And then its face appeared, gleaming and moist. The outline of its wide domed eyes emerged, almost as an apparition, along with the shape of its scooped and bisected mouth. Elisa swayed on her feet like a stubborn leaf, a seagull in an updraft.

The thing trembled before her, nearly indistinguishable from the shifting ferns in its wake, green fiddlehead patterns a thousand fingerprints smudged upon bright sea glass. Elisa reached out, and it reached back, a nebulous motion that brought them within inches of each other. Was it mirroring her now? Impossible to tell, only that they seemed to move as one. Heat radiated from its body of bark and bone, a throb of white starlight that washed over her in a wave that tasted of plant sap.

Another pulsation and it was a razor's breadth away. She could feel it examining every inch of her, inside and out. She still could not see it exactly, but it was here just the same, right here, made up of things from the wood. And as with the forest, Elisa felt renewed in the creature's presence, the way a lost soul must feel when it is saved. Never before had she sensed the presence of God, or anything close to divine grace. Never, except when she was with her best friend, the only person she had ever belonged to without question.

She wrapped her arms around it and placed her hands on its back, where she took up flesh of dew-damp bark and frayed quill, as well as a sticky ooze beneath her cracked nails, her fingers roaming the same way they had explored the forest floor upon waking. Everything in this moment was real, everything wild. She could feel it all, right down to the bone.

"Blue," she whispered.

Her eyes widened, and for a split second she saw him, the old him. Gorgeous and flawed with his crooked wry smile, yes, but more as he was when she'd first met him—younger and fuller of face, a curtain of home-dyed hair draped across his cheek in a crest of blue and black. As soon as she locked on to his eyes, however, the familiar bottle-green ones that had held her so long in their sway, she found herself gazing up at the tree canopy instead. He had slipped from her grasp, her arms still cradled in front of her as if in a pas de deux. But it was him.

"Blue?" she called out. *Where has he gone?*

Movement a few feet away, along the edge of the cliff. She carefully tread along the lichened rocks and followed a vague impression of his retreating shape, his tracks like two fork hoes in the grass and accompanied by a scritch-scratch sound of pen nibs on stiff parchment.

"Wait!" she cried. "What about our child?"

Blue froze by the edge of the cliff. Before she could help herself, she hurried forward and reached for him. She grasped his arm, and a convulsion of energy surged through her.

A nimbus of pulsating light, drawing her deeper into the throne room. High above, the wounded Queen deteriorates in her nest, the sound of her fire-damaged wings thrumming through the catacombs and punctuated by the crackling of embers. Fleshy and swollen tubers hang from the ceiling, discolored opalescent grubs that should be beating with emergent life but are instead puckered and scorched black with decay.

Below the nest is Blue, his flint-gray arms cradling something that looks like a woman, though one that is made of birch. They sway, as if dancing. Its face is Elisa's face, its womb her womb, and inside of it, inside . . .

A keening wail sounded everywhere at once, a dazzling assault so invasive that she fell once more to her knees. She struggled to right herself, afraid she might tumble over the edge to the bay below as the world spun out from beneath her. But Blue was there to steady her. He brought her away from the edge, and gently lowered her to the wet grass.

the unborn
it will
be
safe

Blue, inside her head. The sound of the words excruciating, his multilayered voice intoxicating to the point of nausea.

go
live
in this world
while you still can
you chose to leave
us
once
already

She managed to stand, but he was already bounding away toward the cliff in a flutter of dust and the lightning crack of hollow bone upon rock. The slender line of his spine, a glimpse of his gray paper-birch hide as he vaulted over the precipice as if launched from a springboard. She ran back to the cliff's edge and watched him fall, his protean shape flickering as he crashed through the waves in an arc of bright emerald light.

Elisa placed one hand upon her stomach, then higher to

where the camera rested against her chest. Too late, but she released the shutter nevertheless, in the vain hope of capturing the blur of motion through the dimming waters before he disappeared entirely.

∝

It was midafternoon when she crossed the familiar trail that led past the Colony, the weathered sign in the shape of a light green fairy pointing the way into the woods. She resisted entering the old burned-out husk, and remained instead by the covered well out back, its bucket long since lost to nature. She recalled a fairy tale she'd once heard, about a nixie surfacing from a well; she thought it might have had a happy ending. But that wasn't Elisa's story. She was no fairy. Was Blue? Donald seemed to think so, didn't he? All Elisa was sure of was that Blue was a creature born of this land and below it, a species heretofore unknown to her but as real as any human being.

And what had Blue and Elisa's story been, after all, but a kind of fairy tale, ever since the halcyon haze of their youth? Despite all that had happened to them, that fact had not changed, not really. She and Blue were living a different kind of tale altogether, and she told it to herself as she left the trail to form her own desire line.

Once upon a time, there was a girl who loved to dance, never more so than when she was with her closest friend. But then her feet began to ache and she lost herself, out in the darkest wood. Her friend found her, though, and he brought her to live with his family made of leaf and light, beneath the waves and the land. She never felt so happy.

But down below the world they made another version of the dancing girl. A mirror girl, with her very own face, beneath the roots of

the ocean in the realm of the dying Queen. The dancing girl, she grew
restless, and wanted to see the light of the sun again, but she was
warned she could only leave once.

And so she decided to go. But the mirror girl stayed among them.
Now she was the one who cleaved to the dancing girl's friend, and
they called each other by their secret names. And still they dance to
this day, in the place below the world. Never stopping, never parting,
forever and ever and ever . . .

She didn't know how to finish the story.

Elisa stepped from the forest behind Maureen and Donald's house. As she crossed the lawn she shielded her face from
the low sun magnified off the water in waves of pink and lav-
ender and orange; she felt washed out in the vivid glare, exposed. And, in fact, watched: Jason, up the hill, was tracking
her from the porch of the MacLeod House, in an uncanny
reenactment of when she had wandered out of these same
woods ten days ago. He didn't run to her, but instead stepped
tentatively down the porch steps. There would be no tearful
reunion, no cries for help or calls of prayer to a merciful god.
Not this time.

Gabe appeared on the other side of the door, its dented
screen a dark veil across his face as Jason met her beside the
peony shrubs. The heady scent of the flowers was overwhelm-
ingly ripe, so much so that a powerful and erotic thrill shot
through her. *It all goes back to the land.*

She stared past Jason, past Gabe on the stairs and up to the
house; she tried to make a welcoming smile of its windows and
porch but the façade remained lifeless, its appearance inert.

"Elisa," Jason said, and she was startled by the anguish in his
eyes. Something was very wrong.

"What is it?" she said. Gabe sunk down onto the porch steps, his form compressed like a crushed beer can. He wouldn't meet her eyes. "What's wrong?"

"It's Blue." Jason's face contorted, he was sweating now. "They found him."

"What happened?" She steeled herself. "Where is he?"

"I'm so sorry," Jason said, tears at the corners of his eyes; her pain had always been his, even now. "He's dead."

∽

They'd found the body eight days ago, not long after Elisa had wandered out of the woods. There had been some sort of confusion, the corpse assumed to be one of the half dozen hikers who had gone missing after the forest fires began. It was only upon performing the autopsy that someone thought to compare the samples to DNA collected from Blue's toothbrush. Despite the incompleteness of the remains—much of the body had been carried off by predators, including the teeth—preliminary lab results showed a perfect match.

Jason volunteered to meet with the coroner, but Elisa said she wanted to join him, so she could see Blue one last time. This was patently false, as she had no intention of seeing Blue for the last time, now or ever. Because she didn't believe it was him, not really. Such a thing as never seeing Blue again just wasn't possible; even if he were dead she would see his face in the stars, or the mirror, at the bottom of the sea or in the spidered cracks inside a teacup. No matter what kind of thing Blue might actually be, born of man or otherwise, alive or dead, made of darkness or the light. She would see him again, in everything. The way she had seen him that very morning, on the cliff overlooking the bay.

The coroner, a cotton-haired man of seventy with cauliflowered ears and an aquiline nose, distributed surgical masks to Jason and Elisa before he slid open the steel meat locker door. The walls were finished in immaculate white tile, the floors marbleized linoleum; the space bore an eerie resemblance to the examination rooms in the medical center directly across the street, where Elisa had been kept for observation.

On the far side of the room was a morgue slab, upon which lay the body, a sheet pulled over it like a Halloween ghost. She'd been expecting the corpse to be slid out of some drawer, but no, it was just lying there, waiting. Her stomach seized up, and she put her hand upon her belly, cradled the small mound below her navel as if she were trying to keep herself together, or hold something inside.

"I have to warn you," the coroner said, shifting around the table so the body was between them. "The remains have experienced a great deal of distress."

It was only once he spoke and a cloud escaped his lips that Elisa became conscious of the fact that the morgue was refrigerated, and now that she noticed she grew cold, as if submerged in ice water. The tiled room was like a swimming pool, the cotton mask over her nose and mouth suggestive of a kind of breathing apparatus. "He won't be recognizable to you," the coroner added, and looked from her to Jason. "Viewing victims of fire . . . It can be a distressing experience."

"I understand," she said, but she needed to be sure. "I'm ready."

The coroner pulled back the sheet. Jason, reflexively, squeezed Elisa's hand.

And there it was. A muddy brown amalgam of charred bone and muscle, skin burned off so that the plate of the cranium was exposed. Both jaws were missing, with the bottom of the skull concaved, excavated. The rib cage and stomach had been opened during the autopsy. What was left of the limbs was scorched black, the right shin and foot missing, along with the right hand. Wisps of red muscle were visible along the shriveled and rutted neck, threaded through with a bluish, veiny filament. From one of the eye sockets a single drab of yellow pus had oozed and hardened there like an amber tear. *Breathe*, she thought, *breathe*. She felt as if she were drowning.

"Wait. Please." Elisa put her hand on the coroner's latex-gloved wrist to stop him from pulling the sheet up, though he had made no move to do so. She looked closer. Not at the flame-corroded eye sockets, but into them, through them. The longer she looked, the more convinced she became it wasn't him. The creature she'd seen in the woods, the one she had touched: that was Blue. This was someone else altogether.

"How?" she whispered as she leaned over the corpse. How did they do it? How had he been replicated down to the cellular level, so well it would fool a DNA test? The only answer was that this wasn't a replica at all.

The coroner pulled the sheet up, the body shrouded once more. Jason signed some paperwork and made preliminary arrangements to return the body to New York, once the next of kin—and that could only be Blue's mother—was notified.

"Do you want us to contact her?" the coroner said. "The police will want to notify her directly, but in terms of the burial plans—"

"That's okay." She stared straight down, still fixed on the withered corpse beneath the sheet, the contoured hollows of its abbreviated shape. "We'll deal with it ourselves."

Jason thanked the coroner and stepped toward the door; she could sense him waver there, unsure of whether or not to leave her alone with the body. She remained beside the slab, incapable of looking away from the sheet's snow-white topography, and what lay beneath. *Not Blue*, she thought. *Not Blue Not Blue Not Blue*. No matter who said it was him, no matter how many times. It wasn't Blue. And if he was still alive, that meant she might still be able to return to his world.

"How are you doing?" Jason asked. He returned to her side and placed an arm around her shoulders. "You hanging in there?"

"Trying," she said, a little nod as she pulled the cotton mask from her face. She was too distracted to focus, her head buzzing with possibilities as she forced herself away from the slab and down the hall to the waiting room.

When Gabe saw them he leapt from his seat. There had been no talk between them of Gabe having lured her onto the sandbar, of the believers meeting and the ensuing struggle, Jessed beating on Fred Cronin with Jason looking on. Elisa remembered her promise then, the one she had made to Gabe in the hospital and then repeated out on the sandbar. It was true; she knew that now for certain. They were going to find Blue, or die trying. And she was going to find what she had left of herself, as well as what had been taken.

"Is he . . ." Gabe couldn't finish his sentence. He ran a hand through his matted blond curls, darker and thicker than when they'd first arrived in Cape Breton a lifetime ago.

"Do you want to see?" she asked. Gabe recoiled.

"Elisa," Jason said, a warning.

"What? I'm sure it wouldn't be a problem."

"I don't think that would be a good idea. He doesn't look like anything anymore."

"I don't want to see him," Gabe said, eyes welling up. He

looked exhausted. "I want to remember him the way he was. Just . . . Blue."

"Smart," Jason said, a gleam in his eye. Elisa knew this look well. It was triumph, perseverance in the face of irrationality; illogic always was Jason's most enduring opponent. She wished she could let him have this one victory, not only for his sake but for the sake of their marriage as well.

She turned to Gabe. Distraught as he was, a charged current managed to pass between them. She would have to trust him with her secret knowledge, maybe all of it; he was the one who would believe.

Gabe's face brightened and he drew in his breath, his eyes widening in expectation. "Elisa?" he whispered, his voice that of a little boy. Perhaps he already understood.

"It's not him," she said. "Blue. It's not him."

"Don't," Jason said. His face crumbled as he yanked the surgical mask from around his neck. "Elisa, don't. Please don't do this."

"I mean it." She knew she was going to lose Jason, but Gabe would understand; he'd have to. She'd come this far, seen things she never thought possible, and now there was no turning back. "I know they say it's him. But you have to believe me, it's not."

"He's gone," Jason countered, though Gabe was focused solely on her. "I'm sorry. Really, I am. I know Blue's not with us anymore, but you have to—"

"*No*." She dug into the word like a boot heel into fresh soil. "I'm not talking about his spirit leaving his body. I mean, that body in there was *never his to begin with*."

"I believe you," Gabe said. He wiped away tears with a dirty sleeve, his wan appearance warming under the bright halogen lights. "I do. I believe you. I do."

"Listen, you two are grieving," Jason said. "Don't let your emotions cloud reality. This delusional kind of thinking, it's very dangerous." He looked as if he were about to vomit. "You've been talking too much to Fred Cronin. Both of you. Blue wasn't some kind of alien creature. He wasn't a fairy, or a changeling, or—"

"I know it's hard for you to trust me," Elisa said. "I get that, and I'm sorry. I am. For everything I've done to hurt you. But that body in there? That's not Blue. Because I saw him, earlier today. I saw the Blue we know. I held him, out in the woods." She took Gabe by the shoulders; now they were the ones who were joined, with Jason boxed out. "He's still alive," she said. "He's different now, yes, but it was him."

"Please," Jason said, his voice firm, as if she were an obstinate child refusing to dress for school.

"The body in there, it's the original," she went on, breathless. "It's the real Michael Whitley. He and Gavina, the two five-year-olds, they were taken in and replaced by Blue and a new Gavina."

"He *is* one of them!" Gabe cried.

"Yes. They can make themselves look human, right down to their DNA. The kids, Michael and Gavina, they were raised by the Other Kind, but as their slave labor. Gavina's still out there, I saw her with my own eyes. There's a whole bunch of others too, animals even, they all raced off the cliff into the bay. I think they were running from the fires. That must be how Michael died."

"Please," Jason said one last time, an anguished cry of desperation, and defeat. "I can't," he said, "I can't."

And then he said it again, kept saying it over and over as his voice gradually lowered, the words reduced to muttering, an incoherent mantra.

Jason turned on his heel, dropped his mask to the tiled floor, and marched down the corridor to the elevator.

∞

It wasn't until after sunset that Elisa finally knocked on the door to the pink room and slipped inside. Jason, facing the window, barely looked up at her from where he sat motionless on his side of the bed. He opened his mouth to speak but she shook her head, closed the door behind her, and went to him. She kissed him. Tenderly at first, then with passion; he resisted her, but only for a moment.

She pulled her dress over her head and helped him with his shirt. She had missed the softness of his skin, the power in his broad shoulders and muscular arms. If only they could have shaped themselves together from the start, instead of pretending their unlikely and fully formed selves were some kind of perfect fit. Only then might they have lasted.

Jason laid her out on the bed like one of his old pinstriped suits. He paused for a moment, and she could tell part of him didn't want to do this, could already read the regret on his face. But he relented. He kissed her neck and shoulders, her breasts and navel, lowered her underwear and moved down to the darkly thatched mound of her sex. She gasped and held her breath, squeezed her eyes shut so she saw a Milky Way of shifting stars, followed by pure darkness. Why had she gone so long without feeling this way? Why had she withheld these tremors, this gratification, not only from Jason but from herself? And why now, on this day of horror and awe?

Jason's tongue moved inside her. She arched her back and grasped his hair, which over the past weeks had grown longer than she knew he liked to keep it. Dust motes sparked in the twilight glow from the twin windows, neither branch nor leaf visible from where she lay. Only the night sky unfolding at dusk, wide open above the vast expanse of the cove. She scarcely had time to catch her breath before she felt him hard against her thigh, that part of him that always seemed to act as its own separate animal. The pungent and perfumed scent of decaying peonies wafted from the vase on her bedside.

She rolled on top of Jason and eased him inside. In the narrow channel between discomfort and pleasure, she thrashed against him. She wanted to bite down on his shoulder, to draw blood; she wanted to cut into him with her cracked nails and peel back his skin. She longed to tell him she was sorry one more time, that she understood why he was going to leave her, just as she hoped he would understand why she needed to stay.

But she remained silent, pressed against him as he surged in and out of her. Elisa pictured invading hands, hollowing her out so they could take her unborn child. Down in the underground warrens, through the passageways she could now conjure in her mind's eye, not by sight but by touch. Down there. Her fingers made their way up Jason's sides, the way they had felt their way out of the caverns, surfaces slick with humidity and excreted life. That was where she would return.

"I'm—I'm going to come," Jason said, and sat up, still inside of her. "Do you want me to—"

"It's okay," she said. "It's okay," but he pulled out anyway, ejaculating onto his stomach. They both knew there was no real healing in this.

A few minutes later, sweat cooled on her skin as they held each other across the worn down comforter, Jason focused on a lock of her hair as he twirled it between two fingers. By the time she worked up the courage to tell him she wouldn't be going back home, it was obvious he already knew.

"The body," he said. "We can't leave it here lying cold forever. His mother—"

"He should be returned to her," she said quickly. "Of course."

Elisa had always related to Yvonne's need for Blue, but only now could she begin to fathom a mother's need for her own child. What Yvonne had to face, though, that was too much to bear. The sickly woman had to come to terms with the fact that her son—her first son, her biological son—was truly dead. "Can you . . . Can you bring him back to New York?" Elisa said.

Jason bent to retrieve his clothes from the floor. Next to him was her Konica, the one that contained her undeveloped photographs of the burn-ravaged Gavina, as well as those of the sky and sea: her mad attempt to capture Blue, who never could be truly captured. She reached for the camera but pulled away, and instead let her hand rest on Jason's back.

"I'll do it," he said, without turning to face her. "But I'm leaving tomorrow."

∞

"I guess that's everything." Jason slammed shut the trunk of the Cadillac, its polished veneer glossed with rain. "I don't know what you're going to do without the car, but . . ."

"We'll get by." Elisa looked back to the house where Gabe waited at the top of the porch steps, under the protection of the eaves. "Maureen said we could borrow hers whenever we need it."

"And when I hear from your parents?"

"Tell them everything's fine, that I'll stay in touch. And

not to come up for any reason." Jason nodded, and she smiled. "Thank you."

"Well. Okay, then." He ambled toward her, and started to raise his arms. "Do we . . ."

"Sure." They embraced, firmly and for the last time, perhaps. Though who knew what awaited any of them? There was still so far to go. "Have you made all the arrangements?"

"The coroner's office is going to meet me at the airport. I have more paperwork to sign, but since the autopsy is complete, they're releasing him into my care."

"And what about Yvonne?"

"No answer. I left another message, though, so I'm not sure what her story is. I'm going to bring him to a funeral parlor in the city, and from there . . ." He shrugged. "Maybe Flushing Cemetery, where my mom is. Or maybe somewhere in Brooklyn. I don't know. I'll figure the rest out when I get home."

There was an uncomfortable silence, lightning without thunder. It was really raining now. "I know I've let you down," Elisa said then. Couldn't help but say, really, though there was little point anymore; all she could hope to accomplish would be to agitate the wound. "I know I've been a great disappointment to you." She looked down at the gravel bed of the driveway before forcing herself to meet his eyes. "You must think I'm the most disloyal person on earth."

"You've got it wrong." Jason put a gentle hand on her shoulder, a melancholy smile upon his lips. "I think you're loyal as hell. Unfortunately, it's just not to me."

He leaned in and kissed her forehead, and she felt anointed. "I love you," he said, almost as an afterthought, and opened the car door. The safari hat she'd bought him at Frenchy's rested on the passenger seat.

"I love you too," she replied, her throat an arid plain. And she did.

Jason slid into the driver's seat and eased the door shut, then raised a hand to Gabe, who did the same. He released the emergency brake and the car bucked, eager to descend the hill, off to more promising places. And then he lowered his window.

"Elisa?" He squinted up at her, the dreary sky draped heavily above them. "You really think you're going to find . . . whatever it is you're looking for?"

She laughed, though there was nothing funny about what he had said. She looked out at the cove and Kelly's Mountain beyond; in the mounting rain, it was impossible to tell the road from the shore, the water from the hills from the sky, everything sheathed in a profoundly gray gray. What *was* she looking for, anyway? Blue? A daydreamed child? The state of sublime unconsciousness she'd craved as long as she could remember? Or simply somewhere to call home, a place to dance forever, even if that place was a subterranean grave?

"I'm not sure," she said at last, and combed back her soaking-wet hair. "But I have to try." She wanted to touch him once more, but instead she remained outside the confines of the car, not so much as a finger placed inside its dry interior. It was too late to seek shelter now—in the car, in her husband, in anything. Those days had passed.

Jason faced forward, shifted into drive, and the rental car started its slow crawl. The wheels spat up gravel, and a piece or two pinged Elisa's feet as she stood in the car's wake to watch its progress down the hill. It ground to a halt midway, and her heart skipped. Was he going to turn back? Only then did she see he had stopped in the spot where she had emerged naked from the woods, not so very long ago but still part of some other age.

He leaned in the direction of the passenger seat and stared out the window into the trees. *Still searching*, she thought, presumably for the wife he had lost. *But I'm right here.*

Jason put the safari hat on his head, and the car continued its descent until it reached the turnoff onto the main road. With a glint of light in the slate matte pane of sky and sea and pavement, he was gone.

Gabe appeared at her side and put his arm around her. There was a chill in the air, a real chill, Gabe's body against hers now the only thing in the world that carried any warmth at all. After a while she turned to face him. His cheeks were wet with either rain or tears, it was hard to tell which. She brought him in close, holding him to her as she breathed against his chest, Blue's scent still on his clothes. Her heart swelled, and she inhaled deeply, then forced herself to pull away. There was nothing sweeter in the world.

She looked up at his face, his skin dotted with moisture.

"I know where he is," she said. "Where they all are."

Now she could see Gabe really was crying, his bright blue eyes brimming with newfound joy.

"Tell me," he said. "Tell me everything. And start at the beginning."

Part Four

———

GABRIEL

Chapter Ten

———

The first time Gabe felt the frequency he was six years old. That was back in New Jersey, when he was playing hide-and-seek with his older sister, Eve, one winter's night while their parents were at a church function. He must have searched for her for over an hour before he began to sob, all alone in the dark of the attic as heavy sleet pelted their slanted roof. He wiped at his tears and listened to the rain's steady beating just above his head, until another sound reached him, a delicate scratching noise from someplace close by. It appeared to be coming from an armoire on the other side of the attic, one he'd already searched at least twice. Sure that he'd found his sister at last, Gabe crept over to the armoire, took hold of its tarnished brass handles, and swung open the doors.

It wasn't her. Instead, it was a little boy. About Gabe's age and size, he was naked and backed into one of the corners behind the hanging clothes, knees pulled up to his chin. He was sickly yellow and resembled a smirking grotesque carved upon a cathedral ledge, tilted and perched inside the cabinet in such a way that he appeared to be emerging from the wood itself. Gabe should have been terrified, the intruder cast in shadow with only the whites of his eyes and his tiny sharp teeth fully visible in the dim light through the casements. But instead he felt a soothing energy emanating from the odd little boy, a feeling of rightness and even reunion—as if all the many times over the many years he had gone looking for his sister he'd unwittingly been searching for this other child instead. Gabe's body sung with the sensation; it felt like nothing so much as home.

The yellow boy pulled his smiling lips back into a distorted and clownish leer, which made Gabe laugh. He reached between two of his mother's summer dresses to touch the stranger's color-stripped mop of hair, but it was like plunging his fingers into a pot of boiling water: the boy burned. Gabe yanked his arm back. His hand was on fire, and he screamed. Flames arched across the air, sparks sent scattering over him, across the clothes inside the armoire, the rafters above his head. He waved his arm wildly, tried to step on his fingers to put out the fire but it only served to spread the flames, smoke wisping from blazing paths that rushed higgledy-piggledy across the floorboards in bright veins.

At once Gabe was knocked to the ground, the wind going out of him. When he next looked up he was no longer on fire, his sister Eve beside him and using a blanket to stamp out the flames encircling them until they were extinguished, only the smell of seared wood and meat remaining. He sat up. The naked little boy was gone, the armoire's shadowy depths now barren save the clothes smoldering upon their hangers. Resting on one of the shelves inside was a book of red-tipped matches, the cover folded open with most of the matches ripped from their stems.

Eve, wild-eyed, stared down at Gabe's hand, his fingers puffed up with blisters, round white mushroom caps that swelled as they watched. She screamed, and the sound was hollow and muted, as if she were some distance away. His pain seemed far off as well, a scary story someone was telling in the next room, whispered for effect. Eve rushed him downstairs. She called 911, then lifted Gabe to the kitchen sink, where she ran the faucet cold and submerged his hand beneath the water. "It's okay, it's okay, it's okay," she said, her screams turned to soothing words as the savory scent of burned flesh permeated the room.

When the EMTs arrived, they swathed his hand in ointment and bandages and wrapped the rest of his body in sheets, mummifying him to prevent exacerbation of his wounds. As they loaded Gabe into the ambulance, he craned his head back toward the attic and peered up at the rain-spattered windows. And there was the yellow boy, perched on the sill behind one of the casements. He stared down at Gabe, the boy's spectral face lit from within, bathed in a beatific light. The little visitor pressed a single palm to the latticed glass, two fingers bent in benediction, and bared his teeth in a wide and impossible Cheshire grin.

The boy wasn't real. At least that's what his mother said at the hospital, when he told her about the fire and the visitation that had preceded it. She called him a liar, said he'd set that fire himself using one of his father's old matchbooks. *It isn't real.* She said the same thing three years later, when Gabe was nine and saw what he later determined was a cub-sized griffin tottering along the ledge outside his bedroom window, the tips of its bristled eagle wings tap-tapping against the pane. Gabe put down his Etch A Sketch and went to the window, beckoned by the warmth radiating from the otherwise fearsome creature, the same liquid brilliance that had emanated from the yellow boy in the armoire. Once the griffin had scrabbled on lion's paws past the adjoining drainpipe, Gabe opened his window, stepped out onto the ledge, and subsequently plunged two stories into his mother's rosebushes, nearly cracking open his skull.

After that, he tried to be more careful, not to look too

closely at the strange things he would sometimes glimpse out of the corner of his eye. He learned never to speak of the fantastical beings loosed in the dark of night, the ones only he could see or hear, like the bank of pay phones that cried out in ecstasy in the multilayered harmony of a church choir deep in the bowels of the New York Port Authority. When thirteen-year-old Gabe reached home, the swell of celestial voices still fresh in his ears, his father beat him for sneaking into the city, just as he'd beaten him for the fire in the attic, and for falling out the window.

Gabe grew afraid. Mostly that he was "possessed of the Devil," as his father maintained, though he did wonder if he might in fact be touched by the hand of God instead. Either way, he really had seen angels and demons, them and more. He cautioned himself not to give the apparitions credence, but oftentimes he couldn't help it; they felt too good to ignore.

The sightings continued after he ran away from home at fourteen. A cloud that rained blood over the Hudson River, just off the Christopher Street pier. A bodega cat on the corner of Avenue C and 12th, threatening passersby in what sounded like Aramaic. A man hanging upside down by his foot, high upon the branch of a lacebark pine in Prospect Park one foggy morning during Gabe's stint in Brooklyn as Vincente Castro's kept boy. All with that familiar electric radiance, as if his senses had unwittingly tuned in to a different station.

He even saw the strange yellow boy again. Two years ago, when he was squatting with a displaced coven of Dianic priestesses in a condemned former power plant in Blackletter. The naked child appeared late at night, perched at the foot of Gabe's water-stained mattress. Close-mouthed, it sang to him a lovely little wordless song, one that he recognized but couldn't quite place. *The new frequency.* Something no one else could see or hear, beautiful and powerful and charged with an otherworldly current that rendered the waking world magical and, by turns, utterly mundane. And every time the brief transcendence of the frequency faded, Gabe was left shuddering and adrift, a withdrawal akin to delirium tremens.

When Gabe met Blue, it all changed. Even before, from the very first moment he heard Blue's voice pleading on Vinnie's voicemail for another loan extension, Gabe sensed this was no ordinary man. The difference was that Blue was most certainly real, and therefore the most special thing of all. He radiated the frequency, the very same numinous current, and to be in his presence was to be holy by association. No wonder Gabe ended up building his life around him, leaving Vinnie the Shark for the menial job at Cyan. It wasn't love, not exactly; or rather, it wasn't a common love for another man. It was far greater than that, a need as essential as breathing.

Most remarkable of all was that Blue hadn't even thought himself special, and seemed to possess no knowledge of this fact whatsoever. But Gabe had known. It was hard for him to hide it all that time, impossible not to feel that being with Blue was a prideful form of sin, akin to keeping Christ all to oneself.

Seated at the MacLeod House's dining room table, Gabe popped three sugar cubes into his mouth, sipped off a can of Coke, and scanned Donald's journal, the words *Entomologia Generalis Vol. I* embossed in cracked gold leaf upon purple leather. It was inside this book, past its battered and coffee-stained cover and upon its yellowed pages, that Gabe had learned of Donald's past in Starling Cove. A cataloguing of its flora and fauna, maps of the land and its hidden corners, the story behind the founding of the Colony, and the fire that resulted in its dissolution. That was the best part of all.

The journal's seemingly innocuous content had swollen in meaning since Gabe first came across it almost a month ago, the afternoon before Elisa and Blue's disappearance. Blue had gone to view his grandmother's house, and when Elisa and Jason lingered by the water following a hike, they left Gabe alone up the hill. Stoned and bored, he sauntered down to Donald's cabin, knocked, and let himself inside. No one was there, but something immediately seized his attention: the weathered old journal, resting upon the chair in front of Donald's rolltop desk. Gabe was drawn to the field notes the way he was always drawn to certain objects, beckoned as if ensorcelled by the compelling clean buzz of the new frequency. He knew the journal would be important, and, since meeting Blue, he had learned to look these things right in the eye.

He closed the book and tapped a burn-scarred finger against the cover, the erratic pulse interrupted by the sound of creaking floorboards as Elisa bounded down the stairs. Gabe pulled a half-eaten Mars bar from his pocket and bit off it, the candy gone stale but he didn't much care. He'd been living on sugar for the past month. It was the only thing that kept him going, that made him feel anywhere near as good as Blue once had.

"You ready?" Elisa stopped by the front door and slung her backpack over her shoulder. They had filled their packs light enough to manage: nonperishables and a first-aid kit, surveys and maps and a change of clothes, a pair of canteens, a rusty old jackknife, and a few keepsakes Gabe couldn't help but bring along. Their supplies collected and divvied up between them, they didn't really know what they would need until they needed it.

Despite Elisa's assurances, they still had very little idea what they would find when they traveled to the place where the

Other Kind had taken her. All Gabe knew was that today was the day, the designated time for their walk down to the dock and the canoe that would take them to the Fairy Hole beneath Kelly's Mountain. Elisa had insisted they journey during the new moon and total darkness, just as it was the night of the disappearance. So they were going now, really going, and his heart filled to bursting with the possibility of reuniting with Blue. He couldn't wait any longer.

"Ready." Gabe stuffed the book into his pack as they stepped outside. "Just doing some last-minute thinking."

"Try not to do too much of that."

He glanced up to find her watching him, her expression unreadable. Was it one of wariness, or concern? *Let me inside your head*, Gabe thought. *Let me see what you've seen, so we can see it all and together as one.*

"We're going to bring him home," Gabe said. "Right?"

"That's the plan." Elisa dropped her pack to the porch steps and grasped Gabe by the shoulders. "Listen, if anything goes wrong, I want you to turn back. There's no point in both of us . . . dying."

"Now who's thinking too much?" he said, but she only stared at him. "Of course. The same goes for you. Okay?" He said the words, but in truth he had no intention of leaving her side, aboveground or below. She was the one who was going to show him the way to Blue.

Maureen and Donald's red Toyota rumbled up the drive. They'd closed the house down and were on their way to Halifax for the winter season, the car packed to overflowing, with a plastic storage container strapped to the roof. As Gabe watched the car climb the hill he wiped a black fly from his face with the sleeve of his Liquid Sky shirt, the ratty one with the cartoon alien on the front. Blue's shirt, once, its smell sweet with burned cedar. Seventy-three hours had passed since Jason had left, seventy-three hours spent sleeping in front of the woodstove, Gabe and Elisa sharing Blue's old mattress from the tartan room, which they'd dragged downstairs and positioned before the fire to combat the crisping air. They both wore Blue's clothes now: to bed, out in the woods, while they cooked over the range in the kitchen. Their hands upon the same spice jars as Blue's hands once were, the same pots and pans and spoons he used—anything that might act as camouflage. They took on everything of him they could.

Gabe ambled down the hill to the idling car, the morning sun voided behind the clouds over Kelly's Mountain. "Hey there," he said, once Maureen lowered the windows. "Is this it for you two?"

"Indeed it is." She wore her cheery smile like a mask. "We just wanted to say good-bye."

He rounded to the passenger side and peered inside at Donald, who held his hands tightly to his chest, as if trying to submerge inside himself. He smelled of shoe polish and chicken soup, and looked nothing so much as shrunken. A little like a young child as well, his eyes watery and wide, the reflection of the treetops swaying in their milky depths. *He sees things I can't. What he's seen, it can fill volumes.*

Gabe leaned forward and pressed his forehead to Donald's temple. He tried to look inside the older man's daydreaming mind, but all he could conjure were images of the surrounding woods, of lush foliage, the forest for the trees. Still, it was something.

"Thank you, Donald," Gabe whispered, and bowed his head in a formal salaam. "See you again soon, I hope."

Maureen sighed and looked away, let her fingers dance briefly atop the steering wheel before she turned back to her husband. "Darling, I'll be right back, okay?"

Donald didn't respond, no reaction as Maureen turned off the engine and got out of the car. He only stared out the windshield and into the woods as Olivier tried to settle in the backseat among the suitcases and cardboard boxes. Gabe gave the dog a good scratch behind the ears, then trailed after Maureen as she made her way toward the woods; he tried to steal a glance at her wristwatch, but couldn't catch the time. A dozen yards across the property and she stopped at the border of the lawn.

"Listen, hon," she said. "Donald's not coming back." She couldn't look at Gabe, only at the forest, the water, the mountain high above the cove. "I've booked him into an assisted living facility. Once I get the paperwork done and the doctor signs off on it, he'll be admitted, down in Halifax."

"Oh, wow," Gabe said lamely, though he couldn't feign proper surprise. *He's departing the Summerlands for the Autumnlands. And after that it will truly be winter.* "I'm really sorry."

"Me too." She smiled, but there was no joy in it. "Things have gone downhill pretty fast. No matter how bad he got, he always used to enjoy Olivier at least, and hiking on the trails. Not anymore."

"I tried to get him out more." And Gabe really did. But it was no use; he'd have sooner moved a mountain, or the world. Donald's deterioration, by all accounts a gradual one, had rapidly accelerated in the past few weeks, the same weeks that had passed since Blue's disappearance. Everything was slipping away.

"You and me both," Maureen said. "I've known this day would come, but that doesn't make it any easier."

Gabe slapped his thighs in an erratic drumbeat. They fell into an uncomfortable silence, neither willing to cut the final cord between them, that binding golden thread. Yet there was something Gabe still needed to make right. "Wait here a minute," he said after a while. "I have something for you."

He ran back to the porch of the MacLeod House, where Elisa was rifling through her backpack. "Donald's being put in a home," he blurted out. "I'm not sure he knows, but . . ."

Elisa made a pained face, then dusted off her hands and headed down to the Toyota. She had gone down the hill the previous night to see Donald, and he had invited her inside his cabin. They hadn't spoken, according to her, only listened to opera on his record player, as well as the jumbled sounds of faraway strangers over the ham radio. But after a couple of hours she could no longer visit with him. She developed a niggling cough, followed by a splotchy rash along her fingers and a sore throat; slowly but surely, Elisa's allergies had returned.

Gabe rustled through his pack until he found what he was looking for, and trotted back to Maureen. "Here," he said, and held out the book. "This belongs to Donald."

She looked down at the scarred cover. "His old field notes," Maureen said. "Where did you find this? We were looking for it everywhere."

Gabe opened his mouth to tell her he found it out by the old Colony building, which was the lie he had prepared. But when he tried to speak nothing came out. "I took it from his cabin," he eventually said. "I was going to return it . . ." But that's how it always was with Gabe, until it was too late. By taking the book he had triggered Donald's fit, which in turn led to Elisa's allergy attack. *And that's what took me away from Blue. Maybe forever.* The thought had haunted him ever since.

Maureen looked confused as to how to respond, but then an answer colored her face. "You're a thief," she said matter-of-factly. And Gabe could do nothing but nod in agreement.

Because it was true; he stole things. He couldn't help it, it was simply what he did, had always done, since he was a magpie of a boy. *You and your sticky little fingers*, one of his foster mothers had said, right before she put him back out on the street (though she'd called him a lot worse by then). Fred Cronin said the Other Kind crept up and stole things too—laundry off the line, recycling from the garbage, bright shiny objects that glittered like dew in the early-morning sun.

Turns out I am more like them than I thought. Which means that I'm more like Blue. He fingered Blue's plastic lighter in his pocket; it was one of his favorite keepsakes.

"Well." Maureen refused to meet his eye. "Thank you for giving it back." He handed her the journal but couldn't quite let go of it, and they held it between them. The message Donald had scrawled in the book's margin, though—the secret that Gabe had deciphered last week—it needed to be let loose.

"You're the one who set fire to the Colony all those years ago," he said. "Isn't that right?"

Maureen pulled the field notes free. She shivered and huffed, then squinted out toward the distant sky, the journal disappearing into the folds of her quilted jacket. "Well," she said. "Well."

"There's this whole passage in there about how some experiment ended when the subjects of the sessions were compromised . . . But later Donald jotted something down next to it. He said it ended because of the fire, that someone who lived there named Barbara had burned the place down." Now that he had spoken, he couldn't get it all out fast enough. "When I checked the list of Colony members and saw there was no

Barbara, I realized that he must be talking about you, only by the wrong name. I heard him call Elisa that too, right before her allergy attack."

Maureen, her face turned from him, took a long time to respond. "I suppose that's the problem with swearing someone like Donald to secrecy," she said, her voice wistful. "It's always a race to see which he'll forget first, the secret or the swear."

"Was it the Other Kind? Did they make you set the fire?"

"No, no. It was all Maureen. Uninfluenced, for better or worse." She held her arms as if chilled, and looked at Gabe at last. "The People of the Wood, as we referred to them back then . . . We thought we'd called them up, even though my own kin have talked about them for generations. Everyone knew there was something about their sort that gave you a good buzz, so we figured hey, why not see if we could bring them around. Lots of namby-pamby ritual work, baby pagans playing at forces we didn't understand. So stupid, and not a thought to the cost. My father would've skinned me alive for messing with them, God rest his soul."

"So you believe in them. The Other Kind. They're real to you?"

"Oh yes. They're as real as we are." She exhaled, drawing it out, and for a flickering moment a whisper of condensation escaped her lips. "And they're out there. Through the deep woods behind the Colony, beneath the water and the land. Back then, they would come right to the edge of our property. And like the fools we were, we bought into the illusion of our own power, having 'summoned' them. We started to take advantage of them, their energy . . . There was a lot of dope going around too, so naturally we were reckless. Then we turned *them* into our drug. We tried pulling back from the brink, but it was no use. We were hooked on their vibes."

The new frequency. Maureen and Donald had trod the very same primrose path. He buzzed with a thrill of recognition.

"We thought we were using them," Maureen said, "but *they* chose *us.* I couldn't see it at the time. A couple of years passed before they took the kids away, replaced them with their own kind like a pair of cuckoo eggs . . . And it was like it didn't even matter to anyone. Not even to Yvonne! She preferred the new boy to her own son. It was once we took in Michael and Gavina—the *new* Michael and Gavina—that stuff started getting real scary." A tear rolled down her cheek, and she made no attempt to wipe it away. "I began to see things. Terrible things. Faces under the ground, in the trees. Always watching. Waiting. Even on the good days, I knew it had to stop."

It hasn't stopped for me. Gabe stared up into the sky at a flock of geese traversing the cove, and watched as the birds arranged themselves into musical notes that played a lilting little song in compound time. The cove still radiated with the frequency, if the right person was looking.

He hummed along quietly, and Maureen eyed him as if she were sizing up his mental state. "Once upon a time," she said, "we swore we would leave them be. So much for good intentions." She winced as if pricked, and he was reminded of the dirty syringes affixed to the Colony murals, the spent needles jutting from the wall and pointing in the direction of the darkened hallway.

"You shot yourselves up," Gabe said. "Injected some part of them inside you. Just being around them, it was never enough, was it?" *We're all so greedy, willing to trade in riches for the promise of more. And then all we're left with is an overgrown turnip of regret.* Was he going to make the very same mistake?

Maureen stared at the ground and scanned its broken surfaces, a divination of dirt. "There was an essence inside them . . . Something that was like the holy grail of highs. Donald thought maybe it was pheromonal, or reproductive. Something about *collateral veins*. The thing was, we could only get the stuff out of them when . . . when they . . ."

The geese had stolen across the sky, the lost meter of music along with them. "They only excreted it," she said, "when we kept them in the dark."

"Aw, Maureen, no." The thought was almost too much to bear, and he shook his head until it burst with a galaxy of stars. "What did you do?"

"I stayed away from them, mostly," she said, but he could tell by her haunted undertone that she didn't believe it herself. "After we took in the new kids, we would keep them inside, cover all the windows, which usually did the trick. If it didn't, well, we sealed the whole place up, trapped all of us in until we got what we needed. Could be days, but over the winter we shut ourselves inside the Colony for two months straight, living off whatever we could. Turned ourselves into a compound, like a bunch of crazy end-of-the-worlders, with the two kids locked behind the thickest door we had. We couldn't help it. We were out of control. And oh, how they would scream to be let out! Like a pair of starving dogs, scraping against that metal door—needing to be part of the earth and the forest, like their kind do." She sighed. "We were no better than Flora, I can tell you that much. After a while, I couldn't take it anymore, and I managed to wean myself off them. God, if only you knew how tough that was for me. Even now, once you all came to the cove. How hard it was for me to be around Michael, and how good it felt all the same."

He knew.

She looked at him and her face smoothed, though only

slightly. "So I freed them, and used the fire as an excuse. I figured everyone would think the church folk had done it, but of course Donald found me out, he always did. After the fire everyone had to go cold turkey, and it was a good thing we had other vices to occupy us. Not that anything else came close. Donald did manage to distill some of the essence into the screech, but eventually that ran out. Even then, no one could bring themselves to leave the cove. Most of us still can't."

Maureen bit at her thumbnail. "Once the Colony was toast, I told Yvonne to take the boy and split, and thank God she listened to me. Look what happened to Gavina—well, not Gavina, but the one sent back looking like her."

"What did happen to her?"

"Daniel Jessed did."

Gabe had suspected as much, but now he knew for certain. He thought of Jessed beating on Fred Cronin, and the small man's agonized cries. *The law is a huntsman in disguise. He dresses in the skins of sheep. He hunts the things that creep.*

Maureen fixed Gabe with her gimlet gray eyes. "He's been poking around, you know. Asking about you and Elisa. What you've been up to, what you might be planning. He's called from the station house the last two days, late at night."

Gabe looked up at the sun and attempted to discern the time from its position; it was rising too fast for his liking, which meant it would set too soon. *No moon like the new moon,* or so Elisa had promised. The dark would show them the light. "What does Jessed want?"

She shrugged. "Used to be heroin. All I can say for sure is that since he went on the straight and narrow and joined the Mounties, he's been getting high off that old-time religion instead. And those types around here, they don't approve of the

Other Kind. Think they're some kind of abomination. That's what Flora MacKenzie thought, her and the rest of her church folk, the old-school fire-and-brimstoners. That's been ingrained in them since William MacLeod's day. Flora and Daniel Jessed were both big wheels at the congregation, and got pretty close before she died. That should tell you something. Not to mention Jessed's the point person on the search-and-rescue operation. Those fires on the mountain? They keep popping up in the strangest places. Even during the rains."

Maureen's troubled countenance flared, then just as quickly lifted from her face like a veil. "If it makes you feel better, I told him you and Elisa were heading back to New York. Speaking of which," she said, retreating into small talk, "the housekeeper's coming next week to close down the house. She'll call before she shows up, but you'll have to be gone by the time she arrives, so I wouldn't wait much longer to book your way home. It really is too bad you never made it up north. Newfoundland? You'd love it. It's all edge."

She started back to the car, but Gabe slipped in front of her. "Donald's field notes," he said. "From what I can tell, they say the only remaining entrance to the caverns beneath the cove is the Fairy Hole at low tide."

"Forget it. Foolish to go that way, at any time. Plenty of folks have tried over the years, but I've never heard of any making it. Not even native guides attempt to navigate those passageways. And that's because they know better."

"What about the rum-running tunnels? I pulled some old maps from the Gaelic College archives, but—"

"Oh, they've been sealed off for decades. And besides, they aren't constant. The tunnels down there . . . they change."

"What do you mean, change?"

"I . . . can't anymore. I just can't, I'm sorry." Her voice qua-
vered, and she appeared, for the first time, old. "When you hear
them in their true voices, inside of you, inside your head . . .
There's no coming back from that. No matter how much time
has passed, no coming back. You'll never be alone with your
own thoughts again." She glanced back at the car. "So don't.
Don't go down there."

"Maureen . . ."

"Leave it alone. And let your friend go."

Now it was Gabe's turn to look away. Chastened, he stared
down at a matted patch of grass. "You're under his spell," she
said. "Under *their* spell." When he looked up, her face was grave
with sorrow and longing. "I understand better than you know."

"It's not only me." They turned to observe Elisa at the passenger side of the car. She had her arms resting on the open
door, leaning inside toward Donald so that her head was no
longer visible. Only a bisected torso and legs, one calf crossed
over the other, with Olivier bounding about in the backseat.
When she emerged, a beam of sunshine escaped from the cloud
cover to wash her in amber light, her face radiant as she walked
to where they stood.

Maureen hugged them both, for what felt like the very last
time. "Here," she said, and produced Donald's notebook, gently
pressing it toward Gabe. "I think he would want you to have it
now. It should belong to someone who can still appreciate it."
She started down to the car, then stopped to squint up at Elisa,
a hand over her eyes in the newly bright light. "You're still glowing," she said. Then she nodded, turned back, and continued
down the hill.

Gabe and Elisa stayed close to each other as the Toyota
crawled the rest of the way down the gravel drive and toward

the main road. All was quiet save the birds and their chirrups, the insects and their whining cries. He looked across the cove and everything was still, but when he focused on the surface of the water, it appeared to be moving very rapidly and out of sync, as if the bay had been filmed in time lapse. His vision blurred, and he rubbed at his eyes.

"We have a problem," he said. "Maureen says the trip through the Fairy Hole is suicide. No one's ever made it through there and lived to tell. We've got to find another way."

"There *is* another way," Elisa said. "We have to go through the tunnels. I know that's how I did it, I'm sure of it. It'll come back to me once I'm down there, and then I'll find my way."

You'll find your *way?* he thought, but suppressed his unease. "But see, that's the thing . . . Maureen said the tunnels aren't constant. That they change. Donald confirmed as much in his journal, when he gave up trying to map them in the sixties." Gabe dizzied a bit, and canted his head, which made him see dark spots. He fumbled in his pocket for the remainder of the candy bar. "Even if you could figure it out, I still don't see how we can get down there."

Elisa opened her hand. "Maybe this will help." In her palm rested a slender and ornate iron key, strung from a thong of Tibetan prayer beads that tangled in her fingers like a rosary. "Donald just slipped me this. What do you think it's for?"

"A door." Gabe reached for it and pointed the key skyward, the beads tightening between them. "And I think I know which one."

They went off-trail and across a field of tall grass spotted with purple lupine, the sky lit up by parti-colored rays from a picture-book sun overhead as Gabe watched the brilliant orb whiten from bright yellow like a dandelion forming a seed head. He stole a glance at Elisa, who stared forward, dark bags heavy under her eyes. Over the past few days she had spent her nights screaming herself awake, as Blue once had. She claimed not to remember what her nightmares were about, but she needn't have bothered, really. Because Gabe knew she dreamed of the place to which they were heading. Compelled in her sleep to travel the unmapped terrain beneath the mountain, follow the winding path to the dark place where she had been violated, her unborn child ripped from her womb. He couldn't begin to imagine that forfeiture.

But there was something else. Another loss Elisa had alluded to beyond Blue and the child, some other, unknown entity she couldn't bring herself to remember, or fully relay.

The past three nights he had stayed up to watch her, no trace of the scintillating energy she first exuded upon her return from the realm of the Other Kind. Still, she remained the closest thing he had to Blue. So he kept near. Last night he'd forgotten to sleep altogether, and stayed up watching Elisa until he swore he could see into her dreams, pictures of restless clouds rolling and unrolling in the dark, accompanied by the low growl of faraway animals. *When wolves are heard howling before sunset, expect the rains to come soon.* But the storm was only inside her head.

On the other side of the field they reentered the woods, and soon the crumbling chimney of the Colony appeared in the distance through the ragged scrim of branches. Elisa caught Gabe staring and she looked away, her hands gripped tightly to the straps of her pack, black cotton frayed at the elbow of her sweater. Just then Gabe had the uncomfortable feeling that she was going to bolt. *Is she going to leave me behind?* She did have the key around her neck, after all, and claimed to remember her way through the caverns. *What does she need me for?*

But that was ridiculous. Why would she run from him, when they were in this together? *We both want to bring Blue back.*

Unless she didn't want to come back at all.

Since they'd headed into the woods, he and Elisa had hardly exchanged a word. It was easier for him to keep his mouth shut and follow her, focus instead on the Colony building rising before them. The former loggers' quarters and its charred brick walls looked different now that he knew it was Maureen who had set it ablaze, the wounds fresher, maybe. There had likely been other fires since, however, a succession of desecrations that had contributed to the building's current state of ruin. The same way the MacLeod House had burned over and over across its long history, and the forest fires that seemed to occur whenever the Other Kind reared their heads. *Fire hides all traces and tracks*, and he fingered Blue's lighter again, rolling the thumbwheel the wrong way until the flint sparked. *Fire cleanses all.*

Once they entered the Colony's burned-out shell they headed for the inner sanctum, its remarkably well-preserved walls adorned with the elaborate and phantasmagorical murals. Though Gabe had ventured inside many times over the last month to take in the vivid and complex illustrations, he viewed them now through new eyes. The once-inscrutable images, they told the story of two peoples, human and otherwise. The collages weren't chronological or even directly representational, but he could follow parts of the story nevertheless. It was a secret history of this place, the alluring darkness beneath the land and the promising half-light of the world above.

Here was a spent book of matches clutched in the hands of a voluptuous young woman, her eyes milky gray behind a praying mantis mask rendered in aluminum foil. Other figures circled her, including a man masked as a bear, a woman as a fox, another as a coyote—all huddled around a spent box of hypodermic needles, the syringes gone cloudy with use and age. Farther down the wall, a black-eyed boy was sketched in charcoal, his hands holding down a saucer-eyed child beneath a shellacked and ridged fiberboard relay of waves. Gabe put a hand to the mural but drew it away as if scalded, a faint trace of energy emanating from the brick.

The Gavina replacement, she made all this. Which meant she knew she was going to drown by her false brother Daniel's hands.

Elisa moved toward the hallway, and Gabe hurried to keep up. Down the dark passage were the pair of steel closet doors they'd discovered upon their first visit to the Colony, one door propped open with a cinder block to reveal the ongoing mural. He shined his flashlight inside. A dull bit of metal glimmered on the ceiling: a gold ring, embedded in the wood. It was part of the mural as well, a halo for a painted red angel whose dark red wings crossed the ceiling in two scarlet slashes. Beneath it was written the words *Borealis the Mother was sent up from the Heavens of the Faraway World to bring comfort to the New Children of the Screaming Places*. It wasn't a biblical angel, the kind that Fred's believer friend Tanya prayed to over her woodland altar, begging the heavenly hosts to bring back her husband, dead in a car crash three years past. This was another kind of angel altogether.

He swung open the closet door and watched as a desiccated rag fell from a nail and landed with a dull paper thump. A *stranger is coming.* He recognized the omen from one of his books. The other door remained shut with its burned brass knob locked tight, though the scorched floor below it showed through in a sweep of blackened ash.

Elisa removed Donald's key from around her neck and inserted it into the keyhole, worried it until it caught. When she pulled the knob the door belched open like a crypt, the humid smell of wet earth thickening the air. Gabe pointed his flashlight through the opening. He had assumed the mural would continue inside this space as well, and was surprised to find the closet's interior was in fact a steel chamber, akin to an elevator car. The space was barren, save a spattering of residue at the corners, dried mud splashed halfway up the walls. *Blue and the Gavina replacement, they weren't allowed inside here.*

He got on his knees and ran his hands along the corrugated iron flooring. It wasn't until he found a notch on the back wall and slid his hands inside the gap that he snagged a piece of loose metal on his finger. It was a ring, the same size and golden color as the angel's halo embedded in the ceiling of the other closet. He took it as a sign, and tugged on it. In a cloud of dust and ash the floor began to rise, and Gabe continued to lift what he now saw was a cleverly disguised hatch door that spanned the length of the closet and opened onto a rough hole, no wider than two feet across and dug directly into the earth. The open gates to the underworld, without a Cerberus in sight.

"Do you see any way down?" Elisa asked, but he shook his head, the beam of his flashlight disappearing into the opening's hungry black mouth. There were no means by which to lower themselves, no way of knowing how far the drop was or what might greet them at the bottom. He longed for Fred Cronin's guidance, not to mention the man's elaborate assortment of supplies from the botched believers group expedition.

"Maybe we could go back to the house and grab some sheets," Gabe said. "Tie them to something heavy and then ease our way down?"

"Sounds good. After that, I should be able to get us the rest of the way there." Her quiet confidence buoyed him. All he had to do now was stay as close to her as possible. *She will show me the way.*

There was a nearby crunch of feet on broken glass, followed by the sound of heavy boots mounting the waterlogged remains of the back deck. Elisa and Gabe exchanged panicked looks before they scrambled inside the closet to perch upon the edges of the hatch, facing each other over the yawning hole. He reached out and plucked the key from the outside lock, easing the door closed as he killed the flashlight, the darkness bisected by a slender shaft of muted light through the keyhole.

Gabe struggled to hold his pack as he scrambled for balance. Floorboards groaned down the long hall, accompanied by the hollow clink of beer cans and other detritus being kicked aside as the footsteps swiftly approached. He fumbled to fit the key into the keyhole, this time on the inside of the door, and barely managed to engage the lock before the knob was jerked from the other side. Elisa gasped. *The stranger has arrived.*

"Come on out of there." The words muffled through the blocked keyhole, but still recognizable as belonging to Daniel Jessed, his voice as authoritative as it was menacing. The big bad wolf had come to blow their house in. "You two are making a big mistake." *You two.* Had he been watching them? Following them? Gabe reached to take Elisa's hand, their arms a bridge over the hatch; if one of them jumped, the other would fall as well.

"You're one of their kind, aren't you, girl?" Jessed said from the other side of the door, his words redolent with scorn. "Maybe you both are, now. Like Flora's grandson. The both of you turned devils."

"Your sister, she isn't dead," Elisa called out, and Gabe squeezed her hand but she didn't quiet. "I saw her, out in the woods."

"Liar! Devil!" He struck against the steel, the sound violent as cannon fire.

"Detective, please," Gabe said. "We're not bad people. Just let us be."

"That . . . *thing*," Jessed said. "The one that came back wearing my sister's body. No one thought it was so bad either." A chilling silence, until he spoke again. "Funny, isn't it? How people around here talk about the Other Kind being from nature. But what's so natural about taking the place of a little girl?"

"Listen to me," Elisa said. "The real Gavina, she was hurt in the fires but she's still out there. She's grown now. They kept her alive all this time."

"My sister's dead!" he shouted. "They killed her. You killed her. Your kind . . ."

"She's alive," Elisa said. "I swear to you, she's alive."

"I'm going to give you five seconds to come out of there." But barely a moment elapsed before Jessed threw himself against the door, the reverberation so loud that Elisa slipped from the ledge. *Little pig, little pig, let me in* . . . Gabe grabbed her and managed to pull her over to his side of the hatch. Her breath was irregular, heartbeat a bass drum against his chest and the hair on his *chinny chin chin*.

"I finally found where they're all hiding, though," Jessed

said. "You know that? Took a mighty deep borehole, but I got them." He slammed against the door again, harder.

Elisa's probably never had someone come at her like this, Gabe thought. *But I have.* His father's crazed eyes blinking through the dark of the closet, like so many dark places he'd known. So he did what his mother had taught him to do when he was set upon by his father: he lowered his head, and he furiously prayed.

Our father which art in heaven hallowed be thy name thy kingdom come thy will be done in earth as it is in heaven . . .

Gabe held his breath and looked up through the dim. The door hadn't budged, and for a single, stupid moment he let himself think they might be safe, that they would get to Blue after all. Then, a scraping sound, and something pinged against the wall next to him. Donald's key, pushed through the keyhole, followed by an arc of liquid traveling up Gabe's side. An acrid gas station smell hit him, and Elisa's grip upon his torso tightened with alarm.

"Oh no," she whispered.

Lighter fluid squirted over them in a violent arc, the angry Cyclops eye of the keyhole illuminated once more as a red plastic spout moved from the opening.

"Go!" Gabe hissed. He forced the flashlight into Elisa's hand and pushed her down through the hatch. A moment later he followed, just as a stream of heat and light pierced the darkness, fire erupting through the keyhole in a chemical torrent of blue and yellow flame.

Chapter Eleven

The smell of burned hair trailed him as Gabe half staggered and half slid down the muddy chute, Elisa a rush of air below. He fell in her wake, the echoing sound of metal upon rock as he brushed her arm with his fingertips but she slipped away, his trajectory suddenly blocked. Scrambling to reach her, he met only earth; it was as if the ground had opened up for her and quickly closed, shutting him out. Chunks of dirt pelted him. Bits of rock forced themselves under his fingernails as he continued to slide, until the back of his head slammed against hard stone.

He was momentarily stunned, slapped to life again by a root that caught hold of his heel and twisted him sideways so that he was no longer sure whether he was facing up or down. *Unhand me, sacred trees of the ancients,* visions of snarled branches clawing at him as Gabe shook his leg to free it from the root's grasp. *Who so shall release me, for him I will open the hoards of the earth.* He dropped a dozen more feet before he crashed into wood and glass, his vision going white with agony.

It took him some time to force open his eyes. He'd landed in some kind of silo-shaped storage room below the Colony, on top of a stack of decomposing lobster crates packed with glass bottles. He didn't understand how he was seeing all this, until he noticed the flashlight he'd handed Elisa lying on the dirt floor and illuminating part of the room. He sat up and frantically patted at his hair to make sure it wasn't on fire, a lingering stench of bitter combustion.

"Elisa?" he whispered, then said again with more insistence. The only response was his own voice, echoing off dirt and rock. He hauled himself off the crates, grabbed the flashlight, and aimed it up at the shaft that had ejected him. He could barely make out the curving mouth of the chute, and wondered at what point above Elisa had been separated from him. There must have been a fork in the path, or perhaps she had deliberately shaken Gabe off, as he'd suspected she might. Maybe the underworld had simply accepted her, while he was jettisoned to land in this improvised storage room. *I am Orpheus, who must venture farther below, lest I fail to bring my love back to the world.* Only Elisa wasn't his Eurydice. And Blue was no Eurydice himself: he was more like the Runaway Bunny, having left of what was likely his own volition. *So I'll turn myself into a bloodhound, little bunny. And I will find you.*

The flashlight trembled, and Gabe saw that he was shaking. The hatred in Jessed's voice rumbled in his ears, the terror of countless childhood beatings as a shudder of fear wracked him, having waited until now to fully blossom. The antiseptic smell of his father's aftershave, the whistle of the belt before it lashed him, blood spotting the underside of his parents' bathroom sink: all of it returned in an unrelenting wave. But not the hurt itself, never that; only the constant low hum of his scars, the twin red channels up and down his back that anchored his invisible wings, the ones that had allowed him to fly free. That's where he kept his old pain now.

Something else came to him as well: Blue's captivating scent, the one beneath all the spices and kitchen grease and cigarette smoke. It was all around now, and it was strong, so much so that

Gabe listed. He ran the flashlight beam across the dirt floor and stone walls, a long-neglected gin still in a far corner.

"Blue?" he called out, and held his breath.

The smell was coming from the lobster crates. Or rather from the bottles inside, a few of which had shattered beneath him when he crashed to earth. His racing heart began to race faster. He looked closer, and now he could see the bottles' faded labels. Each one bore the image of a dainty-looking fairy perched upon a rock in the water, the mouth of a cave visible on a distant shore. It was the hidden remains of the Colony moonshine, what Fred and Maureen had referred to as screech, laced with the remainder of the Other Kind's essence. *Donald's secret recipe, the best in the cove.* Vision clouding with desire, Gabe had to pry himself away from the crates.

It was time to find a way out, and to keep his cool while doing so, turn his panic into a little mouse that was really nothing to be afraid of at all. He retrieved a plastic compass from his pack, lifted it to his chest with the reverence of a holy object, and raised his head up high. *Spirits of the East, Spirits of Elemental Air,* he beseeched, *sweep through like a proud eagle and bring forth the sky so that I may spread my own wings and take flight!* High above in another corner of the room was a sliver of light, dim but discernible all the same. He shined the flashlight upward, upon iron rungs welded to brick casing. It was the sealed-off well behind the Colony, slits of daylight visible through the slatted cover. A covert escape route, fashioned by the old rum-runners perhaps, or maybe by the Colonists themselves. And it would be his deliverance.

Gabe packed up his compass and flashlight, threw on his rucksack, and climbed, the rungs cool against his bloody and sweat-slicked palms. He waited at the top, and remained there for what seemed an eternity: listening for Jessed, for any sound but those of the natural world, its whistling birds and rustling leaves. Finally, he said a little prayer and pushed on the rotted wood cover.

One of the planks gave way, then another, and a third, creating an opening large enough for him to get his head and shoulders through. He pried off the remaining pieces of wood and peered over the rim of the well; he was farther from the rear of the Colony building than he would have imagined. After summoning his courage, he raised himself out of the cold stone cylinder, the air soothing his red-raw skin with a velvet touch. For a brief moment it smelled as sweet as the screech had, and he trembled with delight, the brightness of day rendering the trees an emerald city against a swollen backdrop of blue. *This is the forest primeval*, Gabe thought, and now he was Evangeline, in search of a very different Gabriel.

He dropped down to the forest floor and made a run for it, deeper into the woods, until he doubled back and charted a parallel course to the trail. There was only one place he could think of to head next.

❧

He pounded on the cottage door a few times before he let himself inside. The front room was cold and damp and reeked of fried clams and cigarette smoke, among other things, worse things. But Gabe smelled like hell himself, sweat-soaked from fear and the frantic dash through the woods that brought him to Fred Cronin's place before dusk, still picking splinters and shards of glass from his shoulders and arms. With the shades drawn, the living room was even darker than he remembered; he tried the light switch by the door, which did nothing. After stumbling over a disarray of toppled newspaper towers, upended furniture, and emptied beer bottles, he finally made it through the hazardous mess of an obstacle course to the back of the house, where he found Fred lying unconscious on the bathroom floor.

"Fred? Are you okay? Can you hear me?" *Is he dead?* The stench was so strong that Gabe retched, a cloud of stink around the body. But the smell was an admixture of alcohol and body odor and shit, nothing worse. Eyes watering, he hauled Fred up and carried him to the bed. In the gloom, Fred was but a hazy shadow, his body even more compromised than when Gabe had last laid eyes upon him, after Jessed pummeled the diminutive man into the earth as if staking a tent pole. He was pale and desiccated, his beard dirty and knotted and grayer than ever; he looked like a shriveled wizard drained of all his power, leveled by a rival's spell.

Fred opened his eyes, and Gabe's breath caught. "Fred! Are you with me? We need to get you to a hospital." Fred slowly shook his head, his gaze trained away from Gabe and toward the far side of the room, at the single triangle-shaped window set beneath the slanted roof. Against the unwashed glass hung a dream catcher, its feathered and beaded hoop overtaken by spiderwebs; Gabe pictured the spiteful faces of all the nightmares it had trapped over the years, as well as the ones that, against hope, had managed to break through.

"You need help," Gabe panted, but Fred continued shaking his head, until it settled in Gabe's direction. "Are you listening to me?"

"Fuck the hospital," Fred said in a gravel-dragged rasp. "Why are you here?"

"Elisa and me. We were up at the Colony. Looking for a way into the rum-running tunnels. So we could . . ." Fred's eyes began to close again, and Gabe squeezed the man's arm to keep him awake. "Daniel Jessed, he showed up out of nowhere. Attacked us. Tried to burn us alive. We managed to get away, but we got separated."

"Got off easy. That asshole broke my leg in three places. Cracked ribs, knocked out two teeth I couldn't spare." He jerked his jaw, made a face as if he were laughing, though no sound emerged. He looked decapitated, his head that of John the Baptist, a soiled quilt square the platter beneath his chin. "You going after her?"

"I have to. And I have to go now. Elisa said we needed to do it during the new moon. Donald's field notes said the same, something about the tunnels and the tides. I only have a couple more hours." A selfish part of him was glad Fred would never let him call an ambulance; it would make leaving easier.

"And here you thought she was going to help you," Fred wheezed. "I still think she's one of them. Their kind. Did she try mating with you? You know, screwing?"

"What? No. And you're wrong. She's *our* kind, not theirs. I can tell now. Anyway, I'm pretty sure she's gone for good."

"Is she now?" Fred coughed and sent a thick spray of blood across the tattered quilt before he went limp with exhaustion, his head lolling to the side. Merlin on his deathbed. *But this sorcerer, he remains clever and sage. He knows how I can find Blue.*

"Fred!" Gabe shouted, and squeezed the man's arm again, harder this time. "I need you to tell me how else I can get down there. Okay?"

Fred willed himself back to consciousness. He sat up a bit, all spindly limbs and jutting bones, cheeks sunken beneath his beard. Gabe bent over the bed and Fred reached for him, took a handful of Gabe's shirt in his fist and drew him closer until they were inches apart. "That odor," Fred whispered. His watery eyes rippled, and with an unexpected convulsion of strength he pulled Gabe on top of him. "What are you doing with that odor?"

"What? What are you talking about?"

"You smell of them. The Other Kind. Their scent, it's already on you. Oh, God," Fred moaned, and for a moment his eyes rolled back in his head. "Oh, God, that smell."

"Best screech in the cove, just like you said." Gabe pried Fred's hand from his shirt and laid him back upon the stained pillows. "If you ever get around to telling me where to go, maybe I can bring you some of the good stuff." *How low, dangling the promise of a fix before a wilted junkie.* But he was willing to go lower.

"Tempting. But far too late." Fred grimaced, blood at the corner of his cracked lips. "There's a shaft to the old bootlegging tunnels down in Flora's basement. That's the closest entrance to Kelly's Mountain." It was a struggle for him to speak, and they both knew he would soon reach a point when there would be no more words at all. "The last gateway before the sea, at least according to the old maps." He coughed again. More blood. "Be careful there are no surprises there. The bootleggers set booby traps up and down the channels to thwart the law. I also wouldn't put it past Flora to leave some kind of nasty surprise behind herself."

"For Blue."

He nodded. "She knew it was on top of an entrance. Kept guard of it, always witching up some new way to try and get the Kind to show themselves. Finally worked." Fred reached over and slid a cigarette from a pack on the bedside table. He tried to light it with a stick from a box of wooden matches but was trembling too much, so Gabe took out Blue's lighter and lit it for him. He left the lighter on top of the pack as a burnt offering upon a bronze altar, though his fingers itched to take it back.

"It's down below the mountain you want to go," Fred said, and Gabe could see him trying not to cough, not to breathe, all to keep the poisonous smoke inside his lungs. "That's where they live. In the root of the mountain, through the caves below the water. Their nest." He reached to take Gabe's hand, which jittered upon the quilt, Gabe already plotting how fast he could get to Flora's house. Now he was the junkie. Fred's sunken eyes bored inside him. "He's not going to come back with you. You know that, don't you?"

"No. I don't believe that. I can't." He wished Fred hadn't said it. Gabe couldn't focus on that obstacle yet, only upon the journey. "Besides," he said, "I spent my whole life hiding from the things that people told me weren't really there. Magical things. But they were wrong. The Other Kind, they're real. Blue is real."

"You're right." Fred smiled with sorrow. "The thing about the Other Kind, though? They don't care about us. They *can't* care about us. I get that now. The way we see ants? That's how they see us. Something to study, maybe. But not much more." He took a long drag off his cigarette and clenched Gabe's fingers as if in seizure. "Take my truck. The keys are hanging from a nail by the front door. And whatever you do, for God's sake don't let them lay a finger on you. They're not to be touched."

Too late. Gabe's skin goosefleshed with the memory of Blue's hands as they roamed the scars on his back, his secret wings. That night Gabe had lifted Blue's hands from his body, but he immediately regretted it. Indeed, he'd longed for Blue to touch that sacred and shameful part of him, to quiet the scars and their ceaseless humming. "I think you're really great," Blue had said the next morning while they were still in bed, with what sounded like well-rehearsed words. "You're a great person, and friend. But it's probably not a good idea for us to be—" and Gabe interrupted him, told him it was cool, that he understood, it was fine, they were all good. But he knew that would never be true. Gabe was hooked.

"What happened to the others?" he said as he stood beside Fred's bed; there was so little time left. "Colin and Patricia?"

"Colin's back in the hospital. Came down with pneumonia. It's not looking good. Patricia, she won't leave his side."

"And Tanya?"

"I haven't heard from her."

"Maybe—maybe I can carry you," Gabe offered, his conscience interceding. "On my back. Or we can take the boat, go to the mouth of the Fairy Hole after all. At low tide there's a chance we can—"

"*No!*" Fred shouted, his face flushed from the effort. "No. I got some more life in me yet, you little shit. I'm going to finish the rest of these smokes if it kills me." He released Gabe, thrust his hand away like an unclean thing. "So go on already. And while you're at it, try not to drown down there. You don't have to go through the Fairy Hole to get stuck in the wrong place at the wrong time." Gabe opened his mouth to speak, but Fred had already turned back toward the window and slumped down once more in the bedsheets, the cigarette still clutched in his hand. His skull smiled beneath his skin.

Gabe retrieved his pack from the floor, backed out of the bedroom, and headed through the labyrinth of filth and debris to the front door. The car keys were there as promised, as well as the abandoned hiking packs for the believers group descent.

He rummaged through them, and set aside a mining helmet, spelunking ropes, and a pair of rock-climbing spurs, as well as an energy bar, which he eagerly consumed. Gabe envisioned the sugar flooding him with warmth, and with light, all the bright good feeling he would need until he was at Blue's side once more. He inventoried his own pack, bloody fingerprints left upon his flashlight and the underground maps from the Gaelic College archives, the hard and cracked leather cover of Donald's field notes, the aerial photographs of the cove, the compass, and finally his own sketch pad, filled with his special drawings.

And then he left the wizard's cottage, releasing Fred in turn.

❧

Gabe drove the dingy white pickup truck to the far side of the mountain. He raced the entire way, and instead of ruminating about Fred dying alone he prayed, mostly that he didn't get pulled over. He didn't have a driver's license, never had one, and even if he did, the sirens in the rearview were liable to be Jessed's. And then it was *game over*. He felt Jessed's eyes on him, the detective inside his mind, poking around in there. *The huntsman meditates upon his prey. Trying to figure us out, and where we're headed.* But Jessed's attention, like Gabe's, was ultimately on Blue and the others like him. He wanted to kill each and every one of them, the devils that had haunted him since his little sister walked into the woods and something else came back. *Fire cleanses all.*

Gabe pulled into Flora's empty dirt-track driveway unaccosted. He put on the mining helmet, grabbed his pack from the passenger seat, and ran up to the house. Alone, it seemed, though there was a muddy road that made its way around the back of the house and into the woods that might have had recent tire tracks, he couldn't be certain. He scooped up a rock to break a window, but when he reached the porch he found the front door unlocked, as opposed to when he and Jason had attempted to search the property on their canvass. One last look around— at the sun already setting behind the mountain, firs like arrow-heads piercing the sky, thin ribbons of water visible through the branches—and then, afraid he'd spot the faint gleaming of a star if he waited too long, he slipped inside the house.

The interior was dark and unpleasant, but it was a differ-ent unpleasantness from Fred's cottage. Here everything was astringent, the air heavy with the smell of cleaning solvents. The place had been cleared out since he and Jason had peered through the windows, the doors all thrown wide open, includ-ing the one that led to the basement. He turned on his hel-met lamp and started down the basement steps, the light an ever-dimming circle as he descended. *I'm coming for you, little bunny. And I will find you.*

A draft gusted over the back of his neck. He tried to turn, but he was shoved from behind and sent hurtling down the stairs. His helmet flew off, and he collided with the hard dirt floor, sparks scattered behind his eyes. Gabe peered back up, and in the square of light from the open doorway he caught a glimpse of a dark silhouette as it leapt down the last of the stairs, lowering itself upon him like a spider from its web. He attempted to stand but couldn't even get to his knees before an arm crooked around his neck and stanched the flow of oxygen, pinpricks flaring all over him as he choked on the stinging scent of aftershave.

My father, he's hunted me down at last. All the way to this dank basement, where no one should ever be found.

He couldn't move backward, so he pitched himself forward instead, his father along with him in a windmill of motion, head over feet over head as they rolled across the floor. Gabe was pinned down, and he was so much smaller, gloved hands fixed around his throat. He batted at his father's face, no use as the boy's air was choked away, thick fingers pressing into his flesh like a potter molding clay. They might as well have been back in that attic in New Jersey, just another lightless place among many.

There was a bit of light, though, barely: the subdued glow from the mining helmet, its dull beam shining upward from the spot where it had landed under the stairs. And in this light Gabe's sister Eve appeared, a damned expression upon her face. It was a look he knew well, the one that said Gabe better keep his mouth shut and stop struggling, that they'll both be killed if anyone found out what their father does to them up in the attic. So he went limp, just as he always had, every time.

There was no strange yellow boy. Gabe was startled by the revelation even as his life leaked out of him. He'd wished the monstrous boy into the attic as a sacrifice, a replacement his father could violate instead of him. *There was only me up there, me and a book of matches.* It was just as his mother had said; he'd started the fire himself, because he was trying to make it stop, to make the nightmare end once and for all. He'd wanted to see that house of horrors burn bright, for his father to suffer the way he and his sister had for so very long. But instead, he had run. He had stayed alive.

Gabe turned from his father's glowering face in feigned surrender. He reached along the basement floor until his hand found his backpack, fingers worming their way inside the front pouch, where they tightened around a ball-bearing chain. It was attached to a pen, the ballpoint one he'd nicked from the pharmacy in Baddeck the night of Blue's disappearance. That night the pen had shone with the frequency, which meant it was important, so he'd slipped it from the clipboard and pocketed it. *And now I know why.*

He curled the chain around his hand, grasped the pen in a tightened fist, and thrust it up toward heaven.

The pen made a squelching sound inside his father's neck, and he went rigid, his hold on Gabe's throat slackening and moving to the wound. Gabe gasped for air and coughed violently, his hand still firm on the plastic pen barrel. He leaned in and forced it further inside. His father groaned, guttural and hoarse, blood spattering across them both as he floundered for the pen. But Gabe kept grinding it forward, a pestle inside mortar, and pushed himself off and away, the man falling beside him like an exhausted lover. He crawled retching over to the stairs, reached through the wide plank steps to fumble for the mining helmet until he seized it and swung it around, ready to use its hard metal casing as a weapon.

And there he was. Not his father after all, but Daniel Jessed. The detective was in plainclothes, facedown and spread-eagle in a cloud of dust that settled upon him like a shroud, the pen still buried deep inside his neck. Blood was everywhere. Warm and wet over Gabe's hands and face and clothes, in an uneven stain soaked into the dirt floor, as a dark red caul upon the man's face. And still it flowed, still pumping from the wound and Jessed's dying heart.

Gabe, dizzy as hell, felt at the stinging lacerations on his own neck, the newest marks of violence to brand his skin. *And should they scar, then I shall shift my shape, use these fresh welts as gills to swim away from here.* Just as he once used the scars on his back as wings to fly from his father's nest.

It didn't take long to find the entrance to the bootlegger tunnels, an open spring-loaded trapdoor onto a wide hole dug into the middle of the basement floor. He placed the mining helmet back on his head, and shined the light at the crude hole, upon what looked to be a square box hanging from the joists above. As he approached, however, he saw it was in fact a cage, big enough for a large animal or a small person. *Blue's cage.* The one Gabe had sensed that, metaphorically or otherwise, must have been here all along. Closets, bathrooms, attics, cellars, armoires even—because Gabe had been kept in his own cages, he recognized that in Blue as well. The way only someone who had lived such a life can smell a child's fear, from knowing it firsthand.

Draped from the bars of the cage were two knotted gauzes, swaying in an updraft from the pit. For a moment he thought they resembled a pair of hands, holding on for dear life. But they were only cobwebs.

Gabe's breath slowed, and once it steadied he took hold of Jessed beneath his armpits. With a great deal of effort, he hauled the body over to the pit and shoved it over the rim. It plunged like the dead thing it was, landing with a sickening thud somewhere below. *And now I'll use Blue's cage to escape.* He hooked the carabiner and rope to the bars of the cage and lowered himself into the hole. The cage held, and, after twenty or thirty feet, he touched down atop Jessed's lifeless form. He unhooked himself from the carabiner and glanced up at the cage in the basement high above, steel shining in the light of his helmet lamp before he turned back to face the corpse at his feet. Gabe thought to cover him in dirt but soon abandoned the notion; he had neither time nor energy to spare. Jessed would rot in the dank hole's wet air, where eventually he would be discovered. *Until then, feed the land. Do us all some good.*

Gabe retracted the climbing rope, adjusted the helmet

lamp's beam, and started down the tunnel. The ground stuck to his feet. Adhesive and coated with an amber-tinged goop, the striated passageway was awash in a briny seaweed stench. Semen came to mind, but then he thought of spirit essence, of ectoplasm. He began to shuffle through the gelatinous ooze, but his leg caught on something and the sound of groaning earth made him spin around: the trapdoor to the basement above had sealed itself. His stomach tightened in a fit of nauseating claustrophobia. He wanted to scream for help, not that there was anyone to hear him, above or below. Instead he steadied his nerves and forced himself to continue down the tunnel. He couldn't go to pieces now. And so he would make himself into The Boy Who Feared Nothing, maybe even The Man. The journey was only just beginning.

Two more steps along the passageway and his sneaker crunched down on a waterlogged binder, cellophane pages scattered across the wet tunnel floor. It was an old photo album, leaves yellowed from age and filled with snapshots of a little boy with Blue's face, one picture after the next. Tattered newsprint as well: articles on the first disappearance; the Starling Cove Hansel and Gretel; subsequent reports of the fire at the Colony; and more. Gabe removed a single unscathed Polaroid of a smiling young Michael Whitley and slipped it into his sketch pad, his fingertips going numb where they touched the photograph. *My own special merit badge, an amulet to keep me from harm.* It wasn't Blue, but it was close. He needed to get closer.

Gabe checked his compass and headed down the narrow throat of the tunnel. He reached for sweet memories to light the way, recollections of Blue and his shimmering features; it was a bright enough light by which to see. That day before Christmas when Gabe walked across Brooklyn to peer in the window of every storefront up and down Smith Street, fingers pressed to the snow-dappled glass until off on a side street he found the man Vinnie the Shark had been bitching and moaning about, the *ci-drule* chef with the glittering green eyes and the magic touch. And once he had spotted Blue—at work in his open kitchen, which took up half the tiny restaurant—it was impossible to look away.

Blue's flawed and mesmerizing face, his nose with its slight swell at the bridge as if it might once have been broken, dark brows arched over eyes so bright they glowed. All of him seemed to glow. He was so beautiful, like a painting of Gabe's namesake at the Annunciation, his radiance so strong that Gabe already felt himself changing. At once he needed to learn everything about this rare and exquisite creature. Indeed, Gabe had been so enthralled he had barely noticed the Help Wanted sign taped to the restaurant's window.

The dark passageways became increasingly erratic as he pressed forward, neither pebbles nor bread crumbs to help him find his way. Dilapidated remnants of pine-slatted staircases dangled from the ceiling of the uneven corridor at odd angles, alongside crumbling auxiliary tunnels that appeared to have been burrowed by subsurface mammals. Gabe wiped the blood from his face, pulled a candy bar from his pack, and bit it in two. As he let the sugar do its work he tried to calm himself, reassured in the knowledge that he had kept Blue with him. That he was safe, so long as Blue was near, if only as a conjured memory. It kept him walking.

☙

He wondered how much time had passed, down in the cool and dank and endless tunnels; Elisa was the one with the wristwatch. He told himself he was well, that all would be well, there was nothing to be afraid of, not anymore. But he didn't feel it. Any sense of calm had evaporated, and in its place arose an anxious flood of questions about what he would find when he finally reached the root of the mountain. Would the Other Kind be as indifferent to him as Fred had suggested? Would Blue? What would Blue even be like, down in this new and unknown place? He could have changed so much that Gabe might be a stranger to him. It was bad enough how distant and removed Blue had seemed since they first arrived in the cove; the worry that he was slipping away had already weighed on Gabe's mind even before he went missing.

And this was something that he couldn't bear, the very thought sending a heartsick tremor down his legs. Because without Blue, he would be just as lost up above as he was down in these tunnels. If Blue couldn't be reasoned with, convinced that his former life was still worth living, then Gabe was sunk. That was his only plan.

Maybe none of that mattered. Chances were he wouldn't even make it to find out.

All shall be well, and all shall be well, and all manner of thing shall be well. Gabe's ears rang, and he began to tremble as he walked. He had to get to Blue, or he was going to unravel like a corn dolly and fall the fuck apart. *Just keep going,* he thought. *Keep going.*

The light on his helmet started to dim, so he switched it off and traveled in darkness; he still had the flashlight in his pack, for when he really needed it. He began to tire, and after a while his knees started to clack against each other, so he curled into a ball and slept. His dreams were threaded with dark and fitful nightmares of Blue and his kind, which he dreamed of as cartoon aliens, each of them taking a separate piece of him in their wiry fingers and pulling until only scraps remained. *Blue,* he pleaded, *Blue,* but the only response was the rattle of a thousand cicadas, and dirt thrown into his eyes.

Gabe was startled awake; something had crawled over him. But there was nothing there. And it was only then that he realized there was nothing else down there at all: no rats or moles, no bats or voles, no ants or bees or hornets. *I'm the only living thing around. The only one that dares.* He reached for another candy bar and hungrily devoured it, as fetid drabs of water fell on him from the ceiling. *God and our hearts are crying together,* and he wiped the dirty liquid from his face.

He counted his steps, guessed how many he might make in a minute (a hundred?), then an hour (five thousand?). He decided to break for food and a drink of water every five hours, but he lost count so many times that eventually he stopped only when he couldn't go on any longer.

◯✕◯

After a day or so the water from his canteen was drained, and he finished his meager ration of candy bars from his pack. How much farther did he have to go until he reached the root of the mountain? He began to feel queasy, accompanied by the disturbing sensation that the tunnels were shifting around him.

The ground grew soft beneath his sneakers, and he tensed as a slippery current of muddy water steadily rose from the cave floor. He figured the tide must be coming in, seawater seeping up through the earth. Either that or it was groundwater, soon halfway up his shins. It leveled off, however, then receded, heat surging from the earth in the dark water's wake. It rolled over his skin and drenched him with sweat, until he feared he was going to pass out. He swallowed back waves of nausea and persevered.

After another hour or more of wet air choking his throat, the stinging sensation turned strangely pleasurable, an incongruous and ecstatic rush upon inhalation. As with the ambrosial moonshine stashed beneath the Colony, the giddy smell of sweet jam and juniper berries, wild lilac and gingerbread reminded him of nothing so much as Blue. Gabe's spirits raised, and he dizzied with joy, led forward by his nose more than anything else. The pleasing aroma turned, however, lifting him out of his reverie. The air soured, and he almost managed to stop himself, just before he stepped forward into nothingness.

Gabe's stomach dropped out, the rest of him along with it. He was falling, falling, plunging ten feet, twenty feet and more, into a honey-thick liquid that filled his mouth with the suffocating finality of grave dirt. He wanted to scream but couldn't, the taste of rot and decay unnervingly tempered with the fecund scent of the Other Kind. He was dazed until he broke the surface and gasped for air, his backpack newly heavy upon his shoulders and threatening to drag him under. Then he did scream, a lonely howl into pitch blackness that savaged his strangled throat and forced him back into silence.

I'm going to die here, alone.

He fought against the syrupy fluid, scrambled for the side of what he took to be some kind of pit. It was like being back at the bottom of the well outside the Colony, only this time without any rungs to climb, the wide hole slicked and smooth to the touch. He began to force his way around the circumference, an arm extended in search of the mining helmet loosed from his head. He pushed his way through the ooze and took hold of a clump of seaweed, its ghostly strands tangling in his fingers. The drenched mane of a slumbering kelpie, perhaps, who could awaken at any moment and trample him underfoot with its mighty hooves.

When he pulled his hand back he dragged something against him, and he froze. What he took for seaweed was in fact human hair. There was someone else down there with him.

"Elisa?" His heart sped, the sound of his damaged voice an eerie, unrecognizable thrum off the sides of the pit. He moved his hand along the body, which was facedown, drowning or drowned. The hair felt too long to be Elisa's hair, the wrong texture (*but it's wet*), limbs bloated (*oh God*) like plastic trash bags overstuffed to the point of rupture. Gasping, he tried heaving the body over to see if it could still be alive, if he could do anything at all but drown here himself, down in this dark hell. *So long, farewell. Auf Wiedersehen, good night.*

He couldn't tread forever. So he dragged the body toward the side of the pit and attempted to find a handhold, some way of keeping his head above the surface. The effort had exhausted him, and he struggled to open his sodden pack. Once he grasped his flashlight, he held his breath, wiped a sleeve of sludge from his eyes, and turned on the beam.

As soon as he saw the bright red color of her hair, he knew it wasn't Elisa. It was a woman, yes, but one who had surely been dead for some time. Her columnar neck was marbleized and distended, flesh a fishy blue-gray gone white where Gabe's forearm bore down beneath her chin. A necklace was stretched to near breaking against her rubbery skin, the slender chain intertwined with a tangle of eely red hair. Delicate gold links shimmered under the flashlight's watchful beam, which lit up a dangling charm on a penny-size loop. An angel pendant, hovering upon the surface of the amber ooze like its own drowned corpse, the W shape of its wingspan depressed into her swollen cheek like a brand.

Tanya.

Gabe let go of her and swallowed the bile rising from his stomach. The dead woman floated lazily across the pit, her bulging eyes pitched up at the black void above. His legs were tiring, and if he didn't get out of there in the next few minutes, he would meet the same bleak fate. *Adieu, adieu, to you and you and you.*

He fumbled inside his pack for the climbing spurs, fitted them to his hands like brass knuckles, and plunged the metal spikes into the siding above his head. *Spirits of the North, Spirits of Elemental Earth, give my body the strength of a scarab, for we are kith and kin.* The spurs carved out a notch in which to dig in his fingers, and his grip held. Embedding the other spur a foot higher, he hauled himself from the sludge, arms quivering until he could properly tense them. He used Tanya's body for leverage to gain ground against the wall of the pit, and he rose. Soon the notches left by the spurs above became footholds below, and in this way he began to make real progress. *The earth. It's holding firm for me! This dark and merciful land, it wants me to survive.* He continued to climb in gratitude, humming a little tune as he went; though it felt like his larynx was going to rip open, he'd heard enough of the silence.

A few minutes later he had climbed out of the fluid. He clung to a fossilized tree root, his arm crooked around its knotted length, and he rested for a while. Then he continued to climb. When he finally reached the top of the hole and hoisted himself out, he was more tired than he'd ever been, and knelt in the wet muck of the tunnel. He placed his pack and flashlight beside him and swallowed air in great big lungfuls.

His adrenaline began to subside, and soon the welts on his neck began to tingle. He grew light-headed and unsteady, and the hair stood up on the backs of his arms and legs, as if he'd passed through a field of static electricity. He was standing now. *But why don't I remember getting to my feet?* His lips stung, the inside of his mouth heavy with the taste of the honeyed bio-fluid he swallowed in the pit, and he licked his shirtsleeve to try to rid himself of it. But the tarry liquid had already leached into him, penetrating his consciousness. In a newly perceptible light, a procession of volatile shadows appeared to march across the cavern ceiling; the sound of skittering legs filled the air; the earth bubbled like lava beneath his feet, though there had been nothing but firm ground a moment before. *Am I losing my mind?*

But that wasn't it. The land was changing, him along with it. He was sensing things differently, yes, but his perceptions were no less accurate than before. He was feeling the new frequency, indeed he was swimming in it, its current stronger now than he had ever known. He was becoming magical himself, and wasn't that what he had wanted all along? To be part of the swirling life force that was the frequency, the numinous current threaded through every magical thing that bound them together in a golden glow? And yet. He clicked on the flashlight, his only remaining source of illumination outside his own visions.

I'll never really be part of it, though, will I?

Gabe shined the beam down into the pit. Tanya watched him from below, her wide eyes reflective and shocked bleach white, in awe. He wondered if, in her final moments, the poor woman had drowned in fear, or rather felt something closer to grace. Whether she finally got to see the heralding angels she believed so strongly were with her all along, and only just out of reach. *Maybe at the end she felt the frequency too*, and he switched off the flashlight. Godfather Death had snuffed her candle out.

Gabe said a wordless prayer and turned toward his destination.

∽

After some time—three hours, or maybe five—there was a faint suggestion of brightness ahead of him. Daylight? Starlight? His imagination? But no, it was none of those things. An internal radiance flickered from the cavern walls, shining with bioluminescence as if he were approaching the innards of a massive glowworm. All was calm, nothing bright save the iridescent pulsation from the walls and floor and roof of the tunnel, bearded with moss. Gabe reached out his hands and placed them against the opposing walls, his fingers ablaze with green and yellow phosphorescence. An electric thrill surged through him, the same thrill he had felt that first night outside the ceilidh, when he came upon Blue staring into the night forest.

Gabe had stood watching him for what felt like forever, but must have only been a few minutes. He tried to see what Blue saw, to glimpse whatever profound vision his friend was experiencing, so they could share it together as one. It was only meant for Blue, though, and perhaps those of his own kind. Still, Gabe could feel the energy coursing out of the forest, out of his friend and the cove and the verdant life all around them, the dark sky and wet ground and the very air itself. All of it humming. After, Blue rubbed Gabe's head, and it had felt like a holy hand, his touch so powerfully charged that Gabe had to pull away. They headed up the hill to Elisa and Jason, the four of them laughing as they ascended, their own different kind of happy family. The vivifying flow in the air that night, it wasn't just the singular frequency he had sought for so long; it was also the feeling of requited love.

Another mile down the curling passageway and Gabe reached a narrow cavity, a hollowed-out spiral like the inside of an ammonite shell that echoed with rising sound, the roar of air or water and punctuated by a steady dripping. The trail constricted and wound further, a maze of wet dirt and rock and puddled fluid that stank of secreted life.

He moved through the attenuated gap, forced to push his backpack and flashlight ahead of him and slide in a commando crawl. As he progressed, the tunnel altered around him, the walls fleshing from hard earth into the supple texture of sweat-soaked cotton or foam. It became harder to gain traction, and he had to shimmy along the newly padded surface, the hidden depths of which appeared to roil from within. Soon the tissued lining of the canal began to tug at him with what felt like tiny mouths, nickel-size pockmarks ringed with thorny protrusions. Each time he made progress, his movements seemed to tear a new rend, in either his clothes or the flesh beneath. *All shall be well, and all shall be well, and all manner of thing shall be well.* He stifled his cries of pain.

His backpack dropped down ahead of him. He edged forward and became a lowly worm, crawling its way through the earth. *The worms crawl in, the worms crawl out . . .* He pushed himself from the barbed duct and landed before a slim cleft in the stone that throbbed with light. He saw it as a shimmering doorway, an invitation to an enchanted realm that had appeared only for him. He gathered his pack and wriggled forward, slithering through the new opening. *A big green worm with rolling eyes crawls in your stomach and out your eyes.* After negotiating walls coated with gypsum and barite crusts slicked with mucus, he found himself inside a wider channel, the walls backlit by a series of irregular pulsations. Gabe fell silent, only to hear a wailing cry in the distance, like that of a demented loon. He shuddered.

"Elisa?" he called out. "Elisa, can you hear me? Blue?" He slipped out of the passageway and into a dim chamber within the mountain's immense black heart. His spirits began to soar, he'd made it so far! He was almost there, almost there, the last hour of school before summer vacation and Christmas Eve and next in line for the Ferris wheel, all at once. He risked a smile, and straightened to his full height.

In a fluttering of what sounded like torn sails, something dropped from the ceiling. It landed behind him with a wet squelch, its faint shadow rising as the figure lengthened and extended. Before Gabe could react, a cold hand sheathed his mouth, its touch as forceful and damp as the flowstone of the cave. His vision went black, then white, then black again, and he dropped the flashlight. A strobe of liquid sensation washed through him, over him, pleasure, pain, satiety, ecstasy, more. He felt everything.

An icy respiration drew across his ravaged neck, a fast-spreading rash accompanied by the scent of the sea, rolling in, out, in. *For God's sake, don't let them lay a finger on you. They're not to be touched.* His panic mounted, and he feared he was breathing his last breath. *Help me!* he wanted to cry out. *God in Heaven above or benevolent spirits below, fearsome creatures of the land and air, angels or demons or anyone listening, I beg of you!*

But all was silence. The hand's firm grip upon him began to slacken, and soon it fell away altogether. Gabe slowly turned.

It was like looking at a ceramic mask made to resemble

Blue. Or more like a mask of Blue's face that had shattered and been reassembled, something approximate but skewed. Its limbs were Blue's limbs, though somewhat elongated; its wide eyes enlarged, then shrunk, the bridge of its nose knotting before straightening. All of its features appeared to twinkle and alter, along with the wavering curl of a familiar and ambivalent smile. He could tell it was trying to appeal to him, to give him what he wanted to see. But he knew.

"You're not him," Gabe said, his voice coarse. He shook his head in disappointment, if not outright rebuke, anger flaring through his fear. He hadn't searched these many days and weeks to settle for a substitute. "You're not Blue."

The creature shook its head. For a moment Gabe thought it was answering but it was only mimicking him, and once Gabe stilled it did too. Its green eyes brightened and dulled, then brightened and dulled once more, a reflection of the throbbing catacomb walls that was the only light by which to see.

This place, Gabe thought. *It's lit from within.*

The cavern walls, the smell of the sea, the syrupy trickle of biofilm bubbling up from the rock bed: all of it pulsed with mesmeric luminescence. There was no such thing as true darkness down here.

He had reached the place below the world.

Gabe waited for the simulacrum of Blue to say something, or even just to move, but when it failed to do anything he spoke again. "Where is he?" Gabe demanded. "Where's Blue?"

The creature cocked its head as if awaiting a distant command, no longer occupied with Gabe's presence. Something else had its attention, an event of great importance taking place deeper inside the warrens. *If I follow this one, it will lead me where I need to go.* He didn't know how he knew this, only that he did.

It will show me the way. And I will find you. He felt it beneath his skin.

The creature backed away. Its movements were herky-jerky yet deliberate, and as it receded Blue's features evaporated, leaving only shadow and leafage and the suggestion of domed eyes. It crept toward a crack in the stone wall no wider than a foot and poured itself through the breach, disappearing like an envelope passed through a mail slot. Even with his pack in front of him Gabe could just barely fit. He shuffled along the strip of uneven rock between the cave walls, expected the encroaching rock to be damp and cold but instead he found it warm to the touch, almost like flesh. There were places where he felt his way forward that his fingers sunk into the stone. The modest pressure shaped the rock as if it were made of sponge, the walls organic and pliable.

He continued after the creature, waded across the unbalanced topography and into the broad gap of a crevasse until he was almost entirely submerged in brackish fluid, the smell of which was both repulsive and alluring. Jagged ridges stung Gabe's feet through his soaked sneakers, but they enabled him to scale high enough that he was nearly out of the muck altogether. *All shall be well,* he prayed. *All shall be well.*

A labyrinth of passages led him higher, then deeper underground once again, to an unnervingly humid area within the caverns. There was something wrong here, very wrong. And it was only once he stepped down into a papery puddle of ash that Gabe caught the pungent scent of scorched earth and meat. The warrens beneath the mountain had burned through. The signs of fire were everywhere here, seared across flame-licked granite and soot-caked limestone. He was perspiring profusely, the heat beginning to overwhelm him, and he stopped to breathe next to a thin seam in the wall. An arid wind issued from the gap, as well as an unsteady light, sparkling like a candle's flame. *Godfather Death, stay away a little while yet. I need just a little more time.*

Gabe glimpsed something moving through the gloom, an effulgent figure that tramped slowly toward him, its face a shadow against the dark. It was one of them, and it frightened him in a way the first had not. Taller and thinner, there was an imperious, almost regal air to its posture, an aura of knowingness. Its elegant, sticklike arms reached forward and took hold of the stone seam between them, needle-thin fingers stretching and widening the rift slashed into the rock until it was wide enough to cross.

The creature drew closer, and Gabe shook. For the first time he regretted coming there. To the place beneath the world, to the cove, Cape Breton, all of it. He was petrified.

But then, mere inches away, it spoke.

Blue spoke.

Chapter Twelve

found
found
us
you found
us

Blue sounded far away, even though he spoke inside Gabe's head. The words tentative, like an echo, as if his voice were transmitted from a distant planet.

Gabe looked upon him, what Blue allowed to be seen of his flickering form. Limbs those of a praying mantis, fingers the stiff branches of a gray birch, Blue's head bowed with the veined and leafy shape of his brain beating steadily beneath the thin translucent membrane of his skull, electrical impulses flaring across its surface like a solar storm. He was nothing like Gabe had ever seen.

"I knew it," Gabe said, and grinned like a madman. He was thrilled with expectation, tears of relief at the corners of his eyes. It was the very sensation of being alive. "Ever since I first heard your voice, I knew. But I had to be sure."

He stepped forward, but Blue raised a wraithlike gray hand and shrank from him.

no
look away

"I have to see you," Gabe said. No pretense of composure, not anymore, he couldn't have come so close to Blue's dark divinity without taking this last step. There was no enthroned Hades here, no one to forbid him from doing so. "Please. I need to see your face."

After an unbearable length of time, Blue's head bobbed as if nodding before he slowly raised it, and for a moment his old green beach glass eyes materialized in the empty space between them. But then Blue let him see behind the disguise. Gabe's breath snagged, and the air thickened, like breathing in steam. Blue's eyes, they weren't the ones that Gabe had known. Still glowing green, yes, but now the multifaceted eyes of an insect.

What a thing of awe he was, that he should have to be hidden away beneath the earth! And now Gabe knew why Blue's people hid, what would happen to them if they were to surface and show their true faces to the world. They would be devoured, their flesh and blood consumed like cakes and wine; they would be used up until there was nothing left.

"My God." He reached out to take hold of Blue's face, the razor-edged cheekbones that tapered into a bristled ram's horn chin. But when he touched Blue's skin, the world went spinning out from under him. A lightning strike of scattered pictures, along with a rushing of wind and the buzzing of bees, of insects that burrowed and bit. Fires underground, flames and the assaultive stench of smoke, a mournful dirge of dogs baying for their mother . . .

Gabe felt himself falling, and yanked his hand away.
should have
should have stayed
away
"I couldn't," Gabe whispered. Stung, he looked down at the

dim space between them. "You know I had to come. I had no choice." The answer was as plain as the dirt on Gabe's face, the blood and ash beneath his fingernails. He loved Blue. And what's more, he needed him, Blue's honey-sweet energy washing over him even now and stronger than ever. No candy bar or moonshine, endorphin rush or baby's smile, sexual low or heroin high could compete with it. No distance between them, he read Blue's compound eyes like sacred parchment. Gabe, steadfast as ever, would never leave his side again.

Blue's eyes glistened, and instead of words Gabe received an image of Elisa. She was hunched over, hands held fast to someone else, both of them inert. Naked and pale, she cradled the unmoving figure, her bent arms obscuring their faces like the branches of a weeping willow. The pair were dusted with cave sediment, their limbs overgrown with creeper vines, skins flecked with lichen. She was somewhere close. *How long has she been down here?* Gabe thought.

Blue shimmered, and he cocked his head.

time
is not as important
down here
not the way it is
above
you have already been with
us
longer than you know
"Elisa. Where is she?"
with
the others
down
in the

locus
of the
hive

"Can you take me there?" There was so much more to see.

After a few moments Blue grudgingly turned. Deeper inside the hive it was warmer still, and as Gabe trailed after Blue's shifting form he became saturated with sweat. The walls of the cave perspired as well, everything part of the same immense life form and heaving with hot breath. He couldn't keep up but followed by instinct, advancing through the ever-winding paths. It gradually dawned on him that they were traveling in a series of tightening circles like the spiral of an enormous mollusk shell, the Great Snail at the center of the earth. *I have been in a mouse hole and a snail shell and down a cow's throat and in the wolf's belly.* And now he had become his own channel, who could carry others inside of him.

Blue vanished somewhere ahead, and Gabe grew anxious, clasping his hands together to keep them from shaking. He emerged inside a cavern far greater than any he'd seen, the domed ceiling studded with stalactites and vaulted with what appeared to be the concave leviathan bones of a mammoth sea creature. *And now a whale has swallowed me.* Dim shadows scuttled back and forth behind a curtain of thick gelatinous tissue obstructing his path, shadows that undulated and shuddered, expanded and contracted in a network of pulsating lights. From behind the partition came braying wails, savage ululations both mournful and ravenous. Gabe placed his hands over his mouth with a little room left to breathe and pushed himself through the membranous wall.

At once his vision refracted. Phosphorescence blinded him, but at the same time burned through his senses, a kaleidoscope

of emotions flooded one into the next. *The new frequency.* He
blinked hard through scattered visions of trees with sparkling
silver leaves, willing his sight back to him. And what he saw
were bodies. Hung like slaughterhouse meat in the luminous
field of energy, from the walls, the cavern roof, throughout the
viscous webbing strung around him. Human bodies, mostly,
of varying ages and shapes, some naked while others wore the
moldered remains of clothing. Scattered among them were a
few large dogs, as well as other animals, small woodland creatures and subterranean mammals, all suspended in the murky
wall of glimmering mucilage like fish tangled in an invisible net.
Each figure remained perfectly still, only to twitch at irregular
intervals as if jolted by an electrical current.

The howling cries were louder on this side, much louder,
and he removed his hands from his mouth and brought them
to his ears. *Where the hell is Blue?* His breath grew erratic as he
ingested the heavy perfumed vapor that permeated the air, radiant flares sparking at his eyes. He examined one of the sleeping
figures, a nude and elderly woman with gray hair sprouting from
her skull in uneven patches. She was curled into a ball and cradling a meaty, engorged tuber in her arms, as if to shelter it from
harm. The protuberance was semiopaque with the delicate wet
coating of a shelled egg, a dark embryonic shape writhing inside
its beating green core.

Gabe recoiled and hurried along the wall, past more bodies
in stasis. *They're all fast asleep, the whole of the court felled by a
curse of deep slumber.* Each grasped their own writhing tuber, the
mesmeric pulsations within the sacs harmonized in a throbbing
murmur of light and vibration that made the cave walls hum
like a colossal tuning fork. *The thirteenth fairy didn't get invited to
the christening.* Even the animals in their vast assortment clung

to smaller sacs, their furred bodies motionless but for shallow breaths suggestive of hibernation.

He halted beside a man clad in the shreds of a soot-stained union suit and a pair of brittle leather suspenders. The man clung to his own swollen grub, the heart of which drummed steadily with the same phosphorescent green glow, pounding with bass-heavy life. Gabe placed a hand beneath the man's head and lifted it to inspect his face. It was Donald. A somewhat younger version of him, yes, maybe sixty years old or so. Either this was a copy or it was the real Donald, the human one lost to the world above with a replacement sent up in his stead.

Maybe the Donald I know isn't someone who has trouble remembering after all. Perhaps his burden was that he couldn't fully forget who he had once been, and the underworld where he was born. *Maybe it was only his life above that was falling away.*

Gabe leaned closer. He pressed his forehead to the man's temple and tried to see inside. Flittering, sun-bleached images of trees and water, of a brown-haired woman beneath a broad-brimmed hat and two little boys building sandcastles on a far-flung shore, laughter and blinding brightness.

"Donald?" he said. "Can you hear me?"

Oh Charlie, Charlie, get out of bed!

He put his ear to the man's mouth, and though the cracked lips failed to move, Gabe could nevertheless hear a clamorous riot of words tumble forth, chanted with a youthful and cheery vigor in Donald's own voice.

Oh Charlie, Charlie, get out of bed! Oh Charlie, Charlie, get out of bed!

Sudden movement behind him, and Gabe turned to glimpse a shifting, incandescent shape; he wasn't alone with the sleepers any longer. It was Blue, scuttering past as if guided forward on an imperceptible tether. He followed after him, called out, but Blue didn't stop, only continued to stride in the direction of a stone archway. Gabe hurried through the crudely linteled entrance of sparkling black rock, and he froze.

Darkness. But then his eyes adjusted, and he tuned into a throbbing light, many of them, above and below and all about. The balloon-shaped tubers resembling amniotic sacs were everywhere, variegated and bursting verdant green, then sickly yellow in a steady strobe, their casings coated in a viscous film of sap affixing them to the cavern ceiling and walls. There were flickering figures scattered about as well, others like Blue and the creature who had led Gabe upon his arrival.

The Other Kind. Gabe's rib cage rattled, his chest on fire with yearning and fear, and he began to tremble violently. *They're here, they're really here.* And just as he knew this to be true, he also knew that he was in the place Elisa had told him about. The heart of the hive, where Blue and the others had brought her the first time, steam hissing from a dark and gaping pool at its center. He had entered the throne room.

Across the pool, toward the far side of the room and its shadowy recesses, there was a commotion of figures, the source of the violent screams. A constellation of movement in unstable forms, Blue among them, was gathered around a singular and unchanging mass that twitched and writhed as if in its death throes. Far larger than the others, its wet and leathery skin flashed red beneath a spectrum of color emanating from a sagging cluster of black dangling tubers above, as well as from the luminous radiance of the creatures surrounding it. It was the one from Elisa's nightmares, though it also reminded Gabe of the angel painting inside the closet at the Colony. *Borealis the Mother was sent up from the Heavens of the Faraway World to bring comfort to the New Children of the Screaming Places.*

But this mother brought no comfort, not anymore. Wilted antennae horns drooped over the mirrored domes of its massive eyes, once-mighty wings of scaled and iridescent membrane folded over it like a crimson veil and crisped with dark gray ash. Its needle-ridged mouth slowly opened and closed, gasping like a fish flopping on the deck of a boat. Its gargantuan body was being hollowed out, scraped clean by its subjects, jagged mandibles slicing through meat and tendon alike. It cried out in a keening moan, and the whole of the hive rattled, jolted on its foundation.

The Queen. Her subjects were busy devouring her.

Before he could stop himself, Gabe stepped forward and screamed.

"You're killing her!"

Silence fell over the throne room, a thousand eyes cast in Gabe's direction through the intermittent strobe. From the shadowed corners; from where the Queen lay; from the ridged stone walls: they all observed him with a removed dispassion, as if from a warehouse catwalk. In a staggering blur of motion the Other Kind heaved back, each one of them, the collective swarm tensed like a whip about to strike and accompanied by an ear-splitting shriek of what sounded like indignation. Gabe fell to the ground and threw his hands over his head in a defensive crouch. He knew in his heart that Blue wouldn't, or couldn't, save him.

But nothing happened. *Is it a warning?* He risked peering through his fingers. By the stroboscopic light of a single tuber he saw his own features cast upon the face of the creature nearest

him, adhered to the cave wall and tilted at such an inconceiv-
able angle that its head appeared separated from its body. It was
like looking into a distorted mirror, at a wax museum replica of
himself that had begun to melt. Gabe averted his eyes, only to
have them fall upon another with his face, its arms thrown over
its head in cowering imitation. They all had his face now, every
one. *Any one of them can be me. Any of them. Even Blue.*

He stared back at himself from every corner of the throne
room, a thousand Gabriels when even one was sometimes too
much to bear. He could be replaced in a heartbeat. And how
replaceable he had felt, for far too long to remember. How insignificant. As a child, just another mouth to feed, and now grown
he had become something to be taken for granted, or otherwise
mistreated. It was all written there, upon his many frightened
faces, and inside his many eyes.

A moment later their appearances shifted, features fanning
past like the letters on a train station Solari board. One after the
next they had the eyes of insects again, hexagonal compound
mounds of shining twin honeycombs, faces hided in bark with
mouths knotted like wood. Then they changed once more. In
a single instant one stood tall and thin as a bamboo rod, and in
the next another shifted with a sluicing sound into a crouching
figure the size of a small child, an emerald tint to its papery
skin. In a sweeping tide they withdrew their communal gaze and
returned as one to their feedings and cleanings and excretions,
newly cool in their other unknowable ministrations.

*The thing about the Other Kind, though? They don't care about
us. They can't care about us. I get that now.*

The way we see ants? That's how they see us.

They also returned their attention to the Queen. They continued dismantling her with claws and teeth and spaded tongue,

electric green lifeblood leeching down into the pool water and reeking of brine and copper. She fell quiet, her cries silenced for good, and all that remained was a desiccated husk. Gabe turned away in disgust.

Uneasy ripples of brilliant yellow illumination rose from the cavern floor, cresting to one side of the throne room before crashing back in his direction.

"Blue?" he called out, his terror rising. And there was his friend. One among many, Blue glided from his dead Queen with his allotted pound of her flesh in his mouth. He turned in Gabe's direction, compound eyes glowing brightly in the light from the pulsating growths. He had known Gabe would come. Had he in fact waited for him to see this barbaric ceremony, to prove to them both he was no longer of Gabe's kind? He, who had once forgotten so much of who he was, dazzled by the glittering world above.

Creatures fanned out synchronously from the Queen's corpse in an iridescent spray like the eyes of a peacock's tail, their illuminations reflected off the flooded cave floor. Blue leaped from the assemblage. He scaled the wall on powerful legs that thrust him cricketlike to the cavern ceiling, where he suspended himself among the gleaming multitude. Protean in appearance, they nevertheless shared the same indescribable essence, as well as Blue's beveled honeycomb eyes. And all the while, the sound of clacking jaws, of dripping water, taut vellums of skin and sharp bone snapping back and forth in a staccato and melodious relay. The diversity of life in motion. All the inhuman wonders Gabe's father had preached hellfire about and that Gabe always knew were real, but never thought he'd witness in their own dominion.

He spotted Elisa. She was just as he'd seen her in his mind, perched along the cavern wall and clinging not to one of the glowing sacs but rather to another figure, both of them unmoving. Gabe went to them and shucked the viscid creepers from their arms and legs, hacked away at the wet fibrous matter until he'd freed them both from the rough stone wall. The exposed surface of the rock was veined with white branches and etched with esoteric symbols that reminded him of runes, and the lost tree language of ogham.

Elisa coughed and blinked rapidly as if roused from an unfathomable sleep, and she began to stroke the being in her arms, either by training or by instinct. It was a creature her same size, skin the color and texture of paper birch. She warmed it, ran her fingers across its face and limbs, its chest and back. She passed her hand over its stomach, and slowed, rubbing it there in gentle circles. The creature's belly was distended, aglow and writhing with evolving life. It was carrying a child, or something that might one day be. Elisa's child. And Blue's.

A creation of both places, light and dark, above and below. Persephone unborn. A stab of diffuse envy pierced him, and he thought of Jason and what he might have felt, or known.

Gabe helped her lower the creature to the cavern floor, where they both dropped to their knees, the two of them supporting the being between them. He dizzied with intoxication. It was like handling a live wire, a current of emotion roiling him. Wonder and dread shocked through his brain, and he felt Elisa's emotions as his own. Her fear, her amazement, her doubt: all were transmitted to him through the collective consciousness. She had become a part of it, because to be with them was to be a component of the greater whole. All that the Other Kind had seen over untold millennia—visions of the land before and after the time of man—it could fill the unused parts of

Gabe's brain, a succession of floodgates opened. If only he gave the word.

And maybe that's what these parts of my brain were for in the first place: to remain empty, until one day they could be filled by the hive mind. A place where all knowledge is shared, each to each, regardless of kith and kin, or species, or origin.

But something prevented Gabe from seeing it all, some part of himself that held back and wouldn't allow him complete access, though he wanted so badly to be let inside. Maybe he felt that in the end he wasn't good enough.

"It's me," Elisa said softly, her voice worn thin with time though she looked no older, the words spoken so close Gabe thought they might be inside his mind. *It's me.* He assumed she was confirming her identity, but no, she was referring instead to the creature in her arms. It had her face: her sharp wedge of a nose, her chapped red lips, a damp sweep of the same chestnut hair. There really had been a part of herself she'd left down here, another version of herself. Not only her unborn child, but a substitute of Elisa as well, her very own surrogate counterpart.

"You woke us." Her tone managed to convey both surprise and inevitability. "It must be time."

A ripping noise echoed across the throne room, and Gabe's grip on Elisa and her surrogate tightened. The slumbering attendants stirred. One by one they began to raise their heads, and started to peel themselves from the membrane. The younger Donald pressed his skull to the enlarged celeriac tuber in his arms and released a terrible moan like a father who had lost a child, while a woman beside him rocked violently, the soiled and rent rawhide of her smock flapping across her chest as she moved. All of them stuttered through their fitful reanimations, all waking to some subdued version of life. Gabe glimpsed one of the large dogs he'd seen, which now looked to be a coyote, kneading its paws against a pulsating grub as if trying to nurse.

As they dropped to the catacomb floor, human and animal alike, a thunderous rumble sounded throughout the warrens. The roof buckled and released a cloud of white dust that glimmered in the tubers' array of winking lights like fireflies loosed from a jar. Stalactite needles and stone drapery plummeted from the cave ceiling, rocks colliding against the ridged walls and splashing into the dark pool, the vast and unblinking eye at the center of the cavern. It was the sound of a story ending, the whisper of the last page being turned, just before the book was shut tight.

The Other Kind and their followers gathered around the water's edge. Gabe stepped forward as well, the whole of his body convulsing with desire. He wanted to join them. It didn't matter what they asked of him, whether they stole him away from the world above. It didn't matter if he never went back.

no

Gabe fought it.

NO.

He resisted the hive. Tried to think for himself again, though he was having trouble doing so. Because he wanted to give in, to be swallowed into their communal web of consciousness and perpetual brightness; he wanted to be lit from within. Elisa, she had the right idea, a lifetime supply of the frequency. He could join them too, couldn't he? Become another one of their servants. He'd never go hungry again, never want for anything whatsoever. How sweet it would be, to give himself over to their ego-annihilating form of oblivion.

I'd never be alone again.

Gabe studied Elisa's face. She was resigned, her affect flat-tened beyond her palpable fatigue.

Is that what I want for myself? To have to rise by collective com-mand and merrily dance for joy, though my feet may be blistered and my heart no longer my own?

The truth was that he had no people of his own and never would, that he was all alone in this life, a burden not even Blue could help him lay down. He clenched and flexed his tremulous fingers upon the straps of his backpack, the pull toward Blue and the rest of his kin near irresistible. Bells clashed in his ears, church bells and school bells and little brass jingle bells, a ca-cophony of conflicting noise.

The first of the Other Kind descended into the pool, which shivered with new life, a birthing canal in reverse. Another of its kind followed, and another, and another. Opalescent forms tumbled into the water in rapid succession, each dodg-ing the cascade of stalactites and falling dirt with the won-drous elegance of a trained acrobat. Their servants followed. The enchanted workers peeled the pulsating sacs from the cavern walls and carried them forward. They slipped into the black pool, the squirming roots in their grasp, with no appar-ent thought or trepidation. One of them was a badly burned woman, skin mottled beside a star-shaped red birthmark on her back. Gavina Beaton; Gabe recognized her from Elisa's photographs. A swollen tuber cradled in her working arm, she dove beneath the water's surface, the throbbing brightness from the sac and its burgeoning life fading from sight as she vanished.

Blue dropped down beside the fervent procession and ap-proached, his movements dignified and assured. He hoisted the surrogate Elisa from the cavern floor and into his sickled arms, and it languidly molded itself to him, its body lengthening to take hold of his chest. The viridescent ball of its pregnant womb pressed into him like an external organ, its serrated mouth latched on to Blue's neck, and the surrogate suckled at him, a bee feeding on nectar. His eyes remained wide open and lidless and trained upon Gabe.

time
it is time
to go
deeper

"Please." Gabe reached out to stop him, but then thought better of it. "Don't go yet."

time
it is time
for the new
hive
for the new
queen
below

Gabe turned to Elisa, whose expression was one not only of hunger but of a strange satiation. "You're going with them," he said. "Aren't you?"

"You can't understand what it's like to leave all this," she said, and crossed her arms as if chilled, though the hive was sweltering. "Not yet."

His stomach lurched. "Then you've already made up your mind."

"I thought I was cast out the first time, but I was wrong. I chose to leave, to return to familiar things. And once I came back, I knew I couldn't be without them again. Besides," she said, "you can only leave once."

She spoke with the certitude of a fairy godmother, a seasoned practitioner relating a storybook rule involving potions and curses and spells. *Don't stray from the designated path. Don't drink from the enchanted well. You can only leave once.* The rules were always so simple, which was why they bound so tightly.

Elisa's eyes grew teary and heavy with exhaustion. "Tell Jason I said—" She stared at the flooded cavern floor, at the trembling cathedral ceiling, and finally at her surrogate in Blue's arms. "Tell him I found what I was looking for."

She and Gabe embraced. "We found him, though," she whispered in his ear. "I told you we would."

And with that she pulled away. The surrogate dropped down from Blue's arms and attached itself to her, fitting to her body like a second skin. Its distended belly became Elisa's belly, its limbs her limbs. It was as if the creature had moved inside of her, where it peered out from her now-glowing eyes.

Elisa and her twin turned, the cavern pool before them, and dropped as one into the abyss.

Flowstone keeled and toppled to the ridged cavern floor. But the mournful leave-taking continued, a legion of Other Kind gliding toward the black pool as the throbbing lights dimmed and the cave unraveled around a threnody of buzzing tongues and fluttering wings. And their followers as well: a rail-thin young man about Gabe's age in full hiking regalia and bearing an enormous rucksack; a tiny Mi'kmaq woman in native garb, the furred hem of her caribou-skin robe in tatters; a naked and hirsute gentleman, eyes wide with a hand extended before him as if moving through a waking dream. They all dropped down into the dark water, one after the next.

A massive column crashed down right beside Gabe. It was all coming apart now. But still he could not leave.

go

Blue, pleading. Compelling. His dewy wet eyes a fractalized maze of surfaces, all reflecting Gabe's anguished expression back at himself.

go

now

He shook off Blue and his command. Why would he go now? He had nothing to live for above, not when everything he wanted was right here in front of him, down in this scorched world.

But this world was ending. The colony—the real colony—was gone. Just like the old Blue.

And that was the one Gabe wanted. The *old* Blue, the stressed-out, chain-smoking chef who was his best friend, his only friend. The only one who ever made Gabe feel special rather than freakish, who let him believe that all would be well in the end. Now Blue had become like the rest of his kind, both awesome and fathomless, and there would be no more knowing him, not entirely. Not unless Gabe were to lose himself to the colony, and even then it wouldn't be enough. It would never be enough.

I can't leave you. I need you, Gabe thought wildly, *I can't do it without you. I won't be able to make it up there by myself.*

"You don't need me." Blue's voice, out loud; his old voice, at last. The lush shape of his lips returned to his smooth alabaster face, along with the rest of his familiar features, soft and brutal in equal measure. The old Blue had materialized.

"You don't need anyone but yourself," Blue said, and opened his arms wide. "You never did."

The colony was deserted. Only the two of them remained, motionless amid the terrible roar of heaving earth as the hive crumbled around them. But time slowed to a trickle, with Blue and Gabe at its center. The hive stilled, and fell silent.

"It's hard for me to remember what it was like up there. Isn't that funny?" Blue glanced toward the cavern ceiling, then back at the dark pool. "But one of the things I do remember is you. Your kindness. And how that made me feel. It made me want to be kind myself."

"Don't," Gabe said, his heart swelling; he didn't want to hear any more, not if Blue was just going to abandon him.

"You were the only one who saw me for what I was. Not even Elisa did, not fully." He cracked a wry smile. "That's changed."

"What am I supposed to do?"

"You can still come with us, if you want. Is that what you want?"

No.

Blue's smile dissolved. "That's what I thought."

"So that's it?" Gabe wiped away tears. "Now you're just going to leave?"

"I never left. Not you. Not really." He pressed an open hand to Gabe's chest, and his body jolted and sung with rapture as the roar of dying earth commenced. All was well, all was well, everything crashing down around them again but so what? Gabe shielded his eyes with an arm as dirt fell over his face. There was no place else he would rather be.

Blue raised his hand from Gabe's chest and moved it to his cheek, let his fingers linger there for a moment before he stepped toward the lip of the pool, his glistening eyes still fixed upon Gabe.

"Go," he said. "Live."

"Wait." Gabe steeled himself for his final appeal, the last chance to reunite his clan of two. "You loved that world up there yourself once. I know you did. And you know what else? I think you still do."

Blue hesitated. "Maybe."

"So how can you give it up?"

"I don't have to," he said. "Because you're going back for me."

This is an act, Gabe thought. Blue's emotions, they were only for show, fanning past in quick succession, the same way the Other Kind had altered and reconfigured their appearances. *He's only telling me what I want to hear.* The realization cut him to the core.

"You'd prefer cruelty, then?" Blue said. "We can do that." The softness slipped from his face, and with it the rest of his human disguise, his expression now inscrutable. "You don't have a place here. It's not possible. Not unless you give yourself over to us."

"There's a part of me I can't give you," Gabe said. "One that isn't mine to offer." Blue's shape quivered for a moment, unsure of itself. "It's something you'll never have."

we

need

all of you

Blue's wrathful voice in his head was a thousand piercing arrows, and Gabe's nose began to bleed.

every part

of you to be

us

to be subsumed

into service

of the

hive

Gabe staggered back. "I'm not like you," he said, wiping at the blood on his face. "I can't live down here. I can't do it. I can't live in darkness alone."

"We're never alone. Not together." Blue shimmered and tilted his head to the side, dazzling trails of bright green energy emanating from his skull in waves. "Together, we're made of light."

"I must be made of light too." Gabe straightened himself up, almost as tall as Blue. "How else would I have found my way through the dark?"

For a flickering moment, Blue appeared to smile. He began to reach out to Gabe but then withdrew his hand, the smile fading from his face. He fell back and away, his mirror-ball eyes flaring green before he disappeared beneath the water and earth.

Gabe rushed to the edge of the pool, dirt and rocks assaulting him from the cavern roof. He readied himself to leap after him but stopped short. Instead, he stared down blinking into the shadowy mist, and held on to the enduring sensation of Blue's touch like a talisman. He'd seen too many dark places, Gabe's whole life spent crawling from one to the next. His father's house and the run-down foster homes, the hostels and the group houses, the flophouses and squats and pay-by-the-hour motel rooms; the promise of light was the only thing that had kept him alive, the way that Blue once had. And if he gave that up, he would sacrifice all his dearest friend had given him.

The ceiling gave way as Gabe stepped from the pool. He stumbled forward, righted himself, and raced for the stone archway. A cloud of dust chased him through the caverns and down the long and winding passageway, along with the echoing, deafening sounds of the hive's devolution. The tunnels shifted madly, coiling and uncoiling as if he were traversing the thrashing tentacles of an agitated squid. The passages contracted and pulled back, the vast biological organism of the hive retreating down into the throne room and the dark pool at its center, and what lay below. Gabe had to hold fast to the rough dirt walls to keep himself from falling.

He navigated blindly in the dark. But when he stopped thinking so hard he could sense the path's design and he followed it, spiraling out toward the base of the mountain. Once his route was free of auxiliary tunnels and passageways, it became one clean trail propelling him straight up and through the land, and he could do this, he could do this, it was only another way out of the dark, what was one more escape to pull off? Gabe ran in silence, with only the sound of his panting breath to keep pace.

Eventually there was a slender thread of light, just beyond the watery mouth of a cave: the Fairy Hole, leading out onto the bay. He scuttled toward the opening but the gap was flooded, driftwood obstacles tided through the breach. There was no other way out.

Gabe pulled off his sneakers and peeled away the shredded remains of his clothes in the crisp air, exposing each and every scar he'd tried so hard to keep hidden. He discarded his waterlogged pack and the remaining supplies, Donald's journal and his own sketch pad along with them. The pad fell open and swelled with water, black ink blurred and running from drawings of snarling griffins and upside-down hanging men, sharp-toothed boys and rain clouds of blood. His memories. Dislodged and floating in the dimly lit water at his feet was the Polaroid of little Michael Whitley, who Blue never was, not really. And Gabe would leave this behind as well, his final keepsake. That was okay now; for better or worse, Blue was still with him. Written upon his skin, his heart, every place that he had touched. And there he would remain, so long as Gabe still lived.

Lungs bursting with breath, a silent prayer to a distant god, and Gabe dove into the arctic current. His body shot forward like a harpoon from a gun, the water colder than cold, but he wouldn't let it numb him. Everything was feeling now. And that was what scared him most of all: that he would make it to shore and would still be so raw and new to the world, the very world that had tried so many times to wipe him from the heel of its boot.

The impenetrable cold. So cold! It wanted to swallow him up, to make him its own, every part of his body seized with the shock of its angry sting. But still he swam. A cloud of silt enveloped him, and he pictured the scars on his back frosting over as he flailed desperately for the cave mouth, fingernails scraping at rock and moss and mud. His most dreadful scars, the ones he pretended were wings, they sang out to him, urged him forward in waves of empathy. *The old pain, it wants me to live!* And in doing so the pain became exalted.

The scars, they sang in Blue's voice; he was singing Gabe's suffering away, even now. Blue and the rest of his kind, their tribe burrowing far, then farther beneath the earth.

live

Gabe heard them sing on his way. His entire body vibrated.

live

live

Even their dead Queen sang to him. The fires had fatally wounded her, and so her people had consumed her in transubstantiation, enshrining her as an ever-present part of the hive; it was their very own form of communion. She would be reborn in the new place, where a new queen would be birthed from the old, as was the nature of their design.

His lungs ached, twin bloated balloons filled to their skirts with pebbles. He was sure he was going to pass out, but then he remembered the marks Jessed had left upon him, the fresh gills on his neck in the shape of fingers. They helped him to breathe.

Finally, his hands found the lip of the Fairy Hole. Gabe lunged through the cave mouth and hit a wall: the bay was frozen over. Eyes bulging with fear and disbelief, he beat his fists against the ceiling of dark ice, rapidly losing consciousness. Through narrowing eyes he watched in amazement as his burn-scarred hand shimmered and reshaped, fingers webbing into a sharp-edged spade with which to strike. A hidden source of deep strength emerged from within, one he hadn't known existed. In a mad surge of concentrated panic, he reared back and thrust his hand against the hard surface, and the ice shattered in a splintered spray of hoarfrost.

He sucked at the glacial air rushing above him, and let himself bob for a while in the bay's frigid rime-dusted seawater, every pore in his body gasping for oxygen as its own tiny mouth. Finally, he pulled himself up and out of the crude hole and lay on his back across the ice. He opened his eyes.

Stars. They were everywhere, the night sky a pinpricked sheet above snowcapped Kelly's Mountain and the bay, a total absence of moonlight. Gabe heard the song of his scars in the cold, their song his song as it rose into a heavenly choir. *Exaltation, exaltation.* He was alive.

The ice groaned beneath him. He shot up and scrambled for the shore, bare feet slipping on wet frost. He heaved forward and threw himself down on the shoreline as the frozen bay cracked open in his wake, a jagged line zagged across the ice like a lightning bolt sent from above. The chilled night air extinguished the fire of him, blanketing him in the breath of a

Norse giant. His lungs filled and emptied and filled again, and he waited for his speeding heart to calm as frigid water lapped at his shins, legs as unsteady as those of a newly birthed calf. He rolled over, but wouldn't let the sea have him; some other day perhaps, but for now it had taken too much. Supported by the ice-caked stone, he pushed himself up, on hands and knees at first but then to his feet, where he crouched tentatively upon the rocks.

It was the dead of winter. As impossible as it was unmistakable, the white bay spread out before him like an unfurled scroll. The faraway lights from discrete houses twinkled and winked as their own set of infrequent stars, while wisps of smoke wound from stout brick chimneys, in and among the trees. Was this the winter that was fast approaching, or rather some far-flung season, in the future or even the past? *Time will tell*, he thought, unless it no longer did that either. But he was going to find out. He needed to find a new place to put all his love, after all. Blue couldn't be the only one out there.

Gabe shivered and held himself, though beneath his skin he felt extraordinarily warmed. It was a newfound awareness, one that told him that the cold, like so much else, was only another illusion. How much had changed during his days in darkness, his absence from the great and glorious world above?

All was silent. Even his scars, the rended angel wings quieted after all these many years. Gabe reached behind him with a groan of pain and felt at his skin's surprising glossiness, droplets of seawater dappling his shoulder blades. The wet dewy film along his straining muscles glowed like birch bark through the dim of night. It was hard to see in the dark, but it was only once he looked at his exposed and red-raw back that he could really know.

My scars.

They were gone.

Not only the recent ones from these past unquantifiable hours and days, but the oldest scars as well, the wings on his back given to him by his father's belt. He raised his hand in front of him and turned it this way and that, his burn-mottled fingers now smooth and unblemished, his skin shaded yellow in the starlight. All the markings of violence that he had carried with him, that made him who he was. All gone.

But I'm still me.

He stumbled up the embankment, the pines and firs and spruces and birches all stripped of their leaves, everything deadened in the Maritimes frost but still alive, still alive.

Gabe made his way through the trees that were as naked as he was, holding on to the trunks and their rough bark to steady himself as he weaved his way up the mountainside in the direction of the main road.

He emerged from the woods and waited until he could stand on his own. And then he headed north.

Acknowledgments

My parents, family, and friends; my teachers and colleagues; my son and daughter; and the residents of Cape Breton, whose local geography may have shifted during flight. You are my true Friendship Outpost and Artists Colony.

The Summer People: Sarah Kelly and the Starry Heaven workshop, where the good vibes began. Special thanks to my full readers Brad Beaulieu and Greg van Eekhout.

The missing hikers: Rebecca Brown, Sam Zalutsky, Sebastian Dungan, and Barbara Wally, who looked at early pages and told me I wasn't crazy when I most needed to hear it.

The believers group: Liz Hand and my fellow residents at the Atlantic Center of the Arts, where I finished my first draft. Love and blessings.

My fairy godmother, Tricia Boczkowski, who always has my back. If you ever need to hide a body, I'm just a phone call away.

The hive queen, Livia Llewellyn, cofounder of the Vipers of Self-Relevance Writers Group. Until we are protected by the ejaculation of serpents. :F

Jen Bergstrom, Stephanie DeLuca, and the entire Gallery team. Especially my editor, Adam Wilson, who awes me with his powers of perception. I would dive into darkness and follow you beneath the earth.

My enchanting agent, Luke Janklow, and his ever-astounding assistant, Claire Dippel. You guys are better than screech, and without the delirium tremens.

And most of all, to my very own Other Kind, Dan Sacher. You make everything possible, and magical, and sane, and right. You are the new frequency.

There's a piece of you all in this book. Endless gratitude.